HIGH RISK

Matt Dickinson is a film maker and writer specialising in the sometimes perilous world of expedition cinematography. He has an enduring fascination for teams and individuals who attempt extreme challenges in the wildest corners of the planet.

He has produced and directed more than forty expedition films for series such as BBC 1 *Classic Adventure*, ITV *Voyager* and Channel 4 *Encounters*. He has also worked extensively for National Geographic Television and the Discovery Channel, and in 1995 directed the *Equinox* science documentary on avalanches.

His films have won numerous film festival awards.

In the pre-monsoon Everest season of 1996, amid the worst weather conditions on record, he made a successful ascent of Mount Everest's notorious north face, one of the most technically demanding climbs on the world's highest peak. Twelve climbers were killed in the same season. He is the only British film maker to have filmed on the summit and returned alive. His experiences were recounted in his bestselling book, *The Death Zone*.

On another occasion, filming an ascent of Mount William in Antarctica, his team were caught up in a massive ice avalanche, an incident he was fortunate to survive.

By the same author

The Death Zone
(published in the USA as *The Other Side of Everest*)

You are welcome to visit the author's website at:

www.mattdickinson.com

HIGH RISK

MATT DICKINSON

HUTCHINSON
LONDON

1 3 5 7 9 10 8 6 4 2

First published in the United Kingdom in 2000 by Hutchinson

The Random House Group Limited
20 Vauxhall Bridge Road, London SW1V 2SA

Random House Australia (Pty) Limited
20 Alfred Street, Milsons Point, Sydney,
New South Wales 2061, Australia

Random House New Zealand Limited
18 Poland Road, Glenfield,
Auckland 10, New Zealand

Random House South Africa (Pty) Limited
Endulini, 5A Jubilee Road, Parktown 2193, South Africa

The Random House Group Limited Reg. No. 954009
www.randomhouse.co.uk

A CIP catalogue record for this book
is available from the British Library

Papers used by Random House are natural,
recyclable products made from wood grown in sustainable forests.
The manufacturing processes conform to the environmental
regulations of the country of origin

ISBN 009 180117 6

Typeset by Palimpsest Book Production Limited,
Polmont, Stirlingshire
Printed and bound in Great Britain by
Mackays of Chatham plc, Chatham, Kent

For Anna

Acknowledgements

They say that authors should write about what they know. In this novel, by exploring the worlds of Everest and avalanches, I am writing about what has twice almost killed me. But those near-death experiences were nothing compared with the process of living through five drafts of this book and I owe a big thank you to my editors Sue Freestone and Tony Whittome for surviving it with me. My literary agent Georgina Capel gets my thanks too, for venturing out so energetically and selling *High Risk* all over the world. Georgina would sell this novel to the Martians if she could only get them to pick up a phone.

Finally, my thanks to Fiona, whose input to this book was important in so many ways I am not even going to attempt to list them here. Suffice to say that without her enthusiastic help this book would never have fulfilled its promise.

PART ONE

The Power of Nature

1

Alaska

Hal scooped a final shovel of snow from the makeshift grave and clambered out to address the group. He stood, panting a little, a thin vapour of steam rising from his cheeks, feeling at home here in this wild mountain country, the jagged peaks of the Chugach range jutting skywards around him.

'This morning', he told them with a smile, 'I'm going to bury one of you alive.'

He walked down the line, making eye contact with the five shivering clients. 'Now, who wants to volunteer?'

There were no takers. Hal looked at Rachel. 'Want to get those shots?'

Rachel clutched at the Nikon strung round her neck, unable to keep the alarm from her face. 'Maybe I'll do them another time . . .'

'This is the last course of the winter. If you don't do it now . . . ?' He left the question hanging.

Rachel looked down into the icy grave and suppressed a shudder. 'I'm not so sure it'll produce a worthwhile picture . . .'

'That's not what you told me before. All those faces of the rescuers as they dig you out? The point of view of an avalanche victim? Sounds like a pretty unique shot to me.'

She looked at him pleadingly. The camera might get snow in it . . .'

'Rachel?'

'Yes?'

'If you want that photograph, get in the hole.'

'Oh, God . . .'

Rachel picked out the widest lens in her kitbag, her fingers trembling a little as the 16mm Nikkor snapped neatly into its bayonet mount.

Then she stepped down into the snow hole and lay flat on her back, her hands cupped over the camera to protect it. The others gathered round the lip to look down at her, seeming to tower far above, even though the trench was only three feet deep.

'Move your head into that cavity in the side wall,' Hal told her. 'There's enough space for your upper body in there and enough oxygen to keep you going for a while.'

Rachel tipped her head to the side, noticing the scooped-out hollow for the first time. She wriggled herself into it, finding that her head and shoulders fitted easily, with a clear nine inches or so of space between the tip of her nose and the solid ice roof.

'OK.' Hal leaned down to clip an avalanche transmitter on to her ski suit. 'Your beacon's in place. Hopefully we'll find you before the battery runs out.'

'Ha ha. You're killing me, Hal. Get a shift on, will you? I'm freezing here.'

Hal dropped his voice as he bent his head close to her. 'It's been beautiful knowing you. You were the love of my life.'

'You're sick, you know that? Will you just bury me and be done with it?' Rachel turned her face to look at Hal, smiling as she saw his reassuring wink.

'It'll be OK. Just breathe slow and relax,' he whispered, then shouted out for the benefit of the clients: 'You asked for it!'

The sound of a shovel biting into snow. 'This is for all the mornings you never made my coffee!'

A shovelful of snow landed with a thump on her shin. 'This is for that dent you put in the Toyota last week.'

Then another. 'I should have buried you years ago.'

Soon her legs were covered.

Rachel could feel the vibrations as the clients took up their shovels and joined in, hear their laughter at Hal's over-the-top performance.

Gradually the quality of the noise shifted, the metallic scraping diminishing as the burial continued. Snow began to rain down on her waist, pattering as the crystals impacted on the Gore Tex. The weight was extraordinary, the snow pushing down on every inch of her body with an inexorable pressure which was quite terrifying. The light began to dim, the daylight blocked out little by little until all that was left was a gloomy shade of blue, a luminous glow, which would have been beautiful under any other circumstances.

Then there was just the muffled thud as the shovels pounded away above her.

Then silence.

Rachel stared at the blue wall of ice in front of her.

And tried not to panic.

Hal turned to the group. 'There you go. Well and truly buried. Now follow me.' He led them across the snowfield, away from the burial site. 'This is the most crucial exercise on this course,' he told them, 'the ability to locate a buried avalanche victim. Let's assume that this whole area has just been the scene of a big slide and that one of your party is under that snow somewhere. You know she has a beacon but you have no idea where she is.'

He began to zigzag, then turned them in a series of circles until they were completely disorientated. 'That's just in case you were thinking of cheating. Now go to it. Get the search pattern organised and find her as fast as you can.'

The clients looked out across the snowfield, blinking with surprise as they realised they no longer had a fix on where Rachel was buried. The snow was falling fast – fast enough to cover the tracks they had just made. There would be no visual clues to lead them to where she was.

Remembering the training Hal had given them earlier on the course, they quickly organised themselves into a search line, spreading out one metre apart and beginning a methodical sweep of the target area, their avalanche transceivers set to bleep if they got close to Rachel's emergency transmitter.

Three feet under the snow, Rachel was concentrating on her breathing, inhaling slowly and finding, to her surprise, that there was really plenty of air filtering down from above. She forced her mind to think of other things . . . of the surprise news she had for Hal, which, somehow, she had failed to find a moment to tell him.

She couldn't keep the secret much longer but she wanted the timing to be right. Maybe tonight she would cook for him back at the cabin, buy some wine . . .

Rachel could feel the cold beginning to seep into her bones. The back of her head was starting to freeze even though she was wearing a woollen hat. All concept of time was lost to her. She could have been buried for thirty minutes – or thirty hours. And if they couldn't find her? If the avalanche transmitter failed? A brief surge of claustrophobia embraced her. The snow was too hard; she realised there was no way she could dig her way out. 'Trust,' she whispered to herself. 'Hal knows what he's doing.'

Suddenly she became aware of a distant noise, a shout, barely audible. Then the sound of digging, directly above her. Gradually the frequency of shovelling increased as the rescuers worked their way carefully down to her. Daylight broke through.

'We've got her!' someone cried.

Rachel waited until the top part of her body was free and then raised the camera to her eye. She fired off the motordrive – seventeen shots in rapid succession, the wide-angle lens capturing a unique perspective as the rescuers reached down towards her to brush away snow with their hands. The lens got a heavy dusting of snow crystals but she ignored them, knowing they would add to the drama of the pictures.

Finally she allowed them to pull her free, Hal giving her a big hug to warm her up. 'You see?' he said, kissing her chilled lips. 'We had you out of there in less than fifteen minutes.'

Rachel brushed some snow off the camera. 'I just hope the shots are worth it.' She shuddered from a spasm of cold.

Hal called a coffee break, bringing out his flask and filling plastic mugs for Rachel and the clients. 'Take a break. Get a shot of warm fluid inside you. Then we're going to that steeper slope over there to learn a little about avalanche prediction. We're going to ask a simple question – the one that all back-country skiers and snowmobilers should ask themselves every time they go into the mountains: is this slope going to wipe us out today or not?'

'You're not going to get us all avalanched now, are you?' A client forced a laugh as she sipped her coffee.

Hal held out his bare hand, watching intently as the huge crystals fell to rest, unmelting, on his palm. 'Not if I know my snow,' he told her.

The group watched as he gathered together half a dozen avalanche shovels and headed across to the far slope.

'He does,' Rachel told them reassuringly, 'know his snow, I mean.'

'Sure as hell hope so,' one of the others piped in, 'or we're spending a hundred and fifty bucks to get ourselves killed.'

The group were still chuckling nervously among themselves as they fell in line, following Hal's footsteps across the broad valley floor.

2

London

Josie was out on the streets at 4 a.m., her body warming to the rhythm as she jogged north through Kensington and up into Hyde Park. She always ran before dawn when she was working, it was the only sure way to wake herself up sufficiently for the show. Normally she struggled to drag herself out of bed but today had been different.

It's not easy to sleep when you know the person you love is climbing into the death zone on the highest mountain in the world. Josie had been restless all night.

The circuit was five miles door to door, the result of two years' fine tuning, a forty-minute jog if she was feeling lazy . . . thirty-five minutes if she wanted to break a sweat. Today was a thirty-five-minute day: Josie was in a hurry to get back for Sebastian's satellite call at five. She felt her muscles tighten and protest as she pushed the pace.

The middle section was her favourite part of the run, a three-mile circuit of the park, taking her from Queen's Gate right across to Speakers Corner and back along Rotten Row. The grass felt hard beneath her feet, a late spring frost coating the ground. By the Serpentine, dozing ducks briefly awoke as she passed, tucking their heads back beneath their wings when she had run by. Then it was back on to the streets and through the still sleeping back ways to the leafy Kensington Square that was home.

Josie let herself in the back door, away from the prying lenses of the newsmen who waited at the front. She took a shower, dressed quickly and went to the kitchen to fix herself some coffee. While she waited she stood in front of the freezer and looked at the photograph of Everest Sebastian had pinned there the day before he left for Nepal.

'If you ever want to know what it's like for me out there on that mountain' – he had laughed as he put the picture in place – 'just open the door and put your arm in here for a few hours.' Once, missing him badly in the early days of his absence, Josie had even done it, succumbing to a type of self-conscious madness and opening the freezer door to place her hand inside. She had licked a finger, felt the crackle as the thin coating of saliva froze it instantly to the congealed ice.

Now, Josie pinpointed the location that was the highest of the camps. She wondered what it would be like to be transported there, to really experience the extreme cold that froze unprotected flesh in seconds, to try to breathe in an atmosphere where there was so little oxygen that bottles of the stuff were needed simply to keep the human body alive.

High above the camp a seemingly razor-sharp ridge stretched into the sky towards the summit. The peak was surrounded by strata of clouds, the final uplift of rock and ice jutting up through them like the spire of a cathedral rising through a morning mist.

She kissed her finger and imprinted it on the drawing where she knew Sebastian was. 'Just come home,' she whispered. 'I don't care about anything else.'

Despite the run, Josie still felt tired. Her attempts to get to sleep at nine the previous evening had been interrupted by a number of calls from the press. A glance out of the window told her that the photographers were still waiting. She counted six of them, the red glow of their cigarettes visible where they huddled together beneath a tree. Sebastian had been right when he'd predicted his Everest expedition would create a lot of media interest.

The telephone rang. Even as she put her ear to the receiver she knew it was the satellite connection – the faraway echo on the line told her that. Everest calling: a communication out of the ether – out of another world. Josie savoured the hit of the espresso as she waited for a voice to emerge from the static.

'Josie, this is base camp. I have Sebastian on the walkie-talkie from the col, I'm going to link him up to the satphone, OK? Just hold the line.'

Josie waited while the connection was made.

'Hey, Josie. Can you hear me OK?'

'Loud and clear, Bas. How beautiful to hear your voice. Where are you and how's the expedition going?'

'We reached the south col a couple of hours ago and I tell you I've never been so tired, baby. This mountain is sucking every last drop of breath out of my body. But we're still going strong.'

'What's it like on the col? Is it like they say?'

There was a pause as Sebastian was racked by a coughing fit. 'Like they say? Jesus, it's ten times worse. This place is like some kind of Himalayan rubbish tip. There's shit and ripped-up tents all over, and plenty of bodies . . . Plus I've been feeling sick as a dog the last couple of days.'

'You sound like you just swallowed a pack of nails.'

'Few problems with my throat. But you know what? The strangest thing is that I wouldn't be anywhere else, despite what I'm living through here.'

'Are you sleeping?'

A sound like a snort came down the line. 'Did you say sleep? I don't remember the last time I slept for more than two hours at a stretch. But you get beyond tiredness. Like you get beyond the pain. It's awesome, Josie, like the whole thing is fifty times more awesome than I could ever imagine.'

'How's the rest of the team?'

'Phil and Alessandro dropped out. That leaves eight.'

'You getting plenty of photographs for me? You remember the slide show you promised me when you get back?'

Sebastian laughed. 'I wouldn't forget that, baby, and don't think it's all bad. I'm living the biggest dream of my life here.'

'What can you see where you are?'

'What can I see? I can see getting on for a hundred of the world's most beautiful mountains right from where I'm sitting and somehow that makes it all worthwhile.'

'What about the weather?'

'I'm trying to find a lump of wood to touch here but for the moment it's perfect. We have a blue sky with virtually no wind. Almost too good to be true.'

A wave of interference swept across the line so that Josie had to raise her voice: 'So are you definitely on for the summit?' She failed to keep the tension from the words.

Sebastian paused to get his breath once more. 'You bet. We'll be pulling out at midnight so long as the weather holds.'

'You scare me, Bas. The whole thing scares me.'

'Come on. I'm in good hands here. We have a mountain of oxygen cylinders, loads of strong Sherpas. So far the organisation has been impeccable. It really does look good.'

'But it's still Everest and I'm not going to sleep a wink until I know you're back in base camp.'

'It's roped all the way, honey. You just clip on that line and it's the yellow brick road right up to the summit.'

'You sound like you've been brainwashed into believing the brochure.'

'What brain? I'm losing a million cells every day up here.'

'So get it over with. Fast, please.'

'How's the publicity going?'

'Great. We're all set for the summit party tonight and we have big picture spreads lined up with the dailies just as soon as you can wire back some shots.'

'I'll call Mike in an hour or two to fix the final details. If all goes to plan I'll be on top at about midnight your time.'

'This is so amazing, Bas. I tell you I'm going to be counting the seconds until we get that call.'

'I should go now.'

'Yeah. Me too. I'm on air in forty-five minutes.'

'Be brilliant.'

'Thanks, darling, and listen, you take so much care, OK? Think of me every step of the way and just come back in one piece. For me.'

'I love you.'

'Me too. I'll be glued to the telephone waiting to hear.'

'I have to go. There's a queue of climbers waiting to use this satphone.'

'Love you.' Josie blew him a kiss down the telephone and replaced the handset.

She downed the dregs of the coffee and crossed the corridor to her office. She quickly packed her small leather case with her laptop, Filofax and some notes the producer had given her the previous evening. The intercom buzzer rang from the street, the chauffeur calling to drive Josie to the studio. It was 5.15 a.m.

Josie ran down the stairs and walked out into the pre-dawn chill where the half-frozen press photographers were waiting on the pavement. 'Good morning, gentlemen.'

They snapped a sequence of photographs.

'Any news from Everest?'

'There is. It looks like Sebastian is definitely going for the summit.'

'Have you spoken to him? How's he feeling?'

'I have spoken to him briefly. He's feeling confident and calm. Ready for the challenge, I'd say.'

'Are you nervous for him, Josie?'

Josie laughed. 'Sorry. I have nothing more to say. You'll have to wait for this evening and we'll see how he gets on.' She climbed into the welcoming warmth of the limousine, relaxing back into the leather-clad rear seat as the chauffeur pulled away from the house.

3

Hal rubbed his hands to get the circulation going, trying to coax some feeling back into his frozen fingertips. 'Right. What we're going to do next is create our own personal avalanche zone, like a miniature test bed to check out how stable the pack is. This tells you vital information about the chances of a slide.'

Hal gave each of the clients an aluminium shovel and showed them how to cut a vertical profile into the snow. They dug for fifteen minutes, creating a sizeable hole. When they had finished, they had a sheer wall cut into the mountainside.

'OK. What you have now is a cross-section through the season's snowfall. It all looks the same, right? Except it's not.' He selected one of the female clients. 'Wendy. Take this plastic ruler and start to probe it into the snow. Start at the top and move down. Call out when you feel something change.'

Not quite sure, the woman took the ruler and did as Hal said, pushing the ruler half an inch into the pack, then descending a few inches to repeat the action.

'What you're doing is checking the consistency of the snow pack from the top of the face – the most recent snow – to the bottom of the pack where the snow could be weeks or even months old.'

Wendy paused as she sensed more resistance. 'It's harder here,' she said, 'more like ice.'

'Good. What you're discovering is that as snow falls, it creates layers, some hard, some soft, some granular. A deep overnight frost after a fresh fall, for example, would create a hard, polished layer like the one you just found. That layer remains in the snow pack for the entire winter, offering a shiny, smooth surface, which has little adhesion for the weight collecting on it. Keep going lower.'

Wendy continued with the ruler, the squeaky crunch telling Hal that the pack was solidly bonded. But right at the bottom of the profile, conditions were very different. 'Hey! Now it's gone all soft. I can push the ruler right in.'

Hal bent down and showed the group what she had found. 'You see this? Now this is potentially deadly. Just nine inches from the ground there's this thin layer of sugar snow – big, round crystals, loosely packed. I've had my eye on this layer all winter.' Hal took the ruler and worked it round, demonstrating how soft it was, how the granules fell out around it in little showers. 'See how weak this is? This stuff is inherently unstable. And look here! Right beneath it is an iron-hard layer of wind-polished slab. That means that the whole winter's snowfall is sitting on the crystalline equivalent of ball bearings and this layer beneath it is as slippery as glass.'

He climbed up on to the slope and waded through the deep snow to get into a position a few metres higher than the vertical profile the group had just cut. 'This is the acid test,' he told the group, 'a shock loading, which proves the true stability of the pack.' He took a few shuffling steps and jumped as high as he could in the air to let his full weight slam down on to the slope.

Nothing happened. The slope held. 'Goddam.' Hal slid down on his backside, a disturbed look on his face as he contemplated the test. 'Now that is weird. My guess would have been that weak layer would have given way under that much weight. This has been one of the strangest avalanche winters I've known.'

Hal checked the thermometer, which was tied to his backpack. 'And this is the only explanation,' he told the group. 'It's still four degrees below freezing. The pack is frozen solid.'

'What if the temperature rises?' one of the clients asked.

'Well, I have to admit I'm not entirely sure. Avalanche prediction isn't the exact science we'd like it to be. I've seen weak layers like this melt away without causing a single avalanche . . . But it could be a whole lot worse.'

'Like what?'

Hal looked up on to the snowbound slopes above them. 'If the temperature rise was fast enough, the whole winter's pack could end up sitting on a hair-trigger – this fragile layer of sugar snow at its base ready to give up its grip and let the lot go all at once. We could be looking at a climax avalanche scenario.'

'What the hell is that?' Rachel felt her stomach lurch as she saw the serious expression on Hal's face.

'A climax avalanche? That's when every slope that *can* possibly avalanche *does* – virtually simultaneously. It can strip an entire mountain range of its mantle of snow in less than ten minutes. I've never seen one and I sure hope to hell I never do.'

The clients looked around the surrounding mountains in awe, trying – and failing – to imagine what that would look like.

'It probably won't happen. Last time it did was in eighteen seventy-three.'

Hal checked his watch. He would have to be in his office by midday to give his avalanche report to the local radio station.

'OK, guys. That concludes the morning session,' he told the group. 'Thanks for attending. See you next week at the same time.'

As they moved away, Hal bent to examine the weak layer once more. He stuck his finger into the crystals, astonished by the ease with which he could move it to and fro.

'What do you think?' Rachel asked.

'I really don't know . . . But I don't like it at all. I'm going to call an amber alert just in case.'

Hal and Rachel skied the mile or so to the road where the Toyota was parked and set out along forest trails for the ten-mile journey to the cabin – the wood-built home Hal had constructed with his own hands five years before. It sat on the edge of one of the prettiest valleys in the Chugach with a picture window looking out across the range. On a fair day Hal reckoned you could see sixty miles from the living-room. Today the visibility was no further than you could toss a snowball, the shingle roof of the cabin buried beneath the heaviest fall of the winter.

Excited to see her shots from the mocked-up rescue, Rachel made for her darkroom to process the film.

Hal went straight to his office, put on the headphones and switched on the direct feed to Anchorage radio. He looked out of the window at the falling flakes as he waited for the familiar voice of Angie, the studio producer, to cut in.

'You with us, Hal?'

He leaned forward to the microphone. 'I'm here, Angie. How you doing?'

'Busy show. You're on in twenty seconds.'

Hal watched the seconds tick past on his wall clock as the outgoing music track ran the last few bars.

Then he had the presenter, Ben Owen, direct on the line. 'We go now for our regular avalanche update with Hal Maher at Alaskan Avalanche Control. Listen hard if you're going out into the back country this weekend. Good morning, Hal.'

'Hi, Ben. But I wouldn't call this good. We've had more than two metres of snow in under seventy-two hours.'

'What are we heading for?'

'We have a potentially serious avalanche threat in the making. All this new snow is sitting on top of some pretty dubious foundations. If that weren't enough, there's a high-pressure front coming in right behind. If it hits us with some warmer weather then we'll be looking at some monster slides. I'm issuing an amber avalanche warning for the entire state.'

'We going to see your famous climax avalanche, Hal? The big one? You've been promising us that for years.'

Hal forced a laugh. 'I hope not. That's a once-a-century scenario. Last time it happened more than two hundred people were killed in Alaska in one day alone.'

'Scary stuff. There you have it, amber avalanche alert for the entire state. You have been warned. Thanks, Hal. We'll check in with you same time tomorrow.' The radio host signed off and Hal was left, pensive and uneasy, at his desk.

Rachel called through the door: 'Honey. Don't forget you have that session at Kalkeetcha High School at two. It took you half an hour to dig the Toyota out yesterday.'

'Hell, I forgot about that one.' Hal checked his diary and found that Rachel was right, he was due to give a talk at one of the biggest schools in Anchorage that afternoon.

'You want me to call them and cancel?'

'No. I'll get there.'

As he left the cabin Hal paused for a moment, took a deep breath of the freezing air, looking up into the leaden skies, trying to sense which way the next few days would go. If it stayed cold then the threat would hold off. But what if it got warmer? Then all hell could break loose. 'Probably won't happen,' he repeated to himself as he climbed into the Toyota.

4

The chauffeur turned into Park Lane and cut through Mayfair towards Regent Street and Soho, reaching the *Daybreak TV* studio at 5.30 a.m. precisely.

Josie swept into the reception where the walls were lined with photographs from previous editions of the show. Josie, smiling on the couch with the Prime Minister, with Kate Moss, with a beaming Monica Lewinsky, locked in a mock arm wrestle with Robbie Williams.

'Good morning!' the receptionist greeted her with a smile.

'Hiya.' Josie never lost the thrill of being a part of this place. Particularly because it was only by chance that she was here at all. Every time she walked into the building she flashed back to the first time. That moment had been five years past, but was as clear as yesterday in Josie's mind.

She was twenty-two at the time, a cub reporter, looking for a scoop and with the mighty Sebastian Turner in her sights. Her mouth was dry with fear as she approached the studio. Sebastian was hot news. Josie was no one. She had to bluff her way past the security guards to get to the receptionist. 'I'm here to see Sebastian Turner.'

'Do you have an appointment?'

'I don't, but I'm sure he'd want to see me.'

'And why would that be?'

'I want to do a profile on him.'

'Are you the same one who called last week?'

'And wrote to you six times?' Josie gave a hopeful smile. 'Yes, that's me.'

'I'm afraid Mr Turner is extremely busy at the moment.'

Josie held her ground. 'I realise that but . . .'

'He hasn't got the time to see you.'

Suddenly a figure in black motorbike leathers was next to her, his

American accent surprisingly deep for someone in his late twenties. Josie found herself looking into a dark pair of eyes set beneath a tousled head of sun-bleached hair. 'Oh. You're him,' she said.

'Is this the reporter you told me about?' Sebastian asked the receptionist. 'The one who's gone out of her way to be a total pain in the neck?'

She nodded.

Josie flushed bright red. 'I know I've made myself a bit of a pest. But I really want this interview.'

Sebastian looked more closely at the girl before him. She was blond, fit-looking, with the taut shape of an athlete. Her eyes were lapis blue. He held her gaze, noticing the way her mouth creased attractively into a smile at the edges, locks of hair curling around her ears in untamed wisps where they had strayed. 'What magazine do you work for?'

'*New Icons*.'

'Never heard of it. What's the circulation?'

'About four thousand copies a month. It's mostly read by students.'

Sebastian frowned. 'Have I got this right? You're prepared to travel in here and doorstep me on spec . . . for a magazine which barely anyone reads?'

Josie nodded.

'You're the features writer, right?'

'Yeah.' Josie fixed him with her most winning smile. 'Well, I am at the moment. In fact, the magazine is about to go bust.'

Sebastian laughed and looked at his watch. He was already running late. 'Fifteen minutes. But only so long as you understand I don't answer questions about my private life.'

Josie held eye contact, trying to keep the tremble out of her voice and hoping against hope that she wasn't about to blow it. 'Fifteen minutes and I can ask any question I like.'

The words hung in the air for a moment before Sebastian laughed. 'Holy shit. You're something else, aren't you? What's your name?'

'Josie Cameron.' Josie held out her hand.

Sebastian shook it, still laughing as he led her into his office. 'So,' he said. 'What's your angle?'

'I'm doing a series of articles called "Home-made Heroes" . . . profiles on people who make it big against the odds. You know, find out who's really behind the press releases, beyond the public image you try to promote . . .'

Sebastian leaned forward to stop her. 'Whoa! Wait just a minute. I don't *try* to promote a public image. I never wanted to get my face into the newspapers, it just has a habit of ending up there.'

Josie suppressed a laugh at his look of bruised indignation, then opened her portfolio case and brought out a file of press cuttings. 'How about all this? Sebastian Turner arriving at a première with Oscar-nominated actress Miranda DeLane . . . Sebastian Turner naked on a motorbike, posing for a women's magazine . . . standing triumphant with ice axe in hand on the summit of the Eiger. All that doesn't happen by accident, now does it?'

Sebastian gave her a disarming smile. 'So what's your point? I'm not the only person with a public profile who runs a business.'

'My point is there are about six different personalities jostling for prominence in these pages and it's left me a little confused – playboy, mountain climber, television executive, highly successful businessman . . . So which is the true you?'

'You don't mince words.'

'Well, you did say I only had fifteen minutes.'

Sebastian breathed out heavily and relaxed into his chair with a smile. 'OK. All defences down. You can have me in my entirety, probe beneath my skin, penetrate my soul . . . but I can't be held responsible for the outcome.'

'What outcome?'

'You may fall in love with me.'

Josie laughed out loud.

'Or on the other hand you might conclude, like everyone else who tries to scratch too deep, that I'm a vacuous adrenaline junkie who got lucky and who is now heading for a major slap in the face.'

'Let's start from the beginning. When did you come to the UK?'

'Eight years ago. I came to do some climbing with my friend Mike. I had a backpack full of stuff, fifteen hundred dollars and no idea of how my life was about to change.'

'The same Mike who's your business partner now?'

'The same.'

'So how come you ended setting up a magazine?'

'We were broke, looking for a way to make some money. Then we came across the idea of starting up *Flipped*. It was obvious, really.

Here we were in the midst of this community of people who were obsessed about climbing, hang-gliding and extreme sports but there was no magazine covering all that.'

'It was a niche.'

'An unexploited niche. So I persuaded Mike to get off his ass and borrow a camera – then we just went out and did profiles on all these kids doing stuff.'

'How did you fund it?'

'We did the whole thing on zero budget, borrowed the word processors, got the paper on credit, promised the printer the world. Mike did the photos. I did the words. Then suddenly we had this great-looking magazine sitting on the desk. That was a buzz. But you know about that . . .'

'In a small way.'

'So we sold three thousand of the first copy, then ten thousand of the second, then a distributor picked it up and we were flying. Then we got into fashion titles, then into photography and travel, and it just never stopped rolling. We now employ more than five hundred people on both sides of the Atlantic and have a turnover in excess of one hundred million dollars a year.'

Josie scribbled notes on her pad. 'And where did the idea to bid for a television franchise come from?'

'After five years we'd built up the magazine operation as far as we could and we were looking for ways to diversify. Television seemed like the most exciting way to go ahead. So we applied for the franchise, worked our asses off to get the bid together and wrote out a cheque for six million pounds. And here we are, three months into *Daybreak* and going strong.'

An assistant called through the door: 'We're waiting for you, Bas.'

'One more question.'

'OK, OK.' Josie was flustered as she tried to think. 'Oh, I have it. If you had to choose one key moment in your life – something that changed everything – what would that be?'

'A single momentous . . . moment?'

'Yes.'

Sebastian thought carefully. 'I would say that came when I opened a climbing magazine one day and saw a picture of Everest.'

'How did that change things?'

'Because I decided to climb it.'

Josie laughed at his sheer audacity. 'Climb Everest? Just like that?'

'Climb it . . . and fly a paraglider from the summit. A Japanese guy did it a few years back but no American has ever done it. Can you imagine the thrill of that?'

Josie looked at him, not sure if he was joking or not. 'Seriously?'

'Sure. Why not? It's a life mission. Everyone needs one. I'm thinking about signing up for a place with one of the commercial expedition companies – two years' training on smaller peaks, then the big one maybe three years from now.'

'What do you think that decision says about you?'

He turned to her, his face set in a way she hadn't seen before, no trace of humour now in his eyes. 'It defines me. I dare to live the dream. I believe that no target is out of reach if you want it enough.' Sebastian looked at her. 'How about you, Josie? You dare to live the dream too?'

For a moment their eyes locked and Josie knew that beneath his penetrating gaze she could not lie. 'I'd like to think I could. But there's no Everest in my life, if that's what you mean.'

'So tell me about yourself.'

'I thought you had a meeting to get to?'

Sebastian picked up his telephone and punched three numbers. 'Start without me. I'll be through in a while.' He leaned back in his chair. 'So. I spilled my beans, now you can spill yours.'

5

Hal and Rachel had also met by chance, two years earlier, when Rachel had been sent on assignment to Alaska. Her brief was to photograph Alaskans in their working environment and Hal's was a name that kept cropping up. 'You have to meet this guy,' she was told. 'He's like Mr Adventure around here. He teaches people to fly paragliders, he climbs big time, he skies, oh and he runs the Alaskan Avalanche Control unit.'

It was the avalanche work that interested her the most. She'd tracked down his number and left a message on his answerphone: 'Hi, Hal. You don't know me but I got your name from the Anchorage information office. I'm a photographer doing a picture book about Alaska and I've heard about your avalanche control work. So, if it were possible to spend a day with you to get some shots, please get back to me as soon as you can . . .'

Hal had been torn. He knew he should welcome any media coverage – an important part of his role was to raise awareness of avalanche risks – but the last thing he needed was a photographer hanging round his neck. Nevertheless he agreed to meet Rachel the following week at a steak house in downtown Anchorage. 'How will I recognise you?' he'd asked her.

'I'll be stinking of walrus fat.'

'I'm sorry?'

'I'm flying up to Barrow tomorrow to shoot a traditional Inuit walrus hunt.'

'Some people get all the luck.'

Rachel had arrived late, offering a flurry of apologies, with a battle-scarred Nikon round her neck and a Billingham bag full of lenses. She was dark – almost Latino in her looks – prettier and younger than Hal had imagined from her voice. 'Just got back from the north,' she told him, 'five-hour flight. My ass is going to be shaped like an airline seat by the end of this shoot.'

'Economy or business?'

She laughed and offered Hal her hand.

To her surprise, he raised it to his nose to inhale her scent. 'You were wrong about the walrus grease. Unless they've started marinading them in Chanel.'

'You're an endangered species, aren't you – an Alaskan with a sense of humour. If you must know, I managed to get a shower.'

'How was the hunt?'

'Incredible. I've done some work in war zones and it felt kind of the same, you know? The matter-of-fact business of dealing out death; it's frightening how normal it becomes once you get used to the blood.'

'I'd like to see some of your work.'

'Be my guest.' Rachel pulled a small portfolio from her bag.

They ordered the food and Hal flicked through the black-and-white prints. They were mostly portraits, moody and luminous, capturing perfectly the character of a fur trapper in his cabin, of four oil pipeline workers covered in grime, smiling together at some unknown joke.

Rachel watched him as he scanned the shots. Hal was not what she'd expected. Her preconceptions had this mountain man sketched out with a beard and a thousand-mile stare. In fact, he was clean-shaven with a strong, intelligent face and a head of wavy brown hair. Hal was cute, Rachel realised, seriously cute. She felt herself shiver a little as he turned his blue eyes back to her.

'These are excellent,' Hal told her. 'I can see why they gave you this assignment.'

'I do colour as well, but black and white is my favourite.'

Rachel told Hal about the project for the Alaskan book, a six-month assignment, which would take her into the furthest-flung corners of the state, photographing – and writing about – the men and women who made their home in this untamed place. 'The writing is the tough part,' she confided. 'But I have to develop that side. There's a lot more work around if you can photograph and write as well.'

It took Hal approximately three ounces of a ten-ounce steak to fall in love with Rachel. What really captivated him was her eyes. They were deepest brown, with tiny slivers of honeycomb-coloured pigment set in the irises. They had a teasing quality that was utterly disarming, a sparkling intensity that Hal found it difficult to turn away from.

'So. Are you happy for me to join you for a day?' she asked him.

A week. A month. A lifetime. Why set a limit? Hal wanted to ask. 'What did you have in mind?'

'Something visual. Something dynamic.'

'Well, we do a certain amount of helicopter stuff. That might be suitable.'

'What does it involve?'

'It's avoidance work. We go out to known avalanche slopes and detonate explosives. It makes them shed their load before it gets big enough to be destructive. Mostly it's for the highways agencies, but we have a few contracts for ski operators and forestry departments.'

'Is there room in the helicopter for a passenger?'

Hal smiled. 'There could be but we'll have to be fast. We're almost at the end of the season.'

Rachel had joined Hal on his next assignment. And the one after that. And the following one, too. She was a hit with his team, charming them out of their initial reluctance as she shot roll after roll of film.

Hal loved having her around, so much so that the days quickly got to feel empty when she went off on another shoot or devoted time to processing her material in the darkroom she'd built into her rented Anchorage apartment.

Winter ran into spring, the thaw marking the end of the avalanche period.

'So what do you do now?' Rachel asked him.

'In the summers? Different things. I get jobs as a mountain guide. Sometimes I run classes at a paragliding school up in the hills,' Hal told her. 'But this year's looking quiet.'

'How about you invite me on another shoot? There's still a few things I'm missing for my book.'

'Such as?'

'Such as a bear.'

'A bear? That's not a problem.'

'Wait. I don't just want any old bear. I want a bear in the wild, with her cubs.'

'That's a bit tougher. But at least your timing's right. They're waking up right now and feeding up after the winter.'

'Can you help me? I'm prepared to spend quite a few days on this one if that's what it takes.'

Hal considered his hands, suddenly shy. 'Well, I could take you out to a few places . . . if you'd like. Can't claim to be an expert on bears but I reckon I know where to find them.'

Rachel smiled. 'I'd really like that.'

As she drove away in her rental car, Rachel found herself humming 'If you go down to the woods today . . .' She wanted that bear picture to hurry up and arrive.

As soon as the river ice was broken up enough to allow a kayak to pass, Hal took Rachel for a day trip down the Evans river. It was a day of crystal clarity, the sunlight punching through the water so powerfully that Rachel could see the rocky river bottom as clearly as through glass. For lunch, they built a fire on the river bank, pan-frying the arctic grayling, which Hal pulled out by the dozen.

They sat side by side in the early sunshine, Rachel savouring the silence of the wilderness. When she spoke her voice was low, as if to talk normally would disturb the serenity of the moment.

'I could really get into this place.'

'You are really into it.'

'But it'll be over soon.'

Hal looked at her in surprise. 'It will? I thought you had plenty more to do on the book.'

'I do. In fact, I haven't started writing the text yet and I'm shit scared about that. But that's going to have to happen back home in Seattle. I don't have the money to stay much longer.'

'Don't the publishers pay?'

She gave a hollow laugh. 'Ha. Sure, they gave me an advance, but not enough to keep me here for ever. I'll have to go back to the agency work, freelancing, while I write the text and that's the last thing I want to do.'

'What type of work is that?'

'Anything. News jobs, courtroom shots, weddings. I've been doing that for ten years and it doesn't do anything for me any more. But this job is different; it's going deeper, getting under the skin of a place and its people.' Rachel prised a tiny flake of stone – no bigger than a match head – from the weathered rock they were sitting on. She flicked it out on to the glassy surface of the river, watching as the concentric ripples quickly pulsed and died. 'Still think we'll get that bear?' she asked him with a smile.

'Not here, we won't. The smell of this woodsmoke will make them wary.'

After lunch they floated with the current, too lazy to put much effort into the paddling. Hal had sharper eyes than Rachel and it was invariably he who saw the wildlife. They saw a mink, moving with liquid grace along a lichen-encrusted branch overhanging the river. Later they heard the tell-tale alarm slap of a beaver as it dived.

Finally, while they drifted noiselessly, a black bear with two cubs had come down to the river edge to drink and bathe. If the bear had looked up she would have seen the canoe and retreated. As it happened she was too preoccupied with the cubs, enabling Rachel and Hal to watch from close by as the bears splashed in the shallows, the cubs getting into a mock fight and receiving a playful cuff from the mother. They shook themselves dry and melted back into the dark shadows of the forest, still unaware that they had been watched.

Rachel lowered her camera and turned to Hal, wide-eyed with wonder. 'That was . . .' she struggled for the words '. . . a very Alaskan moment.'

'Happens the whole time,' he told her, smiling, with a nonchalant shrug. But she could see from the flushed excitement on his face that he too had been thrilled by the proximity of the bears. 'Did you get it?'

'Get it? Those were the best pictures I've taken since I got here.'

'Well, I'm glad.'

Rachel looked at him intently. For a second, Hal thought she was going to lean forward and kiss him. 'I love it here,' she said finally, 'and I don't want this to end.'

6

'So let's start at the beginning.' Sebastian had said to Josie in that first meeting at the *Daybreak* studio. 'Where did you grow up?'

Josie inhaled deeply to calm her nerves. This wasn't what she had imagined at all . . . Sebastian Turner interviewing *her*? Hesitantly, she began: 'Well . . . I lived in the north of England, a place called Durham. My father was the rowing coach at the university there. We had an old house on a cobbled street. It was right next to the river.'

'Your mother?'

'She left my father early on . . . he was kind of a demanding personality to live with. She's married to some guy that works in UNESCO. They have two kids of their own. She's been living in Buenos Aires for the last twelve years. I don't see her much.'

'So did your father get you into a rowing seat?'

'From the age of ten. I was cox for the university first eight.'

'No shit! Up against Oxford and Cambridge, big league. I can just see you in the hot seat with your megaphone.'

'We beat Oxford at the heads of the river. That was when I was thirteen. Can you imagine the thrill of that?'

'You did that when you were *thirteen*?'

'Yes. Then I grew too big to cox and I started to row.'

'Were you good?'

'I had the staying power, good endurance. But . . .' Josie glanced down at her breasts with a self-conscious smile. 'Let's just say that nature didn't want me to be a championship rower.'

Sebastian sighed. 'Yeah. My championship cycling career was cut short for the same reasons.' He burst into laughter at her concerned expression. 'Sorry. That was below the belt. Literally.'

Sebastian sipped his coffee. 'And the big life-changing moment?'

Josie screwed up her eyes as she thought. 'I'm not sure . . .'

'Pathetic! You're not leaving this room until you come up with one.' He watched her carefully as she struggled, lost for words. Then a memory seemed to strike her and for a fleeting moment Sebastian thought he saw uncertainty in her expression. He was surprised. His first impression had been of her overwhelming confidence. Suddenly she looked like she was about to lose her composure, her ready smile lapsing for a second into something more troubled.

There was an awkward silence.

'You're not asking me to believe you can't think of one?'

'No. Not at all. I can think of several. But yours is so fun . . . and up . . . mine feels, well, morbid by comparison.'

'So tell me.'

Josie looked at him appraisingly. This was outrageous, she thought. What was it about Sebastian that made her want to talk? Was it that she instinctively trusted him? She already knew she did. Wondering if she was making a big mistake, Josie took a deep breath. 'When I was eighteen my father committed suicide. That pretty well changed everything for me.'

Sebastian let out a low whistle, his face creased with concern. 'That *is* heavy. Did you expect he might do that?'

'No. It was a total shock. I knew he'd been a little depressed but not like that . . . Then one day I went down to the boathouse looking for him – he practically lived in that place – and there he was, swinging from the rafters.'

'Was there a specific reason?'

'Not that I could ever find. I know it hit him hard when my mother left him and he'd had some financial problems, but not enough to make him suicidal. There wasn't a hint it was about to happen.'

'What type of person was he?'

'Very driven. Obsessive. An athlete. He was an Olympic-class rower, had a case full of medals and trophies. He was a good coach, too, but he couldn't take losing – he'd throw stuff around the house and drink himself stupid. Then, next morning at six thirty he'd be down there riding his bike along the towpath, yelling fit to bust, coaching us for the next race.'

'How close were you to him?'

'I worshipped him; not surprising, really. After my mother left we were a team. Every race I ever won, I won it for him.'

'It must have turned your life upside down.'

'Well, it did that all right. Everything was so clear up to that point.

I was set up with a college place to do sports psychology but after what had happened I didn't last a year. It all seemed so pointless. So I went travelling round the world. Worked in a bar in Hong Kong, as a lifeguard in Australia, ran a campsite in a game reserve in Kenya. Then found myself back in England and wondering what the hell to do.'

'How did you get the *New Icons* break?'

Josie's eyes lit up. 'Now that *was* a great moment. I saw this ad in a local newspaper and went along. I discovered I love interviewing people and writing about them. And the first time I saw my name in print . . . well, that was the best.'

'But you say the magazine is on the way out?'

'It's probably going to fold. It's a shame . . . I was just getting used to the feeling of belonging to something.' Josie paused, aware that she had opened up far more than she had intended. 'I guess you must think I'm pretty sad, telling you about this?'

Sebastian shook his head, then appeared to be thinking for a while. Finally he asked her: 'You ever thought of working in television?'

Josie felt a hard knot of excitement form in her throat. His words seemed more like a challenge than a question . . . a dare almost. 'In my dreams.'

'We've been looking for a researcher on the showbiz desk. You'd have to come up with ideas for guests, persuade them to come on the show and go out to meet them to discuss what they want to talk about.'

'I don't know what to say.'

'Say yes or no.'

Josie flushed bright red. 'Well, yes.'

Sebastian checked his watch and stood as he gathered some papers together on his desk. He held out his hand. 'Welcome to *Daybreak*. I'll really look forward to working with you. Ask for personnel on your way out.'

Josie leaned forward and kissed him on the cheek in a spontaneous gesture, which surprised them both. 'I mean, wow,' she blurted. 'This is amazing!'

'Don't mention it.' He gave her a smile and left.

'Thanks,' she called after him, but her voice was too choked to be heard.

And that was the beginning.

7

After the trip down the Evans river Hal had invited Rachel back to his cabin for the first time. He was nervous as hell as they bounced up the dirt road into the remote valley and pulled up outside. 'First impression?' he asked her.

The garden was overgrown with cottonwood and willow. 'The word rustic comes to mind.'

'Is that rustic as in old and decrepit . . . or rustic as in quaint and charming?'

'Rustic as in what a *great* place.'

Rachel loved exploring the house at Hal's side, enjoying the moments of discovery, pausing in front of the many expedition photographs hanging on the walls, enchanted by the stunning view from the living-room window. Worn tribal rugs from Afghanistan and Iran were tossed here and there on the wooden floor.

'This is my office.' Hal showed her into the smallest and untidiest of the rooms. 'This is where I do the avalanche control stuff.' The walls were lined with books, many in French and German, and every one devoted to the subject of avalanche science. There were photographs here too, showing Hal and his team at a number of rescues. The desk was home to a powerful computer and a radio transmitter to keep in touch with monitoring stations through the winter months.

'Do you ever write about the stuff you do?' she asked him.

'Not yet, but I have thought about that. There's a pretty obvious gap in the market for a popular book on avalanche avoidance and rescue. All these works are pretty dry. I've been meaning to get a proposal together and approach a publisher.'

'Hey! I could do the photography. That would be a great way to stick around in Alaska and . . .' Rachel bit her lip, realising with a rush of embarrassment that her mouth was running away with her.

'Well, yeah.' Hal grinned. 'That would be a pretty neat way of teaming up.'

'You'd have to let me come on the real rescues. And I'd want to get some awesome avalanche shots.'

'We'll see. I've been thinking about it for years so I guess it's not going to happen in a hurry.' Hal shuffled papers around in a half-hearted attempt to create some order.

'What are these?' Rachel picked up a handful of pebbles, which were sitting in a small dish near the computer.

'Just a memento. Souvenir of a climb.'

'Oh, yeah. I keep hearing that you're a climber but I didn't get round to asking you about it.' Rachel juggled three of the stones. 'So where are these little babies from?'

'Everest.'

'Jesus.' She fumbled the stones, dropping two to the floor. 'You've been to *Everest*?'

'Sure. That used to be the main part of my business.'

'And now?'

'I don't guide Everest any more. I . . . well, let's just say I retired.'

Hal turned to head for the kitchen but Rachel blocked him, standing in his path, determined not to let the subject go. 'So how high did you get?'

'Twenty-nine thousand and twenty-nine feet.'

'Wow. And how high is the mountain?'

'Twenty-nine thousand and twenty-nine feet.'

'*No way*! You've stood on the summit of Everest? But that's . . . stupendous. I never dreamed you'd done that. Why didn't you say something?'

'What am I going to do, introduce myself, like "I'm Hal Maher – I've stood on the top of the world"?'

'No . . . but you could have told me. How many times were you there?'

'Six expeditions. Four times to the summit.'

She held his gaze, her eyes teasing him as they always seemed to. 'So how come you quit?'

'That's a big conversation.'

'How many people did you get to the top?'

'Thirty-five.'

'That's incredible. It sounds like a real success.'

'It was. I was making a hundred thousand dollars a year out of that business. Then I lost one of my clients.'

Rachel could not keep the shock from her face. 'One of your clients died?'

'Yes,' he answered finally. 'Yes one did.'

Hal unpinned a photograph from the pinboard and handed it to her. It showed a lone climber, standing in front of his tent. 'His name was Alex. He was a really nice guy. His death was the worst incident of my guiding career. I still blame myself even now.'

'What happened?'

Hal sighed. 'Oh, he fell on a steep section of ice I thought he'd be able to handle. I'd taken too many novices to the top. There was a lot of bad publicity about the incident. It cost me my business . . . not that I would have wanted to go back after that anyway.'

'Did he have family?'

'A wife and two children.'

'Oh, God.'

'I'm still in touch with them.'

Rachel looked closer at the picture. 'What was it that made him want to take that risk?'

Hal laughed bitterly. 'You'd be surprised. There's always people want to climb Everest.'

'Will you ever go back?'

'After Alex's death? I couldn't face it. There are too many ghosts on that mountain for me.'

'Will you tell me more about it one day?'

'Definitely.'

Hal summoned his courage to ask her a question he'd been thinking about all day. 'Rachel. How long will it take you to write your book?'

'Well. Let's see. I have a deadline to deliver by Christmas. That gives me six months, more or less.'

'I have space here. Stay here if you like. I have to go to South America with a trekking group for a month this summer so you'll have plenty of peace and quiet. After that . . . well, we can see what happens.'

Rachel was delighted, her eyes shining with excitement at the proposal. 'Are you serious?'

'Yes.'

'That's an exquisite idea.'

'I think so too.'

Rachel reached up her hand to caress his cheek, holding his eye contact all the while. 'I'm falling in love with you, Hal. You do know that, don't you?'

Hal gathered her in his arms.

'I wanted to kiss you when we were down by the river,' she told him, 'but I didn't have the nerve.'

'Got the nerve now?'

'Sure. Suddenly I feel very brave.'

8

Josie's rise through the ranks of *Daybreak* was meteoric . . . researcher to producer to presenter in three years flat.

Her relationship with Sebastian had the same heady momentum, from long, lingering nights in Soho wine bars to a breathless offer of marriage less than a year after they'd first met. Josie and Sebastian got married, barefoot, on a Bahaman beach on the south end of Cat Island. An ice-cream vendor and a taxi driver were the witnesses. Josie had a photograph from that happiest of days, pinned to the side of her dressing-room mirror.

Nearby, close to hand, was a trophy in gold: 'TV Times Television Presenter of the Year'. Josie touched it for luck before each show – twice on this particular morning . . . extra luck for Sebastian on Everest.

Josie left her dressing-room and went down the corridor to the studio, savouring the familiar electric charge of adrenaline as she walked beneath the racks of lights, the brilliant glare dazzling her for a moment until her eyes adjusted. 'When you lose that buzz,' Sebastian had told her right at the start of her presenting career, 'that's when you have to stop.'

She stood still as a sound technician wired her up to the radio mike. Then a call rang out: 'One minute. Stand by to go live!'

The floor manager raised his hand as five seconds came round. Josie watched his fingers as he counted down: 'Five four three . . .'

Through the studio monitors came the familiar opening title music. As the final chords died, the red light flickered into life on top of camera one. Josie stared straight into the lens and gave her best early morning smile as she launched into her welcoming piece to camera.

As a presenter, Josie's style was fresh and confident. She was witty, with a cheeky line of backchat, which could turn even the most staid interview into something fun. She was never intimidated by guests, even when they were heavyweight with a capital 'H'. Prime ministers, presidents, Nobel Prize winners, Josie could hold an intelligent and lively conversation with them all. And make them shine. And when it came to showbiz, chatting the chat, she was without peer. The profile she shared with Sebastian, along with the sheer glamour of his fast-growing business empire, drew big movie stars to the studios and generated useful publicity in the tabloid newspapers.

Josie rejected the predictable fashion styles of her predecessors, instead favouring clothes that did her figure justice. Most mornings she opted for tight skirts cut above the knee and pastel-coloured cashmere cardigans cut tight and low on her cleavage. Photo spreads of Josie – bikini clad – had become a regular feature of the testosterone-charged pages of magazines like *FHM* and *Maxim*. Her mailbag was bursting at the seams with protestations of lust from exactly the category of high-earning single males that advertising campaigns seem to love. 'Josie got us BMW,' Sebastian was proud of saying.

Today, Josie wrapped up the show with a beaming smile and the familiar sensation of relief when three hours of live television came to a successful close.

As she left the set, a production assistant called out: 'Mike wants to see you in his office.'

Josie's heart sank. A session with Mike was enough to blow out the high of the show. Like being called in to see the headmaster, it was never about the good news.

She walked from the studio into the main body of the building, the cavernous atrium that was another of Sebastian's dreams. It was five storeys high, boasting four fully grown palm trees – imported from Tunisia – to draw the eye of the beholder up to a glass roof of impressive dimensions. A wrought-iron staircase snaked in a helix up around the walls, draped with greenery and laid with a custom-built carpet, which had the *Daybreak* logo woven into it in miniature. The glass-fronted lift ran up a rail on one side. Set into the back wall of it was an aquarium loaded with a thriving community of tropical fish and – Sebastian's favourite – a sulky octopus. Experts had advised that the fish would sicken and die if subjected to too many trips to the fifth floor and back. In fact, they seemed to relish their up-and-down home. Sebastian had christened the octopus 'Mike' after his business partner – not that he knew.

Josie got out at the fourth floor and walked over to the deep-piled opulence of Mike's office. The room was already filled with the bitter smoke of an early morning cigar.

Mike's domain was as neat and well-ordered as he was, his desk home to a notepad computer and not much more. He was always immaculately groomed, with the type of year-round tan that only comes off a sunbed. His eyes were hawkish, appraising, set behind an elegant pair of gold-wire spectacles. Josie had always suspected there was nothing wrong with his eyesight, that he wore them because he thought they made him look good. He sat in a navy-blue leather swivel chair reading a copy of *Broadcast* magazine, his jacket off to reveal a pair of tartan braces which, along with the Disney cartoon character tie, said 'I'm fun'.

Actually Mike wasn't fun, as Josie well knew. In fact, the faster the business had grown, the less fun he'd become.

Mike was responsible for finding the advertisers who were the lifeblood of the show. Which meant his eyes were forever glued to the ratings sheets. Mike lost sleep every time *Daybreak* lost ground against its competitors.

'Check this out.' He tossed the *Broadcast* on to the desk. 'We slipped two percentage points against the BBC last week. Peaked at three point two million on that Tuesday show when we did the live link-up with Sebastian. Slumped on Thursday with the fashion special. Generally not good enough, Josie. You're letting it slide.'

'Thanks, Mike, you really know how to lift a girl.'

'Come on. We all know what you can do when you really turn it on. You light up the screen. People can't look away. What's up?'

'Well, it doesn't help to have Sebastian out on Everest, you know? It's distracting.'

'Having Sebastian out on Everest is a brilliant idea. Look at the way the ratings shoot up every time we do a progress report. Look at the tie-ins it's got us with the *Daily Mail* and the *Sun*.'

Josie sighed. 'Well, I was talking more on a personal level.'

'Don't worry about Sebastian. He's having the time of his life out there. And he's doing a great job of keeping *Daybreak* on the front page. Where we belong.'

'Did he manage to get you on the satellite earlier?'

'He did. We're all set for the party. Want to come and take a look?' He led her out of the office and they took the stairs to the fifth floor. Normally this was the area occupied by the production personnel but the desks had been cleared to the side to create a large open area for rows of chairs. 'This is where the press will be seated,' Mike told her, 'and this is the *pièce de résistance*.'

A red velvet drape had been strung on a brass rail behind a low podium. Mike pulled a cord and the drape swished to one side. Behind it was a huge plaster model of Mount Everest with a *Daybreak* flag on top. 'We thought you might pose in front of it and pop a bottle of champagne for the press. When the good news comes through, of course.'

'No problem.'

'We're going full out on this one. I've invited all our principal advertisers, and some movers and shakers from the ITC. It'll be massive and the press will go crazy when he reaches the top . . .'

'Fantastic. He'll be really pleased.'

'Be here by nine thirty. I'll warn the photographers.'

'I'll be here.' Josie made for the lift.

'Oh, and Josie?'

'Yes?'

'Be a darling and put on a short skirt, won't you? Doesn't do any harm to remind our male viewers what a great pair of legs you've got.'

She turned and fired a mock salute. 'Yes, sir.'

Mike didn't hear Josie murmur 'asshole' beneath her breath as she walked away.

9

Hal took it easy on the drive down to Anchorage for his lecture at Kalkeetcha High School. It was a couple of hours since the snowplough had been through and there were already six inches or more of fresh snow coating the road.

The school was situated down by the top end of the Cook Inlet on a stretch of reclaimed swamp. In June and early July it was so thick with no-see-ums and mosquitoes that the teachers sometimes gave up the fight and sent the kids home. In winter the flat, uninterrupted stretch of land was scoured by near permanent wind, the prefabricated classrooms virtually disappearing beneath the drifting banks of snow.

Kalkeetcha High, like many of the rougher Anchorage schools, was fighting a drug problem and a growing trend towards indiscipline and truancy among its pupils. Hal knew his reception wouldn't necessarily be an enthusiastic one.

A teacher in a thick red down jacket approached from the main building as Hal parked the Toyota. 'Thought you weren't going to make it,' she said. They carried Hal's two bags of props into the school.

The ninth grade was not in a welcoming mood. Hal was met by rows of indifferent stares and the restless chatter of a class eager to get this session over with. All they'd been told about Hal's visit was that he was going to talk about mountain safety and, frankly, they couldn't have cared a damn. There were more important things to be thinking about, like lunch . . . or the chance of a surreptitious smoke.

The teacher dumped Hal and ran, with a parting 'good luck' and a look that said 'with this lot you'll need it'.

Hal knew he had to get their attention fast. He scanned the room looking for a likely victim and found him in a gum-chewing candidate in the back row. He was oversize for his age, with that finely etched schoolboy scowl, which perfectly conveys the conviction that this whole education business was a criminal waste of his time. Beneath his baseball hat he stared at Hal with an unsmiling pair of delinquent eyes, his silver-sprayed Caterpillar boots perched on the back of the chair in front of him, to the obvious amusement of his sidekicks and the irritation of the girl he was hassling.

'Hey, you.' Hal singled him out. 'Can you handle a knife?'

The room went absolutely quiet as the words sank in. The fourteen-year-old kid turned to his friends for back-up, surprised by the challenge. He gave Hal a sullen look, not sure if he was expected to reply.

'I said have you ever held a knife?'

'Sure.'

'I have an experiment I want you to help me with. Will you come up to the front, please?'

The kid unfolded himself and sauntered to the front, enjoying the attention now, but flushed with the uncertainty of what he was getting into.

'What's your name?'

'Friends call me Zipp. With two 'p's.' A few of Zipp's cronies sniggered at this.

'OK, Zipp. Thanks for coming up.'

Hal handed Zipp a hunting knife. It had a bone handle and a highly polished six-inch blade. Zipp smiled for the first time as he took it, fooling around for his friends by holding it up in a stabbing motion and giving his best psycho look.

Next, Hal opened one of his kitbags and brought out a block of wood, a clean square of pine roughly the size of a housebrick. He placed the piece of pine on the desk. 'I want you to stab this block of wood as hard as you can.'

'Like what?'

'Stab it.'

Zipp didn't need to be told again. He brought the knife up high above his head and rammed it down into the wood. The blade struck with a clean thunk into the grain, quivering a little as Zipp withdrew his hand.

'Now how deep would you say that blade was?'

Zipp bent closer to the wood. ''Bout an inch?'

Hal put a black felt-pen mark on the blade and pulled it out.

'That was a good strike but you see how hard it is to force even this razor-sharp blade into a piece of pine. In fact, you got it in about a quarter of an inch.' He handed the knife back. 'Take another go. Show us what you can do. Use both hands if you like.'

Frowning with concentration, Zipp held the knife in both hands and brought it down with as much force as he could muster. There were catcalls and a ripple of applause as he stood back and bowed.

Hal marked it again and measured the depth. 'Not bad. About half an inch. Thanks, Zipp, you can go and sit down now.'

Slightly bewildered, Zipp returned to his chair.

Now Hal had them in the palm of his hand. 'Later on,' he told them, 'we'll be finding out why I asked Zipp to give us that demonstration. But for the moment I want you to focus your attention on something I have in this box.' He placed a picnic cool box on the desk in front of him and opened the lid. Inside was a small wooden box about the size of a cigar case, surrounded by ice. He took it out and held it up in front of the class with a flourish, handling it with care to indicate that the contents were fragile. 'Inside this box is one of the most powerful natural forces on the planet.'

He paused for effect, making eye contact with as many of the class as he could. 'As powerful as a volcanic eruption. As deadly as a tidal wave. What is inside this box can break every bone in your body; it can suffocate you; it can easily smash down houses, annihilate entire villages; every year it kills hundreds of people around the world.'

Even Zipp craned his neck.

Hal placed the box on the desk and tapped it with his forefinger. 'Now. Who's going to open it up?'

Half a dozen hands were raised.

Hal pointed to an Asian girl in the front row. 'What's your name?'

'Jennifer Yi.'

'OK, Jennifer. Come up and open the box. If you dare.'

Smiling nervously, the girl approached the desk. She hesitated for a moment, touching the box gingerly as if it might give her an electric shock. Then, glancing at her friends for reassurance, she raised the lid. Inside, the box was lined with black velvet, in the centre a minuscule point of brilliant white.

'What do you see?' Hal asked her.

'It's a diamond?'

Hal handed her a magnifying glass.

Jennifer leaned closer to focus on the tiny fleck. 'Oh. It's a snowflake.'

'Correct. Pass it around the class,' Hal told her, 'but please don't breathe on it or it will melt.'

The children passed the box between them, looking curiously at the snowflake as Hal continued: 'So now you're all asking yourselves, "How can a pathetic little snowflake like this cause all the destruction I've just described?" Does anyone have any ideas?'

A ginger-haired boy at the back raised his hand. 'If you try and drive on snow you can crash.'

'That's true, but that wasn't what I had in mind. Any other ideas?'

'Avalanche?'

'Very good. How many of you have ever seen one?'

No one had. Hal placed a VHS cassette in the classroom video deck and pressed play. An image of a snow-clad mountain came up on the screen.

'This looks like a nice peaceful scene, doesn't it? In fact, it's in the middle of the Chugach range not far from Anchorage. But watch what happens when these skiers start to ski down the slope.' Three skiers appeared at the top of the mountain, the amateur video zooming in shakily to get them tighter in frame. They began their descent, carving elegant arcs in the deep snow. 'Watch the lead skier when he gets to the steep section.' The skier paused for a moment, then committed to the slope, plunging with all his weight into a tight turn.

Suddenly the snow around him was moving, breaking up into cracks and fissures as it began to slide. The camera shook noticeably as the operator struggled to follow the unexpected action. Within seconds, all three skiers were caught in the avalanche as the centre section of the slope gave way. The first skier quickly lost his balance and fell. He disappeared from sight, sucked under as the avalanche picked up speed and thundered down the slope.

Hal paused the video and turned to the class. 'Anyone guess who that first skier was?'

They shook their heads.

'It was me. I set that avalanche off by my own ignorance. Now let's see what happened next.'

10

Josie took the lift down to the ground floor where the limousine waited. As the car sped through Soho she realised that the excitement of the show had blocked Sebastian momentarily from her mind. She felt a guilty spasm as she remembered that, eight thousand miles away, Sebastian was even now setting out on the most demanding and dangerous day of his life.

Everest. The mountain had been as much a part of Josie's life as his – as she had lived through the years of planning and training. She had decided early on that it was pointless to fight this fixation of Sebastian's – she could see by the hazy look in his eyes every time the very name was mentioned that this was something akin to a love affair. Sometimes it even made her jealous.

Everest. Sebastian had thought of the mountain as he pumped iron in the gym each morning before breakfast. He was thinking of it as he spent his weekends walking for miles with a twenty-five-kilogram pack on his back. He was thinking of it as he devoured the literature of past expeditions.

'Have you ever thought you might be obsessed?' Josie had asked him finally.

He had considered the question quite seriously. 'Not obsessed. I'd say more . . . committed.'

Sebastian did his research, getting personal recommendations from previous summiteers to find his guide. Two names kept coming up: Rick Fielding of Himalayan Objectives and Hal Maher of Mountain High.

Sebastian was keen to get Maher involved, mainly because he knew that the guide was a qualified paraglider pilot himself and might be able to advise him on the summit flight. But Maher turned Sebastian down flat, telling him he no longer guided Everest.

Fielding, on the other hand, was super keen, knowing that the high-profile client would be good for business. He had flown across to London and briefed Sebastian about what he would need to do to stand a chance of summiting the mountain. He was a wild-looking man, with a mane of shoulder-length golden hair and the type of restless blue eyes only found in mystics and dreamers. He had a nose that had seen the wrong end of too many bar room brawls and, like most guides, a tall, muscular physique, ideally adapted to the rigours of high-altitude work. He had summited Everest three times.

'Ideally you need a three-year training programme,' Fielding told Sebastian, 'gradually getting more and more experience at altitude and increasing your climbing skills.'

'Make that eighteen months,' Sebastian answered with a laugh. 'I have a short attention span.'

'How about the paraflight from the summit?' Fielding asked him. 'How serious are you about that?'

'Totally serious. I'm prepared to carry the paraglider up there myself if necessary. I need my participation to create the maximum possible publicity and the flight element will guarantee that.'

'One thing worries me. How the hell do you get enough speed to take off when you're that high?' Rick wanted to know. 'Because I'm telling you now you won't have the breath to run at twenty-nine thousand feet.'

Sebastian put a VHS cassette in a video player. 'Take a look at this. This is the documentary film of the Japanese guy who did it. He took off from a flat area not far from the summit.'

Fielding watched with interest as the Japanese climber methodically unfolded the fabric wing of the paraglider from a pack and laid it out flat on the ice. The wind was light enough to make the canopy manageable. He checked the lines – which took him another couple of minutes – then strapped himself into the harness and sat, facing down the steeply sloping drop before him.

Fielding was fascinated. 'How's he going to launch?'

'Watch.'

The Japanese aviator gave a final thumbs-up to camera and shuffled forward on his backside until he was balanced precariously right on the edge of the slope.

'Is he going to do what I think he's going to do?'

Without another word, the Japanese lifted his legs and let himself go, accelerating fast on his back for ten, twenty, fifty metres. The paraglider canopy was dragging behind him, inflating as air filled it.

Just before the final ten-thousand-foot drop, the crescent of nylon plumped up and began to rise.

Fielding watched with amazement as the parachute began to fly. Within seconds the Japanese pilot was flying stable and true, out across the western cwm, heading for his landing site far below. 'That's outrageous! He just slid down that slope until he began to fly. He didn't even need to run.'

'That's the technique I want to use,' Sebastian informed him. 'I've been practising it in the Alps and it's not as lethal as it looks. Just get up enough speed and that 'chute will open. It has to.'

'Rather you than me.'

'It's not a new idea. Paraglider pilots have been launching on mountain slopes with skis for years. This is just a variation on a theme.'

'Well, I want the final decision on whether or not you try it,' the guide told him. 'If I think you're not up to it, I'm not going to let you fly. You can walk back down like the rest of us.'

Sebastian smiled. 'Hey, I'm not in the business of throwing my life away. I'll only go for the flight if everything is right.'

'Well,' Rick conceded, 'it's been done before. So I guess it can be done again but I have the final call, OK?'

'OK.'

Fielding pulled together a detailed – and fast – itinerary, which would enable Sebastian to complete the necessary training. Sebastian paid forty thousand dollars to join up for the preliminary climbs. They took him to Argentina, Alaska, Nepal – short, three-week expeditions, which were gruelling and tough. Sebastian was with other Everest hopefuls, all with the big one in their sights. They learned how to control their breathing at seven thousand metres on Aconcagua in Chile; how to cope with temperatures down to forty degrees below freezing on Mount McKinley; how to pitch a dome tent in a force-ten gale on Mehra peak in Nepal.

Finally, the last training expedition over, Sebastian was ready. He wrote a cheque for fifty thousand dollars and mailed it to Himalayan Objectives in Vancouver. 'That's it,' he said to Josie with an excited smile. 'In four months' time I'll be standing on the top of the world, ready for the greatest flight of my life.'

Josie smiled back but couldn't help noticing a tiny pool of cold fear somewhere deep inside her. The training expeditions had been easy to deal with – losing Sebastian for three weeks was not unusual. But Everest was three months. And it was Everest.

Now that it was real, Josie felt uneasy, a feeling she disguised as well as she could from Sebastian, even as they parted company at Gatwick when he flew with the rest of the expedition to Nepal.

'I love you,' he told her, 'and I'm coming back in one piece.'

'Do that,' she said and watched him pass through passport control.

Just before he vanished from sight, he gave her a smile and a little wave.

11

The Kalkeetcha class watched in silence, their attention gripped by the video, as the avalanche filled the screen. Two of the skiers were lucky. Able to remain upright, they skied to the edge of the avalanche line on to an area of the mountainside that was still stable. The first was not so fortunate. He was buried, then re-emerged further down the slope, clearly struggling to keep his head out of the snow debris in which he was trapped.

Now the avalanche was picking up speed, almost racing faster than the camera operator could track, a swirling cloud of powder appearing at the leading edge. A single ski was propelled into the air as the skier somersaulted out of control, then he was sucked under the snow once more and lost to sight. Only when it ran out of steep ground did the avalanche slow, creating a fan tail of debris stretching for several hundred metres away from the face.

Hal paused the video. 'That is why the snowflake is one of the most destructive forces on the planet. Millions of them, poised on a slope under certain conditions, can be set in motion by the slightest pressure. It was my weight that set that particular avalanche off.' He held up a small device about the size of a cigarette packet. 'Luckily I was wearing an avalanche emergency transmitter like this one. Now let's see how it worked out.'

Hal shuttled forward on the tape and pressed play when he reached the relevant sequence. It showed the same avalanche site, with a rescue team arriving in a helicopter. The search team moved in lines, a metre apart, some pushing deep into the debris with long avalanche probes, others sweeping with radio sensors to pick up the tell-tale bleep of the avalanche beacon.

Then the camera picked up a cry from one of the female searchers, her radio catching a faint beep: 'Here! I have a signal.' She crouched down low, sweeping her arm in an arc, listening intently to the strength of the audio pulse on her headphones.

The others went silent.

'OK. It's right here.'

The team hurried over and began to dig into the debris with their aluminium shovels. Less than a metre below the surface they found Hal lying face down and unconscious.

'He's still breathing.'

The camera kept running as Hal was gently pulled from the ice, given emergency resuscitation and stretchered off to the waiting helicopter.

Hal stopped the video. 'That video was taken eight years ago. I owe my life to that rescue team. He paced the floor. 'After I recovered I started to get fascinated by the phenomenon of avalanches. I began to do some research. What causes them? Can they be predicted? How many people do they kill every year? And the more I found out, the more fascinated I became. Now I run the Alaskan Avalanche Control group and that's why I'm here talking to you today.'

Hal paused at the classroom window, a trace of a frown on his face as he saw it was still snowing heavily outside. He rapped a knuckle on the glass to dislodge the flakes, watching them fall with rapt concentration. 'Did you know, for example, that an avalanche can move at more than one hundred and fifty miles an hour? Or that every year in Japan dozens of people are killed by snow avalanching off sloping roofs?'

Hal placed his kitbag on the desk. 'But the moment I realised I was really hooked was when I found this.' He pulled out an object and displayed it to the class. It was a section of a tree trunk, a young pine some ten inches across. Embedded deeply into it was a thin aluminium plate. 'Come up and take a look.'

The children jostled around the desk.

'Can you see anything weird about this piece of tree?'

'There's something sticking in it.'

'You're right. This is a souvenir from Alpine Meadows, the scene of the worst avalanche disaster in the history of America. What you are looking at is the thermometer, which was hanging on the ski patrol office wall on that day. When the avalanche shock wave demolished the building it sent this thermometer flying through the air at roughly the speed of a bullet. It flew for more than three hundred metres across the valley and was punched into this tree to a depth of six inches.'

'Wow.'

'You may remember how hard it was for our friend Zipp to get the knife into the wood. That'll give you an idea of the sort of forces involved.' Hal turned the tree section so the class could see the thermometer more clearly – the aluminium was weathered but the faded markings of the scale were still visible. 'And if you look close enough you'll see something else – the glass tube full of mercury is still intact. That avalanche shock wave drove this incredibly fragile instrument six inches deep into solid wood without breaking the filament of glass. It still works, too – the mercury travels up and down as it should do when the temperature fluctuates.'

Awestruck, the class returned to their seats.

'So that's given you an inkling of the power of the avalanche. Now we move on to the business of trying to avoid them. How many of you have friends or family who ski or take snowmobiles out into the backwoods in the winter?'

Virtually every pupil put up his or her hand.

'Every one of them is a potential avalanche victim but with a little care they – and you – can maximise the chances of staying alive. Let's take a typical slope on a typical winter day in the Chugach mountains and look at the vital signs that can tell you if that slope is likely to avalanche or not . . .'

12

That night, on the fifth floor of the *Daybreak* studios, more than one hundred guests gathered for the party that would celebrate Sebastian's arrival at the summit of Everest. Among them were representatives of most of the major daily newspapers. Champagne and hot canapés were on constant flow, circulated by hostesses dressed in tight red dresses decorated with the *Daybreak* logo.

Josie arrived just after 9.30 to a volley of camera flashes.

At ten, Mike ushered her up on to the podium. 'Ladies and gentlemen, welcome to the *Daybreak* studios for what should prove to be a momentous night. As you all know, Sebastian is now well into his final summit attempt and we hope to be getting confirmation that he has reached the top of Everest in a very short while.'

There was a murmur of animated chat from the room.

'When he gets there, *assuming* he does get there.' Mike paused to give the audience a smile. 'We'll be establishing radio contact so we can speak to him direct. So, as you enjoy the hospitality here tonight, spare a thought for Sebastian and his fellow team members as they battle through the most demanding day of their lives.'

One of the journalists raised his hand. 'Josie. How do you feel about Sebastian joining the expedition?'

'I feel excited for him. The mountain has been a part of him since he was a child and now he's finally got the opportunity to go there. It's a dream come true.'

'What type of expedition leader does he have?'

'I think that's what makes me happiest of all. He's with Rick Fielding's company and Rick has personally summited three times before. If anyone can get Sebastian to the summit, Rick can.'

Another journalist raised a hand. 'How experienced is Sebastian at this type of expedition?'

Josie hesitated for a moment as she considered her reply. 'Well . . . it's true to say that he's never been on a mountain like Everest before.

But he has climbed lower peaks up to seven thousand metres. And, like I said, he's with the best – Rick Fielding has guided more than thirty people up the mountain, businessmen and women, people who have the same dream as Sebastian. So I'm not worried about the fact that he's never been to extreme altitude before.'

'Josie. The statistics show that for every six people who summit, one dies.'

'Sebastian won't fail,' Josie told him straight. 'No matter how tough it gets out there, he won't back down. I don't think he's ever walked away from a challenge in his life and he's not going to start now. It'll be really hard but that's what he thrives on. Sebastian is never happier than when he's getting his teeth into something and he'll be having the best day of his life.'

Eight thousand miles away, on the highest flanks of the summit ridge, still two hours from the summit, Sebastian crouched like a hunchback over his ice axe and vomited the best part of half a litre of fluid on to the snow. He fought for breath, drawing the oxygen into his lungs in great convulsive gasps, his head pounding with an altitude headache. which made his brain feel as though someone was hacking at it with a chisel. He was beyond fatigue, beyond any point of physical reference for the shooting pains that racked his arms and legs.

In front and behind him, strung out along the rope, the rest of the team members were locked in nightmares of their own. They were motionless, sapped of all vitality, broken like soldiers returning from a front.

Sebastian had got to know them well in the last two months – Stuart Mackay the shipping company boss from Hong Kong, Beppe Caro, the Italian clothing manufacturer from Milan, Mireilla Suarez, the Mexican heiress; people from the four corners of the globe who had two things in common: each had the dream to stand on the summit of Mount Everest and each had fifty thousand dollars to spend on making that dream come true.

Although he was with them, Sebastian felt completely alone and he was sure that they felt the same. In the early stages of the expedition, the lower reaches of the climb, having his fellow team members around him was a constant boost. There was always a face, a set of familiar eyes, a slap on the back or a joke to be shared in a moment of despair. Now there were no faces, just the darkly frozen tint of ski goggles and the ice-clad snouts of the oxygen masks, no conversation beyond the odd grunt, no consoling pat of human contact. 'You climb Everest just like you come into the world,' a summiteer had told him, 'all on your own. There ain't no one to help you.'

'I'm not feeling so good,' he managed to gasp to a figure looming in front of him. Hazily, he realised it was Rick, leader of the team.

'Don't pack it in now!' Rick's words were muffled through his oxygen mask. 'Dig deep, Bas. It's in there. You just have to find it.'

Sebastian nodded, feeling a resurgence of strength. Rick was right – no one had said this was going to be easy. 'How far?' he managed to croak.

'Say two hours to the summit,' Rick called back.

It was ten hours since they had left the top camp but to Sebastian it already seemed a lifetime. The night had passed slowly, so slowly that in the end he had given up trying to will the illuminated hands of his Rolex watch to move faster and had instead prayed for the dawn to arrive.

When the sun had risen he had experienced a brief moment of elation but it didn't last. With the first rays of light he had been able to see – for the first time – the true scale of the mountain still to be climbed; the work still to do; the height to scale. The distance was huge. And on Everest, he knew perfectly by now, distance was pain. As for the very summit itself? That was way out of sight, beyond one, two or more false summits, those psychologically destroying tricks of perspective that fooled a climber into believing he was about to reach the top, only to reveal more hours of toil ahead of time. The really hard part was still to come.

Sebastian preferred not to think about that, just to try to make one step at a time. If he dwelled on what it was really going to cost to push his body onwards to the top, he would probably turn back and start down.

There were five teams making their ascent that day, in total more than forty climbers. They were strung out along the fixed ropes over hundreds of metres of the ridge, disjointed figures locked in their own hell, standing as if frozen to the spot for long minutes on end before reluctantly jerking a leg up into the next snow step and pulling the body up another few inches of the twenty-nine thousand and twenty-nine feet.

Sebastian became aware that the guide was tugging on his harness to get his attention. 'Let's go,' he said.

The guide looked ahead for a target Sebastian could aim for, something not too far away. He spotted a discarded black cylinder about thirty metres up the ridge. 'The oxygen cylinder. OK? Then rest.'

Sebastian had to lean around him to one side to see the target. He nodded an agreement.

In one fluid movement, the guide turned and began to climb, kicking the front points of his spikes into the ice as the ridge steepened into a series of steps. Sebastian kicked in behind him, blocking his mind to the pain of the impact as his frozen toes were rammed blow after blow, into the narrow confines of the plastic boots.

Kick in. Breathe. Lungs aching as the freezing-cold oxygen flowed in from its icy cylinder, stripping precious warmth from his core.

Kick in. Breathe and breathe. The nagging pull of cramp tightened the muscles in his thighs.

Kick in. A stumble as hollow ice fractured beneath the spikes, leaving him with no firm foothold for a split second. He felt the rope go taut as Rick held the fall.

Breathe. Breathe. Breathe. The harness was riding up on to Sebastian's midriff, the tight rope constricting his chest. He found a firmer placement and kicked in once more, levering himself up on his ice axe with a grunt and relieving the tension of the rope as he found his balance.

Standing next to Rick once more, Sebastian paused to recover. He expected the guide to start moving straight away but something had caught his attention on the ridge.

Something had changed. It took Sebastian a confused moment to realise what it was. Then he felt it against his face. A gust of wind had embraced them. Up until that moment the night, and the dawn, had been perfectly still. But now ice crystals were beginning to circulate along the skyline. The plume – the streamer of vapourised ice that was so characteristic of Everest's highest ridge – was beginning, ever so gently, barely detectably, to run.

13

Hal got back to the cabin from the Kalkeetcha High lecture at 4 p.m., more restless than Rachel had ever seen him. He immediately went out for another look at the conditions and, as he stepped out into the backyard, the snowfall gradually eased off, ending with a last flurry of huge flakes. Above him, Hal could see that the sky was clearing as the old front moved out, taking the snow-laden clouds with it. He saw a couple of patches of clear blue – a sure sign that the new front was establishing fast. This was precisely what he had feared, the warm front was moving in with a vengeance. He checked the thermometer, which hung by the back door. 'It's getting warmer as the front comes in,' he called to Rachel. 'It's one degree below freezing.'

Hanging from the eaves of the house was a collection of impressive icicles. Some were several feet long. Hal knew he should have knocked them off long ago but Rachel had wanted to photograph them so he'd let them stay. Now he stretched up his hand and touched one gently, running his finger down its length. Hal pulled back his finger and studied it. Was it his imagination or was that a thin smear of moisture on the tip? It was barely visible, but it was enough. 'I'm going to dig another test pit,' he told her. He fetched a shovel from the store and headed for the slope behind the cabin.

When it was finished, Hal crouched at the foot of the slope and took out his plastic snow probe as he had done earlier in the day. There was only one layer he was interested in, that volatile layer of sugar snow right at the bottom of the pack.

The layer had changed dramatically in character with the temperature rise. Hal barely had to exert any pressure to ease his plastic ruler into it. He scooped out some granules and rolled them in the palm of his hand. He was astonished by its texture. It didn't feel like snow at all, more like a teaspoon of caviar – greasy, almost oily. He checked the thermometer once more, the mercury showing just a fraction below freezing.

It was rising fast.

Hal stood before the slope and tried to think himself into the pack in the hope it would offer him some final clue. He knew the history of that winter's fall virtually day by day, the stratigraphy of the cross-section he had cut was embedded in his mind more deeply than any winter before. Because this was not like any winter before.

Then, in a flash of realisation, he had it. Hal knew, with horrifying certainty, exactly how this snow pack was going to behave. And he didn't have to try a jump test to prove it. For a moment he was awestruck, paralysed, almost, by the implications of what he had deduced.

He hurried back to the kitchen door and called in to Rachel: 'Hey, come out the back. I want you to see something.'

'Can't it wait? I'm sorting out supper.'

'Come out, Rachel. You're probably only going to get one chance to see this in your lifetime.'

Mystified, she came to the door and watched as Hal paced the yard like a man possessed. He found two bricks in a corner of the lean-to and stood with one in each hand next to the test bed.

'Don't tell me you're finally going to build that barbecue you've been promising me?'

'No. Even more dramatic. I'm going to try something I've never tried before. Are you ready?'

'As I'll ever be. Just make it fast.'

Hal bowed to her. 'For my next trick I will perform the impossible.' He brought the bricks together so hard that one of them broke in two. Next to him the slope remained immobile. His expression was one of genuine surprise. Rachel laughed. 'Is that it?'

'Wait. Before you give up, let me try another tack. Maybe I need something of lower frequency.' He picked up a pickaxe handle from the woodpile and crossed to an old oil drum, which lay abandoned nearby. He rolled the drum out to the bottom of the avalanche test area, taking care to keep to the side of the trajectory.

'Ready for another go?' He paused, with the pickaxe handle raised in the air above the drum.

'I think you've finally cracked.'

Hal beat a single blow into the side of the drum, producing a sharp booming resonance, which cut sharply through the still winter air.

What happened next was so fast that Rachel's eyes barely had time to recognise it for what it was. Almost simultaneous with the sound wave Hal had created, in a single fluid movement, the entire ten-square-metre area of Hal's test bed avalanched into a pile at the base of the slope.

Rachel had never seen anything to compare with it. The snow, so perfectly inert, had almost seemed to leap down the incline. 'My God.' She walked, dumbfounded, to join Hal where he stood by the debris. 'How the hell did you make that happen? It seemed almost . . . animal, the way it shot forward.'

Hal said nothing, distracted as he kneeled to prod the pile with the axe handle. It was compacted and hard, he could not push the wooden handle in to any depth. When he did turn to face Rachel she could see that his face had drained of colour. There was a haunted look in his eyes that she had not seen before.

'What does it mean?'

'It means that every single avalanche slope in Alaska is primed right now and ready to go just like this one. The temperature rise has turned that weak layer into an ice slick.'

'And what's going to set them off?'

'Oh, pretty much anything,' he said casually. 'A deer chasing across a slope, an aircraft passing overhead, some guy out with a chainsaw.' Hal scanned the high snowfields on the valley walls that surrounded them. 'This is the day, Rachel. The day the mountains are going to fall out of the sky.'

14

As the clock hit 11 p.m. in the *Daybreak* studios, Mike was beginning to get restless and so were the waiting newsmen. It was getting late and most of them had already put in a long day's work. There was a limit to how long they could be expected to wait. 'Where's the call?' he asked Josie impatiently.

'I don't know, Mike. I have as much idea as you do.'

'We have to push the show along. I think we should try to contact base camp direct, at least get an update.' They retreated to Mike's office to make the call.

Eight thousand miles away, at the top end of the Khumbu glacier, the portable satellite unit rang in the mess tent. It wasn't a mealtime but a Sherpa happened to be in there sorting out some equipment from the expedition barrels. He called across the glacier: 'Telephone, Mr Tony.'

Tony Keller, Rick Fielding's base camp manager, hastily pulled on his soft inner boots and within seconds he was out of his tent to get the call. He had thirty or so metres of moraine to cross and, midway, he happened to glance down the glacier to the south. He stopped dead, perplexed by what he saw.

Normally the view from this place was one of the most spectacular in the world: jagged six- and seven-thousand-metre ice peaks stretching away as far as the eye could see. Now there were none, only a fast-moving cloud, pulsing up the glacier. It was a cloud unlike anything Tony had ever seen, supernaturally dark, almost maroon, the colour of a bruise. It had an unreal quality to it, seeming too sharply defined to be anything other than solid. He shivered. Was it his imagination or had the temperature dropped a few degrees in the last seconds? 'Hey, Gyaltsen! Come out here and have a look at this.'

The laid-back sirdar ambled unhurriedly from the Sherpa tent with a metal tea mug in his hand.

'You ever seen anything like that before?'

The Sherpa screwed up his eyes, his normal inscrutable expression changing to one of surprise as he saw the cloud racing in. 'No, never seen. Not like that.'

The telephone was still ringing in the tent nearby but the two men remained cemented to the spot, unable to tear their eyes away from the ominous cloud.

'Maybe some kind of monsoon cloud. But, my God, it's moving awful fast.'

'I think we have to close the tents,' Gyaltsen said.

'You reckon?'

'I'm sure.'

In the studio Josie was anxiously trying to establish contact. 'I'm still waiting,' she told Mike nervously. 'Answer it, Tony. What's keeping you?'

The hiss of static changed, wavering into higher frequencies and 'ghosting' with low-level voices as other transmissions leaked their signals into the beam between the ground unit and the circulating satellite.

'Come in. We need some news.'

On the glacier, Tony had seen enough. 'Everyone out here!' he shouted. 'We need help.'

The two men began to run back towards the mess tent. His call was too late. As he reached the canvas doorway the first hammer blow of the storm hit the camp.

Inside the tent he paused for a moment, unsure what would happen as the screaming intensity of the wind ripped into the canvas. Less than a second later he found out, as the front panel caved in towards him, sending the table flying. Tony watched in disbelief as the heavy white canvas bulged, then split with a rending crack as a seam gave way. The stinging whirlwind of driven ice particles filled the interior within seconds.

'Hold it down!'

Running from their tents, the base camp team joined in as he threw himself at the front end of the tent, snatching at the wildly flapping wall of canvas. Frozen guy ropes lashed through the air as they fought to pin the panel down. A side wall began to flare out, the skirt starting to lift free of its heavy rock anchors as the wind took control. Two of the Sherpa support team began to load it with more rocks, ripping the frozen stones from the glacier ice with their bare hands.

'The cairn!'

The shout was too late. Through the driving blizzard Tony saw a fifty-kilogram equipment barrel rolling out of control. It impacted at the base of the ceremonial cairn the Sherpas had erected to placate the gods of the mountain, scattering the stones and toppling the prayer flagpole to the ground. The wind picked up speed, bringing a new intensity to the howl filling the air.

'Let it go! Someone's going to get hurt.'

Tony watched the canvas panel shoot up in the air and fold back instantly on to the roof with a violent crash. The metal side poles began to bend as the full weight of the wind bore down on the open structure. The interior was being stripped out before their eyes as maps, files and plastic cups were spun into the air and transported away. There was a scream as a down jacket was torn from the chair it had been left on. It too was spirited off faster than its owner could move to catch it. Then the side wall gave up the fight, the brass eyelets holding it to the ridge pole fracturing one by one with a series of sharp metallic rings.

'The satphone!'

Tony found the satellite communications set behind the overturned table, already covered in snow. The ringing had stopped. Cradling it in his arms, he exited the tent just as one of the corner legs collapsed. He couldn't see the accommodation tents even though they were less than thirty metres away. Guessing the direction, he stumbled across the glacier, probing forward with his feet to avoid falling into a crevasse.

The dome tents were just standing, their igloo profiles distorted and bent. Tony unzipped the front of the nearest one and placed the satellite set on to a sleeping bag lying inside. He brushed the snow from the unit and set out again across the glacier, orientating to the whiplash of canvas and the shouts of the team.

As he came out of the blizzard one of the Sherpas thrust an end of rope into his hands. A length had been passed over the roof but even with four people on each end, their combined weight was still not enough to hold the tent down. Inch by inch, it was slipping free, dragging the guy lines until they snapped. Tony slipped and fell on to his hip as the tent billowed and twisted with one final violent shudder, the frame groaning as the metal poles snapped the stainless-steel bolts out of their securing points.

'Let it go!'

The four-hundred-and-thirty-kilogram structure cartwheeled into the white-out and was gone.

Seven thousand feet above base camp, Sebastian tried to will himself into finding the strength to continue the ascent. Looking ahead he could see a line of climbers waiting at the foot of the Hillary step – the ten-metre-high ice cliff which posed the last serious technical obstacle before the summit. There was going to be a long wait here, he realised. A wait he could ill afford as his body was cold to the core, far colder than he had ever been in his life.

Rick was just above him and, to take his mind off the nagging frost pain of his fingers and toes, Sebastian fixed his concentration on Rick's mask. The guide's goggles were mirror-coated and Sebastian realised that he could see an image of himself in the lens, supernaturally thin, distorted as if by a funfair mirror. Fascinated, he leaned closer, absorbed by the rows of great white teeth behind him, rising up, snarling, as if the mountain was about to be engulfed. Between the sharp fangs he could see a boiling mass of black and violet. Was that shadow? He couldn't tell.

A trail of icy vapour passed overhead at that moment, blanking out the sun. Now Sebastian could see more shapes in the goggles, shifting, rising. Rick tensed, stiffening as he focused on something. Sebastian saw one white fang swallowed by black. Then moments later another. 'Rick?' Even as he spoke, Sebastian was not at all sure that the guide would respond, he seemed to have forgotten his presence. 'Rick. What the fuck is that noise?'

A high-pitched, muscular roar was approaching, a sound like the rip of a jet fighter passing low overhead.

'Rick?' Sebastian tugged at his sleeve. 'What's happening?'

'Oh, my God.' The guide's words were barely audible.

'What did you say?'

Sebastian felt the hair on his head stiffen; an electric charge seemed to be running through him. 'My ice axe feels weird. Like it's wired up.'

Rick held up his hand to silence him.

Now the goggles were rippling, a landscape reshaping, redefining itself with every second that passed. There was more black, then violet, then the sparkle of something which seemed alive: lightning. The roar increased in intensity, seeming to echo off the mountain walls that surrounded them. Sebastian could not pinpoint where it came from.

'Get down,' Rick muttered. His speech was clipped as if through clenched teeth.

'What?'

'I said get down.'

Sebastian shifted his body, unable to resist the pull any longer. Rick did nothing to try and stop him as he planted a crampon into the ice and turned full round.

There was not a single mountain to be seen. Instead, the entire sky was filled with a racing mass of black cloud, rising up from an unseen world below. Sebastian watched in mute fascination as the ridge was engulfed at phenomenal speed. He barely had time to crouch for cover as the maelstrom hit.

15

Back at his desk, Hal called Police Chief Robbie McGowan at the Alaska State Troopers department. McGowan ran the police team responsible for handling road closures and evacuations in the case of an avalanche alert. If he'd been hoping for a quiet weekend, he was about to be disappointed. 'Robbie, it's Hal Maher.'

'I wondered if you might be calling. You cancelling the amber alert?'

'Not a chance, Robbie. The temperature's rising and I'm stepping it up to red.'

'You serious? We still have no avalanche activity reported.'

'You will have. Red alert. I'm putting it out on the website now.'

McGowan exhaled loudly down the telephone. 'You better be right on this one, Hal. If it turns out you're crying wolf . . . ? This decision is going to cost my department two hundred thousand dollars before the night is out. I'm going to have to get every single vehicle all chained up, the closure signs out of the . . .'

Hal cut in: 'We're not just talking about dollars, Robbie, we're talking about lives. Get your men out fast. The minutes are going to count.'

Next Hal called up Anchorage FM. His evening report was not due for another hour but the duty producer knew him well enough to interrupt the show that was in progress once he explained the situation. Hal was patched, live, into the studio, the presenter cutting the music abruptly as he greeted him.

'I got a newsflash on my screen here. Seems we've got an urgent message from Hal Maher at the Alaskan Avalanche Control unit. Hal, I know you called an amber alert earlier on today. What can we do for you?'

'I have some important news for anyone planning to travel in the next twenty-four hours and for anyone who lives or works in a designated avalanche risk area. The heavy snowfalls over the last few days have combined with a rise in temperature so that we now have a critical situation. I'm calling to advise your listeners that this is now a state of red alert. I'd like you to broadcast that in your hourly news reports from now on.'

'We certainly can. What does this mean in practical terms, Hal?'

'Unless your journey is absolutely essential, do not travel until the alert has been lifted. If you do try to use the roads, you'll find many routes will have been closed by the police. If you live or work in a high-risk area then you will have been given instructions on how to evacuate via a safe route. Do that as quickly and as calmly as you can. If you are in doubt as to what to do then call your local police department, who also have a list of instructions for exactly this scenario.'

'Are we going to see some big slides in the next couple of days?'

Hal paused, choosing his words carefully: 'I believe we are entering a period of intense avalanche activity. Perhaps the most intense for many decades.'

'Thanks, Hal. We'll spread the news.'

Hal didn't hear the final words, he was already off the line and accessing his computer to update the website. He typed in the carefully worded report and activated the computer code, which would automatically send it, in the form of a fax, to more than four hundred and fifty connections throughout the state. Within minutes, as the modem hummed into action, the warning notice was printing out in mountain rescue centres, at the homes of radio hams who would spread the news and in every police station in Alaska.

'What can I do?' Rachel was at the door.

'You can help me with the AMRs.' Hall pulled a file down and clicked the loose-leaf pages free.

'At Most Risk' was the file containing details on the properties that Hal had identified as sitting in the path of prime avalanche routes. All over Alaska there were hundreds of such properties, some occupied by families throughout the year, others used as holiday cabins. There were twenty-seven that Hal regarded as potential death traps. These were now in imminent danger of destruction and there wasn't a moment to lose. 'Take half these numbers and call the owners,' he told Rachel. 'Tell them who you are and that I've called the red alert. Tell them to follow the instructions I've left with them and to get the hell out. If anyone has any problems with that tell them that if they don't move I'm going to call their nearest police station and get them pulled out if necessary.'

'OK.' Rachel exited to use the living-room telephone.

Hal began working down his own quota of numbers.

It wasn't an easy task to tell home-owners to evacuate their properties but over the years Hal had built such a strong rapport with the AMR residents that they knew he would only ask them *in extremis*. Some were glad to be told, having watched the snow build for days.

'Do I have time to pack?' one woman asked him.

'Not if it takes more than five minutes,' he answered. 'Put on some warm clothing, get into your station wagon and drive back to the city. Half an hour packing right now could mean the difference between life and death.'

She knew from his tone that he meant it.

Then he reached the last name on the list: Stan Carroway.

The stubborn old bastard. Hal had lost count of the number of times he had tried to persuade that turkey-necked old grizzler about the risks of avalanches. But would he listen?

Carroway and his wife Louisa had one hundred and fifty years between them and every winter of their married lives they were up in the remote cabin in Cooper Valley. Since he'd retired from the coastguard Carroway had spent his summers fishing for salmon and in the winter they took a ton of the stuff in their old van up to Cooper Valley to cure in the smelter he'd built in the yard. He got through fifty sacks of beech chippings each winter. They were happy there, Louisa setting up her easel when the weather allowed and painting delicate watercolours of the winter landscapes, Stan curing his fish and setting out each morning with his cross-country skis for a precisely timed hour of recreation. 'This is what keeps us alive, son,' Carroway told Hal the first time they met, his eyes fixed beadily on the adversary. 'You won't get us out of this cabin come grizzlies, hell or high water.'

'I'm not trying to get you out, Mr Carroway,' Hal had said patiently. 'I'm just trying to tell you that one day there may not be a cabin here at all. You're plumb beneath one of the worst avalanche gullies I've ever seen.'

'You think I don't know that? We been here through all kinda weather and we've seen plenty of slides.'

'Any of them ever hit the cabin?'

'Well. no. But we've taken the risk for thirty years and we'll take it for a few longer, thank you very much.'

'Son, we're too old to change,' Louisa chipped in, 'We'll put it down to fate. Besides, if we heard one of the big ones coming we'd be up and out of there in thirty seconds flat.'

Hal couldn't help smiling at the thought of the two old timers racing out of the cabin in their nightdresses with an avalanche snapping at their heels. 'With the greatest respect, you won't have thirty seconds. If that gully goes you'll be buried under thirty metres of snow before you so much as hear a thing.'

'Poppycock.'

Hal treated the Carroways in precisely the same way as the other AMRs who refused to budge: he carefully built a relationship with them so that if it ever came to the big one, he might still be in with a chance of getting them out in time. They came to have a grudging respect for Hal and he developed a fondness for the cranky old couple. Beneath their grumpy exterior the Carroways were good people. Hal would never forgive himself if they were wiped out by an avalanche. The one small victory he had scored was to get them to agree to have a telephone line installed. Even that had taken four years of nagging to achieve. Hal's departmental budget had covered the cost.

Now, Hal picked up the telephone and dialled them. 'Stan? It's Hal Maher.'

'Thought you might be calling. No sooner do we get a few flakes of snow up here than you start squeaking.'

'I just wanted to touch base. I know you don't have a radio up there, it being the work of the devil and all that.'

'We know about radios, son. We just don't like 'em.'

'This is prime avalanche weather, Stan. I know I sound just like a boring old scratched record to you two but I want you to pack your things, get in your vehicle and drive out of there.'

'No chance in hell. We're staying put.'

'You can see how much snow you have on that hillside just outside your back door?'

'Yep. It's heavy all right, but I don't see no harm in that. That's what Alaskan winters used to be like before they punched that hole in the ozone layer.'

'Won't you do it for Louisa's sake?'

'No way. We've got the fire burning, we're all hunkered down, nothing's going to . . .'

With the softest of clicks the line went dead.

'Stan . . . ?'

Hal felt a cold spasm turn his guts. 'Stan? Answer me!'

He slammed down the phone and dialled again, cursing as he got no connection.

'What's wrong?' Rachel came into the office.

'I was talking to the Carroways and the phone went dead.'

'Shit.'

He dialled the operator and gave the number. 'Can you tell me what's wrong with this line?'

The operator came back to him after thirty seconds: 'It's cut off and I can't retrieve it from this end. They've probably got a post down in Cooper Valley.'

'Thank you.'

Rachel put her hand on his shoulder. 'You think they've already been hit?'

'I don't know. But if they're still alive I want them out of there.'

'Why don't you call up the helicopter?'

'It's too risky. The rotor noise alone could be enough to set off that slope.'

'So what are you going to do?'

'I'm going over to get them.' Hal picked up his car keys from the desk.

'There's hardly any daylight left.'

'If I'm fast I can make it over before dark.'

'Let me come with you.'

'No chance.'

Rachel stood in the doorway, blocking him. 'I need the photographs for our book, Hal. I need an evacuation.'

'This pack is right on the edge, Rachel. I don't want you to risk getting injured for the sake of a few shots.'

'You promised me when we started the project together. No restrictions, remember?'

Hal could see from the obstinate set of her face that she was not going to back down. He sighed and looked at his watch. He had less than an hour of daylight left and Cooper Valley was a good thirty-minute drive away. 'I'll put in a quick call to Robbie

McGowan at the State Troopers office to tell him where we're going. But after that I'm out of here. If you're not ready I'm going without you.'

Rachel ran to get her camera.

16

At 11.30 Josie dialled the Inmarsat number again. This time it did not ring.

'That's odd. It sounds like the machine has been switched off.'

Over the months that Sebastian had been away she had got used to the vagaries of the satellite connection, which linked the expedition – tenuously – to the outside world, but this was the first time she had heard a continuous tone.

Mike looked through the glass door at the party where the unlimited champagne was beginning to take effect. The noise level and the sound of laughter were rising as the guests steadily became drunk. 'Bloody satellites,' he said. 'We were always running a risk by trying to do this all live.'

'Don't panic. We'll get through.'

'But when? We can't keep this lot here all night.'

'We can if the champagne doesn't run out.'

'This is getting out of hand,' Mike protested. 'We have to give them some news soon or they'll start to leave.'

The telephone rang. Josie practically leaped across the room to get it. 'Yes?'

'Josie. This is Claire down on the switchboard. I have a gentleman from CNN's London bureau on the line. He says it's absolutely top urgent that he speaks to you.'

'Not a chance. We're waiting for a call from Everest on this line . . .'

Claire's voice shifted uncomfortably. 'Er, he did give me a brief idea of the context of the call and I think you should take it.'

Josie was perplexed. 'Very well. Put him through.'

The journalist was connected. 'Josie Turner? My name is Ron Purdey, I work for CNN's London bureau.'

'We have an important press launch under way here, Mr Purdey, so please keep it brief.'

'I know about that. A couple of my colleagues are there. I'm the sad one who gets left behind on the graveyard shift, except this time I'm the one to get the hot news first.'

'What news?' Josie sat down on Mike's desk.

'We have a network of stringers, as you know, and one of them is based out in Kathmandu. I just got an e-mail, which could be interesting to you.'

'What e-mail?'

'You mean you don't know?'

There was a long pause. Josie tilted the chair forward, her attention gripped. 'Know what?'

'This is not confirmed, right? My source could be wrong.'

'Tell me for Christ's sake.'

Purdey took a deep breath. 'Apparently, the mother of all storms is raging on Everest as we speak.'

Josie watched the seconds ticking away on the wall clock.

'Virtually all the lines into base camp are down,' he continued. 'I have numbers for the Italian team there and for some American expedition. I can't get any of them.'

Josie thought fast. 'What about the Everest websites? Is there anything on any of them?'

'Nothing in the last hour. My stringer got one of the last calls out of a Malaysian team but since then, nada.'

'Is there any news of Sebastian and the rest of his team?'

'According to my stringer, he's missing. And so are about thirty other climbers.'

'Jesus.'

'I'm sorry to bring you this news.'

'Have they reached the summit?'

'According to our guy no one reached the summit. The weather turned before they got there and there was a big queue of climbers all trying to get through a bottleneck – what's it called, the Hillary something?'

'The Hillary step.'

'That's the one. Anyhow, now they're still up there and God help them. We'll be running a report at midnight on this. I'm trying to pull it together now. Can I get a quote from you?'

'I haven't got the time for that right now.' Josie put down the telephone.

'What the hell was that?' Mike asked.

'That was . . . that was not good news.'

'Which means?'

'It seems a storm has hit the mountain. I don't think Sebastian's going to reach the summit now. Not today at least. And he's certainly not going to be paragliding anywhere if what I've just heard is true.'

'Where are they?' Mike asked.

'Making their way back down to camp four.'

'In a storm?'

Josie nodded.

Mike pursed his lips. 'That's all we need. We're going to look bloody stupid now, aren't we?'

'I'm sorry?' Josie's voice was cold and emotionless.

'You know what I mean.'

'You're worried about looking foolish in front of our guests?'

'Not myself. I'm worried about the company looking stupid. How are we going to handle this?'

'Mike. It hasn't occurred to you to wonder about Sebastian? About the fact that he's probably going through hell on that mountain?'

'You didn't say he was in trouble. You just said there's a storm. He's paid fifty thousand dollars to the people you say are the best so what *is* the problem? They'll just retreat to a lower camp and hang out for a bit before they try it again.'

'They might not get another weather window to try again.'

'So then the whole thing's been a monumental waste of time and we've ended up with egg all over our corporate faces.'

Josie took a deep breath and consciously tried to calm herself down. 'All right. All right. We're not going to make anything better by rowing about this. You're right, there's no reason to think he's actually in *danger*. The storm has obviously put the communications gear out of action but that's all. And he *is* with the best. Rick must have been in similar situations plenty of times. They'll probably be arriving at camp four as we speak.'

Mike strode from the office into the conference area and took the podium. 'Thank you for your patience, ladies and gentlemen, and I can only apologise for the delay in proceedings here tonight. I do have some news from Everest but it is not the news we had been expecting.'

The room went quiet.

'Some minutes ago we got a message from Everest to inform us that weather conditions have deteriorated rapidly in the last hours and it seems that Sebastian's summit attempt is postponed for the moment.'

There was a collective groan from the audience.

'I'm sorry to be the bearer of that news but that's where we are at present.' He pointed to a raised hand. 'You have a question?'

'I'm from CNN and I've just been speaking to my colleague Ron Purdey on my mobile here. His version of events doesn't quite tally with what you say. He indicated firmly that the weather change on Everest is in fact a very serious storm. Can you comment on that?'

'I believe that there is a storm on the mountain at present but since we have not managed to get a telephone call through we are in the dark as to the current status.'

A dozen hands were raised as the babble of conversation erupted.

'I'm sorry.' Mike had to shout to make himself heard. 'But since we have no more news than you do, we have to call this press conference to a halt.'

'Can we have a word from Josie?' another call went up.

Mike glanced through the glass partition to where Josie stood. She shook her head firmly from side to side. 'Josie will be leaving right away. But we'll all be here tomorrow to resume the conference, hopefully with the good news from Everest that Sebastian and his fellow team members are fit and well, and that they will be attempting the summit again. Thank you very much.' With that, Mike left the stage and fought his way back through the clamour as half the pressmen in the room tried to get to speak to him. He escorted Josie away from the ruck and into the lift for the ground floor.

'I have to get home,' she told him. 'If base camp get their telephone working they'll call there first.'

'You'll let me know as soon as you hear anything?' Mike asked her.

'Yes.'

'I don't expect you to be here for work in the morning. Take the day off. I'll get a replacement presenter.'

'No. I'll be here. The show goes on, right?'

Josie sat in silence during the limousine drive back to the house, praying like she'd never prayed before.

17

Past the Little Salmon river turning the road had not been snow-ploughed. Hal put the Toyota into low-ratio four-wheel drive, the crawler gears whining as the transmission strained to give the vehicle a purchase into the deep snow. A series of red marker poles had been placed along the edge of the road to indicate its position and now Hal used these as a guide to tell him where it was. Without them they would have floundered into the deep drifts which lurked on either side. Only the very tips of the marker poles were visible even though each was two metres high.

The light was fading fast as they entered the narrow confines of Cooper Valley, an eight-kilometre-long cut into the mountains in which only the Carroways had built themselves a home. The valley sides were steep and forbidding, in places more like a canyon, with exposed black rock jutting out through the trees. There was some pine planting by the forestry department on the lower slopes but the upper ones were bare and laden heavily with snow.

Hal stopped the Toyota and got out to inspect the track. 'Doesn't seem like a vehicle's been down for a while.' He switched on the headlights as they continued, the brilliant yellow beams illuminating a haze of tiny crystals falling from the trees where their branches interlocked above them.

'It's snowing again,' Rachel said.

'That's not snow. It's tiny droplets of water. The temperature's still rising.'

Hal put on the windscreen wipers to clear the glass as they powered in second gear through the gloomy half-light of the forest. Old man Carroway had cut the track himself and as he hadn't had the money to blast away obstacles there were plenty of twists and turns. Hal was kept busy at the wheel, weaving with the track as it dodged boulders and snaked around the larger trees. Here and there he thought he could hear the muffled rush of the Cooper river where it ran, unseen and newly melted, beneath the snow to the side of the track.

Halfway up the valley they found the cause of the cut telephone line; a telegraph pole had fallen under the weight of snow, severing the cable. 'That's the first bit of good news,' Hal said as they passed. 'Now we just have to pray that the top end of the valley hasn't avalanched.'

They passed through the narrowest part, a section so choked with massive glacial boulders that a tunnel had been dug through them. It was only fifteen metres long but Hal knew it had taken Carroway three years to excavate it. The sides of the Toyota scraped along the rock walls as they drove through.

Towards the high end of Cooper Valley the track degenerated into a succession of steep rocky ramps where a series of spring floods had partly washed away the route. Beneath the snow, boulders and slippery rocks snatched at the Toyota's wheels, rocking it violently on its springs as it skidded upwards.

With its engine groaning under the strain, the vehicle made it to the top of the wash-outs and up on to the plateau, which formed the final feature of the valley. They were driving up into a dead end – an almost perfect natural amphitheatre with a few scrawny pines and huge, intimidating walls on each side. In this open arena there was more light than in the forest, the snow almost pink with the reflected cloud bounce of an unseen sunset.

Hal brought the car to a halt. 'Every time I see this place it sends a shiver down my spine.'

'It looks so peaceful.'

'It's beautiful, that's a big part of the problem. I can understand why old man Carroway wanted to build his winter dream home here. No one could ever believe that such a place could turn against you.'

Across the flat terrain, still several hundred metres away, the Carroways' wood cabin was clearly visible, its dark shingle roof shovelled clear of snow. It sat at the foot of the largest of the valley walls, dwarfed by the immensity of the slope above it. The welcoming amber glow of gaslight was visible through the single window and smoke was trickling from the chimney. Hal viewed the scene with his binoculars, easing them skywards as he tried to assess the condition of the valley walls above the cabin. 'That slope is absolutely stacked.'

Not far in front of them was the Carroways' station wagon, parked neatly beneath the protection of one of the larger trees. From there a path led through the snow towards the cabin. Hal drew up next to the tree. 'You all set?'

Rachel was checking her light meter. 'There's not much light left. I'll have to use the ultra-fast stock.' She pulled her Nikon from the bag and loaded it up with the sixteen hundred ASA film, fixing a speedlight flash unit to the top for good measure. 'Ready to go.'

Hal gently clicked the car door shut behind him and, with Rachel by his side, set off across the snowfield towards the cabin.

18

Josie checked her answerphone – one message, sent ten minutes earlier: 'Josie, this is Deborah Fielding at Himalayan Objectives. Can you call me in Vancouver as soon as you get a chance?'

Josie punched the numbers; if anyone would have news it would be Rick's wife. Running the Himalayan Objectives office, she would be the first to know. 'Deborah. This is Josie.'

'Oh, thank goodness you called. You've heard about the storm? I'm just calling all the clients' families to let you know that we're monitoring the situation. As soon as we get any news we'll be straight in touch.'

'What the hell is going on out there? Why can't we get them on the satphone?'

'I don't know. I have to say I've never known that happen before.'

Josie felt a sudden surge of anger. 'How could Rick let them get caught in this way, Deborah? Haven't they got weather information? It sounds crazy to go for the summit on a day like that.'

Deborah sighed. 'Josie, I don't know what went wrong. But I do know how you feel. My husband is up there too. You're not the only one, you know.'

Josie held back her temper. 'Sorry. You're right. I just . . . I just can't stand not knowing . . .'

Deborah was soothing. 'Don't worry. Rick is the man for that situation. If I know him, he'll have the whole team snugged up at camp four all nice and cosy. In a few hours' time we'll get a call to say they're all fine.'

Josie thought she sounded just a bit too bright, just a bit too sure, like she was trying to convince herself. 'All right. But promise you'll call me as soon as you have information?'

'Better. I'll get base camp to call you direct once they have the communications sorted out.'

Josie put down the telephone with a detached, hollow sensation inside her, the sick feeling that this couldn't really be happening, that Sebastian would call her in just a moment and say it was all a big joke.

She ran to the sitting-room, where the resonant tones of Victor Melzac, CNN newscaster, boomed out of the television: 'News just in from Mount Everest indicates that up to forty climbers are missing in what has been described as the storm of the century. Among them is media mogul Sebastian Turner who is attempting the mountain for the first time. Let's go to our Kathmandu correspondent Pia Rothwell for the latest.'

An image of the stringer came up on screen next to Melzac. 'Pia, what can you tell us about the storm?'

'Well, it seems the storm hit the Everest region completely unexpectedly. Weather reports for the day had not predicted it so the expeditions actually on the mountain had little warning that it was on the way.'

'What are conditions like?'

'I have just been speaking to the Malaysian expedition base camp – their satellite connection seems to be one of the few that is working at present – and they told me they have recorded wind speeds of up to one hundred and forty miles an hour and temperatures as low as seventy degrees below freezing. And that, don't forget, is thousands of feet beneath the high camps where many of the climbers are.'

'Are the climbers safe in a camp or are they still stuck somewhere out on the peak?'

'There's no way of telling that as of now, Victor, but initial indications are that a significant number of climbers have not made it back to the top camp after their abortive summit attempt.'

'And how about Sebastian Turner, is there any news of him?'

'None whatsoever. Sebastian was part of a commercial expedition run by Rick Fielding, one of the leading figures in the Everest guiding scene. But as of this moment there is no news of Fielding or any of his team. All we know is that they did leave for their summit bid at about midnight local time and that they did not reach the top before the storm arrived.'

'Pia, thank you for that. We'll be talking to you later as this story develops. In the meantime we have Ed Haston on the line.'

A still picture of the bearded climber came up on screen. 'Ed, thank you for joining us at this late hour. You were one of the early pioneers on Everest. What is your reaction to the news we are getting tonight?'

Haston's gravelly voice filled the air: 'My reaction is that this is something I and many others have been predicting for a very long time.'

'That an unexpected storm could sweep the mountain?'

'That an unexpected storm could arrive while the mountain is overcrowded. In the last five years the tendency has been for more and more commercial expeditions to set their sights on Everest and, sooner or later, that was always going to end in disaster.'

'Because of the sheer numbers?'

'That. And the inexperience of the so-called clients. Everest is not just the biggest mountain in the world, it's one of the most dangerous. But that seems to have been forgotten along the way. As I understand it, some of those commercial companies will take just about anybody so long as they've got a big enough chequebook.'

'Ed, by my reckoning there isn't much daylight left out there on Everest. What is your expert assessment of their situation?'

'Their minds will be on one thing: getting to the safety of camp four. Not many people have survived a night out at those sort of altitudes and they'll be desperate for shelter. Normally it would take about four to five hours to descend from the summit to that camp but if they have poor visibility then that might be extended significantly. In the winds they've got up there they'll be moving at half speed at best, so I figure they'll still be a way off the camp.'

'Which means?'

'Which means they are many hours away from any shelter with night about to fall.'

'How serious is that?'

'How serious?' Haston found it hard to keep the sarcasm from his voice. 'About as serious as it gets.'

'How about a rescue team coming up from camp four?'

Haston paused to consider his response. 'If the information we have about this storm is correct then no one is going to be moving up from camp four in those conditions. It's too far. It's too cold. And those climbers at the south col will already be exhausted.'

'Are you saying that a rescue is impossible?'

'Nigh on impossible. Once you're in the death zone, by which I mean above eight thousand metres, you are truly beyond reach. Right now their oxygen bottles will be running out, their goggles will be useless in the driving blizzard and they'll almost certainly be without life-sustaining fluids or high-energy foods.'

'As a mountain guide, what will Rick Fielding's priorities be?'

'Right now, assuming they haven't already been blown off the mountain, his priorities will be to keep his team moving and, above all, together. It's horribly easy to get separated up there.'

'And a final word. How do you rate their chances?'

'It depends on the storm. If it blows out, then they've got a fighting chance of survival.'

'And if it doesn't blow out?'

'If the storm keeps going then I'm afraid that many people are going to die on Everest tonight.'

19

Hal carried a powerful flashlight with him. As he walked, he turned it on and directed it towards the cabin in the hope that the Carroways would be forewarned of their approach. There had been no sign from the occupants that they had heard the Toyota driving up the valley and he wouldn't put it past the old man to reach for his shotgun if he thought a stranger was unexpectedly at the door.

The snow was soft and yielding under Hal's boots, his feet sinking in above the ankles as he followed the path. Reluctant to let his eyes be drawn up to the looming hulk of the mountainside with its frightening mass of hanging snow, they were fixed on the cabin and the white lace curtains that covered the window.

He was a hundred metres away when the lace twitched and he thought he caught a glimpse of Stan's face glancing out. He had no doubt that Carroway would recognise him – even at his advanced age he was a sharp enough customer to realise that Hal was the only person with a reason to be up in that remote spot so late in the day. But would they agree to evacuate? Hal had his doubts but he was determined not to leave them overnight in the death trap they called a home. He would convince them one way or another.

Stan Carroway had spent a bit of time some years before building a flight of wooden steps up to the cabin veranda – they were useful in the summer months when the flat ground of the plateau got boggy and in winter the hand rail helped Louisa haul herself up the short rise to the door. As Hal and Rachel reached the bottom of the steps Stan Carroway emerged. 'What the hell you two doing up here at this time of the day?' he called down.

Hal put a finger to his lips. 'Keep it down, Stan. This isn't the right time to be making a lot of noise.'

Stan reluctantly shook Hal's outstretched hand and gave Rachel a starchy kiss. 'You didn't need to drive all this way to give me the same old lecture,' he said.

'I did. Your telephone's out of action.'

Stan beckoned them into the living-room, where the wood-burning stove had pumped the temperature up to something just a shade below the average sauna. Louisa emerged from the bedroom, where she'd put on a hasty layer of make-up, and graciously accepted a kiss on the cheek.

'You gonna say what I think you're going to say?' Stan fixed Hal with his beadiest stare.

'I'm sorry, Stan, but you can't stay here with the snow conditions like they are. I came up to fetch you down.'

'You know I'd fight you tooth and nail . . .'

'I know you would Stan and believe me, I understand why you don't want to . . .'

'. . . if it wasn't for one thing.'

Hal paused. 'I'm sorry?'

'We're coming with you,' Louisa told him. 'We've already got the bag packed.' She gestured to an old leather suitcase standing by the door.

'So why the change of heart?'

'I never seen Stan go so white . . .' Louisa held tight on to her husband's hand as she spoke.

'That's true enough,' Stan confirmed. 'I don't normally spook easy but I heard something about an hour ago that fair made the hairs on my neck stand up. I'll tell you, Hal, the quicker we get out of here the happier I'm going to be. I would have driven us out myself but I couldn't be sure we'd make it down the track. I figured you'd be along soon enough.'

'What did you hear?' Hal asked, the hairs on his own neck rising involuntarily.

'It happened just after you rang. I went out to check the wood store and I was just standing there admiring the first bit of clear sky we've seen for days when there was this noise from the mountain.'

Hal felt his stomach turn. 'Can you describe it?'

'Don't reckon I could, exactly, but I never heard a more terrifying sound in my life. It was like a "whoomph", a crack, like a thunderous great boom of a noise, but deeper than thunder and it was all around the valley . . .'

'Did you see anything at the same time?'

'Well, this is the thing. Along with the noise I could have sworn I saw the mountain shake, like the snow was settling down . . . but not just a little patch . . . I mean the whole goddam snow pack moved in a single mass. It dropped about a metre, then it stuck.'

Hal looked out of the window at the surrounding slopes. 'It's worse than I thought. Get your boots on now. We haven't got a moment to lose.'

'What about the fire? Shouldn't we put out the fire?'

'Leave it. We don't have time.'

Hal ushered them to the door and out into the chill of the evening. Rachel took a series of photographs as they negotiated the steps.

The sky was darkening rapidly as night fell, the first stars faintly brilliant to the east as a crescent moon rose over the ridge. Hal switched off his flashlight, realising, once his eyes adjusted to the silvery blue light, that they could all see perfectly well without it.

At the bottom of the steps Louisa paused, looking back at the cabin. 'Are we ever going to see this place again?' she asked.

'Sure we will,' Stan told her. 'We'll be back when the snow conditions allow.'

'So where are we going to stay in the meantime?'

'You're both coming home with me and Rachel,' Hal said.

Hal had left the side lights illuminated on the Toyota and the two pinpricks of white light acted as a friendly beacon across the plateau. They walked towards them without a word, Stan striding purposefully ahead, upright and military with the leather case, Louisa making slower progress behind, leaning on Hal for support.

Rachel went ahead by a few steps, turning occasionally to fire off a photograph.

20

Josie sat cross-legged, watching the telephone, motionless as she had been all night, ignoring the pressure in her bladder and the cramps in her legs. The television news had run every hour but little new information had emerged from Everest. She had never felt further from someone she loved.

Sebastian was locked in a world he knew nothing of, and which – Josie was now beginning to understand – he might not be destined to survive. He himself had told her that any mistake up there was likely to be fatal . . . even the tiniest error of judgement. But to try to summit when a storm was rolling towards them across the Himalayas? How had that happened? How could they have put their necks so far into the noose?

A huge well of anger began to build inside her as she pictured Sebastian, crouched in some scooped-out hollow, his skin cracking like the hide of some abandoned animal carcass as it turned to ice, his arms reaching out towards a place of safety . . . and finding nothing but the clawing bite of the wind.

She imagined she was there, how she would shelter him with her body, embrace him to mask the power of the blast. Then she could feel him being physically blown away from her, the wind ripping him from her arms, tearing him from her embrace, his fingers slipping from hers as the last screaming pull of the storm whipped his body into the air and carried it, broken, away into the night.

Some time before, during the Gulf War, Josie had interviewed the wife of an RAF pilot who had been shot down and captured by the Iraqis. It was the height of the war and her husband had been paraded, bloodied and bruised, in front of the television cameras like some kind of sick exhibit in a freak show. Josie remembered the question she had asked: 'Is it possible to articulate how you felt when you knew that your husband was being held – possibly even tortured – by the Iraqis?'

The woman had thought for a very long time before replying with as much dignity as she could muster: 'I wanted to share his pain. To take some of it away from him. But I knew no matter how hard I tried I could never take away even a single blow; that was the hardest thing, the frustration of knowing that he was being hurt but that I couldn't do anything to prevent it.'

Now Josie recalled the infinite sorrow of those words, understanding them more deeply than she had ever done before. Like the pilot's wife, she would not give up hope.

Sebastian would survive. She was so desperate to hang on to this that at first she allowed herself not even the merest glimmer of despair, not a scrap of uncertainty to undermine the fragile edge of faith, which tied her to the spot. She clung to the certainties, ticking them off against a mental list one by one. He had the best clothing. He was with the best high-altitude guide in the business. They had walkie-talkies, ropes, Sherpas to help them every inch of the way. The ground was known. Hundreds of people had climbed it. It was 'the yellow brick road' – wasn't that what someone had called it, 'a highway in the sky'?

The very idea that all of that could somehow be rubbed out . . . erased and nullified by a storm? That was the type of fate that befell Scott of the Antarctic, in an era before weather satellites and mobile communications. Sebastian and his team couldn't get killed by something so simple as a storm . . . could they? She kept that fire burning inside her all through the night.

While Sebastian fought for his life.

21

Stan's account of the 'whoomph' noise had given Hal plenty to think on and the more he considered it the more he felt like gathering Louisa up in his arms and breaking into a run for the Toyota. In the occasional avalanche awareness courses he gave for cross-country skiers Hal always talked about the 'whoomph' factor. Basically the advice was this: if you were ever crossing a slope and you felt the whole lot shift in a sudden jolt – and got that 'whoomph' at the same time – that was your one-minute warning to get the hell off and go ski somewhere else. It was like the tell-tale puff of gas a volcano emits before the big bang. To a layman it might look like a harmless emission of smoke – a shower of small stones. To the volcanologist it is the clue that tells him the mountain is about to blow its top.

There was something else preying on Hal's mind: as Stan had described it, the sound had come from *every* direction at once. Normally the 'whoomph' would come from one particular slope – the localised effect of a weak layer snapping under the strain. Hal had never heard anyone describe it as coming from all around. What did that mean? He had a hunch he knew but he sure as hell didn't want to stick around to find out.

When they reached the Toyota, Hal opened the tailgate to let Stan place his bag inside while Rachel helped Louisa into the back: 'There you go.'

Hal took his place in the driving seat, slipped the clutch and put the Toyota in gear. 'Let's go, Stan.'

The old man paused where he stood at the back of the vehicle, looking back at the still glowing gaslight in the cabin window, some unknown thought passing through his mind.

'I'll get him in,' Rachel said. She walked round to Stan and placed a hand on his shoulder to usher him gently into the car. Then she reached up, placed her hand on the tailgate and slammed it down hard.

And that was all it took.

The shock wave was a feeble one but, under the circumstances, it was enough. The wave of sound created by the slamming door raced through the air, hit the valley walls and sprung the mountain into life with all the explosive force of a finger triggering a gun. An answering retort came back, an explosive detonation that rent the air like the crack of some celestial whip. It was unlike any sound Hal had heard before: nature's ultimate fury unleashed. And it came from all around, as Stan had said.

'That was the noise . . .' Stan's voice cracked with confusion as his mind tried to comprehend what his eyes were seeing, 'But this was bigger . . .'

'Get in the car, Rachel!'

The crack became a rumble, a sub-bass note, which made the ground shake. The windows of the Toyota began to reverberate and rattle as the sound waves pulsated aggressively through the atmosphere.

Hal squinted out into the half-light, trying in the adrenaline rush of the moment to assess what the accumulated mass of snow was going to do. It could still hold, but he knew it wouldn't. Terror gripped him as ink-black fracture lines ripped across the valley walls.

'Avalanche!' Hal yelled the warning in the split second after the slope began to move. He turned in his seat, shouting back to Rachel: 'Get into the car!'

Rachel was transfixed, scarcely able to comprehend the magnitude of what she was witnessing as millions of tons of snow gathered speed and began to race down towards the valley floor. She raised her camera and started to shoot.

'Sweet Jesus,' the old man muttered, 'That's a slide all right. I guess we can kiss the cabin goodbye.'

'Rachel! Forget about the shots!'

As he spoke the avalanche swept down towards the cabin like a hawk tumbling out of the sky on to its prey. For a second or two, even in the blue cast of the moonlight, it was possible to appreciate the scale of the billowing cloud – hundreds of feet high – before it descended on the cabin and obliterated it into so much matchwood. There was a flash of orange light – perhaps the stove exploding as the pressure wave blew the cast-iron chamber apart – then it and the cabin were gone and the mushroom cloud was hunting across the plateau towards them, a boiling, livid mass, travelling faster than Hal had ever seen an avalanche move before.

Next thing Rachel knew, Hal was bundling her into the front seat of the Toyota and racing back to the driver's seat where he slammed the vehicle into gear. The 4x4 leaped forward and began to forge across the plateau, the engine screaming at high revs as Hal pushed his foot to the floor. In his rear-view mirror he could see the avalanche gaining on them, the roar intensifying with every second as the pressure wave powered after them at more than one hundred miles an hour.

Hal made for the edge of the plateau, willing the vehicle to go faster, changing up through the gears as the tyres bit into the snow and picked up speed. He was faintly aware of a gasping, panting sound from the back seat – Louisa hyperventilating with fear as Stan struggled to get her seat belt fastened. He knew their only hope was to make it to the steep broken ground of the wash-outs where the plateau dipped down and the track descended. If he could get the Toyota into the lee of one of the ramps then there was a chance – just a chance – that the pressure wave would be deflected and the mass of the avalanche turned to the side.

In the mirror he saw the avalanche hit the Carroways' station wagon – the one-tonne vehicle and the tree it stood beneath were tossed thirty or forty feet in the air, before rolling and cartwheeling in the bow wave for a few seconds and then disappearing into the turmoil that followed. Now Hal knew there was no chance they would reach the edge of the plateau before they were swallowed up. There were just a few seconds to count before the first wave hit them from behind and try as he might to coax more power out of the Toyota he knew that there was no escape.

Suddenly Rachel screamed: 'Hal look to the side!'

The shock of her call caused Hal to spin his head round for a split second to glance through the side window. Coming towards them, its pressure front even bigger than the one closing up on them from behind, was a second avalanche. Illuminated by the blue-grey cast of the moon, it seemed ghostlike, almost spectral as it speeded directly towards them.

A beat later Hal turned his head and made eye contact with Rachel. Her face was bloodless and white, the proximity of death in her eyes as she held tightly on to her camera. They exchanged no words, there was no time because at that same moment, over her shoulder, Hal saw the third avalanche tumbling across the plateau.

He realised in that heart-stopping second that he had been so preoccupied racing to beat the avalanche coming up behind them that he had not even considered the possibility that they were threatened from the sides. He knew with sickening certainty what had happened: all three sides of the bowl had been released at the same time – the entire amphitheatre had ripped out in one avalanche, which had formed three separate fronts, one travelling down the valley, the two side ones racing down from each wall to meet it at ninety degrees.

Hal slammed the Toyota into third gear and continued on his direct line for the plateau edge, driving straight across country and abandoning the track, which wasted time weaving around minor obstacles. He crashed straight through the middle of a cluster of juvenile pines – the crunching of the wood as the trees were beaten down under the front bull bar hardly audible against the ever increasing rumble that now surrounded them.

22

Sebastian lay on Everest's summit ridge, locked in a state somewhere between confusion and terror, with the wind-blown figure of Rick huddled next to him. They were buried in fast-drifting snow.

They were out of oxygen, out of fluid, two insignificant specks of barely functioning life in the vastness of an unseen terrain.

The storm had not stopped, as Rick had promised it would. If anything, it had grown in ferocity as the hours had gone past, the wind rising from occasional gusts reaching one hundred miles an hour to an almost constant hurricane force blast in excess of one hundred and fifty miles an hour. The conditions were beyond Sebastian's imagination.

He was in a state of shock.

He tried to focus, a niggling pulse of life force telling him that if he let his mind drift away he would be finished. They were on the ridge . . . that much he knew. Beyond that the only two certainties were that Rick was still with him and that the storm was still raging all around. Of the other climbers there was no sign – Sebastian had not seen them for hours since they had become separated in the confusion of the white-out.

Rick was shivering violently – a phase Sebastian had experienced himself as he passed through the early stages of hypothermia.

Now, Sebastian was hovering on the borderline of acute mountain sickness – the altitude-related condition that begins with disorientation and, if the victim does not descend, ends inevitably in death. Dimly, he was aware that something was changing, changing inside him. His feet and hands had lost all sensation some time before but now the cold was eating into his core with more urgency. He could feel its frozen talons squeezing the warmth out of his guts.

Until this day Sebastian had always thought of cold and wind as two separate entities. Now he realised they were not. They were one, slicing through the nine protective layers of Gore Tex clothing as sharply as the keenest blade. Sebastian felt the enemy clawing into him, like a creature burrowing its way to his vital organs. His mind blanked out for a while, then he realised that Rick had forced himself to his feet again. Sebastian squinted up at him, seeing that the guide's face and wind suit were so encrusted with ice that he was almost perfectly white. Sebastian felt himself pulled upright.

In the early stages Rick had yelled words of encouragement: 'This storm won't last long!' Sebastian could remember, and, 'You'll die if you lie down, Sebastian, do not lie down now.' Once the guide had even hit him hard on the side of the head, to rouse his client from the stupor into which he was inexorably slipping.

Now Rick wasn't yelling anything at all. He couldn't; earlier, he had taken off his oxygen mask to give Sebastian his last air and in the course of inhaling a deep breath had frost-burned his lungs right to the deepest tissue. He was having severe trouble breathing as he hauled Sebastian to his feet and dragged him blindly in a direction chosen at random.

Neither of them could see further than a metre at most, there was too much wind-whipped ice in the air for that. Rick was lost. It was seven hours since he had seen a landmark he could recognise.

As he stumbled after the guide, Sebastian could physically feel his tendons cracking where the frozen flesh in his legs was tearing itself apart. Somehow he knew, instinctively, that this would be the last time they would move – that they had already given too much. And besides, what were they looking for anyway? Sebastian didn't really know. A tent? There were no tents this high. More oxygen? All of their bottles were out. A fixed rope? They wouldn't have the strength to descend it. He was losing the will to carry on.

The ground was falling away more steeply once more, with blue ice beneath them. Sebastian could see rough steps had been cut into the slope. Rick used his body weight to push his axe as far as he could into the ice and turned a loop of the rope wearily around the shaft. He indicated for Sebastian to climb down.

Sebastian turned awkardly to face him at the top of the section. His feet were now so frozen that they barely responded to the commands of his brain. He leaned back and placed his front spikes into the ice, stepping down mechanically as Rick eased the rope around the axe belay. Less than halfway down Sebastian could no longer see Rick's shape above him, just the thin red lifeline of the rope disappearing into the white void. Looking up, he misjudged a kick, snagging a crampon spike of his right foot on the neoprene overgaiter of the left. An enormous gust of wind struck a vicious blow from the side. Unbalanced for a critical moment, Sebastian spun sideways into the face, striking it hard with his shoulder and hip. The blow winded him, making it impossible to shout a warning to Rick as his weight shifted on to the waist harness. Sideways to the ice, Sebastian could not spin himself back into a standing position and his attempts to secure a foothold merely ended in glancing scrapes with the spikes.

Rick continued to lower him slowly down the step until Sebastian felt his body roll on to the broader shelf at the base. Still gasping for air, he slumped on to the ice on his side, too winded to move. The rope went tight across his shoulders as Rick tensioned it from above. Sebastian stared at it, then closed his eyes as the wind picked up in a new assault. Where was he and what was he supposed to do . . . ? Then a figure was climbing down from above, so slowly that an hour seemed to drift by as the crampons punched one after another into the ice. Sebastian fought panic. Find a point of reference, he told himself again. Focus your mind . . .

Rick shook him. 'Don't sleep,' he shouted at his client. 'Sebastian, don't sleep . . .'

But Sebastian merely buried his head in the crook of his arm, trying to find a refuge from the bruising velocity of the storm. He sensed Rick lying down beside him.

Slowly an image seeped into Sebastian's mind, a picture as cruel as it was beautiful. As close to him, and as far from him, as it would ever be. It was Josie, tears running down her face. Suddenly he was overwhelmed with an unbearable sense of loss. 'Josie,' he whispered, his lips cracking like parchment, the single word sucked away immediately by the wind.

Sebastian let his head rest back on to the ice.

23

One more glance in the rear mirror told Hal everything he needed to know. His entire rear vision was filled with the cloud of pulverised snow as it snatched at their back bumper. He could feel the steering loosen, the wheel fighting against his grip as the other end of the vehicle was lifted from the ground. Suddenly the rush of noise increased massively on Hal's side and in that instant he saw their one infinitesimal chance of survival: that the avalanche which had come from the left-hand wall of the bowl was going to collide with the one behind them and that it might even knock it off course. Nothing on earth could neutralise the destructive power of the force about to annihilate them, but if the two avalanches collided before the vehicle was hit . . . ? Hal had no idea what would happen but in the following ten seconds of madness he was about to find out.

The crescendo reached its peak as Hal gave up his battle with the steering wheel. From behind the vehicle all hell broke loose as the shock wave of the two avalanches colliding caused the rear windows to implode. Briefly, above the deeper roar there was a high-pitched hissing sound, the finer particles drumming against the metal body, punching pinholes into the aluminium. Then the interior was a circulating mass of ice as the windows blew out of their rubber seals one by one.

Hal felt the pressure blast as it enveloped the car, the faint thud of an explosion as one of the tyres was ripped apart by a razor-sharp shard of ice. He threw himself across the cab, using his body to protect Rachel as best he could, as larger chunks began to hit the bodywork, the entire vehicle slewing sideways as a slab the size and weight of a truck spun with a sickening crunch against the passenger side. Then the Toyota was airborne, tossed into a three-hundred-and-sixty-degree roll, which crushed the roof down in a scream of rending metal. Next thing he knew, Hal felt the car dumped back upright, then sent spinning into a glissading skid that ripped them backwards across the plateau at awesome speed. The slide went on for what seemed an eternity, the vehicle demolishing clump after clump of the saplings, pushed forward by a turbulent blast of hurricane force wind. A bone-jarring impact shook them, smashing Hal's shoulder against the dashboard as the vehicle was pounded into something hard, then it slipped sideways down an incline and ground to a halt.

Hal shook himself free of the snow blocks covering him and raised his head. He could sense from a movement beneath him that Rachel was still alive. The Carroways were both crying in the back, Louisa screaming in short bursts as Stan tried to help her upright in her seat. Somewhere in the violence of the impact they had clashed heads and both were bleeding profusely.

Hal looked around to try to orientate himself, realising with astonishment that they had been thrown right off the plateau. Some hundred metres away, a white mushroom cloud was now racing *away* from where he stood and towards the other side of the valley.

What the hell was going on?

At first he could make no sense of it . . . but then his mind clicked in; the side avalanche had not only demolished the one coming directly down the valley, it had *swallowed* it whole, changed its direction and the combined force of the two was now running for the far wall, straight into a head-on collision with the slower-moving third arm.

It happened a second later: a cataclysmic coming together of forces. Sixty million tons of ice travelling at one hundred and forty miles an hour smacked straight into forty million tons of ice travelling at ninety miles an hour. The reverberations were picked up by seismographs as far away as Seattle, the rumble heard twenty miles away in Anchorage. And that, Hal now comprehended in a blinding moment of truth, was what caused a climax avalanche – the climax avalanche that was about to wreak havoc across the state; the climax avalanche that was about to peel every ounce of snow off the walls of Cooper Valley and send it on a mission of destruction, which would leave no tree standing and no creature alive.

On both sides of the valley, avalanches were beginning to shoot down towards them, the sides peeling away neatly in a funnelling effect, which formed a perfect trap. Bruised and dazed, Hal watched with a mixture of wonder and terror as the world came in towards him. Far away, in unseen valleys, he could hear a distant rumble as slope after slope was fired into action.

He realised he had just two options: sit there and wait to be destroyed . . . or drive.

He pulled himself upright in the driver's seat, remembering as he did so that somewhere along the line the engine had stalled. He turned the key, cursing as it failed to fire. He tried again, gunning the accelerator as the engine came to life.

The Toyota lurched out of the dip with a graunching protest of twisted metal where one of the front panels had been smashed in against a wheel. Hal ignored it, gunning straight into high revs and piloting the vehicle directly down towards the forest at the base of the valley. Just a short distance inside it was the rock tunnel and now Hal fixed every part of his being on one single intention – to get the Toyota into that tunnel before the next wave of avalanches hit them.

Both headlights were shattered. He had to punch the remains of the windscreen out on to the bonnet to give him any vision at all. The slope was peppered with embedded boulders and hollows, the Toyota careening from one impact to another as Hal fought to keep the momentum going. The smell of burning rubber filled the cab as the exploded tyre shredded itself on the rim, the metal wheel glowing red hot as it spun over rock and ice.

Then he was in the forest, weaving around the larger trees, smashing down the smaller, branches lashing continuously against the front so that the interior was filled with pine debris and the smell of crushed resin. There was barely enough light to see by, the moonlight filtered out by the higher branches; Hal twice came close to running straight into trees, which would have stopped them dead. The rumble from Hal's right-hand side grew rapidly, changing in pitch as the sound of splintering wood reached his ears.

The tunnel was just ahead, the black entrance visible through the trees. Hal pushed harder on the accelerator. To the side he could sense the whiplash of the trees as the force moved in among them. Suddenly the Toyota was sliding out of control, a mass of snow catching the rear and spinning the vehicle backwards towards the tunnel mouth.

In his last moment of consciousness Hal realised that they had been spun around to face directly into the pressure front, into the oncoming face of the avalanche. Out of the oblivion the splintered end of a seventy-year-old pine tree flew vertically towards the Toyota, its trunk at least a metre wide. As it punched through the front of the vehicle Hal felt the first particles of powder enter his lungs in one drawn-out suffocating breath, then all was black.

24

Josie retreated to the living-room sofa, wrapped herself in a blanket and switched on the television to see if there was any more news. There was, but not from Everest. Frustrated by the lack of pictures, CNN had switched its focus to another breaking story, this time in Alaska, altogether closer to home. She was dimly aware of a disaster being reported on the television screen in front of her. The pictures were night-time scenes, illuminated by the harsh glare of television lights. They showed terrible devastation, houses, cars and railway tracks shattered, twisted and destroyed in frames of spectacular carnage. At first she thought it must be an explosion, but as they cut from scene to scene she realised that the images were not from one catastrophe but from many.

A reporter was standing in front of what was once a ski lodge, the building in ruins and strewn down the piste. Josie turned up the sound to listen. '. . . early reports indicate that more than forty people have been killed this evening in the worst series of avalanches to hit Alaska since records began.' The camera cut to a hospital entrance where victims of the disaster were being brought in. They looked like car crash casualties, heads and limbs bandaged and in some cases soaked with blood. '. . . throughout the state, hospitals have been stretched to the limit as hundreds of victims are brought in by private car or ambulance.'

A shaken-looking police officer flashed up on the screen. 'We're only beginning to gauge the true scale of this disaster. Seems like just about every valley in the south of the state has avalanched all at once. We believe that there may be as many as a hundred or more people still missing. Probably buried in cabins or cars which have been caught.' The commentary continued as the pictures cut to library shots: 'Among the missing is Alaskan avalanche expert Hal Maher. He issued a red alert just hours before the killer slides began but now his whereabouts are unknown. Police fear he may have been caught himself as he tried to warn others of the impending disaster.'

25

The impact had smashed several teeth. Hal could feel their shattered remains as he ran his tongue around his mouth. He spat out the sharp, alien pieces of broken enamel, coughing up the compacted powder snow from his airway and pushing his right arm into the hard mass of ice around him to create an air pocket.

All was silent. It took his mind an unknown passage of time to understand where he was – and that he was still alive. Twisting the muscles in his shoulders and neck, Hal tried to move his head, only to find that it was pinned tightly in position. He could feel that his left arm was behind his back, stressed close to breaking point if the pain was anything to go by.

The final moments came back to Hal in a series of vivid images; the speed at which the avalanche had swept the Toyota backwards towards the tunnel, the tree coming out of the wall of white, the steel-hard impact of his face against something metal as he was dragged, spinning uncontrollably, out of the vehicle. Then the blackout.

Hal realised he wasn't even aware of feeling cold. The prospect of slipping off into a deep sleep was warming and attractive. He forced himself to resist the temptation because he knew that would be the end. Blood was dribbling into his eyes, a steady, thick fluid tracing a warm path from his mouth. A stubborn electric pulse of memory fired up in his mind as he tried to blink free from the stinging plasma – a handful of half-forgotten words from the winter survival course he ran each year. The blood was running *down* from his mouth to his eyes. That was when Hal figured he was upside down, which would explain why his temples were tight with the rhythmic pulse of his heartbeat.

Experimenting, he moved his left leg above him, finding to his astonishment that it was free. So, as far as he could ascertain, was the right. Hal paused to summon his strength, jamming his left leg into solid terrain and tensing the knee to push. The violent movement twisted his torso round at the waist, forcing his head and shoulders free from the snow debris in which they had been buried. He lay on his side, shocked and bruised, panting with the exertion. The world was completely still, the phenomenal roar of the avalanche long gone. It was colder than before and from somewhere above him persistent showers of spindrift were sweeping down, dusting him with freezing powder. Near him was the driver-side door, torn from its hinges.

Rachel. The Carroways. The thought of them brought Hal to his feet. He stood, swaying, resting against a fallen tree trunk as he spat out another mouthful of blood, swearing beneath his breath as the exposed nerve endings reacted painfully to the cold air. The moon had risen higher in the night sky and, as Hal's eyes adjusted, he was able to make some sense of his location. He was standing a few metres from the tunnel entrance, which was now partly clogged with snow and the debris of broken trees.

Inside the tunnel he could see the glow of a red light – one of the tail lights of the Toyota. It seemed too high off the ground. Hal blinked in confusion. Around him, the forest had been razed to the ground. Like the aftermath of some devastating hurricane, not a single tree stood, just chewed-off stumps by the thousand, the ground a mass of fallen trunks.

Hal took a few faltering steps into the tunnel entrance. 'Rachel!' His shout came back to him, mocking, in the form of an echo from the far wall. He screwed up his eyes, struggling to pick out detail in the dim red light. Now he could see it, the wreckage of the Toyota was visible inside, partly crushed beneath the weight of the huge tree, which Hal now recalled had hit them in the final seconds.

He started to fight his way through the splintered trees, clambering over and under the confusion of broken branches, falling into unseen pits between them. Sharply fragmented wood was everywhere, cutting and gouging him for every careless movement. He spotted a torn piece of white metal. It was a section of the front wing, embedded in the snow. Hal rocked it to and fro until it worked free. The sharp piece of aluminium would make a useful tool if he had to dig.

He reached the vehicle, his heart sinking as he saw that it was upside down, half buried in the snow which had been forced into the tunnel. Thank God for the tail light, Hal thought, at least he had some illumination to work by. He tapped the wing section against the axle in three sharp knocks, praying for a response to tell him that someone was still trapped in the wreckage . . . and still alive.

A muffled cry came back.

Hal couldn't make out the words but it was definitely Stan Carroway's voice. 'I'm getting you out, Stan.' Hal began to dig as fast as he could, knowing that if Stan was alive there was still hope for Rachel and Louisa. Even if they were unconscious, they could be trapped in an air pocket and he knew of avalanche victims who had been successfully rescued after hours under the snow. The smell of petrol was strong – Hal figured the fuel tank must have been ruptured as the vehicle rolled. He concentrated on the passenger side, scooping and scraping away the compacted snow until he was breathless with exhaustion. Finally he got down to the window frame where he could reach into the area of the back seat.

A bony hand grabbed him with a feeble grip as he heard Stan's voice, weak and shaking with shock: 'Louisa's still alive . . . I can hear her breathing next to me. For Chrissakes get us out of here before this thing goes up in flames.'

'You're going to be all right, Stan,' Hal told him. 'I'm digging you out as fast as I can.' Then he shifted his body so he could ease his hand in further towards the front, reaching up into the constricted footwell of the passenger side where snow had failed to penetrate.

An air pocket.

At first he felt nothing. He moved his body head first down into the cavity to get better access to the space. Then he felt a tiny movement . . . and the warmth of life.

A groan of pain. Rachel was also alive.

Hal pulled back and began to dig once more, slicing into the frozen pack with the torn piece of metal until he had exposed the entire side of the Toyota on the passenger side. It took him an hour to achieve this and a further hour to extract Stan and Louisa from what remained of the back passenger area.

Stan was in deep shock, Louisa alive but unconscious. Hal found the bag they had brought with them and spread clothes on the snow before laying them side by side. Stan pulled Louisa into his arms to warm her as best he could.

Then Hal returned to the task, digging a new hole so he could get access to Rachel. It was a delicate job to manoeuvre her out of the constricted space without damaging her body further.

Finally, borne out of the wreck of twisted metal and shattered trees, Rachel was free. Hal could see immediately that one of her legs was broken. Shaking from the exertion of retrieving her, he placed her gently on the clothes next to the Carroways to try to assess her injuries. She was deeply concussed, possibly already in a coma, and he could see from the damage to the side of her head that the tree trunk must have caught her as she tried to duck down into the floorwell of the car. Hal ran his fingers down the side of her head and was relieved to find no tell-tale jutting of bone that would mean a fractured skull. She could live. They could all live if he could get them to hospital.

The radio. Hal experienced a surge of hope. He left Rachel, to squirm back down into the wreckage of the Toyota only to find that the unit was smashed, the internal circuitry spilled out in a mess of twisted wire and broken circuit boards.

Suddenly Hal heard a noise from the valley outside, the muffled clatter of rotorwash as a helicopter flew overhead. A rescue team was out looking for them. Now Hal remembered his last conversation with Robbie McGowan at the State Troopers office – he had told McGowan he was heading out to Cooper Valley to try to get the Carroways out. But how would they possibly be seen in the dark? The Toyota was hidden in the tunnel and there was so much debris on the valley floor that even with their thermal-imaging camera the rescuers would not see the heat of one tiny human figure.

Hal could hear the helicopter sweeping up and down the valley in a search pattern, the intensity of noise rising and falling with each pass. Then the acrid smell of petrol gave him an idea.

Fire.

Hal knew he had to move fast; the helicopter wouldn't search for long once they saw the scale of the destruction.

Strapped in the back of the Toyota was a gallon can of spare fuel. Hal retrieved it quickly, thankful it hadn't ruptured in the roll-over, as had the main tank. But how to ignite it?

Carroway. The old man smoked a pipe. Hal crossed to him and shook him by the shoulder to rouse him. 'Stan! You have a lighter?'

Stan looked at him in confusion and did not respond as Hal began to search his pockets. He found a brass Zippo in the old man's back pocket and made his way as fast as he could through the broken trees to the tunnel entrance. The helicopter rotor was already getting fainter as the aircraft searched further down the valley.

Hal beat his way to a safe distance from the tunnel, unscrewed the cap and began to shake out the petrol. When he'd covered a sufficient area he took some paces back and sparked up a flame on the Zippo. He tossed the lighter on to the fuel, stepping back as it combusted with a big roar. Soon, the flames were rising five metres into the night sky, the orange light casting jagged shadows among the fallen trees.

The helicopter was too far away, the flashing strobe of the tail light a mere pinprick in the night. Hal sat on a tree trunk, praying it would make one more pass. Slowly the sound of the rotorwash increased once more as the machine made its way back up the valley. Abruptly, it changed tack, moving away from the straight-line course up the middle and heading directly for the fire. Hal stood, feeling dizzy and weak, waving his arms above his head, as the searchlight of the rescue helicopter picked him out. Then it was hovering directly over him, the propwash creating a mini whirlwind of leaves and broken fragments of bark.

Hal saw a figure being lowered from the open door on a winch cable. He wanted to shout a greeting, but the world was spinning too much. By the time the paramedic reached him, Hal had collapsed to the ground in a faint.

26

Despite having had no sleep, Josie decided she would go ahead and present the show as she had promised Mike. If nothing else, it would give her a chance to escape the pressure of this endless wait.

Before dressing, she crossed to the window and pulled the thick curtains back a few inches. Across the road, wrapped up warmly against the gloomy drizzle of the night, four or five press photographers were gathered in a group, staking out the house on the orders of their picture editors. They wore their cameras round their necks, ready for action, the long three-hundred-millimetre lenses ready for a chance shot if Josie should try to leave. Another car drew up, two more photographers inside, the back seats also loaded with their cameras and lenses.

With a sickening lurch, Josie realised that this day – this day that felt like the end of the world – was really the beginning of the story for the press. From now on she knew that no amount of pleading would keep them off her back.

As she went down to answer the chauffeur's call, the telephone rang once more. It was Everest base camp again: Tony, still sounding as though he was speaking from the deck of a storm-tossed ship. 'Sebastian and the others are still not back at camp,' he told her, his voice flat and emotionless. 'Not even Rick. Another team have reported they saw bodies huddled together near the south summit.'

'Oh, Christ. Can't you get them on a radio?'

'We did get a snatch of radio from Rick about four hours ago. We think he's still alive – possibly with Sebastian.'

'What did he say?'

Tony sounded strangled by his own grief: 'He was distressed. He didn't make sense. He said he was in trouble and wanted oxygen before he could move. He told us he can't feel his feet.'

'Can anyone get oxygen to them?'

'I think not. There's no chance in hell of anyone making it up there in these conditions even if they were willing to try. We're preparing for the worst, Josie, I can't pretend otherwise.'

Josie wanted to lash out, to swear at this, the only voice she had to rage at. But she knew it would not help.

'Thank you for telling me.' She put down the phone. There was nothing more she needed to say.

Moving like a robot, she was too shocked to notice the flashes of the photographers as she walked to the limousine. She ignored their frantic questioning.

Mike was waiting for her at the studios. 'Well done for making it,' he said. 'We've had thousands of calls coming in all night. The whole world will be watching this morning. Are you sure you're up to it?'

'I can't think what else to do.'

Mike noticed how ashen Josie was. 'Have you had any news?'

'It doesn't look good, Mike. Sebastian could die up there today.'

'Come on. Stay positive. You know how tough he is. He'll be back with a hell of a story to tell. The whole country is behind him. He'll come back a hero and we'll send the ratings through the roof. You'll see.'

Josie looked at him blankly and allowed herself to be escorted to make-up where a television was running with CNN.

'You want me to turn it off?' the make-up girl asked her.

'No. Leave it on.'

27

The rescue helicopter had flown Hal, Rachel and the Carroways straight to Anchorage General Hospital, where the casualty department was in a state of pandemonium. New avalanche victims were being brought in every few minutes.

Hal, revived by the paramedics during the flight, watched as Stan and Louisa were quickly examined and pronounced to be in no serious danger. Rachel was worse. Much worse. A surgeon took one look at her injuries and had her spirited away to an operating theatre. In the confusion, no one tried to stop Hal as he followed the stretcher along the corridor. He sat outside the operating room, trying not to bleed on to the floor as he waited. One or two passing nurses tried to persuade him to get his own injuries treated but he stubbornly refused to move.

It was an hour before the surgeon emerged. 'Your wife . . . ?'

Hal forced himself to concentrate. 'My partner.'

'Your partner has suffered multiple trauma. We pulled a six-inch piece of metal out of her thigh and she has numerous fractures to the legs and ribs. There are superficial injuries to the head but so far as we can ascertain there will be no lasting effects.'

'She'll make a complete recovery?'

'She'll be mending for some months, but I believe she will make a complete recovery . . . in time.'

The surgeon looked at Hal appraisingly, as if trying to assess if he was strong enough for the next piece of news. 'I'm afraid for the baby there's no hope.'

Hal looked at him in confusion. 'The baby?'

'Your partner was pregnant, Mr Maher, but I fear that her abdominal injuries are such . . . ?' He gave a small shrug, the gesture of a professional man used to the imparting of bad news.

'Thank you for telling me.'

'Now may I suggest that you get your own injuries seen to? I appreciate you've wanted to stay with your partner but I really think you need patching up.' He took Hal by the elbow and led him through to the casualty ward where a dozen other patients were still waiting. A camera crew was there, locked in an argument with a nurse as they tried to film. The nurse was doing her best to persuade them to leave but the reporter was insistent. 'These pictures are going out live,' he told her, as the cameraman panned around the room, finally fixing on Hal.

28

Josie watched the television screen in a daze as the camera panned around a casualty room, finally focusing on a tall figure, bloodstained and clearly injured, his clothes ripped and torn. 'What about Everest?' she wanted to scream out loud, why were they so obsessed about this avalanche when her beloved Sebastian was in so much . . . Then something in the victim's face made her realise that his pain was like hers.

She turned up the volume as the reporter's voice explained the scene: 'As the night wore on, hospitals all over the state have been taking in the wounded, including Alaskan avalanche expert Hal Maher.' The reporter moved closer to the confused-looking man. 'Hal, you've been saying for years that a catastrophic series of avalanches like this was a statistical possibility. Are you satisfied that enough was done to prevent more bloodshed?'

Hal spoke slowly, in obvious pain from a mouthful of shattered teeth. 'The police and the authorities did everything in their power,' he said. 'But what we have witnessed here is a freak event.'

'Where were you when the avalanche began?'

'I went up to the Cooper Valley to try to persuade an elderly couple to move out of an avalanche zone.'

'And that was when it started?'

'Yes.'

'Can you describe what you saw?'

Hal paused and considered the question before shaking his head slowly. 'No words can describe what I saw up there.'

'Did the old couple make it?'

Hal appeared to be swaying on his feet and his voice was groggy as he answered quietly: 'Yes, they're both alive. Can I go now, please? I think I need medical attention.'

The reporter was persistent, unwilling to let his victim go before he had squeezed every last drop. 'Have you any comment on the forty deaths confirmed so far?'

Hal looked at him in horror. 'Forty deaths . . . I had no idea it was so high . . . oh, my God.'

The cameraman focused in tighter on Hal, framing in on a big close-up, which had his face full screen.

As the shot lingered, Josie found herself becoming uncomfortable, willing it to cut away since his obvious devastation was almost too painful to watch. How many times had she seen the same helpless expression in war zones, after bomb explosions, the face of a man who has seen his world ripped apart.

For a second he looked up at the camera, his expression fleetingly angry, then the tears began, flowing in rivers, cutting dark tracks through the bloodstains on his cheeks. He whispered a few distracted words: 'It was my fault . . . I should have called the red alert sooner . . . if only I'd . . .'

A nurse took him by the arm and away behind a screen as the camera panned away to find a new victim.

29

They toned out the bags beneath Josie's eyes, just in time for her to take her place on the sofa. As the clock ticked round and the red cue light came on, Josie forced her face into a smile. 'Good morning and welcome to *Daybreak* . . .' Josie's voice suddenly faltered as a sob caught in her throat. For a brief instant she stopped, as she saw herself reflected in the lens of the camera. She thought she could see the figure of Sebastian by her side.

And that was when she knew. He wasn't coming back. Sebastian was dying, probably already dead. She was as certain of that now as she had been earlier that he would survive.

The hope died.

Everest had killed him.

The tears began: agonised, rending sobs, which came from a deeper place than she knew she had inside her.

The camera lingered on her face for a while before the gallery realised Josie was not going to recover. They faded to black as she ran from the studio.

PART TWO

The Siren Call

30

Twenty-four hours after the avalanche, Hal discharged himself from hospital. He was as stiff as hell, beaten and bruised from being ripped out of the Toyota, with one fractured rib, two broken fingers and a mouthful of sawn-off teeth. The staff nurses had forbidden him to leave, suspecting he would suffer from delayed shock, but no power on earth could have kept him on that ward.

He waited until a shift change and slipped out of a side door on to the street from where he walked, with some difficulty, to a nearby garage owned by Denny, a member of his rescue team. Predictably, Denny was out, helping with the post avalanche clear-up, but his wife Tina gave Hal the keys to her Ford Bronco and forced him to down a couple of Advil. 'You sure I can't run you back to the hospital?' she asked him, watching in horror as Hal eased himself, with evident pain, into the driving seat.

'No thank you,' he replied. 'But tell Denny I'll be coming along to help with whatever they're doing as soon as I've cleared the calls at the cabin.'

'You take the car for as long as you need, you hear?'

'Get Denny to call me on the radio when he's free.'

Hal drove up to the cabin and went straight to the office. He could see the computer e-mail server flashing urgently at him, the LED read-out telling him there were more than ninety messages needing his attention. Hal knew that every one of those callers would be seeking his help or advice.

The telephone rang.

'Hello?'

'Thank God I got you, Hal. This is Deborah, Rick's wife down in Vancouver. I've been trying to get you all through the day. I didn't know if you were dead or alive until I saw you on the TV.'

Deborah. Hal was relieved it was a friend on the end of the line. 'I'm sorry. I've been at the hospital and only just got back.'

'Is Rachel all right? I saw from one of the reports that you'd been caught in one of the avalanches.'

Hal decided he could not hide anything from her. 'She was pregnant, Deborah. But not any more.'

'Oh God, Hal. I am so sorry.'

'I blame myself. If I hadn't let her talk me into taking her with me . . .'

'What's her condition?'

'She'll be in traction for quite some time. Her left leg is well smashed up but it seems they saved it.'

'Is she conscious?'

'Heavily sedated. I saw her briefly this morning before I checked myself out. She could recognise me but they're stacking her up with morphine.'

'Does she know . . . ?'

'About the baby? Yes. They told her when she came round from the first big op.'

'Have you talked about it with her?'

Hal sighed. 'Not yet. That's something we'll have to deal with later.'

'Have you seen any other paper or news today, Hal?'

Something about the desperation in her voice finally alerted Hal that she was not calling merely to commiserate. 'I've deliberately avoided them. This is all too big to handle . . . so many people have died.'

'I know you've just been through hell, but I have more bad news for you and I want you to hear it from me and not from some newspaper or whatever.' There was a sob from the other end of the line.

Hal realised for the first time that she was crying. He sat down heavily on his chair. 'It's Rick, isn't it? You heard something from the expedition?'

'The climb was a total wipe-out, Hal.'

'A wipe-out? How do you mean?'

'Six died in a storm. Rick was one of them. I know this is . . .'

Hal felt his heart pump hard in his chest. 'Rick *died*? I can't believe it.'

Deborah took a big suck of air. 'You're not the only one, Hal. I can't believe it, the rest of the climbing world can't believe it, but there it is in black and white. He's not coming back and neither are five of his clients.'

'Rick died on Everest? Was he injured?'

'No. But it seems he stayed with some clients when they got lost. They ran out of oxygen . . .' Deborah's voice cracked up into tears. 'Oh, Hal, it's all so desperate.'

'How did it happen?'

'Don't ask me. I've spent the last twenty-four hours on the telephone trying to find out what the hell's been going on on the mountain. Most of the time the satphone's been down from the storm. The press have been crawling all over the place, mainly because Sebastian Turner was one of the fatalities.'

'The media guy?'

'Yeah.'

'The press won't let that one go in a hurry.'

'I know.'

There was a long pause, broken finally by Hal. 'How are the children taking it?'

'Totally distraught and in shock, like me. Rick was invincible, Hal, we all knew that. How could that happen to him?'

'I can only think he must have been trying to save some clients. It must have been one hell of a storm.'

'Why, Hal? Why that day, at that time, just when they were at their most vulnerable? Can you answer that?'

Hal knew there was little more he could say. 'Anything I can do, just tell me, OK? I'll come down to Vancouver, go out to Nepal. Anything, you hear?'

'Oh, Hal, thank you, but it's enough just to hear your voice and know that you understand. Fact is, you've got a nightmare of your own to handle up there. It sounds like the whole state just avalanched.'

'That's not far from the truth.'

'How long will it take to clear things up?'

'God only knows. Could be a month. Maybe more. I have nearly one hundred messages on my machine here and every one of them is going to be someone reporting an avalanche, wanting help with body retrieval, or advice on whether more slides are on the way.'

'I have to go, Hal. I'm going to make some more calls. There are still people I need to talk to. But listen, whatever happens, you must come down to Vancouver for the memorial service.'

'When will you have it?'

'Six . . . eight weeks from now. I'll let you know.'

'Just for Rick?'

'For the whole team . . . I mean, everyone who died. Rick always told me that that's what I should do if the worst ever happened. Will you come?'

'I'll be there.'

'Thank you. I'll call again when we both have more time.'

Hal put down the receiver and looked at the flashing LED in front of him.

He pressed the button and the first message rang out. It was Robbie McGowan at the police centre: 'Hal. An update. We have one hundred and eighteen reported avalanche sites scattered mainly through the southern part of the state. Forty-one fatalities confirmed and a further six people missing. At least twenty-six cabins have been destroyed, a full half a mile of railroad track up at Jasper and plenty more. Call me as soon as you can.'

Hal stared out of the window.

Where to start?

31

Three days after Sebastian's death Josie finally summoned the courage to return to work. A question of pride, she told herself. She knew it was what Sebastian would have wanted.

Six uniformed security guards and a pair of self-conscious-looking policemen were waiting at the studio, along with approximately fifty newspaper photographers. A volley of flashes blinded Josie as the photographers jostled with the security guards to try to get prime position. Josie kept her head down and ran for the studio entrance. She swept into reception where the smiling photographs of great moments in the history of the show now seemed like nothing more than a sick joke – Josie knew she couldn't quite muster that winning smile today.

Mike was there, along with several of the show's senior producers.

Mike embraced her. 'My deepest sympathies, Josie, and from everyone here at *Daybreak*.'

'Well. What can I say? Sebastian lived on the edge . . . we all knew that. And sometimes people who live on the edge pay the price.' Josie bustled away, moving quickly towards her dressing-room. She found a black outfit on the rail – Jacqui, the wardrobe assistant had been sharp enough to think that one through.

When the telephone rang she picked it up in a daze. 'Josie?' It was the receptionist. 'We're getting hundreds of calls of commiseration from viewers.'

'Make sure you thank them for me.'

The technicians were gentle with Josie when she walked through to the studio, the soundman miking her up while at the same time telling her: 'It takes a lot of courage to do what you're doing here today. I know the show goes on and all that but I tell you, not many people could sit in front of that camera after what you've been through.'

His words boosted her confidence. Sitting in make-up she had experienced a last-minute burst of doubt – was she doing the right thing? Or should she give up and succumb to her grief alone at home?

Josie took her place on the sofa just as the last seconds were counted down. She breathed in as deeply as she could in a final bid to calm her nerves, realising too late that she hadn't had time to run a check on her hair or clothes.

The red light flicked on and with it Josie's face came to life as it had done hundreds of times before. 'It's six o'clock on the twenty-eighth of April and a very warm welcome to the *Daybreak* breakfast show. For the next three hours we'll be easing you into the day with our unique mix of news, celebrity guests and special features, so sit back and relax as we kick off with a round-up of the latest news.'

The master camera indicator went off, leaving Josie to dab at her forehead with a handkerchief as she tried to reduce the sweat. The prospect of having to jolly her way through the next three hours was one which made her feel faintly nauseous. 'Don't lose it,' she told herself, a quiet voice inside warning her to be calm. 'Sebastian wouldn't want that.'

And so the first days passed, filled with flowers, telephone calls and grief. Each morning Josie held it together through the three hours of the programme and then collapsed as soon as she reached the sanctity of the house.

Sleep was elusive. For the first time in her life she began to drink late at night – two large vodkas to help her slip into oblivion. She spent hours staring vacantly at the television, as if she was waiting for some miraculous news to emerge from Everest.

The press was insatiable. The sensational story of Sebastian's death ran on and on, as the journalists ripped every last piece of meat off the bones. Not that there was much for them to go on. The fatalities had come right at the end of the pre-monsoon season and no one would be visiting the high ridges of the mountain until the weather once again allowed. But that didn't stop the speculation – much of it hurtful to Josie: 'Sebastian Turner – was he murdered?' was one front page 'exclusive'. 'Last message from the death zone,' ran another, carrying a fictitious radio call from Sebastian. The quality broadsheets went for in-depth analysis of the disaster – bringing in 'experts' and reconstructing, as far as they could, the final hours of the climbers. Rick and his company came in for a great deal of criticism, and Josie saw Rick's wife Deborah quoted frequently, defending his record and rebutting the critics who were already accusing the dead leader of negligence.

Josie didn't want to get involved in the debate but, on Mike's urging, she did give a number of interviews to mass circulation women's magazines. 'You've got to be careful about your profile, Josie,' he told her. 'Keep the sympathy going and your viewers will stick with you.'

She spoke of the emptiness of a marriage so brutally destroyed and of her determination to be strong, of her love for this man who had been so cruelly taken from her. That was what they wanted, after all, along with the grief-stricken photographs – without make-up – dressed, always, in black.

The tabloid photographers were the worst – hounding her at home and at the studio. Some louse went through her dustbin and found an affectionate letter she had been meaning to post to Sebastian. One of the gutter papers, unforgivably, printed it. Josie had never felt so foolish or ashamed.

Every day she added an extra loop to her habitual run. It was the only therapy she could think of. Before long, she was out there running for two or three hours a day.

32

Hal parked in the hospital car park and made his way through the antiseptic corridors to Rachel's room. He hoped he wouldn't be challenged by security – with his beat-up face he looked like a vagrant wandering in after a late-night fight.

Rachel was asleep, the lighting in the room subdued. On the table next to her an untouched meal was waiting to be cleared. Her left leg was heavily plastered, hauled up in a complicated traction device that made Hal wince it looked so painful.

He pulled up a chair and sat there looking at her, seeing that even through her black eye and swollen lips she was still as beautiful as ever. He ran his hand over her forehead, feeling the heat, the film of sweat as her body's immune system struggled to make some sense out of the trauma inflicted on it.

Finally her breathing altered, becoming more shallow as she came out of the sleep and turned to see him. 'Hey, Hal,' she whispered.

'Are you OK?' he asked her gently. 'You want me to call the nurse for some painkillers?'

'No. I'm stacked up with pills. I can't feel a thing. But you look like you could use some yourself.'

'Listen. They told me about the baby. You don't have to worry about telling me about that, OK?'

Rachel closed her eyes. 'It was eleven weeks. I don't know why I hadn't told you . . . I was meaning to . . . that night . . .'

Hal brushed away the tear that welled from the corner of her eye.

'I never even asked you,' she continued. 'Do you like the idea?'

'I love the idea,' he told her, 'and when we get you out of here we can start again.'

'It might be more difficult. I'm pretty banged up inside . . .'

'They told me.'

'It was the camera, Hal. Isn't that weird? It was that camera that killed our baby.'

'What?'

'I've been thinking about it. They told me the injury was caused by a blunt object about three inches wide being punched into my stomach when the vehicle was crushed. That was the lens of the camera . . . I had it in my lap. Oh, Hal, I'm so sorry . . .' She reached out to hold his hand as she began to sob. 'And the worst thing is the whole avalanche was my fault. I was the dumbass who slammed down that door. That was it, wasn't it?'

'Anything could have set it off, Rachel. I told you . . .'

'But it was me. I was so stupid I didn't think . . .' She looked at him for a long while. 'Hal. How many people died?'

'They're still counting. It's going to be more than forty. But those lives are on my conscience, not yours.'

'The Carroways?'

'They're OK. Louisa has concussion and plenty of bruising. Stan is as right as rain. He's already asking them when they're going to let him out of here.'

Rachel smiled. 'Thank God.'

'I went back out to Cooper Valley with the helicopter today to get their clothes and possessions out of the tunnel. I retrieved the camera too. For what it's worth.'

'Thank you.'

They sat silently for a while, Hal holding Rachel's hand.

'What about the rest of the AMRs?' she asked him.

'The AMRs? They're all alive. Thank god they got out when we told them. I only wish we could have helped the others . . .' Hal stood, pacing the room, agitated now. 'If only I'd been faster off the mark. I should have called the red alert twenty-four hours earlier, then those forty people might not be dead.'

'No one in the world could have known for sure, Hal. If the temperature hadn't risen so fast, maybe nothing would have happened at all. It was a freak event, like you said yourself.'

'Maybe. But if I could turn the clock back . . .'

'There's nothing we can do – either of us.'

Hal returned to the seat and laid his head next to Rachel's. They lay like that for a long while, Hal finally breaking the silence: 'There's one more thing you have to know.'

'What?'

'On the same day as the avalanche there was a storm on Everest. Rick Fielding was killed.'

Rachel was stunned. 'Have you spoken to Deborah?'

'Yes, she called me. I'm sorry to give you more bad news but I knew you'd want to know now rather than later.'

'Deborah . . . she must be destroyed.'

'Pretty much. We'll go down to Vancouver when you're healed and spend some time with her. She may need help.'

'That's a good idea . . . My god, I never would have imagined that could happen to Rick . . .'

Hal left soon after, not wanting to tire Rachel out.

But his visit had left her disturbed . . . particularly the news about Rick. As she lay on her hospital bed, Rachel recognised that however bad this time was for her, it must be infinitely worse for Deborah. Deborah had lost the man she loved. Rachel thanked God that Hal was still alive. Hal was right, she realised, they should make sure they went down to Vancouver to spend some time.

When she was healed.

33

Sebastian's memorial service was held in a West End chapel three weeks after the storm, Josie inviting more than two hundred guests from *Daybreak*. 'Sebastian wouldn't have wanted this to be miserable,' Josie had told the organisers. 'Let's try not to make it too morbid.' But the weather was conspiring against her; it rained solidly all day, drenching the congregation as they hurried through the streets of Marylebone to the church. The interior was dark and sinister, with what seemed to be half of the congregation sniffing and coughing with colds. She found the echoing hymns deeply depressing.

The speeches were from Mike and a vicar who was supposed to be fashionable with the celebrity set. Josie thought him smarmy and unctuous, his clever words of praise about Sebastian irritating, as she knew the two had never met. At the end of an interminable hour, she was relieved when they were able to spill out into the street and breathe fresh air.

A drinks reception was held afterwards at the *Daybreak* studios. Josie drank a glass of wine fast, trying to numb the feeling that she had somehow let Sebastian down with this lacklustre day. 'I've never seen such a totally despondent crowd of people,' she told Mike when she got a chance.

'They're all scared,' he said. 'No one knows what the future is going to be like now Sebastian's not around. Just about everyone in this room depends on *Daybreak* for their jobs and I suppose they're terrified there's going to be some big changes.'

Josie wasn't slow to pick up on his words. 'Are there? Is that your way of telling me?'

Mike sucked in his cheeks, his habitual preamble for bad news. 'Between me and you, yes, there might have to be. The magazine market has been declining steadily over the last few months and *Daybreak* isn't yet as profitable as we'd projected.'

'So what are we looking at. Cuts?'

'Well, we'll see.'

'You can trust me, you know? I'm not just another employee. I'm not going to go blabbing to all the rest.'

'It's a question of confidence. Sebastian was very much the public face of the company. His profile made things like raising money relatively easy. Without him, we're going to have to fight twice as hard.'

'Has *Daybreak* still got debt problems?' Josie knew that Sebastian and Mike had been fighting to keep borrowing under control.

'Every company has debt problems,' Mike replied, 'and we're no different. That's why the advertising revenue is so critical. The difference between profit and loss for us is the difference between three million viewers and three point five.' He saw an important client at the other side of the room. 'Anyway. Don't want to bore you with business stuff. I'll see you later.' He weaved his way through the crowd, leaving Josie pondering on his words. When Mike dropped a hint there was normally a damn good reason for it.

There were going to be changes, Josie knew. Cuts. But what? And who would have to go? Looking around the room, at the people she worked with every day – the researchers, the studio technicians, Josie could not think of a single one who deserved to be sacked. Damn Mike. Why did he have to bring this up today of all days? Josie wished she had avoided him.

Nervous and distracted, she left the reception early, driving herself away from the studios feeling curiously hollow inside. At Hyde Park corner she should have branched off through the park and down towards Kensington. But a sign for the M1 caught her eye. On an impulse she followed it, up the Edgware Road and through Kilburn to the motorway. After all, she reasoned, there was nothing for her at home. She began to drive north, grey miles of tarmac rolling by.

Josie was still a little drunk from the wine. She had eaten nothing for the last day and a pressure headache was beginning to establish itself in the back of her skull. When she stopped to fill up with petrol at Watford Gap, the attendant had to come running after her to return the credit card she had forgotten on the counter. The memorial had left her feeling empty and it wasn't hard for Josie to figure out why. There had been no body, Sebastian hadn't even been there. His grave – his real grave – was in some unknown, godforsaken part of Everest and that was why the memorial had felt such a sham. What did the shrinks call it? She struggled for the word: closure. Definite lack of closure around here, she realised.

A hundred miles clocked past. Two hundred. She left the rain clouds behind, hitting blue skies in the mid-afternoon. Then Josie was back in familiar territory, the rolling hills of Northumberland, the country of her childhood. Sebastian had been here with her, in the early days of their relationship. That, at least, was something.

Josie turned off the motorway and headed for the coast, passing through villages of warm stone, winding through narrow lanes, dry-stone walls on each side. Then came the sea, the wild coastline that had excited Sebastian so much. 'Great flying conditions,' he had told her. 'Onshore breeze and rising hills.' Rounding a corner, she saw the bluff of headland she was seeking, here, on these cliffs, with the water beating endlessly against the jagged rocks below: the place where Sebastian had taught her to fly.

Josie drove up the track, hoping there would be no one around. She was lucky, there were no pilots flying that day. She lay on the grass, surprised at the warmth of the early summer sunshine, and let her mind go back.

It had been a glorious summer day, just the two of them together. In the back of the car, Sebastian's dual paraglider was packed and ready to go. Josie was more scared than she had let on. Turning off the coast road they drove up a dirt trail, gaining a thousand feet or more on the winding track before reaching the launch site.

'Here's the place.' Sebastian pointed to a bare patch of mountainside where a number of brightly coloured paraglider canopies were being laid out on the ground in preparation to fly. 'This is one of the best spots in England to paraglide,' he explained. 'On a mild day like today the breeze hits the cliffs and creates plenty of lift.'

As they pulled up, one of the pilots launched himself into the air and flew off towards the sea one thousand feet beneath him, the elegant fan tail of kevlar cords catching the light as the canopy plumped and filled with air to support him. Within seconds he was rising, soaring on an invisible up-current until he was hundreds of feet above the launch position.

'I don't have a very good head for heights,' Josie admitted to Sebastian.

'What is it that scares you?'

'Oh, not much, really, just the prospect of being dashed to the ground and killed.'

'Control your fear. Like I do.'

'How?'

'By thinking of the surface of the planet like a great big soft marshmallow. Then you don't care whether you hit it or not.'

Josie helped him to unravel what seemed to be a cat's cradle of strings and within a few minutes they had the bright-yellow and red canopy stretched out on the grass. 'It seems so fragile,' she said, running the material through her hands wonderingly. 'Can this really keep us up in the air?'

'Let me put it this way. If this thing collapses like a bag of washing at seven hundred feet we're not going to be in a position to take it back to the manufacturer and complain.'

'You have a neat way of reassuring your passengers.'

'Here's the seat. Put both your arms through this loop and do up the buckle here between your legs.'

Sebastian helped her into the harness and then buckled himself in. 'We're going to fly side by side,' he explained, 'but first we have to get the canopy inflated.'

As soon as he judged the wind right, Sebastian pulled up on the two guide lines. The canopy unruffled and filled with wind, and a few moments later was flying, suspended above their heads like a kite.

'She flies!' Josie was ecstatic.

'When I give the command we're going to turn and run.'

'I'm scared, Sebastian.'

'Now!'

They took a series of stumbling steps, almost tripping each other on the bumpy ground as they rushed forward. Josie felt the hard pull of the shoulder straps on her harness as the wing took their weight. Then they were airborne, swooping out across the sea.

'Wow! This is incredible!' Josie screamed in delight.

They were flying parallel to the coast, with the rounded flanks of the mountains to the left and the shore directly below. Josie could see the white surf beating against the beach and feel Sebastian next to her.

'I love you,' he told her.

It was the first time he'd said those words. As they began to soar upwards on a thermal Josie felt she had never been happier.

34

Five weeks after the avalanche, Hal's clearance work began to ease off and, at the same time, Rachel was finally ready to go home. Her left leg was still pinned but she was mobile enough to get around in a wheelchair. Hal picked her up from the hospital, pushing her out to the car park where a brand-new Toyota was waiting. 'Check this out,' Hal said, 'The insurance company paid every cent. I picked it up yesterday.'

'Great.' Rachel made herself sound as enthusiastic as she could, but she couldn't help wishing Hal had chosen a different model. This one was the same as the last – down to the smallest detail. Rachel knew that every time she climbed into it she would think of the avalanche.

They drove out of town, Hal noticing every detail of the newly arrived summer; the rivers flowing strong with meltwater, the shoots of cotton moss standing tall above the shallow boggy areas next to the road, a wispy white plume crowning each one. At Eagle Junction he stopped at the post office. 'I haven't had time to pick up the mail this past week.'

The postmaster was new and looked at Hal curiously when he gave his name. 'You're Hal Maher?'

'The same.'

'Your post box is pretty much bursting at the seams.'

'I'm not surprised.' Hal knew that most of the letters would be from insurance companies – all wanting his expert witness on avalanche claims following the disaster.

The man fetched the mail for Hal, a stack which fairly covered the desk. 'I'll give you a plastic bag for that,' he offered, reaching under the desk to find one.

'I'm obliged.'

'You're the avalanche man, aren't you?'

'Some people call me that.'

The postmaster held out his hand. 'Jim Parry. I heard a lot about you.'

'Well, be seeing you.'

'So long.'

Hal climbed into the Toyota. 'You know what he called me?' he asked Rachel.

'No.'

'He called me the avalanche man. That's what I'll always be around here. Isn't that frightening?'

'Just drive, Hal. Let's get home.'

They finished the journey in silence, Hal pondering over the postmaster's words – Rachel trying not to show the pain she felt every time they hit the smallest bump in the track.

'Looks like you haven't had much time for housekeeping,' Rachel told him, seeing the state of the cabin.

It was true, Hal realised, the place was looking pretty dilapidated. As summer had arrived, the cabin garden had quickly become overgrown. In the frenzy of the clear-up operation Hal had not had the time to devote to any care of the property and he was ashamed, as he saw its tatty state, that he hadn't thought to do something about it before Rachel's return.

The guttering along the side wall had fallen from the eaves and he noticed that a handful of shingles had been loosened on the roof – probably in the winter gales. Damp had caused the side door to swell in its frame and Hal had to shoulder it to get it to budge.

'What a welcome!' Rachel sounded wry. 'I can see if I'd spent another month in hospital this place would belong to the termites.'

He lit the wood stove to take the chill off the air as Rachel wheeled herself from room to room. Everything was as she remembered it: the tiny handful of stones from Everest next to her laptop on the desk; the bonsai, now shrivelled and dried out in its pot, a few fallen leaves scattered in a sad pattern beneath it; the bottle of wine on the shelf – the wine they were going to drink that evening, she realised, on the day of the avalanche.

What had been stolen from them that day, Rachel wondered, as she wheeled herself into the bedroom? Bones would mend in time but what unseen damage was still to be discovered? They had a lot to adjust to, she knew, and an unborn child to mourn. If that was the right word.

Hospital had not seemed the right place to talk. Hal had visited as often as he could, but their conversation had been stilted on each occasion. They talked about Rachel's progress as her legs healed, the work Hal was doing with his team, the five long sessions at the dentist's which had restored his teeth to a state where he could smile without making people scream. Most of all they talked about Deborah and the death of Rick (mainly, Rachel suspected, because it was a loss greater than their own).

Alienated and lonely in the hospital, Rachel had longed to get home, to be in Hal's arms by the fire, to talk freely and openly about the deeper wounds they had both suffered. But their conversation that night was anything but easy. Hal was distracted and monosyllabic, Rachel overtired and permanently on the verge of tears. They ate together but neither could enjoy the meal.

'I'm going down to Vancouver next week,' Hal told her, 'for the memorial service. Will you be OK?'

'I'll be fine. It'll give me a chance to get the cabin straight. At least on the inside.'

Finally Hal helped her into bed and they fell into an awkward silence. They had not shared such close contact for a very long time but there was no spark of physical desire between them.

'You wondering what I'm wondering?' Rachel asked him.

'Maybe.'

'Like, who's feeling worse?'

'Yes. I hope you have the strength to begin, because I'm not sure I do.'

'We don't need to rush in. Best to spend some time getting used to being around each other again.'

'I'll get Rick's memorial out of the way, then we can sort ourselves out.'

In the end, neither had the emotional energy to say anything more that night. And, although Rachel held his body close to her, he didn't feel like Hal – *her* Hal.

'Sleep,' he told her, 'that's what you need.'

But Rachel could not sleep, not when every time she closed her eyes she saw the avalanche tearing down the valley to annihilate her.

The avalanche . . . the day the mountains fell out of the sky. Rachel could see that billowing force running towards the Toyota as clear as day, and Hal's face as he turned to meet her eyes in the seconds before they were hit. The look that told her they were probably both about to die.

A lifetime might not be enough to heal. She knew that now.

She listened to Hal's fitful breathing, and wondered if things were ever going to be the same.

35

After a while, lying there on that Northumberland hillside, Josie half awoke, roused by a breath of wind coming in from the sea. She blinked sunlight out of her eyes, disorientated and confused until she saw a lone seagull soaring high above. She closed her eyes once more, willing herself back into the dream and the day Sebastian had taken her into the sky.

Flying the paraglider, the only sound was the singing of the guide lines, a curious, gentle, high-pitched whistle as the air passed through them.

Sebastian had the two control grips – one in each hand. They began to circle as he pulled down on the left line, banking the paraglider round. He piloted the glider in a figure-of-eight circuit as they climbed. 'You want to try?'

'I've never flown anything before.'

'Take the controls.'

Before Josie could protest, Sebastian slipped off the control grips and handed them to her. She held them high above her head, paralysed with the fear of making a catastrophic mistake. 'I really don't think this is a good . . .'

'Pull down gently on the right hand.'

Josie did as he said, feeling the broad arc of the wing turn into her movement. It felt good – more precise than she could have imagined. 'Hey, it did what I told it,' she said.

'This wing will always do what you tell it. Now level out and keep both hands even.'

They flew back towards the mountain for a while.

'And now the left hand down and we're going back into the loop to try to catch that thermal again.'

Josie pulled down on the left side, a huge smile cracking across her face as she realised she was actually flying the wing. 'This is more fun than I thought.'

'OK. This is nice. Can you feel we're climbing now?' A sudden powerful surge lifted them.

'Yes. I can feel it.'

'We're right in the thermal, gaining one hundred feet a minute. It's not the strongest in the world but it'll give us another ten or fifteen minutes' flying.'

He talked her through the movements as Josie piloted the canopy in circles. 'Don't be hesitant,' he told her, sensing her lack of confidence. 'You have to make your movements positive but relaxed.'

'Positive but relaxed.'

But Josie had not been fast enough. Her flying circuit took them momentarily outside the rising column of air, the canopy dropping fast as it came out of the thermal. 'Whoa!' she handed the controls back to him as they were buffeted for a few seconds, before regaining the calmer static air.

'Don't be afraid,' he encouraged her. 'Get back into the thermal and try again.'

Josie didn't make the same mistake twice and on her second attempt managed to soar for more than five hundred feet. The extra height enabled them to fly further, Josie delighting in the experience as she began to feel at one with the paraglider. She continued to fly, Sebastian quiet now beside her.

Soon she started to notice the conditions changing around them. The blue sky began to be peppered with dark clouds, the warm breeze replaced with something altogether colder. Still they were rising, the ground falling away dramatically beneath them.

'It's time to come down,' Josie said. 'I'm getting cold.'

Sebastian made no reply.

Josie shivered and tried to imagine what she should do to make the paraglider descend. 'Talk to me, Sebastian. Tell me what to do.'

Still he was silent. Still they rose, ice crystals forming on the rigging around Josie's hands. Now they were among the clouds, thunderheads around them, the canopy beginning to be tossed from side to side as turbulence struck. 'I don't know what to do!' she screamed. 'Help me, for Christ's sake!'

Then Josie noticed Sebastian's fingers where they clutched the hand control next to hers. They were blistered and black, the flesh hanging off them in strips where they had frozen to the core.

The paraglider continued to climb and now there was more

ice forming on the canopy, and on Josie too. She could feel her hair congealing, her lips beginning to seal with the intensity of the cold.

The canopy was becoming too heavy to fly.

'Sebastian, what's happening?'

She turned and looked into his face, the bones of the skull visible through a frozen outer layer of ice where the flesh should have been, the eyes deep sockets of unknown depth.

Above her the canopy was completely encrusted with ice. Josie could no longer move her arms. Then they were falling like a stone, the fabric of the wing wrapping around them like a shroud, the lines hopelessly entangled, as the ground rushed up . . .

Josie's scream echoed around the hills as she woke, sweating and disorientated, from the dream.

In the car she found a warm can of Coke. She drank it down hungrily, getting little relief for the thirst that had crept up on her. She sat in the front seat for a while, her forehead against the hot leather of the steering wheel, trying to will the horror of the dream away. Then she drove on, still perspiring even though all the windows of the car were open. More lanes, a near collision with a slow-moving tractor and back on to the motorway and the turning leading down the sweeping hill to the cathedral city nestled in an ancient oxbow loop of the River Wear.

Durham. Josie parked her car on the Palace Green, right by the castle, ignoring the signs warning her she would be clamped or towed.

The path down to the river was just as she remembered it, a cool, green tunnel of beech and alder. Through the foliage she could hear the roar of the weir – the same one friends had dared her to walk across as a child. Then there were the muddy brown waters of the river itself, the towpath of gravel and compacted clay, the damp stillness of the moist air, so refreshing after the burning sun on the coast. Josie rested her cheek against the mossy bark of a tree, relishing the coolness it brought to her face.

The boathouse was just a short walk away, nestled beneath the dripping arches of Elvet Bridge. The sliding doors were open to the slipway, the two eights out on the river. There was no one around. Josie walked slowly into the dark interior, her eyes gradually adjusting to the unlit space, seeing the faded flags and photographs on the walls. There was a faint musty tang of mildew in the air and above her, higher than she had remembered, the rafters, mottled green with age.

36

Police Chief Robbie McGowan looked at the envelope which Hal had placed on his desk. 'Is this what I think it is?'

'I want out, Robbie. I'm quitting the avalanche work.' Hal took the seat McGowan gestured to.

'You sure this isn't a knee-jerk reaction?' the police chief asked him. 'I know how tough the last month has been for you.'

'I can understand why you might figure that,' Hal answered, 'but this is from the heart. Something happened the other day to make me question what the hell I was doing.'

'To do with the clearance work?'

'Not that. It was the most stupid thing but it really got to me . . . It was something some new guy said at the post office up at Eagle Junction.'

'What's he got to do with it?'

'He called me "the avalanche man" and that's about all I am around here. There's hardly a family in the state won't know someone who died in that slide. And when they see me coming I'll be the public face of that catastrophe, the guy who was right in the middle of it all.'

'They know you did your best. You got all the AMRs out safely for God's sake.'

'The AMRs yes. But plenty more died . . . in places where avalanches had never been seen before and that leaves a lot of questions unanswered, a lot of grief unspoken. Believe me, I know.'

'Yeah. It was as hard for you as anyone, I guess. But that's why I don't want to lose your expertise. Stay on the job, Hal. You know the subject. Alaska needs someone with your skill, you understand the way avalanches work . . .'

'I thought I did. That was my biggest mistake. But I didn't predict that slide would be so huge. I never thought it would happen the way it did.'

'No one did and that's the truth of it.'

'But it was my job to get the prediction right. How do you think that has made me feel when I've been pulling the bodies of young children out of shattered buildings these last weeks?'

'You want me to arrange for you to see a counsellor? We got one lined up for some of the other officers who saw bad stuff on the clear-up and I can get you on the list if you . . .'

'That's kind of you, Robbie, but I don't think it's the answer. I can't face another winter of avalanche work and that's the long and short of it.'

'OK, but the offer stands if you want it.'

'Thanks.'

'So what are you going to move on to?'

'I'm not sure yet. I need to talk to Rachel.'

There was a long pause before McGowan rose and offered Hal his hand. 'I respect your decision, Hal, but I want you to know that there's a job for you here. Any time you want it.'

'I appreciate that. I really do. But I won't be changing my mind.'

'You'll be missed.' McGowan watched Hal walk out of the office.

Hal drove back to the cabin to find Rachel hard at work in her darkroom. It was the first time she had put any effort into her photography since the accident.

Hal sat drinking tea in the sitting-room until she emerged on her crutches. The wheelchair had been put aside the week before.

'Did you give McGowan your resignation?' she asked.

'Yep.'

'How did he take it?'

'I think he understood.'

Rachel took a sip from Hal's cup. 'You're going to be mad at me,' she told him.

'Why?'

'Because I printed up the Cooper Valley shots. I managed to get the film out of the camera.'

'Jesus. I thought we agreed you wouldn't do that?'

'Well, we did. And I was going to destroy the roll. But the more I thought about it the more I thought what a waste that would be. I went out there with you for a reason and, well, that was my job.'

'Are you going to show me?'

Rachel hesitated. 'Yes. I should. But I'm not sure if you'd want to see them . . . they're pretty strong.'

'Maybe it'll help. Let me see them.'

'They're on the drying rack.'

Hal went to the darkroom and returned with the black-and-white prints.

The first shot was taken just outside the cabin, the tension of the departure written indelibly across the Carroways' faces. There was Louisa in close-up, her face bewildered and scared, then other wider shots as they had walked to the Toyota.

The next print was the avalanche shot.

'My God.' Hal looked at the picture in awe.

The photograph was the one Rachel had taken just as the avalanche had begun – the frame filled with the racing pressure front as the cloud of ice thundered down the valley towards the vehicle. It was grainy, printed up from sixteen-hundred ASA film to squeeze every last detail out of the gloomy light and as atmospheric as any photograph Hal had ever seen. It contained an eerie sense of menace – the certainty that the photographer had risked life and limb to get the shot.

'That was an expensive photograph,' Rachel said sadly, 'but at least I got the shot.'

'How do you feel now when you look at these?'

'Sad. Angry . . . that we lost our child.'

'What are we going to do with them?'

'I suppose we have the straight choice. We can use them in the book. Or we can destroy them for good. What do you think?'

'Destroy them,' Hal said, his voice more bitter than Rachel had heard before. 'I never want to see them again.' With that he rose, leaving the room without another word.

37

Out on the River Wear, sitting in the number five seat of the university first eight, Dominic Walden's day was going from bad to worse: six foot five and two hundred and fifteen pounds of finely honed muscle rendered virtually useless by a two-ounce strand of damaged tendon buried somewhere in his shoulder. The injury was an old one and sometimes Dominic could punch through the pain barrier. Today, as the training session picked up a little pace, that was clearly not going to be an option.

Dominic tried to keep the rhythm, sliding back and forth on his seat with the rest of the crew, gritting his teeth against the searing agony shooting down his arm. Finally the tendon gave way and Dominic caught a crab – his oar locking underwater, slewing the sleek craft to one side and causing the rest of the crew to lose their rhythm.

'Mr Walden,' the cox called out, 'may I remind you that this is not a fishing expedition?'

Dominic cursed himself; catching crabs was for pussies. Any more like that and he might be out. The eight shipped their oars, waiting for the cox to command a restart.

The coach was watching, exasperated, from the towpath. 'Come to the side,' he called through his megaphone. 'I'm putting the reserve in your seat, Dominic. You shouldn't be training with your shoulder in that state.'

At the river bank Dominic unclipped himself from the frame and climbed out of the boat.

'I want you to take some time out,' the coach continued, 'and get that shoulder sorted for good. I don't want you back in that seat until you can guarantee me you're one hundred per cent fit, you hear?'

'I hear you.'

'Go take a shower.'

Dominic jogged back towards the boathouse, cursing his bad luck. This summer session was a vital part of the selection process for the upcoming term. He had to be in that seat come hell or high water. Problem was, it could require surgery. Then how long would he be out of action?

Dominic was so preoccupied with his own problems that he almost tripped over the comatose figure of the girl lying prone on the boathouse floor. 'Shit!' Dominic recoiled in shock.

He stared at her in astonishment. She was blond, dressed in a neat black designer outfit with a short skirt and high heels. In her hand she was holding one of the faded black-and-white team photographs from the wall. To Dominic she looked amazingly like Josie Turner, the *Daybreak* presenter. She had Josie Turner's legs . . . that much he could definitely see. He kneeled by her side, trying to remember some first aid. She clearly wasn't dead, which was a good start. Dominic felt for her pulse, noticing the sweet smell of alcohol on her breath.

The girl murmured something incoherent as she began to come round.

She'd fainted, he decided, nothing worse than that. But what the hell was she doing in the boathouse dressed like she was going to a funeral? Dominic arranged her in the recovery position and fetched a mug of water from the sink. He brushed her hair back from her eyes and sprinkled a little of the water on her brow. He walked to the door to see if there was anyone he could enlist for help. He should call an ambulance, he guessed, but he didn't want to leave her alone while he did it. There was no one to be seen.

His mobile telephone was in his study, part of the university college accommodation not far off. It would be just as easy to carry her there. She didn't look that heavy. Blanking out the protestations of his shoulder, Dominic gathered the girl in his arms and carried her up to Palace Green where he walked impassively through a crowd of curious Japanese tourists. He took her straight to his study and laid her on his bed. 'Holy caramba.' He whistled, now he could see her whole face. It *was* Josie Turner.

Josie woke up and looked at him for a while, her eyes focusing and defocusing as she came out of the faint. 'Who the hell are you?' she whispered, looking around the neat study in confusion. 'And what is this place?'

'I found you down in the boathouse. You fainted,' Dominic told her. 'I think you should drink some of this.' He helped her to sit up so she could drink the water. 'You want me to call an ambulance?'

'No! I'm fine. Really.' Josie flushed with panic at the thought of the publicity this would generate.

'You seem pretty dehydrated to me,' he said. 'I'll make you some tea.'

Dominic busied himself at the kettle while Josie composed herself, brushing some of the dirt from her dress.

'So, if you don't mind me asking, what the hell is Josie Turner doing lying flat out on a boathouse floor in Durham?'

'Please don't talk to the press about this,' Josie urged. 'I was just taking a walk and felt dizzy . . .'

Dominic came and sat next to her on the bed. 'Listen. I wouldn't do that. What do you take me for? It's just not every day you come across a famous presenter lying in a faint. What were you doing there, of all places?'

Josie suddenly felt another wave of dizziness come over her. Part of her wanted to get out of this place, get away from this giant stranger with the kind eyes. But another part was crying for rest. 'I'm sorry.' She yawned. 'I haven't slept for a couple of days and I've been under a lot of pressure.'

Dominic suddenly recalled. 'Now I remember the publicity. Your husband died on Everest, right? Not long ago.'

'Right.'

'That's why you're wearing black?'

'We had the memorial this morning.'

'Do you have to go somewhere now?'

'My car is on the green. I suppose I should go and . . .'

'You're in no condition to drive,' Dominic contradicted, 'but let me move it before you get towed.'

He prepared her the tea and after she had drunk it told her: 'Get some sleep. I'll leave you alone for a few hours and see how you're doing later.'

She gave him the car keys and flopped back gratefully on the bed. When Dominic met the rest of his crew returning from the river he didn't say a word about Josie.

She slept for fifteen hours straight, waking up in surprise on Saturday morning to find Dominic had spent the night in a sleeping bag on the floor.

They shared breakfast – croissants, takeaway cappuccino and fresh orange juice. Dominic told her about himself, about his postgraduate course in English, about the shoulder that was threatening his rowing career, about the fact that – at the age of twenty-five – he was beginning to wonder if he should get out of full-time education and find a future in the real world.

'And you?' he asked her. 'What brought you here?'

Josie told him as best she could why she had come back to Durham, about her father being the rowing coach, about the compulsion she had felt to be close to the place where he had died . . .

Dominic was a sympathetic listener, calm and somehow reassuring. Even on this brief acquaintance Josie was confident he would not sell the story to the press. 'I was lucky it was you who found me,' she told him. 'You've been wonderful. Come and see me when you're in London.' She gave Dominic her home number.

Josie never told him how close to the edge she had been. Or how that darkness beyond the rafters had seemed so beckoning. Instead, she thanked him profusely for his help, kissed him warmly (she had to stand on tiptoe to do this) and walked to where her car was parked feeling self-conscious in the black dress.

She drove out of the town feeling she had got off lightly from this journey north. It had been bad enough with the paragliding nightmare and the incident in the boathouse, but it could have been a lot worse.

Why had she come here? Josie wasn't really sure, but she knew that in Dominic she had been extremely fortunate. One photograph of her unconscious on the floor of that boathouse would have been enough to make her life even more of a living hell than it already was.

On the journey south her mobile telephone rang – Rick's wife Deborah, calling from Vancouver. Damn, Josie cursed herself. She had forgotten about Deborah and the memorial service for the expedition. She had promised her a decision a week ago. 'I don't want to pressure you,' Deborah said, 'but I need to know for numbers. Can you make it or not?'

After the sheer depression of Sebastian's memorial, Josie hadn't planned to go to the ceremony Deborah had organised in Vancouver. She had a feeling it would only create more press interest at a moment when the surge of media frenzy following Sebastian's death was just beginning to get under control. But the more she considered it, the more she realised that the journey might help. There would be other families of those who had died. Perhaps with them she would find more solace than she had done so far and maybe even the answers to some questions.

'I've kept this very quiet,' Deborah assured her on the transatlantic call. 'As far as I know there will be no more than a couple of local press guys present. Please come, we'd all make you very welcome.'

'That decides it,' Josie told her. 'I'll be there.'

She booked the ticket and flew to Vancouver the following week, leaving an infuriated Mike to find a stand-in presenter for the show.

38

Hal made it to the memorial service in Vancouver with an hour to spare, the flight down from Anchorage having been delayed.

Deborah met him at the aiport, looking more drawn and exhausted than Hal had ever seen her before. 'Hal, I'm so glad you could get here.' Deborah held him in a tight embrace. 'You prepared something to say in the service? I can't think of anyone who could do it better than you.'

'It will be an honour.'

Deborah drove Hal back to the home she had renovated with Rick over the years. It was on the coast about ten miles from the city – a converted yacht club, situated on a quiet wooded bay. When they had bought it the slipway was just about rotted through but Rick had restored it during the long months when he wasn't out in the Himalayas.

Rick's tatty old boat was moored out front, a weathered thirty-foot ketch with a shallow draught perfect for cruising the small inlets and island moorings that lay within a few hours' sail. Seeing the boat fired happy memories for Hal. He and Rachel had spent long days sailing in it with Rick and Deborah – days that passed in a haze of red wine and laughter.

'Where are the kids?' Hal noticed the house was quiet.

'At my mother's. I didn't want to force them to come today – they've been through enough these last weeks.'

'Rachel sends you all her love,' Hal told Deborah, 'and said she's sorry she can't be with you today.'

'How is she?'

'Oh . . . healing, I guess. Slowly.'

'You should both come down and stay. It would be lovely to have you here again.'

Deborah went to change for the service and, while she dressed, Hal took a look around the Himalayan Objectives office. It was neat, the files packed away tidily, a tall pile of brochures waiting to be mailed out in the corner.

That was Deborah's work, he knew – if the office had been down to Rick it would have been a mess. In fact, if it had been down to Rick alone, the business would have folded long ago – it was no secret that it was Deborah's organisational ability that had kept the company going as it had lurched from one financial crisis to another. 'Rick can lead the expeditions,' he recalled Deborah saying to him with a smile on one of his first visits to the house, 'but I have to run the business.'

Now what would Deborah do? Hal could not imagine that the company would survive now Rick was dead.

Hal and Deborah drove to the church where they met the other mourners – more than one hundred in total. Most were close family of the climbers who had been killed, some were climbing friends of Rick's, people whom Hal had known for years.

The service began at three in the afternoon. Hal took the pulpit after the first few hymns. 'Deborah has asked me, as a friend, and as someone who climbed frequently with Rick in the Himalayas and elsewhere, to say a few words about him.' He paused and looked around the church. 'Rick Fielding was one of the finest high-altitude climbers in the world. I know that for sure because on more occasions than I can remember he proved himself to be stronger, braver and more committed than anyone around him. Those of us who climbed with him measured ourselves by his standards and rarely felt we matched him.

'He was generous to a fault, to the point where he was prepared to risk his life for others. There are many climbers alive today who would otherwise be dead if it had not been for Rick's assistance.

'Rick loved Everest. He must have done, he'd made it to the summit on three occasions and his infectious delight in the mountain was something he infused into every one of the clients he took there. There was no cynicism in his approach, he truly believed that every step he ever made on that mountain was a privilege to be earned. His were the standards the rest of us aspired to.

'He was gentle with Everest. Perhaps his only mistake was to assume that Everest would always be gentle with him. Rick, you will always be in our hearts and our memories of you will be ones we will treasure for all time.'

Hal left the pulpit, taking his seat next to Deborah who, finally, had dissolved in tears.

'That was so beautiful,' she whispered to him. 'Thank you, Hal.'

After the service was concluded Deborah invited the guests back to the house for food and drinks. Finding himself claustrophobic in the crowd, Hal went down to the jetty to breathe a little sea air. There he found one of the mourners, sitting alone, looking out across the calm water. 'Mind if I join you down here?' he asked her.

'No, go ahead.'

Josie turned to scrutinise him, sure, for a moment, that she had seen him or met him somewhere before this day. 'I was really moved by your speech,' she told him. 'Almost made me want to forgive the mountain.'

'You lost someone in the storm?'

'My husband Sebastian.'

'The *Daybreak TV* guy? Rick told me about him before they left, said he liked him a lot.'

'That's him. Well, that was him. We had a memorial service for him in London. But this has a much better feel to it. I'm already glad I came.'

They sat in silence for a long while.

'I admire Deborah,' Josie continued. 'This has to be the most difficult day of her life. Everyone here has lost someone they loved. She must know that deep down we can't help blaming Rick.'

'She knows that. But she's got the courage to face it.'

'When you lose a friend in the mountains, how do you cope with it?'

Hal let his gaze wander to the horizon where a blue mist was hanging, inert, above the sea. 'As best I can.'

'I keep getting this terrible urge to point the finger at someone – at something. To be able to say it was this, or that, which was ultimately at fault. To begin with I was angry with Sebastian, raging at him for that damn stupid obsession which took him there in the first place. Then I was mad at Rick, at his company. Then I got furious with the mountain. I fantasised about destroying it, spending the rest of my life smashing every last stone with a sledgehammer, or flying above it and dropping a bomb, which would blow it into the sea.'

Hal laughed. 'I've wished that myself from time to time. But it's a hell of a waste of energy to get mad with a mountain. Because in the end all you're going to do is find all that energy bouncing back on yourself. Whatever you take to the mountains you're going to find coming back at you sooner or later.'

'How do you mean?'

'That if something's inside you then a mountain will find it out and push it back in your face. If you go to the mountains because you're angry then you'll come back angrier than ever. If you go because you want to cure a broken heart you'll come back worse. And if you go caring more about the summit than you care about the people around you, then the mountain will strip that out of you and force it down your throat too.'

'You mean it brings out extremes?'

'In a way. It's an arena. A hard arena. It encourages the best and the worst sides of humanity.'

'So how should you go there?'

'That's something I'm still trying to work out myself. If you listen to one Tibetan friend of mine, he'd say that you should go with nothing. Strip your whole self inside out until every scrap of greed, selfishness, pride and ego is scrubbed clean and gone. Then, and only then, are you worthy enough to bring yourself before the highest peaks.'

'And have you ever achieved that?'

Hal laughed again. 'Are you kidding? I'd have to spend so long getting myself cleaned up I'd never make it to the bottom of the hill.'

'Whatever you say. I imagine I'll always hate Everest in some way for what it did to Sebastian and all the others.'

'Maybe that's healthy. Better than blaming yourself.'

Josie sighed deeply. 'But I do blame myself. It was me who encouraged him to go. I wanted it to be perfect for him. I wanted him to reach the top. When he had doubts about it it was me who told him everything was going to be all right. Then it wasn't.'

She thought for a while. 'You know Everest, right?'

'I know a bit about it.'

'You've been to the summit?'

'Four times.'

'Can the bodies ever be recovered? I'd do anything to get Sebastian back.'

'That's a difficult thing. I'd say not. I've never heard of anyone being retrieved from high on Everest.'

'It's hard for me to understand that.'

'I know. It's hard for anyone who hasn't been there to understand that.'

At that moment Deborah came down from the house, carrying a glass of red wine.

'How's it going in there?' Hal asked her.

'Oh, warming up. People are starting to talk, starting to drink a little. That's how Rick would have wanted it. The church thing is so heavy.'

'Have I missed the food?' Hal asked her.

'Not yet, you haven't. But speaking of which, Hal, you look like you haven't eaten for a month. You'd better do it now or it'll be gone.'

'I'll do that.'

Hal left the two women by the waterside and returned to the reception.

39

Josie watched Hal as he walked back to the house. 'I'm sure I've seen him somewhere recently,' she told Deborah.

'Hal? Well his face was all over the television when the big avalanche hit Alaska.'

'The avalanche?' Suddenly Josie remembered the shot of Hal, bloodied and bruised. 'God, I do remember seeing him, interviewed at a hospital. That was the same day as the storm.'

'His girlfriend Rachel was injured that day.'

'In the avalanche?'

'Yes. In the front seat of the Toyota Hal was driving.'

'Oh, my God.'

Deborah took a sip of her wine. 'She lost the baby she was carrying.'

'And here I am taking about nothing but Sebastian. He didn't even mention about his girlfriend.'

'That would be about right. I remember Hal coming back from an expedition to the mountains when three of his best friends had been killed in some kind of disaster, a rockfall or something. Rick asked him if he wanted to speak about it and all he said was "I'll speak about it when I'm over it".'

'But he never did speak about it, right?'

'Right.'

'I feel the opposite. All I want to do right now is talk about Sebastian, how he died, how it happened . . . why it happened.'

'They'll put it all together before long.'

'Hal told me that the bodies will never be recovered.'

'I know. It's brutal isn't it?'

'It makes it harder to grieve, when you can't even picture where your loved one died. I'm beginning to realise what type of void that leaves. It's like he's just abandoned there, one more piece of rubbish left behind. I went past a graveyard on a train the other day in London and I actually felt *jealous* – if you can believe that – that all those people had their loved ones there, in a known place, in a place where you can go and talk to them, to be close. I never thought I could feel that way but now Sebastian is gone that's how I am.'

'I know. At least I've been there. I can understand it more.'

'You've climbed on Everest?' Josie looked at her with surprise.

'Not exactly. I went to base camp one year with Rick.'

'Oh.'

'I was sick – so sick I could hardly get out of the tent to see the mountain. But it really helped to understand what it was about it that meant so much to him. Now it helps even more.'

'I can see that. To me it's just another name on a map; that and what I've seen on television. Sebastian might as well be on the moon for all I can imagine of Everest.'

'I'm thinking about trying to organise a memorial of some type at base camp.'

'What would it be?'

'They build cairns, with a plaque with the names, or an engraved stone, I don't know. At least it would be something.'

'I hadn't thought of that. It's a really good idea.'

'I'll be writing to all the families to let them know about it. I'll contact you with the details when I know.'

'Thank you. I'd appreciate that.'

The guests left before midnight, Josie returning to her hotel by taxi. Hal was the only one of Rick's friends Deborah invited to stay. They sat in front of the fire, drinking the last of the wine. Deborah looked tired but at the same time relieved that the memorial had gone as well as it had. 'You think Rick would have been happy with today?' she asked him.

'I reckon he'd have been delighted. You did it just right,' Hal reassured her.

'I've rehearsed this day in my mind so many times that it almost felt like I'd done it before.'

'It was perfect. Really.'

Deborah poured Hal another glass of wine. 'There's something I wanted to ask you. Another favour, in fact.'

'Go ahead,' Hal replied.

'If I organise a memorial plaque, will you take it up to base camp for me?'

Hal hesitated for a few moments as he thought it through. 'Of course. I'd like to do that for Rick.'

'Thanks. I know you said you'd never go back and I'd be the last person to want you to break that promise to yourself. But it's only to base camp. I could get someone else to organise it but it wouldn't be the same.'

'I know what you mean. Don't worry about it. If the same thing had happened to me I'd sure as hell expect Rick to drag his ass up there on my behalf.'

Deborah smiled. 'How long would you need to sort it out?'

'The trek would be three maybe four weeks, but we'd have to wait a couple of months for the rains to finish. I'd have to be sure Rachel was going to be OK.'

'She can come and stay here, if she likes. One more plate at the table won't make much difference and I'd love to have her here.'

'That would work out well – the old couple I pulled out of the avalanche could stay in the cabin while she was here.'

Hal stirred the remaining logs on the fire to create a little more heat. 'How about you?' he asked her. 'Have you thought about what you're going to do with the business?'

'The business is as good as finished. Who in their right mind is going to go to the mountains with Rick's company after he and five of his clients have been wiped out on Everest? There's been that much publicity about this that I can't see us ever getting another client again. And who would I get to lead the expeditions?'

'Which leaves?'

'Which leaves me I don't know where. You know, the company was our only source of income and Rick wasn't insured. I have to see the bank manager next week to talk about it but I can't see how I can sustain this place for more than another six months without some kind of money coming in. And then there's the real nightmare possibility that one or more of the families will try to sue.'

'Have they talked about that?'

'There's been whispers in the press. And one half of me thinks, well, they haven't got a chance. Those clients signed on in the full knowledge of the risks. But the other half of me thinks, well, shit, you only have to trip up on a loose paving stone in the street to make a case against a local authority. Maybe Rick *was* negligent up there.

Maybe he *did* make a mistake that killed those clients. Perhaps they have got a case.'

'I don't think you should lose sleep over that until it happens. And if it does, I'll help you fight it.'

'Thanks. I appreciate that. In fact, I appreciate everything you've done for today . . . the memorial speech and all that. Everyone mentioned how moving it was.'

They sat in silence for a long while, staring into the dying embers of the fire.

Finally Deborah stirred. 'It's been a long day. I prepared the spare room for you.'

'Thanks.'

In his room, Hal opened the window. Outside he could hear the sound of the sea breaking gently on the pebble beach.

Base camp. Everest again. History repeating . . . Hal fell into an uneasy sleep.

40

Josie's decision to ask Deborah if she could join the trek to base camp was one which took the entire summer to make. It had begun with the barest seed, sown at the memorial service in Vancouver, a tiny germ of momentum inside her, which was so alien that for weeks she really did not recognise it for what it was. So she ignored it.

She ignored it as her performance on *Daybreak* gradually lost its edge – her normal polished delivery missing its sparkle a little more with every show. She ignored it as her relationship with the show's producers deteriorated to the point where they barely spoke.

Mike was not slow to bring up the subject: 'You look terrible, Josie, and your appreciation index is way down. I know you're having a hard time after Sebastian's death but, hell, we can't have a presenter looking permanently like she's just come from a funeral. You have to get back on form or I'm telling you we're heading for a problem.'

Josie sat there despondently. One of Mike's lectures was the last thing she needed on this day she was planning to break some news.

'After Sebastian died there was a huge amount of sympathy for you, Josie,' he continued. 'You put a brave face on it and people respected you for that. Your appreciation figures even went *up* for a couple of weeks – do you remember? At that stage I thought we'd all pull through it and go ahead. But now I'm not so optimistic.'

'I know, Mike. I'm not turning it on in quite the same way. But it's not just me. Morale in the whole building has been steadily going downhill.'

'Not that I've noticed.'

'Well you should do. There's tension in the air. Half the production team are saying they're going to be out on the streets by Christmas.'

'And you blame that on me? If the staff are nervous it's because our audience figures are dropping and the advertisers are getting jumpy.'

'I'm just trying to point out that it's not all down to me.'

'But you're the figurehead. You *have* to make it look like it's one great big jolly party or why are we paying you two hundred thousand pounds a year?'

Josie plucked up her courage. She knew Mike would not react well to the news she had to give him. 'I'm thinking about taking a break.'

Mike gave her an exasperated look. 'Running away from it isn't going to help.'

'I think it might. Particularly the journey I have in mind.'

Mike's curiosity was spiked. 'What journey?'

'I've been thinking about going to Everest base camp.'

'What!'

'Someone from the company is trekking there next month to put up a memorial to the climbers. I've been toying with the thought that I might ask to go with him.'

Mike gave her a hard look. 'To the *Himalayas*? You don't know the first thing about mountains. Jesus, Josie, I know you need a shock to the system but isn't that, literally, going a bit too far?'

'Apparently not. I've been reading up about it and they say any reasonably fit person can get to base camp.'

'So how long will this take you away for?'

Josie looked sheepish. 'I think it's about a month.'

'A month! Jesus. The viewers will have forgotten who you are by the time you get back.' Mike lit a cigar. 'So what is this really about? You want to confront the mountain?'

'In a way, yes.'

'So it's about anger? Payback time.'

'If that's an adequate word.'

'And what else?'

'I don't know. A chance to get my head together. They say mountains do that, don't they?'

'Hell of a long way to go to sort yourself out. Can't you do it at a health farm?'

'It's deeper than that. It's a Sebastian thing.'

'Look. I'm no psychologist but it strikes me that you're playing with fire. Surely you should be trying to put the whole episode behind you rather than revisiting old . . .'

'Old what . . . ghosts? Is that what you were going to say? I think it will help. I'm having the most dreadful bloody nightmares about Sebastian lying there all abandoned and frozen. Something inside me wants to get close enough at least to say goodbye. I feel he needs me to do it, that he'll know I've done it.'

'I thought he was near the summit.'

'Well, when I say close I mean base camp.'

'I don't know, Josie, I think you should think about this really long and hard. It's against *Daybreak*'s interest. Unless . . .' Mike suddenly brightened.

'Unless what?'

'. . . unless we treat it as an opportunity. Maybe there's a twist to this that we can work to our advantage.'

'How?'

'Send a cameraman out with you to wire back video. Run it as a series of daily updates on the show! "Josie goes to lay memorial at Everest base camp." Brilliant. Shots of you in front of the mountain. I can just see it.'

Josie blanched. 'Well, I was thinking of it more as a private thing . . .'

'It would just be one guy. He wouldn't get in the way. Better still, he could take stills as well . . . We could set up a deal with the *Daily Mail* or *Hello!* Don't you see? It's perfect . . . you get your journey and *Daybreak* gets a publicity-generating special series.'

'I can see the logic, but . . .'

'It's a brilliant plan. Like a pilgrimage, almost. I think the viewers will be very touched by the idea.'

Josie thought for a few moments. 'I suppose you're right. It does make a kind of sense. How would it work?'

'We'd send one of the crew out with a digital camcorder. Pack him up with one of those new satellite transmission systems – they don't weigh much more than a briefcase these days – and you feed back five minutes of video every day. A sort of diary.'

'Who will you bring in to host the show?'

'I don't know. I'll have to talk to the producers about that. God knows we've got enough presenter showreels on file. We'll get somebody good, don't worry.'

'I'll have a think about it.'

'You do understand I'm not just talking about a travelogue? The viewer is going to want innermost thoughts as well.'

'I know what the viewer is going to want, Mike. That's what frightens me, having three million people watching my every step on what is supposed to be a personal trip.'

'You can handle it,' he insisted.

'I'll sleep on it and let you know tomorrow. But I don't want this turned into a circus, you understand?'

He called after her as she walked out: 'Make whatever decision you think right, Josie, but think about this. Whatever happens I want the ratings up . . . and this could be a good way of doing it.'

Later that day Josie called Deborah in Vancouver. They had talked frequently since the expedition memorial service and Deborah had already agreed in principle that she could accompany Hal on the journey to base camp. Now, Josie confirmed that she would do it.

Putting down the telephone, there was a pulse inside her that she hadn't felt since Sebastian's death . . . a bright core of something so close to optimism it almost felt like a betrayal.

Everest base camp. A focus. A target. A reason to believe . . .

41

Kathmandu was a shock, louder, more polluted and yet in some ways more charming than any other city Josie had ever been to. She flew with Hal and cameraman Jeremy, arriving in the first week of September and checking into Hal's old haunt, the Yak and Yeti where, despite his long years of absence, many of the staff still remembered his name. 'Welcome back to Kathmandu, Mr Hal,' the manager greeted him. 'You have been gone for too long.' Garlands of sweet-smelling flowers were placed round their necks and a rough china clay bowl of raki was offered to drink.

Josie moved forward to take it and at the same time was daubed with a dot of bright vermilion paste in the middle of her forehead by a Sherpani girl dressed in exquisite silks. 'I feel like I've stepped into another world,' she whispered to Hal as they waited for the receptionist to give them their room keys.

'You have,' he said, 'the most special country on earth.'

For forty-eight hours Josie wandered the streets in a daze, which was part jetlag, part disorientation and part intoxication with the sheer exotica the city laid out before her. Hal was busy chasing up some old contacts so she was left with Jeremy as a companion. He, too, was on his first trip to Nepal and he didn't waste any time in starting to build his portfolio of shots for the first of his video sequences.

He was taking stills, too – part of a deal with the syndicate of magazines Mike had sold the story to: Josie on a bicycle rickshaw; Josie outside a temple decked with thousands of candles, bathed in a glow of natural light with the haunting eyes of the Buddha painted on the stupa behind her; Josie bargaining for trinkets at a stall selling spices and souvenirs.

'This is going to be *some* assignment,' Jeremy told her, dripping enthusiasm as he framed up his Bronica medium-format camera for the hundredth time that day. 'That's it. Just lean back against that temple wall and look wistful.'

Josie was a nervous flyer. She had to resist the temptation to hold on to Hal's hand as the tiny Twin Otter had lifted unevenly off the runway at Kathmandu airport and turned towards the dreaming snow-capped peaks of the Himalayas. The persistent drone of the engines was seductive. She found it numbed her brain against the fear that height induced inside her. She steeled herself to look down from the tiny aircraft window. Thousands of feet below them terraced fields were etched into the mountainsides, green with the shoots of a late Himalayan harvest.

The rounded foothills soon gave way to more rugged valley sides. Outcrops of rock formed dragon tails along the ridges. Deep in the shadow-filled canyons Josie could see silver threads of light, rivers dancing their way to the plains of India.

'Take a look ahead.' Hal's voice pulled her from the reverie. 'That's Lukla airstrip.'

Josie raised herself as far as the seat belt would allow and peered over the pilot's shoulder through the front window. The plane had banked steeply and was now heading straight for the side of the valley, aiming at the heart of a large village. Carved into the valley side was a narrow brown strip which, foreshortened by the angle from which she now viewed it, seemed to Josie to be no more than fifty metres long. 'You're kidding.'

'No, I'm not.' Hal laughed out loud at the expression on her face.

Josie's terror turned to hysterical laughter as the pilot throttled back the engines. Turbulent air currents tossed the tiny plane from side to side and then they were on the ground, the engines on full reverse thrust, kicking up dust as the pilot fought to bring the show to a halt before the sheer face of a cliff did it for him. He turned abruptly off the airstrip on to a field and parked next to the shattered skeleton of a Russian helicopter, which had crashed some months before. He cut the engines.

'That's better than sex, isn't it?' Hal couldn't wipe the smile off his face.

Josie was still trembling as they made their way up the hillside towards the lodge.

In the hour before sunset Hal took Josie on a walk around Lukla. The Sherpa village was shrouded in a haze of woodsmoke, the air filled with the laughter of children kicking a ball around on the airstrip.

Josie found herself enchanted by the beauty of the Tibetan faces that surrounded her, by the jet-black hair of the women, plaited elegantly in long tails to the waist, by the ready laughter that filtered from doorways and windows. A young girl with red and green ribbons in her hair took Josie's hand as they wandered past the trading stalls, each laden with fabrics and clothing from India and China. They climbed up a small trail leading away from the village as the chill of evening set in.

'Is she going to be able to get home all right?' Josie was concerned about the girl, who could not have been more than five or six.

'She is going home.'

There was just enough light left for Josie to see the low wooden building surrounded by a stone wall. The young girl ran ahead, calling in her high-pitched voice. A woman and several more children came out to greet them. Hal spoke to her in her own tongue, the first time Josie had heard him use the Sherpa language for anything more than a casual greeting. They were escorted into the house.

It took Josie's eyes a while to adjust to the low level of light – the only illumination came from the flames of the hearth. They sat cross-legged around the fire as the Sherpani added split logs and chatted amiably to Hal. Josie held her hands towards the flames, relishing the way the warmth drove the chill night air out of her. They drank tea and ate a simple meal of rice and lentils. The children were shy, keeping to the shadows and talking in whispers. Only the young girl with the ribbons dared to stay close to Josie. She put her head in Josie's lap and went to sleep.

Suddenly the door burst open and a figure appeared, panting for breath. There was just enough light for Josie to register that it was a Sherpa boy – strikingly handsome, perhaps eighteen or nineteen years old. On seeing Hal his face lit up. 'I heard you were here!' He crossed the room rapidly as Hal stood, with a smile, to embrace him.

'Nima! Great to see you. Did you run down the valley?' Hal asked him.

'As soon as I heard you landed. They will get mad at school but I wanted to come.'

Josie stood to take the newcomer's hand.

'Josie, this is Nima, the oldest son of the family.' Josie could not miss the glimmer of pride in Hal's voice.

'Pleased to meet you, Josie.'

They sat once more while Nima greeted his family and caught his breath.

'He just ran about ten kilometres in the last couple of hours,' Hal explained, 'but that's not unusual for Nima. He's as strong as a lion.'

Nima's mother handed him a bowl of tsampa – the glutinous barley paste that is one of the staple foods of the Sherpa people. Nima ladled the doughlike stodge into his mouth with a huge wooden spoon, smiling all the while at Hal and Josie. 'So where you go?' he asked through a mouthful.

'Base camp. Slow trip. No hurry.'

Nima nodded. 'I come with you.'

Hal laughed. 'Wait a minute! What about school?'

Nima gave him a sideways glance. 'Not first time I leave school to go to base camp.'

Hal turned to Josie. 'Nima's following in his father's footsteps,' he explained. 'His dad was Ang Phurba, one of the all-time greats. Pretty well the strongest Sherpa I ever knew. He was killed in the ice fall on my second Everest expedition and I've kept in touch with the family since.'

'This good man.' Nima laughed, punching Hal playfully on the shoulder with surprising force. 'Many leaders, Sherpa killed, do nothing. Hal come back, look after us. He like a father to me.'

'And if I was your father I'd be insisting you got back to school.'

'No. I come to base camp. You can't stop me. Have to train. Last year I go to Everest with Italian team – twice above eight thousand metres, big loads, no problem for me. Only weather stopped me from going to top.'

'You want to go to the summit?' Josie asked him.

Nima looked at her as if she were mad. 'Of course. My father reach summit three times. I will go there for him very soon.'

'When you've finished your education,' Hal protested.

'Everest eight thousand eight hundred and forty-eight metres high. What else I need to know?' Nima gave him a cheeky smile but Josie could see the thick streak of stubbornness in his intensely black eyes.

Later she learned from one of their Sherpa porters that Hal had supported Nima and his family financially since the death of Ang Phurba, paying for Nima's education at the best school in the

Khumbu and wiring money for the upkeep of the family through an intermediary in Kathmandu.

'If you think you can square it with the teachers, you can come with us,' Hal told him.

'Very good. And next time you go on the mountain you make me sirdar, yes?'

'I'm not going back on the mountain.' Hal's voice was firm.

'You not resist.' Nima spoke earnestly. 'One day you will go back to Chomolungma. And I reach summit with you.'

42

They trekked for eight days through the Khumbu to Namche Bazaar, the great Sherpa trading centre, then struck out on the narrower and steeper trails, which led to the Tengboche monastery and beyond. The physical process was harder than Josie had anticipated, the vast valley walls seeming to stretch on for ever as her body struggled to adjust to the rigours of hard walking for eight to ten hours every day. The altitude was another shock. Even at ten thousand feet she found herself breathless when she moved too fast.

'You have to slow yourself down,' Hal advised her. 'Imagine you're moving in a type of slow motion. That way your muscles will be able to cope.'

There were days when she thought she had made a big mistake, when her entire body seemed locked in a rigid spasm of cramp as she tried to get out of her sleeping bag. Nima was very sympathetic, bringing her sweet tea in the early morning and offering to carry her rucksack when the afternoons gave way to long hauls of uphill work. She stubbornly refused his offer, insisting on carrying her own pack even when the straps began to chafe open sores into her shoulders.

Gradually, once her body had begun to acclimatise and she had mastered the art of packing endless amounts of fluid into herself to prevent dehydration, Josie found her condition improving. She began to notice more about the landscape through which they were trekking, to appreciate the dank green intensity of the rhododendron forests, to turn up her eyes and drink in the majesty of Ama Dablam, the icy sentinel towering over the approach to Everest.

Finally, she settled happily into the rhythm of the trek, enjoying the physical exercise in a way she had never done before.

Cameraman Jeremy was her constant companion, snapping her at every opportunity and consoling her by having an even tougher time on the trek than she was. He was kept busy filming scenes in the villages and recording Josie's diary pieces along the way. Each night he set up the satellite transmitter and beamed five minutes of material back to the *Daybreak* studio.

Hal kept himself to himself, choosing to trek alone and spending his evenings with Nima and the rest of the Sherpas, rather than with Josie and the photographer. Every time Josie tried to get time to talk with him he managed to avoid her. At mealtimes she would pointedly sit next to him, only to have him rise and take his plate outside the mess tent to eat alone.

On the trail he was just as elusive, either leaving long before Josie and Jeremy, and setting such a pace that they could not catch up, or lagging far behind, taking tea in every village along the way. The more Josie pondered on it, the more she was irritated by Hal's behaviour. Then, on the tenth day of the trek, an incident occurred which brought them into outright confrontation.

It happened in the village of Pheriche, an untidy collection of stone-built houses on a high plateau just a few days from base camp. Josie and Jeremy arrived an hour ahead of Hal to find that a colourful ceremony was under way. Almost all the inhabitants of the village were gathered in one of the larger fields, the women decked in their finest red and yellow silks, the men in white robes. There was singing and drumming, and the high-pitched ululations of the women echoed off the surrounding valley walls.

Delighted by this riot of local colour, Josie and Jeremy both got out their cameras and were busy filming away when Hal arrived. 'What the hell do you think you're doing?' he hissed at Josie, pulling her bodily away from a group of dancing women she was in the process of filming.

'Ow! Be careful, you're hurting my shoulder. What's your problem?'

'You're pissing all these villagers off, that's what. Jeremy! Put your camera down.'

Jeremy continued shooting his stills until Hal walked over and snatched his camera away from him.

'I said stop.'

'Hey. I have a job to do here. This is the most colourful little festival we've seen so far. We can't miss this.'

'It's a funeral. These people are mourning.'

'They are?' Josie said. 'So why didn't they say something?'

'Because they're far too polite. If you'd asked their permission to take photographs they would have politely declined. But as it was, you both just launched in there without so much as a thought for their feelings.'

'You're too much!' Jeremy yelled at him, snatching his camera back and retreating to a tearoom where he spent the rest of the afternoon in a sulk.

'I think you're overreacting,' Josie flared. 'You think you're their guardian protector or something? They're perfectly capable of letting us know if they don't like what we're doing.'

'You treat this place like a photo opportunity.' Hal's voice was calm but furious. 'And that's what it will be. Some kind of overblown Disney park full of colourful folk with pretty faces. But that's not the way to travel through this country. This is their home, Josie, and you should respect the fact that we are the strangers here.'

'You've been waiting for this, haven't you?'

'For what?'

'For a chance to have a go at me. I know you just think of me as a spoiled little rich girl out here on some kind of media shopping trip.'

'Well, the thought had occurred.'

'You bastard. I'm here to pay my respects to my husband, if you remember.'

'That might have been the original intention, but you've turned it into a glamour shoot. Every time I see you or Jeremy you have your lenses pushed up against some Sherpa's face. You give out pens and sweets to the children like some visiting charity. If everyone who came here behaved like the two of you, before we know it this part of the world would be filled with beggars and satellite dishes.'

'And you're so great? You see yourself as the big white protector of the Sherpa people but has it ever occurred to you that it is expedition leaders such as yourself who've been responsible for the deaths of dozens of Sherpas? They've died working for you on mountains like Everest. How do you square that one up with your great perspective on the rights and wrongs of the world?'

'I don't trample over their culture. I respect it.'

'You're a snob. You think you deserve to be here and I don't. In fact, you wish I weren't here on this trek at all!' She stormed away to join Jeremy in the tearoom, leaving Hal on his own.

43

The next day was a rest day, a chance for the small team to recuperate from the long trek and to garner their strength before the final three-day session up to base camp. Following the row, the atmosphere was dreadful, the communal meals punctuated by long silences and theatrical sighs from Jeremy.

'We'll leave at six tomorrow morning,' Hal informed them. Those were the only words he spoke all day.

Leaving Pheriche was a big psychological boost for Josie. She had hated the confrontation and the cloud it had cast over their small team. Paradoxically, she found herself in a good mood and resolved to find an opportunity to try to make peace with Hal. She waited for late morning, when Jeremy was lagging far behind, and put on some speed to catch him up.

They had been trekking for three or four hours and Josie felt strong. She fixed her attention on Hal's leather boots as she followed him up the trail. The path was loose and rocky, and she needed to concentrate hard to avoid twisting an ankle. The sky was clear and blue, with not a hint of cloud. Josie was trekking in a T-shirt and shorts, such was the warmth of that Himalayan autumn day.

After a while, the path eased off into a grassy valley with a scattering of Sherpa houses. It was mostly grazing pasture, with stonewalled fields on which yaks and the occasional horse could be seen. Hal selected a comfortable-looking field of grass and they sat down to rest.

'I want to say I'm sorry,' Josie told him, settling herself, cross-legged, beside him.

Hal looked relieved. 'Yeah, me too. I guess I overreacted a little.'

'But you were right. We were being intrusive and there's no excuse for that.'

'It's just that every time I come back to this country I see a little more of the soul has gone. Like it's being eaten away, piece by piece.

Every photo takes a little more; every unthinking action by a trekker. It depresses me.'

'Is that why you don't come back any more?'

'Hell. It's one of the reasons but there are plenty more.'

'I know you think of me and Jeremy as excess baggage on this trek. You'd probably prefer us not to have come.'

Hal sighed. 'Not really. I understand your need to come to base camp, I really do. Shit, I'm here for the same reason . . . on Deborah's behalf for Rick.'

'Yeah. I didn't like to say that.'

They sat without speaking for a while, the only sound the clanging of the yak bells as an expedition passed by on the trail.

'So,' Josie asked him softly, 'is this a pact? Are we going to treat each other like human beings? Apart from anything else, there's not enough oxygen here to waste any breath on shouting.'

Hal smiled; 'OK. I apologise.'

Josie looked pleased. 'So how do you feel I'm doing? Think I'll make it to base camp?'

'You're looking a lot stronger than you were the first days,' Hal admitted, offering her a swig of his water bottle.

'I'm feeling better, too. The altitude really knocked me for six but I feel like I'm adjusting.'

'I'm a bit worried about Jeremy,' Hal said. 'He's not coping so well.'

'I noticed that. He's puffing and blowing all over the place but he's still adamant he's going to get there.'

'I'll keep a careful eye on him,' Hal promised. 'If I think he's getting altitude sickness I'll have to turn him back.'

By the time they roused themselves to continue the track was filled with numerous teams, all heading in the same direction. Josie found herself trekking next to a Danish woman dressed in state-of-the-art mountain gear. 'You going to base camp?' she asked her.

The woman paused, leaning against a boulder to catch her breath. 'That's the start,' she said.

'You're climbing Everest?'

'You bet.'

Josie was surprised. The woman seemed no fitter than she was – in fact, as they continued up the track, Josie found she was easily capable of keeping up with her, and she couldn't help noticing that the other's rucksack was lighter and smaller than her own.

Later, when she mentioned it to Hal, he laughed. 'That was Else Vellir. She's Denmark's leading woman climber. She's climbed Broad Peak, K2 and plenty more.'

'She has?' Josie was astounded. 'But she looked like she was going through hell and we're still two days from base camp.'

'You seem to have this impression that climbers going for the summit are somehow superhuman. In fact, the chances are that they suffer at these lower altitudes just like anyone else.'

'So what has someone like her got that I haven't?'

This time it was Hal's turn to laugh. 'She has the desire to stand on the summit,' he said simply.

'And?'

'And that's it.'

'So that's all you need?'

'You need the physical attributes too, of course. But it surprises me how many people forget that motivation is *the* driving force.'

That night was rough for Jeremy. He coughed violently and vomited several times.

When Hal had a good look at him the next morning he made the decision to send him back. 'Your lips are starting to look blue,' he told the disappointed photographer, 'and that's the first sign of acute mountain sickness. Your blood is not carrying enough oxygen to keep your vital organs going so I'm afraid you have to descend.' Hal appointed one of the Sherpas to accompany Jeremy back down to Namche Bazaar.

'But what are we going to do about the filming at base camp?' Josie asked nervously. She still half feared that Hal would tell her that was just tough luck.

Hal thought it over, then said, 'I'll do it.'

'You mean that?' Josie gave him a hug. 'Thanks, Hal. That's really good of you . . . bearing in mind, well, the argument and that.'

'I can't promise they'll be great shots but I'll try my best.'

Hal, Josie, Nima and two other Sherpas trekked up through Gorak Shep – the final human habitation on the route – and made their way for a long and, for Josie, memorably painful day alongside the decaying ice spires of the Khumbu glacier, arriving at base camp just after 4 p.m. on an afternoon as cold and bleak as any Josie could remember.

'Oh. Is that it?' Josie stood, panting and light-headed, as they saw their first view of base camp. It was a bigger area than she had expected, a sprawling tented city of colourful domes, vivid against the dirt-grey of the ancient ice. 'But we can't see the mountain!'

Hal laughed. 'Everyone says the same. They expect base camp to be at the foot of this great pyramid. In fact, the route goes up there to the right, through the ice fall.' He pointed up through a narrow defile, protected by what seemed to Josie to be an impregnable flow of twisted, tortured ice.

'Oh.'

While Nima set about building their small camp Hal took some video footage and stills of Josie with the ice fall behind her, then more of her standing in front of a ceremonial cairn decked with Tibetan prayer flags.

Although she didn't feel like it, Josie did a quick diary piece to camera, forcing herself to sound a great deal happier than she really was.

Then, with night falling, they retreated to the mess tent where she was handed a plate of food she knew she would not be able to eat. 'So,' she asked Hal, 'when was the last time you were here?' She saw Hal and Nima exchange a glance.

'Six years ago,' Hal told her. 'That was the time I decided I wouldn't be coming back.'

Josie looked at him searchingly. 'Will you tell me about it?'

Hal thought for a while, then began . . .

44

Alex was a star client – Hal had liked him greatly, right from the first phone call in which he had enthusiastically expressed an interest in joining the expedition to Everest the following year.

'Let me get this straight,' Alex had said, his crisp East-Coast accent loaded with the pleasure of an impending joke. 'I pay you thirty-seven thousand dollars and in return I get to spend three months puking my guts up on the highest mountain in the world? I get cerebral oedema, my lungs fill up with fluid, my fingers and toes shrivel up, go gangrenous and then drop off? Or have I missed something?'

Hal smiled. 'You might get a summit photograph thrown in.' He knew the type. Alex was what he called a 'corporate mountaineer' – one of the growing band of high earners who had an Everest-sized stash of disposable income to help them take their pick of the world's summits.

'I see this as part of my personal development,' he told Hal, 'and it's kind of a unique item to put on a CV!'

Alex was slow to acclimatise – so much so that it was only in the very last days of the expedition that he was ready for a summit bid. Hal's other clients had already completed the climb and were back down at base camp by the time he and Alex left camp four. Hal had sent his exhausted Sherpas down with the rest of the team, confident he could handle Alex's ascent without them. On that day they were completely alone, the only people on the mountain. Hal relished the chance to experience Everest without the normal crowds.

Not long after sunrise they came to a rising bluff of blue ice – a wind-polished wall steeper than anything they had tackled so far. Calling to Alex to stop, Hal climbed up to him. 'You OK to climb this section unroped?'

Alex looked up at the dauntingly steep terrain. 'You sure you don't want to fix it?'

If Hal had been sharper, just a few per cent more alert, he might have spotted the momentary stumble in Alex's habitually optimistic tone of voice, the tiny catch of uncertainty contained within it. 'We're running a bit slow . . . We can't afford to lose the time. Just take care and you'll be fine.'

Alex began, his earlier quickfire pace diminishing dramatically as he hit the sharp rise of the blue ice. Shards of chipped ice skittered down the slope, showering Hal with fragments as his client kicked into the glassy surface. From his vantage point Hal followed Alex's progress, clearly seeing the metallic cluster of sharp crampon points as his client raised his feet to bite into the surface.

He was no more than ten metres above Hal's position when he tripped and fell, but it happened so fast that Hal was caught completely off his guard. Alex shot down the slope, his only warning cry a scream of abject fear. Within seconds he was travelling too fast to arrest himself with his ice axe, a blur of flailing arms and legs rocketing past Hal with no hope of regaining control.

Hal lurched forward to try to catch him. He was a fraction of a second too late. 'Use your axe,' he screamed.

But the axe had already been ripped from Alex's hand. Now he was tumbling in a series of shattering cartwheels towards the crevasses, which sat waiting at the foot of the slope. Fifty metres, one hundred, Hal had the sickening certainty that his client would not survive. He could barely bring himself to watch as the tiny figure was flung in the air. Hal thought he heard the briefest of cries. Then Alex plunged out of sight into the cobalt-blue interior of the first crevasse.

Silence. Hal felt the bitter taste of bile in his mouth. He was shaking, looking down in shock, as if Alex would climb from the crevasse and give him a cheery wave. Still numb with the terror of watching his client fall, and already saturated with guilt at his mistake in allowing him to climb unroped, it took Hal more than an hour to climb down and make his way into the interior of the crevasse. Alex was still alive, but only just. He was lying on a bank of powder snow not far below the lip of the crevasse. He had hit the far wall at catastrophic speed and regained only partial consciousness as Hal reached him.

'I guess I fucked that one up . . .' were Alex's only whispered words as he briefly recognised Hal.

A fast examination confirmed that Alex's physical condition was as bad as Hal had feared – a compound fracture of his left thigh, massive contusions and internal bleeding down the left side, including, Hal was almost sure, a ruptured kidney.

Hal knew that to move Alex could cause more damage but to leave him where he was would mean certain death. Hal half carried, half dragged his stricken client to the edge of the crevasse and paused to review his options. He called base camp on the walkie-talkie to tell them of the disaster. Three Sherpas immediately offered to come to assist a rescue but he knew it would take them two days to get back up. He asked them to try, in case by some miracle Alex might last that long.

Now, getting Alex to the protection of the tent was the only hope. For the next five hours Hal manhandled Alex's dead weight across and down the west face – a feat of enormous physical strength fired by desperation. Finally reaching the lone tent, he tended to Alex's injuries as best he could. The leg wound was severe – the shattered end of the bone had ripped through the flesh of the thigh. Injecting him with morphine against the pain was the best Hal could do. 'Sleep, Alex. Help is on the way.' Hal gripped Alex's hand to reassure him as he passed once more into oblivion.

Hal had little hope that Alex would survive. His injuries were such that, even if two or three of his strongest Sherpas got up in time, they could never get him out alive. By midday on the following day the margins of Hal's own survival were getting increasingly thin. Not anticipating this crisis, he had instructed the Sherpas to leave only enough food and cooking gas to cover the summit attempt. Now, the supplies were finished.

Hour by hour, Alex's life was slipping away, his pulse becoming weaker, his breathing shallower as he passed into a coma. Hal knew at this point that his client was going to die. He radioed the Sherpas and told them to turn back. Hal felt an all-consuming sadness as he watched his fellow team member fading in front of his eyes. His skin was parched and yellowing, his lips blue, he had the tell-tale bubbles of pulmonary oedema exuding from his mouth.

By three that afternoon Hal was aware of the pressing need to make a decision. If he stayed another night at the present altitude he would be risking his own life. He was already extremely debilitated and he was a long way from the safety of the lower camps. Periodically he looked out of the tent flap to see if any figures were climbing up towards the camp. He knew there was one more team waiting for a chance at the summit and that they would probably share their oxygen and food with him once they understood the situation. That, at least, would enable him to stay another night with Alex. But as the afternoon wore on, a bank of light cloud swept across the flanks of Everest. Even if climbers were approaching, Hal would not be able to see them. It was time to go down while he still could.

Alex was already effectively dead, Hal told himself, the systems of his body even now shutting down. There was no way he would ever regain consciousness. He probably wouldn't last for more than another hour.

But another voice wanted to hold Hal back. What if Alex *did* regain an awareness of where he was, even for a fleeting moment?

Hal prepared his rucksack.

To find that Hal had abandoned him?

Hal put on his plastic boots.

To find he was dying alone?

Hal forced himself through the entrance of the tent and zipped it behind him. He set off for the route that would take him down. And he didn't look back.

And there the story of Alex might have ended – another casualty of the death zone, an anonymous statistic to add to the list – if it hadn't been for the two climbers who loomed out of the cloud in front of Hal as he descended.

They were from a Catalan expedition – the one that Hal had half suspected might still try for the summit. He recognised one of the pair: Miguel Font, the expedition leader.

'Where is the other?' Font pointed up into the cloud. They had heard at one of the camps that two of Hal's team were overdue.

'He's not coming back.' Hal shook his head. He could think of nothing else to say.

The Catalan placed a hand on Hal's shoulder; 'You want us to help you? You need something?'

'No. I'm OK.'

He shrugged, 'So, we go now.'

Hal began his descent once more and didn't give the two another thought, although he would have done had he known the identity of the second man.

Font's fellow climber was Xavier Pujol, a photojournalist for the Spanish newspaper *El Periodico*. He was there to cover the Catalan expedition. Unlike the expedition leader, Pujol was not a seasoned mountaineer who had seen it all before. He was seeing it for the first time and when he unzipped the front of Hal's tent and found Alex was still – just – alive, he was not slow to spot the opportunity. Pujol shot digital photographs of Alex's dying face in the tent, and a couple of the tent exterior for good measure. As soon as he could, he wired back his pictures and story by satellite transmission.

The following day *El Periodico* ran it front page under the banner headline, LEFT TO DIE. The piece was a scathing indictment of the guide who abandoned his client to a lonely death: 'Hal Maher lost no time in accepting Alex Chesman's dollars,' Pujol wrote, 'and lost no time in turning his back on his wounded team-mate when he needed him most. Maher saved his own skin, but at what price?'

A London-based syndication agency picked up the feature from *El Periodico* and added their own file photographs of the mountain. Within twenty-four hours the story of Alex Chesman was distributed around the world and Xavier Pujol was a wealthy man.

It nearly broke Hal Maher.

There was no defence, of course, or at least not one that Hal could possibly justify. To stress how close he himself had been to that critical point at which the effects of altitude become irreversible was something only those who had been there would truly understand. A few fellow guides and some big guns of climbing wrote spirited defences of Hal. Kowing the integrity of the man, *they* had no doubts. But from the layman's point of view and that, it seemed, of every leader writer in the popular press, Hal Maher had a case to answer. 'Where there is life', wrote the *Daily Mail*, 'there is hope. Alex Chesman deserved better than to be left to die alone.'

Hal returned to Anchorage, put a message on the Mountain High answerphone to say the office was closed for a couple of months and embarked on a series of long solo treks through his beloved Chugach mountains. It was a lonely summer and at the end of it he had decided he would close down the company and concentrate on the avalanche work, which he had been on the fringes of for years.

Hal drained his hot drink and looked at Josie. 'And that was the story of my last Everest expedition,' he told her, 'and the reason why I decided not to go for the summit again.'

'I'm so sorry,' she said. 'Watching him die before your eyes like that . . . I really can't imagine what it must have felt like.'

'About as bad as it gets.'

Later, when she saw how the telling of the story had depressed him, Josie regretted asking the question. An uneasy silence fell over the mess tent, which not even the cheerful Nima could dispel.

45

Curled up in her sleeping bag, Josie spent the lingering hours of darkness fighting the urge to vomit, wondering why she felt that the whole endeavour had been a waste of time. She tried to analyse it: what exactly had she been hoping to achieve by this journey and why was there an aching sense inside her that it had come to nothing? She had wanted to be close to – wanted to touch – this place that meant so much to Sebastian. She had imagined base camp would ease a pressure inside her, untap the lake of grief that was still locked inside. But the reality was something else. She felt no sense of communion with Sebastian, of coming to terms with the mountain, of belonging to the place, only the blank, indifferent stares of the expedition team members as she wandered like a lost soul through the jumbled moraine of the glacier.

'They're not very welcoming, are they?' Josie had observed to Hal as they gathered for breakfast.

Hal laughed. 'As far as they're concerned we're just another couple of trekkers. They don't want to get too close or they might catch a virus.'

'Are you serious?'

'Yes. This is a closed community. You get the colds and flu over in the first month and you avoid strangers like they've got the plague. There's plenty of people have put their summit failures down to an imported flu bug from a visiting trekker.'

'So am I going to get to see the mountain?'

'Don't worry, we're going up to Kala Pattar, the classic viewpoint where all the photographs are taken from. That's where we're going to put the memorial plaque.'

'Why not here?'

'Because this glacier is moving, a few feet every year. If we built a cairn here it would be destroyed pretty quick.'

After forcing down some muesli and hot chocolate, Josie followed Hal across the glacier and on to the ash cone that would take them to the summit of Kala Pattar, the outcrop of rock – some six thousand four hundred metres high – which would, she hoped, give her the longed-for sighting of Everest itself.

The effects of altitude were more noticeable with every passing hour of the climb, Josie's chest tightening, her ribs beginning to ache as her breathing rate increased to cope with the thin air. She climbed, fixed on the shallow impressions Hal's boots left in the trail, trying not to raise her hopes too high. Hal had already warned her the mountain could be covered in cloud – even though they were climbing in bright sunshine.

'You promise you haven't sneaked a look?' Hal had made her swear she would wait until they reached the viewpoint.

'No way!' Josie smiled and concentrated on her breathing. The rocks gave way to finer packed gravel, like volcanic ash; then they crossed two small patches of snow, crusted and dirty with wind-blown dust.

Hal stopped a couple of metres from the top and waved Josie through with a theatrical bow. 'The viewpoint is yours, ma'am.'

'May I turn round and look now?'

'Yep.'

They sat side by side on the warm platform of rock where a few prayer flags and a broken piece of ski pole had been left by previous trekkers.

'Welcome to Kala Pattar and your first view of Everest.' Hal was playing the tour guide to perfection.

And there it was. Josie turned up her face to savour the majesty of that moment. The mountain that until now had existed for her only in photographs was sitting right there in front of her, terrifyingly, impossibly huge. This was not like base camp, Josie realised in a moment of perfect understanding. *This* was what she had come for. She struggled to find the words but none came. To say anything would have demeaned the mountain and herself. Hal understood. They sat side by side in silence, watching the perfect triangle of rock and ice, soaring effortlessly above the jagged ridges of its neighbours – many of which were themselves some of the greatest mountains on the planet.

'Have you really stood on that summit?' Josie was the first to break the silence.

'Yes. And it's the most beautiful place in the world.'

'Is that why you climbed it so many times?'

Hal placed his lightweight rucksack behind him and rested back on it with his hands behind his head. 'I guess so.'

Josie arranged her own pack and leaned back next to him; she felt intimidated and small. It seemed inconceivable that there should be any real connection between her and the mass of ice and rock that now transfixed her. 'How can anyone sit here seriously and contemplate climbing that mountain?'

'Too many people can do that.'

A cold realisation hit her. 'I'm looking at where Sebastian is. I'm looking at his grave. He's up there somewhere.'

Hal said nothing.

Josie concentrated on Everest, registering every feature – the gullies, the couloirs, the hanging glaciers of ice poised to avalanche – as if by knowing them she could find an answer to the question that had haunted her since the journey had begun. What was the hold this mountain had had on Sebastian – the obsession that had drawn him halfway around the world?

Time passed. A hint of cloud began to play around the face, thickening rapidly even as they watched.

'We should put the plaque in place,' Hal reminded her. In his backpack Hal had the brass plate that Deborah had designed in Vancouver. It was fourteen inches by twelve, deeply etched with a motif of the mountain and with the names of the members of Rick's expedition engraved in alphabetical order upon it, along with the date on which they had all died.

Josie held it in her hands, looking at it for the first time. 'It's nice. Deborah did a good job.'

Nima had been up to the high point a couple of hours before them to deposit a small one-kilo pack of cement. Now Hal scooped a hollow out of the gravel and poured the powder in before adding a cupful of water from his bottle and mixing it with a small trowel he had brought for the purpose. When it was the right consistency he would use it to fix the plaque to the rock face nearby.

'You've done this before,' Josie remarked.

'A few times.' Hal paused from his work to look at her. 'Enough that I'm sick of erecting these monuments.'

'Sorry.'

They placed the plaque in a good location, a small ledge cut into solid rock and facing the mountain. It was a short way from the main viewing area and would thus not attract too much attention. Hal had told her that some plaques – particularly those bearing famous climbers' names – had actually been stolen by souvenir hunters. Hal smoothed the cement into place and pushed the plaque into position. Then they stood side by side to look at his handiwork. It was a neat job, the metal set flush with the face. He took out the video camera and filmed Josie looking at the plaque, then fired off some still shots for the magazines.

'So, that's it?' Josie asked.

'Yep. That's it. Now we go home.'

The mountain was now behind a mask of cloud, depriving Josie of the one last look she craved. She said a prayer for Sebastian and followed Hal down the slope to the trail, which would take them back down towards the lush valleys and Kathmandu.

That night, when she closed her eyes to try to sleep, all she could see was that great pyramid of rock and ice as it was revealed from behind the clouds. What had she understood in that fleeting glimpse of Everest, she wondered? Why had that awesome vision imprinted itself so indelibly in her mind? What had it spoken to her?

It would be many months before she understood the chemistry of that moment and, when she did, the spark it had created would seem so natural that it might have been a part of her very being.

The desire. Wasn't that what Hal had called it?

46

Hal watched the Rockies rise out of the dawn, the familiar ridges and furls of the continental divide reduced, from his vantage point five and a half miles high, to a mere wrinkle on the surface of the earth. There was already a sprinkling of snow on the high ground, as he had expected. He massaged his neck with the fingers of both hands where it was stiff from sixteen hours of air travel and the effects of skewing his body to look out of the glazed plastic of the aircraft window. Along with the rest of the passengers, he breathed a sigh of relief when the captain announced twenty minutes to landing and began the descent into Vancouver airport.

In the terminal, Rachel and Deborah were waiting for him, Rachel out of the wheelchair and walking with a stick.

Hal kissed them both.

'You lost some weight,' Rachel said.

'And you learned to walk. Take a trek down the concourse here and let me see you.' Hal was pleased. In the month he'd been in Nepal, Rachel's leg had healed well. There was a distinct limp but that was nothing considering the damage the leg had sustained. 'You'll be dancing by Christmas,' he told her.

They drove back to Deborah's place and sat around the kitchen table to catch up with news.

'So how did you all get along while I was away?' Hal asked.

'It was a great success.' Deborah stated. 'Rachel was a hit with the kids and it's been a real pleasure to have her around. So did you get the memorial put up?'

'Everything went fine,' Hal answered. 'I shot a couple of stills of the plaque for you. I'll get them processed in the next few days.'

'Oh, I'd like that. Thank you Hal. You don't know what a relief it is that you managed to get that done, not just for me but for the other families as well . . .'

'How was Josie?' Rachel enquired, 'Was she a pain in the neck?'

'She was OK in the end. We had a few flare-ups but generally she was all right. I think the journey helped her quite a bit.'

'Did she have trouble with the altitude?' Deborah asked.

'Her cameraman did – I had to turn him back before base camp. But Josie was strong, stronger than your average trekker by far. She made it up to Kala Pattar like it was a Sunday afternoon stroll.'

'And the filming?'

'Oh, we got the occasional bit of feedback from London, all very positive. It seems that several million viewers were following the daily updates. How about here? Have you had any problems with the press?'

'Like you wouldn't believe,' Rachel confirmed. 'I've had to act as a minder to Deborah these past weeks. The telephone must have rung a thousand times with journalists, radio reporters, all wanting just that short little conversation with Rick Fielding's wife. There's six books in production about the storm and that's just the ones we know about.'

'There's some pretty hurtful stuff flying around,' Deborah conceded. 'I knew Rick was no saint but it's one thing to know that and another to read about all the affairs he had with his female clients when he's dead for God's sake. What purpose does that serve?'

'The children have been getting teased at school too.' Rachel added. 'Can you believe that?'

'All too easily,' Hal replied.

Rachel gestured to a pile of correspondence sitting on the kitchen table. Hal figured there must have been more than two hundred letters in the stack. 'There's another twist to this. Guess what they are?'

'Letters of condolence?' Hal suggested.

Deborah laughed bitterly. 'Not quite. These are requests for Himalayan Objectives brochures. There's about a hundred e-mails too. And guess which mountain everyone wants to climb?'

'Everest?'

'Spot on. In all the years of running this company we've never had as much interest in that mountain. It's almost like the disaster has made people more keen in going there rather than the opposite.'

'Now I've heard everything.'

'So it raises the question of what I'm going to do about it.'

'Have you decided to hold on to the company?'

'I don't know what else I *can* do. Nothing apart from this is going to keep this place running and the kids just seem to get more and more expensive as they get older. The company has a loyal clientele – the ones who aren't thinking of suing us, that is. I could find leaders to take on McKinley, Aconcagua and so on. Probably make a living that way. It'll be tough to run it myself but it'll be a good distraction.' Deborah stood. 'Anyway, enough of my problems. You two probably want to spend a bit of time together after this last month apart. I'll take the kids into town to do a bit of shopping and give you some peace and quiet.'

'Thanks, Deborah.'

When they were alone, Rachel cupped Hal's face in her hands, kissing him tenderly. 'Oh, Hal, I'm so glad to get you back. Deborah and the kids have been very welcoming but I really missed you all the same.'

'I missed you too.'

'You didn't fall madly in love with Josie? She's quite beautiful from what I've heard.'

Hal laughed. 'I don't go for blondes, remember?'

'So you say . . .'

They kissed again.

'So how has Deborah really been?' Hal asked.

Rachel sighed. 'Courageous, but I think she's closer to cracking up than she lets on. She's been going through hell with all this press attention. And the rumours of a lawsuit are still flying around.'

'Yeah? I thought that would have died down by now.'

'No chance. There's some hotshot lawyer talking to the relatives of people who died in Rick's group. He's stirring things up nicely.'

Hal shook his head sadly. 'That's the last thing Deborah needs when she's trying to get the kids through all this.'

Rachel took Hal's hand in hers; 'Hal, do you mind if we spend some more time here? I know Deborah wouldn't ask us in a million years but from what I've seen she desperately needs more help over the next few months. There's the kids, the business, the house. I get the feeling things are going to get worse for her before they start to get better. I spoke to the Carroways on the telephone a few days back and they're happy to stay on at the cabin for a while longer.'

'That's fine by me,' Hal agreed, 'I don't want to head back to Alaska now in any case. The guys will be running around getting the avalanche team together for the winter and I'm not sure I could stand by chewing my nails while they do that without me.'

Rachel looked at him intently. 'What are you going to do next, Hal? Did you come up with any great ideas on the trek to base camp?'

'Not exactly.' He laughed. 'All I know right now is that I want to help Deborah get through these problems and that we should spend a big chunk of time together sorting things out between us.'

'You really mean that? While you were away I kept getting this strange idea that you'd want to end our relationship when you got back.'

Hal looked shocked. 'Why?'

'I don't know . . . I guess I just can't quite see where we're heading at the moment and that makes me nervous.'

Hal reached out to hold her. 'I know what you're saying. We still haven't straightened things out after the avalanche. But don't worry, it's just a question of time.'

'I hope you're right, Hal, I really do . . .'

47

Josie got back from base camp to find that plenty had changed at *Daybreak* in the month she'd been away. The first clue was the black cab that arrived to take her to the studio – limousines were off the payroll in Mike's new regime.

'We were losing a quarter of a million a month,' Mike told her by way of explanation. 'So certain things have had to go.'

'Certain people, too?' Josie could scarcely hide her dismay. 'I really couldn't give a damn about the limousine but have you cut some of the staff?'

'Oh, a couple of lighting technicians, a few sound people, a handful of researchers. The producers have been very good about it – putting in double shifts to help out.'

'Why did you wait until I was away to do all these things? Because you knew I'd object?' Josie could not disguise her anger.

'Not at all. That was just an accident of timing. And I don't have to ask your permission, in case you were wondering.'

'Can we keep up the quality with less staff?' Josie asked.

'Don't worry about that, the viewers won't notice the difference.'

Josie picked up her running order for the day and went through to make-up. She could see at a glance that the show would be bland; a second-rate politician, an actress launching a West End play, a pet spot featuring a parrot. 'This is a terrible line-up,' she said to the make-up girl. 'The viewers are going to sleep through this lot if they bother switching on at all.'

'Morning, ladies!' Tarik, the producer of the day, put his head round the door, his nervous smile vanishing as he saw Josie's expression.

'We can do better than this.' Josie tossed the script on to the make-up desk in front of her. 'That's a B-grade running order and you know it. I can't work miracles out there. You have to give me the quality guests. No one is going to turn on the television for this.'

'There's nothing I can do about that now,' he countered. 'Mike booked most of those guests.'

'And what is "Junior Commando"?' Josie pointed once again to the script and a ten-minute item scheduled in the second half of the show.

'A cartoon series.'

Tarik retreated before Josie could react.

Josie blinked as she entered the set. The lighting was way too harsh and would have her squinting into the camera. Everyone seemed stressed. There was none of the banter which normally ran around the studio.

'One minute.'

Josie looked into the camera and let her mind wander back to Nepal. She imagined herself in one of the rhododendron forests, trekking up a cool mountain trail, with the glistening peaks of the Himalayas ahead. The trek to base camp had been a great healer, she now realised. Getting back to this was the last thing she needed.

She snapped out of the daydream just as the transmission began. 'Good morning and welcome to *Daybreak* . . .' She smiled as she read the autocue, falling easily into the routine patter she had delivered hundreds of times before.

Her gut instinct had been right, the show *was* tedious, so much so that in the middle of the interview with the politician Josie completely lost the thread of the conversation. As he droned on, she found herself daydreaming once again about Everest, becoming so lost in the reverie that she blinked in confusion when he stopped talking.

'Are you listening to me?' he asked. 'I have the impression you haven't heard a word I've said.'

Josie went white, stammering as she attempted to recover the situation, trying to block her mind to the fact that millions of viewers had just witnessed her blunder.

And that was the new *Daybreak* for Josie as the weeks went by, the constant fight to keep her mind from wandering, the falling morale as the staff talked among themselves about more cuts and an ever increasing diet of cartoons introduced by Mike to disguise the lack of quality guests. The violent content of the cartoons – made with the sole purpose of marketing a range of action figures

– finally earned them a strongly worded rebuke from the ITC, the regulatory body that had awarded Sebastian and Mike the franchise in the first place.

No wonder Mike was looking increasingly sour. 'We slipped eight places on the top one hundred last week,' he told her one morning. 'I just got the figures. The BBC breakfast show is starting to pull up on us.'

'We're not putting on a good enough show,' Josie repeated. 'We need better guests.'

'The guests are the same, Josie. I just don't understand where we're going wrong. Unless it's the viewers responding to your evident lack of interest.'

'The problem, Mike, is that we're so preoccupied trying to fill in for the people you sacked that we don't have a moment to concentrate on getting the best people on the show. I've now got one researcher where I used to have three. I don't have a production assistant any more. Big news stories come and go and we can't even get our act together to cover them.'

'Well, one way or another we need to solve this problem . . . If BBC breakfast catches us it'll be a disaster.' Mike stormed off.

'Welcome back to the real world,' Josie whispered to herself as she watched him stomp to the lift.

48

Hal and Rachel settled easily into the routine at Deborah's, Hal running the Himalayan Objectives office and Rachel helping Deborah with the children and the house. During the days they were happy, relishing the busy simplicity of the daily routine, but when they were alone the more fragile world of their own relationship was difficult to escape. Each night they would lie in each other's arms, wanting it to be the same as it had been in Alaska, wanting the passion to come back, wanting to erase the black void that had existed between them since the avalanche. But it was elusive. Rachel would lie awake, listening to the sound of the sea beating against the shore, knowing that Hal was also incapable of sleep.

They had not made love since the accident. Damaged goods. Rachel had often heard the expression and now she knew what it meant. They were both damaged goods . . . and so was their relationship. The loss of the baby – and the blame they shared for it – weighed more heavily on them both than they could express.

Rachel was beginning to fear that their relationship might never recover.

One morning she was up at dawn, early enough to catch the sunrise. There was a thin layer of sea fog sitting in a perfect blanket over the water and, in the places it had drifted over the islands, leaving cedars standing as if on cloud. She had a camera with her, the Nikon SLR with a 28mm wide-angle lens, which she knew would capture the scene perfectly if she got the exposure right. But as she clicked the aperture ring to get the light reading, she realised that the photograph would be as nothing compared with the timeless grandeur of what she was witnessing. She lowered the camera and continued to drink in the scene.

A few moments later Hal was beside her.

'I thought you were asleep.'

'I came looking for you.'

Rachel breathed in the early morning air. 'Isn't that the most beautiful thing you've ever seen?'

Hal leaned against the boathouse and wrapped her close in his arms. 'Perfect.'

'Some things are too good to be photographed. It's almost like a violation to do it.'

'I feel the same. The first few times I went to the big mountains I deliberately didn't take any stills. I wanted to be sure I was really seeing it for myself.'

Rachel turned so she faced him, noticing the way the early morning light was red on his tanned face. 'Hal, do you think we can sort things out between us?'

'Maybe. I certainly feel it's time to talk.'

'I know. We've both been dreading it. There's too much we have to confront.'

'To decide who takes the blame? I'd take it all if I thought it would help.'

'It's not as simple as that, is it?'

'I guess not, or we'd be over it by now.'

'It was all such a dream, meeting you like that, falling in love. I should have known it was too good to be true. Something was always going to fall out of the heavens to destroy it.'

'You think we should split? You asked me the question, perhaps it's time for me to ask you?'

'I don't know. But I do know you're not happy and I feel like our relationship hasn't got a hope in hell while we're like this.'

'Maybe we need a therapist.'

'No, we don't.' Rachel pulled back to look Hal in the eyes. 'I think we need each other. We're burning up with guilt over what happened and ignoring the one thing that can help us.'

'Which is?'

Rachel kissed him gently on the lips. 'Which is our love for each other.'

'You think that still exists?'

'I hope so, Hal, I really do. That avalanche already took away so much. If it took that as well . . . ?'

'I think there's two ways we can be.'

'How?'

'One is to be in a sort of suspended animation, like now, going neither forward nor back.'

'I don't want that way.'

'Nor do I.' Hal gave her an awkward smile. 'The other way is to go on the offensive.'

'Like how?'

'Like realise we do still love each other and try to start again.'

'Try to get pregnant again?'

'Maybe.'

Rachel watched the sea fog shift as a breeze wafted through it. For the first time in a long time, she felt a flash of happiness inside her. 'You mean it? You really want to start again . . . a clean slate?'

'Yes. Yes I do.'

Rachel threw her arms round Hal's neck. 'Will you take me back to bed?' she whispered. 'The rest of the house is still asleep.'

Back in their bedroom Rachel handed Hal a small bottle of oil, slipped off her shirt and lay face down, naked from the waist up. She felt the drops of oil running in a line up her spine and then the gentle power of Hal's fingers as he massaged the liquid into her. She pulled her hair up away from her shoulders as Hal dripped on more oil and moved his fingers in small circles on either side of her neck, unravelling a tight knot of tension, which she had lived with for so long she'd almost forgotten about it. She let out a long sigh of contentment. 'Hal?'

'Yes.'

'I want you. Now, please.' Rachel rolled on to her back and cupped her hands round Hal's neck. She pulled him to her, her spine arching as his lips ran in a series of slow kisses along her neck. Then their mouths came together.

Hal pulled back from her, holding her gaze as they both savoured the longing.

'You were wondering if I was ready? To start again?' she asked him.

'Uh-huh.'

'Well, I am. Want to see how much?' Rachel guided Hal's hand gently between her legs.

Later she lay in his arms, her head nestling against his shoulder. 'I think everything is going to be all right now,' she whispered.

'I think so too.'

49

Josie was dreading Christmas and the New Year, knowing how empty they would be without Sebastian.

Then, a surprise: Dominic called from Durham with a proposal. 'Do you get any holiday over the New Year?' he asked her. 'Me and a couple of friends are going down to the Canaries for a few days' sailing. I'm sure you'll be fixed up with something else, but I thought I'd ask you anyway.'

Josie was delighted. Since their bizarre first encounter Dominic had kept in touch – even coming to see her a couple of times in London. She enjoyed his company. 'Let me check which days I'm working.' She pulled out her Filofax and flipped the pages. 'I'm free from the twenty-eighth until the second.'

'Five days. That's enough. You sort out your flight to Tenerife and I'll arrange the rest.'

'Who else will be there?'

'My sister and a couple of mates from the rowing crew. You'll like them; it'll be a laugh.'

Dominic was right, it *was* a laugh. In fact, Josie felt more relaxed in their company than she had done for a long time.

They sailed in a forty-seven-foot ketch called *Jessamine*, chartered out of Los Gigantes at the southern end of Tenerife. Josie hadn't done much sailing but she quickly learned to make herself useful on deck and spent long hours at the helm, enjoying the feeling of power as the wind filled the canvas, turning the craft into a living thing.

Dominic was in his element, drinking a few beers, frying up excellent steaks in the galley and making Josie laugh as she hadn't done for months.

Josie was fond of him after the kindness he had shown her at their first meeting and knew secretly that Dominic hoped their relationship would cross the line one day – that they would be more than friends. And why not? she thought, I can't spend the rest of my life alone.

He was attractive – Josie had to admit that – a truly gentle character locked into that powerful athletic frame. He was patient, too. She knew he wouldn't push the pace too fast. One day, she thought, when I'm ready.

On New Year's Eve they threw a party, midway between two islands, getting happily drunk on sangria and something Dominic innocently referred to as 'fruit punch', which seemed to Josie to be the most alcoholic drink she had ever tried. Dominic let off some fireworks, then swam beneath the boat for a bet, before they all collapsed on the deck, huddled in blankets for warmth. Feeling chilly in the early hours, Josie pulled Dominic closer to her for warmth. They lay, innocently entwined, holding hands in their sleep as the boat drifted with the current through the night.

The following evening, at La Gomera, they found the most perfect harbour, lined with palm trees and with moorings for just a handful of yachts. The village square was a stroll away, dotted with cafés and restaurants, and with surprisingly few tourists around. It was a mellow night, warmed by a hot breeze from the south. Josie and Dominic went for a walk, ending up at one of the waterside restaurants where they ordered tapas and wine.

Dominic raised his glass. 'So. Did you make a New Year's resolution last night? I saw you gazing out across the sea looking kind of dreamy at midnight.'

Josie was hesitant. 'I . . . I think so.'

'You think so. What does that mean? Either you did or you didn't.'

'Well, all right, I did. But don't ask me what, OK? I don't want you to think I'm insane. And it's a secret.'

'OK, I won't pry. But let's drink to this year being a better one for you than the last.'

They chinked glasses.

'Sorry. I didn't mean to be so short with you,' Josie told him. 'I just find it hard to open up with you . . . well, with anyone, in fact, since Sebastian died.'

'Don't you get any support at *Daybreak*? You must have plenty of friends there.'

'Ha. That's a bit far off the mark, I'm afraid. Most of my friends have been cleared out by the man at the top.'

'That must have been a blow.'

'It was. Fact is, things are getting pretty strained at *Daybreak*. Ratings are down, debts are up, we've had an official complaint from the ITC, advertisers switching to other shows, that sort of shit. There was even a diary piece in the *Mirror* saying I was about to be sacked.'

'How can you still put on that smile every morning if it's as bad as that?'

'Oh, I can still smile but my heart's not there like it was in the beginning. I was so *into it* then. Sitting in front of that camera and watching that little red light going on was the most thrilling thing in the world.'

'And now?'

'Now it's hard to care. The show is getting really tacky. All those cartoons. It's heartbreaking when I think back to what Sebastian wanted the channel to be.'

'You still have a loyal following,' Dominic reassured her. 'Well . . . I still watch you every morning. That's one fan at least.'

'That's sweet of you,' Josie said, 'but it's not the same as it was. I have other things on my mind these days.'

'Like?'

Josie toyed with her glass, turning it in her hands and wondering if Dominic would ever understand.

'It's Everest. After that trek to base camp I can't get the mountain out of my mind. You know how it feels when you fall in love with someone . . . you obsess over them, you see their face every time you close your eyes?'

Dominic took a breath. 'I'm familiar with that, yes.'

'So that's how it is for me with that mountain. I remember being astonished by how strong it was for Sebastian and now I've got it the same . . . A couple of weeks ago I called Hal – that was the guide I went to base camp with – asked him if he would take me to the mountain this spring. He told me he wasn't going back but I still tried to persuade him.'

Dominic practically choked on his wine.

'Wait a minute! Am I getting this right? You're saying you want to climb *Everest* . . . I mean really climb it?'

Josie felt herself ridiculous.

'Well . . . it's only a dream.'

Dominic drank in stunned silence for a while, looking at Josie as if she were a creature from another planet.

'Have you asked yourself *why*?' he asked finally.

Josie frowned as she thought of an answer.

'I suppose I feel I can't start again – I mean *really* start my life again – until I've been close to Sebastian one more time. I want to say goodbye to him and to understand where . . . and perhaps why . . . he died.'

Dominic whistled. 'And you're prepared to risk your life to do that?'

Josie looked at him sadly. 'I feel I might as well not *have* a life unless I do that.'

'You really loved him very deeply, didn't you?'

'I still do and God, it's lonely without him.'

'You think you might get to a point where you could begin again with someone else? I mean, hypothetically speaking.'

Josie chose her words carefully, smiling as she did so. 'Hypothetically speaking, I think that might happen. But not for a while. There are things I have to do first.'

'Like Everest, for example?'

'Yes. Like Everest.'

'I'll be gutted if you go.'

'You will?'

Dominic looked at her intently. 'Mainly because you might not come back. And that would leave me feeling very sad.'

'Don't worry, it's still just an idea at the moment. And if it does happen, I'll be with one of the best guides in the business . . .' Josie bit her lip as she realised she was repeating Sebastian's words.

'Well, I'll be waiting for you,' Dominic continued shyly. 'I know I can never compare with Sebastian but I'll be waiting and hoping you get back safe just the same.'

Josie took his hand. 'I would never compare you with him,' she told him. 'I wouldn't need to do that.'

'I haven't got much to offer.' He smiled. 'More or less penniless, a postgraduate arts student, for God's sake, only thing I can do is row.'

'And make me laugh. And make me forget the bad things while I'm with you.' Josie brought him close to her and hugged him tightly. 'I won't forget what you said,' she assured him. 'I promise. I'll be thinking of you . . .'

'On Everest?'

'Yes.'

Dominic looked away across the harbour to where *Jessamine* was rocking gently on her mooring.

50

Early in the new year a letter arrived for Deborah at Himalayan Objectives. 'Come up to the office,' Deborah invited Rachel and Hal. 'I have something I want to show you.' They followed her upstairs. 'Take a look at this.' She handed Hal a document, thick and official-looking. It had the address of a legal firm in New York on the letterhead.

'What is it?'

'The worst-case scenario. Himalayan Objectives is being sued by the families of two of the victims over the Everest disaster. They believe they can prove negligence.'

'Rick gave his life trying to *save* those climbers,' Hal said, his voice low with bitterness. 'When are people going to understand that?'

'I don't know.' Deborah slumped into the chair and put her head in her hands.

'How much are they asking for?'

'Does it make any difference? Fifty million. A hundred million. Who cares? The result will be the same.'

'What's their case, exactly?' Rachel asked.

'That Rick had a professional duty of care. That he should have known not to keep the team going forward when the storm was coming. There's even a suggestion in there that he cut and ran when the storm hit, that he died alone . . . trying to save his own skin.'

Hal was outraged. 'That's an out-and-out lie. Rick would never do that.'

'You know that. But they don't. Everyone died. There's no one to give an eyewitness account.'

'But they know where the bodies are. Sooner or later someone will work out who died where and I'm sure it'll turn out that Rick was with his clients. He would have fought until the bitter end.'

'That's something I may have to prove.'

'How?'

'I'm not sure. Get some hard data on which members ended up in which spots on the mountain. It's still a mess. No one has really looked. Now do you see why I'm a little depressed?'

'You don't deserve this.'

'I won't buckle under. I'll do anything to prove that Rick was a fine and honourable man, a total professional. That's ultimately what I care about, not the money. It was the mountain that killed those climbers . . . not my husband.'

'I'll give you any assistance I can.'

Deborah turned, looking at him intensely. 'If I asked you to go to Everest and map out where the bodies were, would you do it?'

Hal let out a slow breath of air in a long sigh. 'I did say never again . . .'

'I know that, Hal, and the last thing I would ever want to do is to pressurise you into it. I'm just saying that I might have to organise an expedition for this spring to go and find out who ended up where on the mountain. There's so many rumours that I don't see how we can make a defence until we map out the sequence of events as far as we can.'

'What do you think you can prove?'

'That Rick died protecting those people. I'll bet when his body is found, he'll be hunched over one or more of them, trying to save them from the wind and the cold. That'll tell them everything they need to know about duty of care.'

'How are you going to fund it?'

Deborah sighed. 'That's the problem . . . I'm not sure. We could get a bunch of clients together but then you'd have your work cut out looking out for them.'

'How about Josie Turner?'

'What?'

'Get this,' Hal said. 'A while back she approached me about the idea of a private expedition. Just the two of us . . . Maybe that's the answer.'

'What's her objective?'

'She's talking about the possibility of visiting the site where Sebastian died. It's only an idea but . . .'

Deborah whistled in surprise. 'That's virtually the summit. She'd need to be in pretty good shape to get that high. You think she's got what it takes?'

'I think she has. She was surprisingly strong. But chances are she won't make it.'

'So what? If she burns out then that's her problem, to be blunt about it. It'll still give you a chance to get up and find Rick's body and with just the two of you there's no big numbers to worry about. How would she fund it?'

'That's the good part. She asked me to put a figure on a custom-built expedition and I told her a quarter of a million dollars.'

'And?'

'She didn't blink. Said she inherited money when Sebastian died and would cover it herself.'

'That's high.'

'It's potentially a clear hundred thousand of profit. That would be for Himalayan Objectives, of course – it could go towards the legal costs of fighting the case.'

'You think she's serious?'

'From what I learned about her on the trek to base camp, I'd say she's deadly serious.'

Deborah turned her back and looked out of the window. 'If this works out there's something else I'd want you to do,' she said.

'What is it?'

'I'd like to get Rick's ring back. It would mean so much to me. It was a symbol of our love. It's a small thing, but if we do go ahead and organise an expedition that will be one of my objectives. What do you think?'

Hal looked at Rachel questioningly. 'I think Rachel and I need to have a long hard talk about this.'

Rachel shook her head. 'No we don't.' She crossed to the window and put her arm round Deborah.

'You don't need to make a decision now . . .' Deborah began.

'Yes we do,' Rachel continued. 'You could lose everything if these people win their case against you. We can't let that happen.' She turned to look at Hal. 'Do you want to do it?'

'For the chance to get something right? Maybe. Can you bear it?'

'It's not a question of bearing it, it's a question of what's right. How long would the expedition be?'

'Three months.'

'You can continue to stay here if you want,' Deborah told Rachel. 'You're almost a part of the family . . .' Deborah stepped to the door, tears in her eyes. 'I should leave you two to talk about it. I'll go and put some coffee on.'

Rachel took Hal's hands in hers. 'Hal. You have to do it. They'll destroy her if they get a chance. Without us, she hasn't got a hope.'

'I know, but Everest . . . ?'

'Think about it. You make a big success of this and we can truly start again. Go back up to Alaska for the beginning of the summer and make a completely fresh start. You've been so down about the avalanche that I don't think you're thinking straight. Everest is something you know intimately, you told me before that you feel alive there – renewed.'

Hal looked at her directly, thinking for a while. 'I'll do it. For Deborah and for Rick.'

Rachel kissed him softly on the lips. 'And for me. Please.'

51

Josie walked into Mike's office, her head held high, feigning a confidence she definitely didn't feel. Hal's telephone call the previous evening had been a bolt from the blue – she'd almost given up hope that he would agree to take her to the mountain. But would Mike give her the three months she would need?

She sat opposite him at the desk and watched him working at his computer for a while until it was clear he wasn't going to be the one to speak first. 'Mike, you remember the trek to base camp? How I had it in mind that it would help me put Sebastian behind me?'

Mike glanced up and gave her a blank look. 'And?'

'Well, it didn't. If anything, it left me feeling more restless than before.'

Mike put on his bored voice. 'I can't sanction you going on another holiday, Josie. We need you in front of the camera, not on some jolly jaunt to the ass-end of nowhere. If you've got itchy feet, why don't you wait until the summer hols like everyone else . . . ?'

Josie let him finish. Then she went on: 'I'm thinking about climbing the mountain. For real this time.'

He looked at her in shock as the words sank in. 'You can't be talking about *Everest* for God's sake?'

'What other mountain is there?'

'Don't be absurd, Josie. You'll kill yourself.'

'That is a possibility, yes. But I'm ready to take the risk.'

Mike burst into laughter. 'My God. You and Sebastian really are two of a kind. I haven't heard anything so crazy since Sebastian sat in that very chair and told me the same thing.'

'This isn't a joke, Mike. I'm completely serious about it.'

'When would it happen?'

'In the spring – that's the pre-monsoon season. It takes three months.'

Mike scribbled some notes on a pad. 'The ITC meet to decide on our franchise renewal in July. If we play our cards right, we can get three months of sky-high ratings out of this before they meet. The timing is spot on.'

Josie got that familiar sinking feeling. 'You want me to cover the expedition for the show?'

'Of course.' Mike gave her a quizzical look. 'Why on earth would we agree for you to do it if it wasn't for the ratings?'

'It's a bit more complicated than that . . . who the hell will we get to shoot that high? Jeremy didn't even make it to base camp.'

'We'll take some advice. There are specialists for high altitude. Besides your guide . . . what's his name . . . ?'

'Hal.'

'Yeah, him. He shot some good stuff. We'll pay him more to use the camera up high.'

'He might have other things on his mind. Like making sure I don't get killed, for example.'

Mike tutted with frustration. 'You did it for the journey to put up the memorial. What's the big deal?'

'Sure, I went along with it for the trek but that was a lot less serious. This is much more committing. I'm not totally sure I can handle the climb, let alone the idea of filming and reporting on it at the same time.'

'So where does that leave us? A show without its star presenter for three months? At a time when the BBC is catching up on us? We're treading a very thin line here, Josie. I'm not sure you've grasped that.'

'Oh, I have. I know the show's in trouble. But I don't want to promise you a series of reports that I can't deliver.'

'You're a pro, Josie, that's your job. Besides . . . how often do you think I can put a stand-in presenter in your seat before I feel I have to offer them something more permanent?'

'Is that a threat?'

'Just trying to make you see sense.'

'This expedition is different, Mike. It's my dream to go there, not yours . . . not *Daybreak*'s. Maybe I want something for *me*, did you think of that?'

Mike pursed his lips and Josie knew she had made him angry. 'Look at it another way. Sebastian made you what you are, Josie. You owe everything to him. You think he would have wanted you to stand by and watch his business slip away before your eyes?' Mike's eyes were cold as stone as he glared at Josie through his glasses. 'This new project can give *Daybreak* a real shot in the arm, Josie. But only if you play the game. Now, yes or no?'

Josie bit her lip. She would rather die than let Mike see her cry at this moment. 'What choice do you give me?' she said quietly.

'That's my girl!'

Mike picked up the telephone and barked an instruction to his secretary: 'Get the press in for four o'clock. Tell them we've got a surprise announcement. I want the works . . . agencies and all.' He was smiling as he put down the receiver. 'I'm going to get this spinning so fast we'll steamroller our competitors out of the frame. We'll have five million viewers hanging on to that mountain by their fingertips by the time we've finished.'

'Do we have to move so fast? We've still got three months before the expedition can happen.'

'We need the exposure now. There's not a moment to lose. Can you get hold of some high-altitude gear for the press conference . . . you know, ice axes, oxygen masks, dress up a bit?'

'This isn't a bloody pantomime, Mike. I'm not dressing up to look an idiot in front of the world's media.'

'OK. Keep your crampons on, sweetie. Just be back here by four.'

Josie turned on her heel and left.

Fifty-seven journalists were there by the time she returned to the studio that afternoon. 'I wish you could have waited for just a while,' Josie told Mike. 'I'm not sure what the hell I'm going to say to all these people.'

'Don't panic. This conference is going to change all our fortunes for the better.'

'I really hope so, Mike.'

Mike swept past her and took the floor, the room going quiet as he stood with the microphone before the sitting journalists and photographers. 'Ladies and gentlemen. Thank you for being here at short notice. As you know, there has been a great deal of speculation in the press recently about the future of *Daybreak*, and indeed the future of Josie Turner as our presenter. Let me make one thing clear. I have not called this press conference to give you bad news. Quite the opposite, in fact. What I am going to tell you about is an exciting project, which we hope all *Daybreak* viewers will be enjoying over the coming months.'

Mike savoured the moment, pausing before the dramatic announcement. 'In three months' time Josie Turner will be leaving for Nepal for an attempt on Mount Everest. And we're not talking about base camp this time. You're heading for the summit, Josie, isn't that right.'

The room buzzed with excitement.

Josie smiled nervously as she stepped up next to him and took the microphone. 'That's right. It's time for a big challenge . . . and, let's face it, what could be bigger than Everest?' There was a polite ripple of laughter from the room.

Mike addressed them again. 'As we did before with Josie's base camp trek, this will be covered in a series of daily updates here in the studio, coupled with live reports from the mountain itself.'

One of the journalists raised his hand. 'What's the objective, Josie?'

'Well, I will be visiting the place where my husband died to pay my last respects to him. And, if all goes well, I may – and I stress this is by no means a foregone conclusion – I may try for the summit itself.'

The room erupted with questions.

Josie pointed to one of her favourite feature writers. 'Jack. Go ahead.'

'Josie. I have to ask you. You're not a climber. You've been to base camp but what you're proposing is very different. What makes you think you can pull this off?'

'I loved my late husband and I can only repeat his words. He said "There are no limits" and I believe the same. I want to hold his hand one last time. To tell him how I feel about him one last time. And if I have to climb into the death zone to do that, then so be it.'

'Attagirl,' she heard Mike whisper excitedly by her side as the pressmen scribbled down the words.

She pointed to another questioner. 'Cynics might say that this is a classic diversion tactic. Word has it that *Daybreak TV* is in danger of losing its franchise. Isn't this new Everest expedition a smokescreen to buy you all some breathing space?'

Mike jumped in before Josie could open her mouth. 'That's an honest question and I want to give you an honest answer. This is not a cynical exercise. It's true that we are having a difficult time.

But that is why I want to remind the viewers of the original spirit of the company. Sebastian Turner was that spirit. He was brave. He was adventurous. Now, Josie is taking that spirit to new heights.' He pointed to another hand.

'Josie. Are you scared? I'd be bloody petrified.' The room hummed with laughter.

'Everest is frightening, I agree. I'd be lying if I told you I didn't have some nerves about this. But somehow, when I think of Sebastian, I hear his voice telling me to go for it, to put my fear aside . . . to confront the dangers of the mountain like he did.'

The press burst into a spontaneous round of applause; Josie felt a lump harden in her throat and knew she could not trust herself to say anything more. 'Thank you very much for listening to me this afternoon.'

Mike ushered Josie out of the room before any more questions could be fired at her. 'Well done Josie. You did the job,' he told her, offering her a handkerchief.

'Was that OK?'

'It's exactly what we need. If that doesn't bring back the viewers, nothing will.'

'Just so long as you're happy, Mike.'

Back home, Josie found the adrenaline still pumping strong. She put on her running gear and hit the streets, aiming for a four-hour session. She would have to squeeze every last ounce of fitness training out of the next three months if her body was to stand a chance of the summit.

As for her mind . . . Josie had no real idea how to prepare herself for the enormous strains the expedition would bring. Even as she ran, she was already wondering if Everest was going to be the biggest mistake of her life.

PART THREE

Summit Fever

52

In late March, three days before they would leave for Nepal, Hal flew into London with Todd, the high-altitude camera operator he had chosen for the demanding task of shooting the *Daybreak* reports.

Todd was a native of Denver who had trained as a professional cameraman and now specialised in wilderness documentaries. An experienced expeditioner and climber, he would also act as logistics and communications manager while Josie and Hal were climbing together. He had the serene look of a man who was heading for the world he loved. He was blue-eyed, bearded, with the physique of a rugby player and a handshake that left Josie's eyes watering.

'We're not talking about a Jeremy clone here,' Hal told her with a smile. 'Todd's an old friend. He has filmed on K2 and plenty of mean mountains. He'll be good for the col and maybe more.' Todd was taken into the *Daybreak* studio for a briefing from Mike while Josie and Hal went shopping for the last pieces of personal equipment she would need.

The following day, on Mike's insistence, an on-air party was thrown in the studio to mark Josie's departure. Hal was invited in to talk about some of the highlights the viewers could expect over the coming three months and he got Josie to dress up in all her high-altitude gear. She felt like a spaceman, swaddled completely in the ultra padding of the down and Gore Tex, sweat running off her in rivers beneath the lights. The party went surprisingly well and she finished by reading out, live, a few of the thousands of good luck messages she had been receiving from viewers.

Josie said her emotional goodbyes to those of the staff who remained and walked out of the studios, knowing she would not be back for three months. It was a great feeling of relief finally to have gone. The atmosphere at *Daybreak* had deteriorated yet further in the weeks of waiting and Josie was desperate to get out.

On the Royal Air Nepal flight she ordered three glasses of champagne and proposed a toast: 'To the expedition.'

'I'll drink to that!' said Todd.

Hal smiled and chinked her glass.

Josie was feeling good; she felt sure they would all get along just fine.

When they landed in Nepal, Nima was waiting for them. He'd received Hal's letter inviting him to join the expedition and, having finished his schooling, he'd trekked down from the mountains to help Hal with the provisioning in Kathmandu. He was delighted to see Josie again, clasping her in a tight bear-hug and kissing her effusively on the cheek. 'You see what I say?' he told her. 'Hal no resist go back to Everest. And now I go to summit! I'm very happy.'

'I can see that.' Josie laughed. 'Well, if you're happy, I'm happy too.'

'I take good care of you. I think you not know much about big mountains.'

'You're right. I don't know much at all.'

'So don't worry! With me and Hal you are very safe, very good. All come back alive. All reach summit. Keep fingers and toes.'

Nima introduced Josie to the six other Sherpas who would be accompanying them on the trip and to Tashi, the expedition cook. They were all seasoned Everest hands; some – like the veteran high-altitude porter Lhakpa – had been on more than ten Everest expeditions and summited multiple times.

But it was Nima Josie most warmed to. He was a youthful shot of enthusiasm, smiling fit to bust, shuttling backwards and forwards between the market and the hotel garden with hundredweight sacks of onions, oranges, beans and flour. He was astoundingly strong, never once complaining even when his back was bent double under a huge box of canned food which must have weighed more than the average fridge.

Nima loved the city and took pleasure in taking Josie with him when he had friends to see. Most of them were high-altitude porters and guides from his own village – tough, wiry men who had made fortunes in the mountains and now ran shops or trekking companies to cater for the tens of thousands who came for a brief Himalayan adventure. 'One day, I run a big company like these men.' Nima puffed out his chest. 'But first climb Everest.'

Every day, the mountain of supplies grew a little more in the hotel garden. Tons of food, one hundred and fifty oxygen bottles, twenty-eight equipment barrels stuffed with ropes, tents and climbing hardware. Hal was quartermaster, accountant and quality-control supervisor rolled into one, waiting with his check pad and pencil to log in and count every item. 'See these potatoes?' he said to Josie one day.

'What about them?'

He opened the sack and showed her the top layer.

'They look fine,' she told him. 'What's the problem?'

Hal dug deeper and pulled out a handful more, each with a tiny green shoot sprouting from the side. 'Trying to pull a fast one on us,' he said, instructing Nima to take them back and find better. 'Those will be rotten before we reach Namche Bazaar.'

Ten sacks of cabbages, eight of rice. Two hundred double A batteries for radios and torches, five jerrycans of petrol for the generator, seven oxygen masks imported from Russia.

'Ex-Soviet Air Force,' Hal explained to Josie. 'Cheaper and better than anything you can buy in the West.' One hundred kilos of sugar, twenty-six gallon cans of dried milk, two pounds of dried mint, sixty pounds of salt.

'Fresh meat we can get up there,' Hal assured her, 'so long as a yak dies on the trail.'

'Lovely. I'll look forward to that.'

Hal gave Josie plenty to do, starting off with the tents. There were eighteen lightweight dome tents, three larger cooking tents and one huge ex-Indian Army canvas monster, which would be mess tent and general canteen at base camp. All were heavily used and it was Josie's job to erect each one in the hotel garden and check for damage. Ripped seams had to be sewed or patched, holes covered up with Gore Tex and glued firmly in place, tent pegs counted, straightened and checked for metal fatigue. 'One rip in one of those tents could mean death at high altitude,' Hal explained. 'A storm gets up and it'll find any fault.'

Josie paid attention, checking and double-checking to make sure she missed nothing. Then she did the same with the oxygen bottles, patiently attaching the special gauge to each orange cylinder and marking the pressure on the exterior with a fine paintbrush and black paint. Of the one hundred and fifty, it turned out that three were empty, which had her wondering: 'Hal. What would happen on summit day if one of our oxygen bottles were empty?'

Hal thought carefully. 'Well I'd say that would put you in serious risk of frostbite and might even cause a fatality.'

Josie checked all the bottles again, just to be sure, and threw the empty ones back in the hotel store marked 'Do Not Use' clearly with black paint, to be extra sure.

At last Hal pronounced they were ready to roll. Two green trucks backed into the hotel car park, belching noxious diesel fumes. The boxes, barrels and containers were loaded up and driven to the airport, where a cavernous Russian transport helicopter was waiting.

'What are these holes?' Josie asked Hal, as she ran her hand over the dented fuselage.

'Bullet holes. Most of these helicopters are veterans of the Afghan war,' he replied, 'and so are the pilots. They earn more here in dollars than they could ever make in the former USSR.'

Before Josie had time to wonder if she was really going to fly in this clapped-out piece of iron, Hal ushered her into an interior which was not only devoid of seat belts but also of seats. 'The fun starts here!' he shouted to her as the helicopter took off and headed north for Lukla and the trail that would lead to Everest.

53

The trek to base camp was different, very different, from the time before. Josie felt she could have been in another world. It was not yet spring, the land bearing the remnants of deep winter drifts, the high peaks around them still wearing their winter plumage of ice with hardly a sliver of rock to be seen.

The last journey had been seven months before, in the lush warmth of the Himalayan autumn, with green terraced fields of barley and millet surrounding each village. Now the flowers were gone, the rhododendron forests frosted and dark, the skies threatening snow or storm at any time. The animals were kept inside, still feeding on their winter stores, their grazing pastures as hard as iron and with no shoots to offer. It had been a tough winter; you could tell by the subdued mood of the villagers that spring wouldn't arrive a moment too soon.

In the lodge at Lukla there was no sugar, flour or tea – all had run out long ago and the owner was grateful to Hal for a few of the expedition's supplies as payment for accommodation. Nima's mother was also out of winter stores but her wily son had smuggled plenty of rice and vegetables on to the helicopter for her. Josie was there when he gave her the sacks of food. They could have been gold for the smile she gave him, while his younger brothers and sisters held tomatoes and onions as if they couldn't quite believe their eyes.

Hal was busy recruiting, haggling with porters and yak drivers for the long haul up to base camp. Josie chose this for her first video report for *Daybreak*, knowing the viewers would enjoy the spectacle as he was surrounded by the crowds of Sherpas, each claiming he could earn more working for other expeditions and what the hell was this insulting rate Hal was offering anyway? Josie was pleased to find that Todd was competent and relaxed behind the camera and the rushes were successfully beamed out that night from the lodge.

Eventually a sort of calm came over Hal as he ticked the last of the loads off his list and on to the back of the yaks. When they set out they had no fewer than thirty-eight beasts of burden and twenty-nine porters carrying loads.

'It's always a relief to finally hit the trail,' Hal told her as they walked side by side out of Lukla. 'The knowledge that the shopping is finished and the climbing can begin.'

'Hal, may I ask a stupid question?'

'Shoot.'

'Why don't you get all this heavy stuff shipped up to base camp by helicopter?'

'Because a helicopter big enough to take the weight can't fly much higher than this. There's not enough air to support the rotors and it certainly couldn't land.' Hal gestured to the caravan in front of them. 'Besides, who'd want to miss out on all this? This is really *something* don't you think? Makes you feel you're part of an epic voyage into the unknown even if you know thousands have been here before.'

Josie had to smile at his enthusiasm. 'I know what you mean.'

The trails were quiet – some of them so deeply buried in snow that they were hard to locate. Compared with the autumn, when the tracks had been alive with merchants, porters and trekkers all making their way noisily between villages, it was virtually dead. Now, the only people using them up into the deeper part of the Khumbu were those who, like Josie and Hal, had Everest in their sights. That gave it a serious feel, Josie realised, as she watched the long caravans of yaks and porters pulling up the slippery inclines. In fact, the whole enterprise had a damn serious feel. Part of Josie liked that sensation. Part of her was scared rigid by it.

Past Namche Bazaar the cold set in with a vengeance. Big sections of each day were spent trekking through falling snow, often accompanied by a wind which cut to the bone. Josie had to concentrate hard to keep herself going when the cold got bad, focusing on just one step at a time, feeling the frost as it crept down into the warm passages of her throat and lungs, managing her cold-weather clothing so that she didn't freeze to the core. By the time they got to base camp Josie's normal everyday wear consisted of three sets of silk longjohns and Capilene thermal gear, jogging trousers and top, fleece layer above that, an all-in-one Gore-Tex and down wind suit and sometimes more. On her head she wore a silk balaclava and a wool cap, on her hands three layers of gloves, on her feet four layers of socks. Nevertheless, she felt her teeth chatter when she stood still for too long.

At night it was not unusual for the thermometer in her tent to go down to thirty degrees below freezing. 'Base camp is cold in early April, make no mistake,' she said to camera on one of her daily reports, her teeth literally aching from exposure to the frigid air.

After a few days she began to feel her body slowly adjusting to the altitude, her appetite returning, although it was strangely selective. One day she could have a craving for cheese . . . another for muesli or olives. Other foods – particularly canned tuna – turned her stomach, and the slightest whiff of a cigarette was enough to make her want to vomit. But at mealtimes she tried her best, picking at the plates of rice and beans, and forcing down what she could.

'That's good,' Hal approved every time he saw her eating. 'Feed yourself up. The higher we go the more sick you're going to be. The more calories you can get inside you down here the better.'

When it came to fluids Josie also took Hal's advice, drinking copious amounts of liquid – several litres a day – to combat the dehydrating effects of the dry air. Hot chocolate was her favourite, as the cook Tashi soon discovered. 'Hot chocolate! Hot chocolate for Josie!' he would sing from the mess tent, luring her in to drink and chat until the kerosene fumes from the stove drove her back out, her head reeling, to the clean air of the glacier.

She watched her body change day by day as the freezing temperatures and dust of base camp took effect; her fingernails became brittle and cracked, her eyes red and sore from the constant wind, her lips chapped, no matter how much lipsalve she applied. Two of her teeth lost fillings to the cold – the metal contracting at a different rate from the enamel, leaving annoying holes which felt a mile deep. Another back tooth was destroyed completely when Josie bit on a small stone in her rice.

Hal taught her some of the little tricks to make life more bearable: the square of cardboard he placed beneath his boots at the mess tent to give his feet an extra ten minutes before they froze, the small hole scooped into the glacier where the hip bone lay at night, enabling Josie to sleep comfortably on her side, and – best of all – the bottle of hot water placed in the sleeping bag as a warmer before going to sleep. That was a real luxury on the days when the interior of Josie's tent was so cold her breath froze as it left her mouth.

'Get to know your gear, Josie,' Hal warned her. 'Familiarise yourself with every last piece until it feels like an old friend.'

Josie did as he asked. There were the crampons – the savage metal spikes strapped to her plastic boots – the harness, with its stiff straps and oversized buckle, the ice axe, wrapped round her wrist with a small sling. Everything had to be fastened, clipped and doubled back with frozen fingers. Nothing could be lost or dropped. Hal had drummed into her the perils of mislaying even the smallest and seemingly least significant piece of kit.

Hal took her out to train – it was time to learn some of the basic mountain craft she would need. He found some steep ice and taught her how to arrest herself with the ice axe by rolling so that her body weight forced the sharp end into the surface. He showed her how to walk properly with the crampon spikes – to learn the wide-legged gait that would prevent them from tripping her if a sharp tooth should jag against the fabric of her wind suit.

There was a lot to think about and, higher up, it would get more complicated still. Once they reached an altitude that demanded supplemental oxygen, the dozens of pieces of equipment would be joined by oxygen bottles, regulator valve, feed line and mask: more straps, more buckles, more things to drop, to break, to freeze, to go wrong.

'At least twenty per cent of people who fail on Everest do so because they have a problem with equipment,' Hal lectured. 'Never assume that someone else will be carrying a spare of anything. Always treat every last thing as if your very life depends on it.'

Josie's mind buzzed as she sat in the base camp tent for hour after hour, going through each piece of gear again and again. 'Got to get this right,' she told herself. 'No mistakes at all.'

54

During the second week at base camp, on a morning calm enough for voices to be heard, a big meeting was held on the glacier. All the team leaders were there, Hal included. He invited Josie along. 'For fun,' he explained. 'These pow-wows can be quite sparky.'

Josie could sense the mood was tense and confrontational, for days the gossip had been bubbling away that some teams were not happy with the way others were behaving.

Eric Silverman was one of the more experienced commercial leaders. He appointed himself chairman of the meeting and launched off without further ado. 'Two important issues need to be resolved,' he said. 'The question of who's going to pay who for the work that's been done to put a route through the ice fall and the question of slots – which teams are going first.'

The French team leader stood. 'Last year there was a figure of one hundred dollars per head for each team member going up the ice fall. I propose the same, to be split between the three teams who have roped it. Namely my team, Eric's team and Stephan's team.'

There was a clamour, led by a vociferous New Zealander. 'That's not on, Michel, and you know it. Some of us have got twelve clients or more. We can't be paying over a thousand bucks to get them through the ice fall. Your team are rich enough already. Some of my guys have sold their homes to get on this trip.'

Someone else shouted: 'And besides, who are you to lay down the law? We would have roped up the ice fall ourselves if we'd had a chance. You're profiteering and it's as simple as that.'

Eric called for calm. 'No one's profiteering. It's just that some teams – my own included – have taken risks and spent money to put in ladders and ropes. We want our fair reward for that, that's all.'

'So what about higher up?' A Malaysian climber raised the point. 'Maybe there it is us who put in fixed ropes on the ridge. You pay us for that or no?'

'My team are likely to be up there first,' Eric said, 'so I imagine it'll be my Sherpas again who put in ropes on the ridge.'

'So you want to rope the whole mountain and be paid for whole mountain? What authority you have to do that? You get permit from Nepal government for that?'

'My team will go up that mountain and we won't pay a penny to you scabs!' The New Zealander was back in the fray. 'And anyone who tries to stop us will regret it.'

Hal kept quiet as the debate raged, a sad expression on his face. The arguments bounced backwards and forwards for an hour but became even more heated when the subject of 'slots' came up.

'We're putting our names down for the eleventh of May,' Eric announced grandly, 'and I'd appreciate it if other teams could avoid that time.'

'The hell we will!' Now an Austrian leader was red with rage. 'If that's the weather window, then that's the window we want too. You think you are God? You want everyone else to go in the bad weather or what?'

'No. My objective is to make the mountain safe. We all know what happens when there are too many people on the summit ridge.'

'If you don't like sharing the mountain why don't you go home?' yelled a Russian woman.

'We also put our name down for the same day,' someone else called. 'Where's the list? We want to put our team on the list.'

The Malaysians argued with the Indians, the Canadians with the French. The American teams bickered among themselves and the dishevelled Iranian team stood back in astonishment, unsure what the hell was going on.

A tall, slavic-looking climber began shouting from the back of the crowd: 'You are crazy, you people! This mountain for everybody. I not pay one dollar to you. You try to exploit real climbers like me. I say you all go to hell! I climb ice fall without your fixed ropes.' With that, he stormed away.

'Who on earth was that?' Josie whispered to Hal.

'That's Andrei Vasylenko. He's Ukrainian, a bit of a lone wolf. He's bought into one of the other team's permits but they won't want him to climb with them.'

'Why not?'

'Let's just say he's got a chequered history. He says he summited

K2 but no one believes him. He's strong but he doesn't know when to stop. That's why he's always getting into trouble. He's been rescued off more mountains than I've had hot meals.'

The meeting broke up in disarray, some in agreement with the proposals and others obstinately determined to make their own agenda regardless of overcrowding on the higher slopes.

Josie was left shaking her head. 'You wouldn't think people had so much breath to spare,' she told Hal. 'Shouldn't all their energies be focused on the mountain?'

Hal laughed. 'You bet. And that's where we'll have an advantage. We'll just pay our share for the ice fall, nice and easy, and not get involved in the fight.'

'I never knew this place could get so political.'

'Political?' Hal gave a snort. 'Base camp is like a hornets' nest. Every team wants to make their claim, every leader wants to give his clients the best chance of the summit.'

'So what's your tactic?'

'My tactic is we don't get involved in the scrum. We're going to hold back, let the hordes take the early slots and we'll wait for the crowds to disperse. There's always a late weather window towards the end of May and that's what we'll go for. No congestion, no problem.'

'Sounds good.'

'It's just a question of being patient.'

Later that day a blizzard swept in, the start of four days of atrocious conditions, which had the entire base camp pinned down and motionless.

'You see what happen?' Nima pointed out to Josie. 'Many people shouting, getting angry, say bad things, then gods send bad weather. This how mountains work.'

Looking out of the tent at the driving snow, listening to the mean howl of the wind, Josie could only agree.

55

Josie tugged the sleeping bag tightly around her as she heard the footsteps approaching across the glacier. From a tent nearby she could hear a radio tuned in to the BBC World Service news. It was the twenty-fifth day of the expedition and the climbing was about to begin in earnest.

Nima spoke softly from the entrance as he unzipped her tent: 'Josie. It's four o'clock.'

'Let me have five more minutes.'

He laughed. 'OK. Here's your tea.'

Josie hated early morning starts. Ripping herself out of the snug warmth of her sleeping bag into the freezing pre-dawn required a colossal act of will-power. Particularly today. This was the day Josie had dreaded for a long time: the first trip up through the Khumbu ice fall to get to camp one. The pre-dawn start was a safety measure, Hal had told her, the ice fall became more active during the day. She ate a fast breakfast of Granola in the mess tent and then joined Hal, Todd and Nima as they prepared their equipment ready for the climb.

'How are you feeling?' Hal asked her.

'Dead scared.'

'I understand. I still get freaked by the ice fall myself.'

'How many times have you been through it?'

Hal thought. 'I don't know. Thirty, maybe forty times.'

'Ice fall very bad place,' Nima added, 'Full of bad spirits. My father killed there.'

Josie felt the knot in her stomach take another twist. *Thanks Nima,* she thought. *You know how to make a girl feel really safe.*

'So how are you fixed with your gear?' Hal asked her, seeing she needed a change of subject.

'Oh, getting there, I think.'

Hal helped Josie with her crampons, made sure she had her harness fastened correctly and checked she had all the right gear in her rucksack.

As they walked away from the tents, Josie had never felt more out of her depth. What the hell was she doing here? she asked herself . . . a novice climber about to enter one of the most dangerous mountain environments on earth. It was the first time in her life that she had experienced the fear that comes with the possibility of imminent death. It brought a metallic taste to her mouth and an urgent desire to defecate. That would have to wait, she realised, as she saw Hal was already striding ahead.

Hal led the way up the glacier away from base camp, Josie following on with Nima and Todd behind her. The night was clear and although there was no moon, the stars alone created enough light to see the silver silhouettes of the mountains that surrounded them. The silence was broken by the creaking and groaning of the glacier. A flowing body of ice, perpetually on the move, it was subject to phenomenal pressures within. At random intervals a report like cannon fire signalled that a new fissure had opened up. Josie hated the sudden sounds, they put her already stretched nerves more on edge. As always, Hal set a slow but steady pace. Josie never found he was going too fast. She followed without speaking, feeling her body warm to the activity as an hour passed.

They reached the first of the fixed ropes and Josie learned to clip herself on to the line with her carabiner. At her initial attempt she got the Gore Tex fabric of her outer glove stuck in the snapgate. Hal patiently showed her the trick of snapping it on with her thumb to avoid the problem.

By dawn they were deep in the ice fall, the shifting maze of crevasses and seracs forming a natural barrier to Everest when approaching from the south. Massive blocks of teetering ice are the overriding danger; some are eleven storeys high – leaning at impossible angles prior to collapse. The crevasses widen continually, sometimes by as much as a foot a day as gravity drags the billions of tons of ice down the valley. Early reconnaissance expeditions had pronounced the ice fall too deadly to penetrate and turned their attention to the northern side of the mountain. Now hundreds of climbers took their chances there each season. Josie knew that more than thirty people had lost their lives in this place and she couldn't wait to get out the other side.

Hal picked up a fist-sized piece of ice and handed it to Josie. 'You feel how heavy that is? It's like iron.'

He was right, the ice was incredibly dense, compacted by the extreme pressures of the glacier. He gestured to an overhanging serac they would have to move beneath – a gravity-defying tooth-shaped mass the size of a large house.

'Now you know why those things hurt when they fall on top of you.'

'Are you trying to make me feel worse or is that just a by-product of your natural sadism?'

Todd brought out the camera and filmed Josie as she moved as fast as she could on the trail beneath the serac, her heart pounding with the knowledge that it could fall at any time.

A tortuous trail of fixed ropes had been laid through the maze. Where crossing large crevasses was unavoidable, aluminium ladders were in place. Josie crossed them with her eyes trained resolutely on the far side, trying not to think of the chasm beneath her.

She was shocked by how unstable the environment was, 'small' pieces of ice were fracturing and falling in a constant fusillade of crashes and bangs. A bathtub-sized section of a wall collapsed without warning just ten metres from their position, exploding into thousands of pieces and disappearing into the gaping crack of a crevasse.

'Ice fall very bad place,' Nima muttered again and again.

They were two-thirds of the way through when it happened. Somewhere above them an ear-splitting 'whoomph' rent the air, the ice beneath them shaking with the violence of the impact as a thousand-ton chunk of glacier split free and fell.

'That's a big one.' Josie saw Hal's head whip round, scanning above them, trying to compute, in those milliseconds, whether the debris was going to sweep down on them. They were unsighted, positioned in a gully whose high walls did not allow a clear line of sight up the glacier. If they were lucky, the avalanche would run its course and miss them.

And if they weren't . . . ?

The terror ran through Josie; the feeling of total helplessness in the face of phenomenal power. The memory of that fist-sized chunk of ice flashed through her mind; how would it feel when a piece the size of a car smashed into her body at two hundred miles an hour? Would she sense anything at all as she was destroyed? She heard a roar like water rushing from a burst dam. It was diminishing as it ran a course away from them, the air becoming still as the avalanche died somewhere down the glacier.

Silence. Josie looked around. The gully was full of airborne ice particles but there was no other sign of the power that had been unleashed around them. They stood side by side, Josie trembling as the adrenaline of shock subsided.

Hal was the first to speak: 'Me and my big mouth. We were lucky there.'

'You think it reached base camp?'

'I doubt it.'

Josie looked up into the ice fall along the route they still had to negotiate. 'This place is evil.'

'We've had our scare. Now we've got the odds on our side.'

'That's one way of looking at it.'

Hal led on, giving Josie no choice but to follow.

Five hours later they made it to the top of the ice fall where the Sherpas had prepared four tents on the flatter terrain of the western cwm.

They sat side by side, sipping hot tea, looking up at the Lhotse face – the next big obstacle, revealed for the first time now in all its fearsome glory.

'This place makes me so . . . small,' Josie said.

Hal smiled. 'It's good for the ego to feel that way.'

'And when I see how much climbing we still have to do it seems like mission impossible,' she added.

'You'll be fine,' Hal told her. 'You did really well today, handling yourself, the ropes and ladders. That was an impressive day's climbing for a novice. I think you're going to go high.'

'You really think so?'

'Yeah. I really do. If you can handle the strain of four more trips through the ice fall.'

Four more trips.

Josie sat there, sinking quickly into a depression at this prospect. Then she thought about Sebastian, how it would feel to be with him again, and knew that she would find the strength.

56

That first trip to camp one was only the briefest of introductions. They returned to base camp the next day where Josie lay on her back in the tent for twenty-four hours to recover.

'Feel like you've run a marathon, eh?' Hal asked her, seeing how stiffly she moved when she finally emerged, 'That's what oxygen deficiency does to your body. If we did that same two-day round trip at sea level you'd probably have recovered in half the time.'

Josie thanked God she'd taken her fitness campaign seriously. At least she had the stamina to survive.

Five days later it was back up through the ice fall to camp one again: one night there and the nine-hour climb to camp two; one night there, then back down to base camp and so on . . . a programme which would give their bodies maximum chance to adjust to the altitude, and maximum chance of readiness to climb high.

The Sherpa team were working twice as hard. Often, as Josie, Hal and Todd were making their way down from an acclimatisation trip, the Sherpas would be coming back up, their backpacks loaded with oxygen, tents and equipment for the high camps. Josie admired them hugely, for as the whole expedition got higher their work load could only increase. Each excursion demanded a longer recovery period; every trip to altitude pushed muscles and tendons harder than the one before, each time Josie had to dig deeper to find the required reserves of strength.

At last, after three weeks on the lower slopes, they pushed up the steep flanks of the Lhotse face towards camp three. They were higher than seven thousand metres, twenty-five thousand feet, and still not using supplemental oxygen.

Josie was so drained by the thousands of feet of ascent that she collapsed straight into her tent without a word. An infection had inflamed her sinuses and throat, making it difficult to swallow or speak. Todd tried to do some filming but he too was gasping for breath and badly dehydrated. Hal brewed them both tea and forced them to eat some food.

That night was memorably unpleasant. The tent was pitched on an incline, with Hal and Todd jostling for space and restless beside her. The slope gave her the sensation that all three of them would roll down the Lhotse face to their deaths if the guy ropes of the tent gave way. The wind was blowing hard, sending a ghostlike moan through the camp. When Josie did fall into a sort of sleep she soon lurched out of it with a horrible gasp – gulping down great lungfuls of air to fight the sense of suffocation.

'That's a syndrome known as Cheyne-Stokes,' Hal told her. 'It's when your brain has a sudden panic attack because there's so little oxygen. It wakes you up to make sure you're breathing.'

'Can't we use some of the bottled oxygen?' she begged. 'I really feel I can't breathe.'

'Not yet. We haven't got the gas to spare this low down. We'll be using it from the col and above.'

This low down.

Josie pondered on those ominous words. Later she vomited every last morsel of food from her stomach, only just making it to the tent door in time. 'Hal, I'm sick,' she told him, feeling weaker than she could ever remember.

'That's normal,' he answered. 'Don't worry about it.'

Later Todd was sick too, retching horribly for what seemed to be hours.

Josie lay without sleep, wondering, dreading, what it would be like when they got really high. But for now, camp three was the turning point, the end of the acclimatisation programme.

'Next time we come up, it'll be for real,' Hal promised them as they began the return descent through the western cwm.

Two days later they were back in base camp, resting and letting their bodies recover. Josie saw a medic from one of the bigger teams and was prescribed antibiotics for the infection in her throat.

'There could be a bit of hanging around now,' Hal warned. 'We're not getting caught in the rush hour up there and if that means we sit on our asses for a few days down here then so be it.'

The days stretched to a week, the week to ten days, but Hal still wasn't ready to give the go-ahead.

Josie found the waiting difficult. Her desire to find Sebastian had turned to gnawing impatience. So much down time was beginning to chew on her nerves. Team after team went for their summit attempts and still Hal held back. 'Are you sure we're doing the right thing?' she demanded. 'Perhaps those teams know something we don't. Maybe we should be going up with them?'

'Josie, I know how you feel,' he assured her. 'It's not easy to watch all those people going up when we're sitting here, but believe me, we'll be better off without them. They'll get stuck one behind the other on the summit ridge, all queuing to get up the Hillary step, and we'll have a clean run at it, no delays.'

'OK. You're the boss.' Josie threw him a mock salute but his words didn't make the waiting any easier.

Hanging around at base camp, she began to get cravings – as if she were pregnant – for oranges, bananas, fresh croissants, steak. Instead there were just the endless beans, rice and pasta, garnished with Tashi's home-made sauces of unknown origin. When a Sherpa offered to go down to Pheriche and try to find some eggs, it felt like Christmas. Josie and Hal ate the omelettes in silence, doused in real Heinz tomato sauce donated by a neighbouring team, relishing every last mouthful as if they hadn't eaten for a month.

The weight was falling off Josie at a rate of almost a pound a week.

'That's normal for someone your size,' Hal told her. 'Your body is eating up its own fat. That plus the altitude does strange things to your stomach – I read somewhere that you only digest thirty per cent of anything you eat above twenty thousand feet. So, even if you're a good eater, which you are, you still lose all your subcutaneous fat.'

After two months Josie was aware of her clearly prominent ribs, her breasts shrunken noticeably from their former size, her thighs like matchsticks. 'You're missing a trick, Hal,' she teased him. 'The real money isn't in climbing . . . it's in the Everest weight-loss programme. I know plenty of women who'd pay good money to lose a pound a week. Bring 'em here to base camp and watch those stones roll off.' She started to wonder if her body would ever regain its accustomed curves.

She began craving butter, fats. Tashi tried her on 'yak tea' – a local drink prepared with rancid yak butter – and despite its foul taste Josie found her body accepting it for the fats it gave her. From then on, it was yak butter tea and not hot chocolate for her mess tent drinking sessions.

Hal spent hours sitting outside the tent watching the mountain through his binoculars. He monitored the radio conversations of the other teams, constantly intrigued to know who was where on the slopes and how they were doing. One day he sauntered casually into the mess tent. 'We go tomorrow,' he said. 'That OK with you?'

'Well . . . yes.' Josie felt a spasm of terror run through her.

'Nima. You feel OK to go up with Lhakpa tomorrow?'

'No problem. You go high, I go high. And if the gods are with us we go to summit.'

'Why tomorrow?' asked Josie.

Hal handed her the binoculars and took her to the tent door. 'See that crocodile of climbers retreating through the ice fall?' he asked. 'That means it's time to go for it. A nice empty mountain waiting there just for us.'

Josie spent the rest of the day in a state of nervous activity, packing and repacking her rucksack, running through the list that Hal had helped her compile. The course of antibiotics had come and gone, but with little sign of impact on the infection in her sinuses and throat. To make matters worse, she had developed what Hal called 'climber's chest', a racking cough that made her ribs ache. For now, she put those problems out of her mind. She'd just have to climb with them and that was the end of it.

Finally, at two o'clock in the morning, light-headed and very afraid, she stumbled out on to the glacier and looked up at the surrounding peaks. 'Send me a sign, Sebastian,' she whispered. 'Am I doing the right thing?'

But the mountain was implacable, sulking behind its night shroud of ice and snow. Josie shivered and went to her tent for a few fitful hours of sleep, the cough troubling her throughout the night.

57

A frosted mist of ice coated the polarised glass of Josie's mask, causing her to squint as she tried to focus through the distorting rime. Her eyes were tired. It was a relief to close them as a sudden blast of wind snapped her head down.

'Look at that.' Hal was holding his pocket altimeter in front of her face. 'We just reached eight thousand metres.'

Josie did not have the breath to reply at that moment, nor did she have the emotion to feel the excitement she knew she should feel. Eight thousand metres. Hal had told her how few people ever reached that high. 'The most rarefied club in the world,' he had added.

Altitude had dulled Josie's sense for anything other than an appreciation of the depth of her own pain.

'Can you see the tents?' Hal's voice was hoarse and frayed.

Josie looked up once more, felt the momentary pull as her eyelashes levered apart the bonds of tiny ice crystals that had glued them together. Then she saw them, a cluster of red domes far across the flat expanse of the south col. Camp four. Beyond, soaring far steeper than she had imagined, was the brutal, intimidating mass of Everest's final pyramid.

Josie let her eyes follow the natural climbing line up from the col, through the fault lines of ice-encrusted gullies on the flank of the south-west face and then sharply upwards to the south-east ridge. From there a series of knife-edge switchbacks, alternately black rock and wind-sculpted ice, rose in a line of seemingly vertical steps to a summit shrouded in a plume of cloud. The deep moan of high-altitude wind resonated from the uppermost slopes, the phantom call of the jet stream which beats an easterly path across the skies of southern Asia. Only Everest is big enough to interrupt its flow.

Josie knew she should feel something at this instant of confrontation. Awe perhaps, terror, inspiration, dread; she had lived with all of them since her decision to come to find Sebastian in this highest place on earth. Yet now they were absent, replaced by a numb core of apathy. Altitude, and the eight hours of climbing since dawn, had drained her of the ability – in this moment at least – to care.

The red domes of the camp caught her attention once more. Josie fixed her eyes on them, trying to imagine the pain it was going to cost her to reach them. 'They're miles away.' Her voice was flat, emotionless.

'One hour, maybe less.'

He was lying, she knew. One of Hal's hours was invariably two. 'Let me rest.'

'Not now. Rest at the camp.'

A bank of cloud swept across the col, obscuring the view. Josie welcomed it. The ten weeks of the expedition had taught her that climbing into a void was easier on the mind.

Hal shifted his position so he faced her, his vivid blue eyes locked on to hers in a questioning moment of assessment.

'You still got the chant going?'

Josie nodded.

'All right.'

She felt an encouraging pat on her back through the down layers of her suit. Then came the tightening tug of the short rope on her waist harness as Hal moved up.

The mantra was so much a part of her now that she no longer knew whether the whispered words were real or merely a series of impulses on a loop in her brain: 'Every metre up . . .'

One step. No more than one plastic boot's length – except somewhere in the last hours the plastic had turned to lead. 'Is a metre . . .'

Another. The muscle tissue of her calves and thighs protesting under the strain. 'Less to go.'

Another. Dig the metal crampon spikes hard into the ice. 'Every metre up . . .'

Josie stopped, straining for more air as a coughing fit struck. The throat infection had been getting steadily worse since leaving base camp, creating spasms of such violence that she feared she would crack a rib.

Hal waited patiently as she slowly recovered. Then they began again.

The slope they were climbing was at the top end of the Geneva

Spur, the bulging ridge of snow that forms a natural ramp between the Lhotse face and the south col of Everest. The angle was not steep, at sea level Josie and Hal could have ascended it in minutes. Here, at eight thousand metres, their progress was reduced to little more than crawling pace.

By 3 p.m. the cloud had cleared and they were cresting the rise on to the flatter terrain of the col, a wind-blasted shoulder of the mountain strewn with the debris of rock falls from above and the abandoned equipment of expeditions past.

Josie surveyed the plateau, only now appreciating its sheer desolation. 'Is there a lonelier place than this?'

'I doubt it.'

Josie was surprised. The col was so much bigger than she had expected it to be. At last she understood how easy it would be to get lost here in a storm.

Hal unclipped the rope from her harness. Now they were off the ice slopes of the Lhotse face there was no danger of a fall. She followed him as he picked his way across the gently undulating plateau.

Abandoned equipment was scattered around the col in large quantities. Josie had to be careful not to snag the spikes of her crampons in the shredded fabric of wind-torn tents. The orange and yellow cigar shapes of exhausted oxygen cylinders were strewn in abundance, the faded names of the expeditions they sustained still stencilled on their sides. She tried to ignore the piles of human excrement and the deep-yellow stains where urine had frozen into the ice. The wind was rising a little and small flurries of ground blizzard blew across the polished ice in front of them as they walked.

Even though she was no longer ascending, Josie still found herself struggling to put one foot in front of the other. The camp stayed obstinately in the distance until she feared she would never reach it. She began to believe she had been wandering the plateau for hours – in fact, Hal had been leading her across for less than forty minutes.

Suddenly there was a cry from ahead. A figure in a yellow wind jacket was approaching from the camp, his face obscured by an oxygen mask. It was only when he stood just inches in front of her that Josie recognised whom the laughing eyes belonged to. 'Nima?'

'Yes, ma'am. Welcome to col.'

Hal slapped the Sherpa on the back. 'How you guys doing up here?'

'Lhakpa very tired, maybe sick, but me and Todd OK. You want tea?'

'Definitely.'

Nima took the small rucksack from his back and brought out a flask. He poured the sweet brown liquid into the plastic top and handed it to Josie. She sipped it slowly, trying to ignore the pain as the hot tea hit the raw tissue of her throat.

Twenty minutes later they reached the three dome tents of camp four where Todd and Lhakpa – the team's second climbing Sherpa – were waiting. Todd had the digital camera out and was filming as they arrived. 'Hey, Josie. You made it. How are you feeling?'

Josie wanted to be bright, to say something meaningful for the camera but all she could manage was: 'I'm a bit sick.' She sat down heavily on the ice and put her head between her knees. She fought the wave of nausea for a few seconds then succumbed, vomiting up the tea in a violent spasm.

Todd laughed. 'I don't think that shot's going to make it to prime-time TV.'

'Sorry. There was nothing I could do to stop it.'

'We'd better get her on the gas.' Hal took a full bottle of oxygen from the small pile next to the tent. 'Give me a mask and regulator, will you?' He screwed the thread of the aluminium regulator valve into the bottle and connected the rubber hosing leading to the face mask. 'OK, Josie. Welcome to wonderland.'

She took the mask and held it against her face.

'I'll give you two litres a minute.'

Josie had to fight a moment of panic. The mask felt suffocating and alien. She took a tentative breath. Then another with more confidence. Hal watched, smiling, as she drew the oxygen into her lungs.

'That's incredible.' Josie could scarcely believe the chemical changes happening inside her as the oxygen took effect. Within a minute she could feel the pounding sensation in the back of her head subsiding and fading away. After three minutes the nausea, which had been with her for so much of the expedition, was also easing off. 'I feel warm, Hal. I can feel my toes!' Josie drew another deep breath, relishing the richness of the air.

Hal assembled his own oxygen equipment. For some time they sat facing each other, saying nothing, letting their bodies recover from the long day's climb from camp three.

Todd brought out more tea. 'Lhakpa's having a pretty hard time. He can't hold down any food or drink. He's been bickering at Nima all day like an old woman.'

'Did he sleep on gas?'

'So far as I know.'

'Let me see him.' Hal crawled into the tent entrance and found Lhakpa lying prone in his sleeping bag. 'Hey, Lhakpa. What's the problem?'

'No sleep. No eat. No drink. Only sick.'

'You got headache?'

'Headache. Everything ache.'

'Do you think you can climb tonight?'

'Maybe. Not sure.'

'All right. You take care, you hear? I'm going to cook up something that'll sort you out later, OK? For the moment try and sleep.'

The Sherpa rolled over with a groan.

'Call us if you need something, OK.'

Hal backed out of the tent and consulted with Todd. 'You think he's up for tomorrow?'

'I'm not sure. He was really bad on the climb from camp three, cursing and swearing like I don't know what.'

'Lhakpa too old,' Nima said quietly. 'He come to Everest too many times. Should buy shop in Kathmandu and rest. He no good for big mountains any more.'

Todd looked at Hal. 'Let's see how he feels at midnight.'

'OK. How's the weather looking?'

'Pretty good. Some slightly odd patterns lurking around in the north but I don't think they'll affect us.'

'So we're on?

'Definitely.'

Hal crossed to Josie and crouched before her. 'It's time to make a decision. It looks like the weather window we need is with us.'

'Good.'

'You still want to go through with it?'

Josie gave a small nod.

'Because if there are any doubts inside you then maybe just to be here is enough. You've already done more than anyone could have expected.'

'No. I'm sure about it. I can handle it. I feel Sebastian is waiting for me up there. I want to finish what we've started.'

Hal smiled as he saw the fierce determination in her eyes. 'OK. We leave at midnight.'

Josie rested, absorbed in watching the mountain as Hal and Todd prepared her sleeping bag in the tent. The summit was still bathed in a last glow of light, the snow plume running lazily in a veil of pink from the ridge. 'I'll be with you tomorrow,' Josie whispered.

58

The roar of the gas stove dragged Josie out of her half-sleep just before midnight. The straps of the oxygen mask had twisted as she slept, cutting into the flesh of her left ear. She lifted her head to ease the tension, flinching as the movement sent a splash of ice-cold spit down her neck from the vapour reservoir in the flange of the mask. Sleeping with the plastic mask had been hard work for her, the tight fit of the device against her face taking her back to the claustrophobia she had suffered as a child. Yet much as she hated it, she knew she had no choice. Hal had already explained in chilling detail how quickly her body would die without it at this altitude. Sebastian was proof of that.

Hal was sitting up in his sleeping bag, tending to the stove, which was in the front alcove of the tent.

Josie watched him, illuminated by the soft blue light of the gas, as he broke fist-sized chunks of ice off a larger block to add to the meltwater. A horrible realisation hit her. 'You haven't slept, have you?'

'Nope. And neither have you. At least not what I'd call sleep. You were tossing and turning, mumbling all sorts of shit.'

The tent rocked suddenly as a blast of wind ran across the col. It brought Josie's mind sharply back to the day that lay ahead. Summit day. The very words created a cold pit of terror deep inside her. On this climb there would be no room for anything other than a total singularity of mind. Climb. Nothing else. She suddenly remembered something Sebastian had said before leaving for Nepal: 'It only takes one tiny mistake up there. And that's it.' One tiny mistake: one dead body. Along with the one hundred and fifty-four other dead bodies that this mountain had so effortlessly added to its slopes. What gave her the insane idea that she would be one of the lucky ones?

In those moments of doubt Josie wished the wind would pick up, that Hal would turn round and tell her the weather didn't feel right, that she had the strength to open her mouth and tell him she wanted out. She buried herself deeper into the sleeping bag, trying to ignore the primeval reaction that so much raw fear had created. Trying and failing. 'Hal, I need to go . . . well, you know.'

'Funny how summit day has that effect on people.'

'It's not a laughing matter.'

'I know. I had to go myself an hour ago.'

Hal checked the small thermometer, which he had hung on a cord in the alcove. 'It's thirty-three degrees below freezing out there. I recommend you make it fast.'

Josie braced herself and unzipped the sleeping bag. The cold bit into her straight away. She put on her thermal jacket and slipped her feet into the soft inner linings of her boots. Then, already shivering violently, she moved carefully past the stove into the bone-chilling cold of the Himalayan night.

After she returned, it took Hal forty minutes of massaging her fingers and toes to restore them back to life. He forced warm drinks down her, one after another, then made her eat two foil sachets of high-energy food. He supervised her as she dressed, making sure every layer of clothing was right. The sock system was one that he himself had devised: four layers in total, starting with silk against the skin, then a vapour barrier plastic sock to prevent moisture freezing. Next came a Capilene thermal layer and finally one of thick wool.

It was 1.15 a.m. by the time they had wriggled into the huge down suits, zipped the Pertex wind layer over the top and exited the tent. Josie was surprised by how restricted her movement was inside the multiple layers. Hal checked that her oxygen cylinder was correctly positioned in her rucksack and fastened her harness for her.

Todd came out of the adjoining tent where the two Sherpas were preparing themselves.

'How's Lhakpa doing?' Hal asked him.

'He's grumbling a bit, but Nima had some sharp words with him and it seems he's going to try.'

'How much oxygen are they carrying?'

'Sufficient to leave two bottles at the south summit.'

'Good enough.'

Hal looked up at the stars. There was not a cloud to be seen. 'Shame we haven't got a moon.'

'You can't have everything.'

Nima and Lhakpa joined them. 'This the most exciting day of my life!' Nima told Josie through his oxygen mask. 'Maybe go to summit with you.'

'Oh, I hope so, Nima, I really do.' Josie said.

Hal ran a final check on his own rucksack, satisfying himself that no vital piece of equipment had been left behind.

'Got the dexamethasone?' Todd asked.

Hal patted his pocket, feeling the outline of the syringe in its plastic case. 'Check.'

'What's that?' Josie asked.

'Emergency medical kit,' Hal replied, 'A steroid for treating acute mountain sickness. Just a contingency.' He checked to see if the two Sherpas were ready. 'Shall we?'

Josie nodded, wanting desperately to get moving.

Todd approached her. 'You're in good hands, Josie. Keep your mind positive and you'll do well.'

Josie gave Todd a hug. 'You sure you don't want to come with us?' she asked him.

'Someone's got to man the radios. Besides, I quite like the thought of climbing back in my sleeping bag.'

Hal gave Todd a thumbs-up sign, then turned his back on the camp to begin the trek across the col, their path lit by the circular pools of yellow light from the head torches. The four of them moved unroped on the flat plateau, picking their way with care across frozen fields of ice and rock. At one stage Josie thought her beam of light had picked out the remains of a human body among the collapsed wreckage of a tent.

Hal set an easy pace, establishing a slow but consistent rhythm early on. Josie fell in behind him, content to let him lead. She had learned weeks ago that her own tendency was to push too hard, exhausting herself by moving too fast. She sensed her body losing the stiffness of the night. She felt good for the moment but she knew from previous days on the mountain that this meant little. Sometimes she had been exhausted after just four hours of climbing. On other days she had gone strong for seven hours and then hit the wall.

This was summit day. Ahead of them were a mammoth sixteen to eighteen hours of unrelenting physical activity. They would barely have time to rest, save the short stops to cram calories and fluid into themselves. She had read somewhere that summit day put the human body through the equivalent of five marathons. Josie knew she might hit the wall somewhere up there. When it happened, how would she react?

She prayed that when the time came she would not fail.

59

By 2.30 a.m. they were leaving the flat terrain of the col. Hal cut across the snow ramp at an angle until his head torch picked out the first of the fixed ropes. Nima was right with them, but Lhakpa was already lagging behind.

They waited fifteen minutes for Lhakpa to arrive, Nima getting increasingly impatient. 'Why he so slow?' he repeated. 'Should be faster like us.'

'I want you to stay with him,' Hal instructed Nima. I'm worried he might not make it if he's on his own.'

After allowing Lhakpa time to get his breath, they began the climb. They clipped their jumar clamps on to the fixed ropes – the sliding device which would lock into position in the event of a fall.

As the angle of the slope increased Josie was deeply shocked by how little oxygen she seemed to be getting. Every step up was causing her pain. Her lungs were demanding far more air than she seemed able to supply. Soon she was panting far too quickly and beginning to feel faint. 'Hal. I think there's a problem with my oxygen.'

Hal stopped and shone his head torch on to the tiny toughened glass window set into the oxygen line. Inside was a pea-sized red bead, set on a spring. 'You see that indicator? When the red ball is in the middle the oxygen is flowing fine. Everything's OK with the equipment. It's the way you're breathing. It's a common mistake to pant too fast. Then you're just recycling exhaust gases from the mask and not getting any new oxygen. It's like diving; you have to breathe as slow and deep as you can.'

Josie consciously tried to calm herself down. It was true that she had allowed herself to lose control. She took a long slow breath, inhaling as deeply as she could. Then another. 'OK. I see what you mean. That feels better already.' Reassured, she stepped up behind Hal once more, using the impact marks of his crampon spikes as a reference point to judge the length of her own stride.

With her breathing under control, she found her body responding much better to the work but it was still a pathetically meagre supply of oxygen that she was getting.

She realised her expectations of the bottled gas had been far too high. She had assumed that using it would virtually eliminate the effects of climbing at altitude. In fact, it merely diminished them. Josie struggled with the thought that they still had three thousand vertical feet to go. How would she feel once there was even less air? The thought that they might run out of oxygen began to prey increasingly on her mind. She was in no doubt now that she could not cope with that.

The snowfield stretched up endlessly, far bigger in reality than Josie had estimated it to be when she saw it from the camp. Gradually they pulled away from the two Sherpas, Nima keeping his word to Hal and staying alongside Lhakpa at the back, even though it frustrated him to do so.

At 4 a.m. Hal called a rest, pouring Josie a cup of hot chocolate from one of the two flasks he was carrying and insisting that she eat a power bar even though the thought of it made her want to retch. 'Look. There's the Sherpas' head torches.' He pointed down.

Josie stared at the tiny dots of light, realising that they had gained quite a bit of height above Nima and Lhakpa.

'I don't like the speed Lhakpa's moving at,' Hal told her, 'I'm not sure he's going to get much higher than the south summit and he might not even make that.' Then Hal spotted something else. 'Hey. Look behind the Sherpas. There's another light.'

'Where?'

'Way down there, just coming off the flat ground.'

Josie strained until she could see the third point of light. 'Oh, yes, I see it. That's weird. I wonder who it can be?'

Hal thought. 'Maybe it's Todd. Perhaps the Sherpas left something behind and he's trying to catch them.' He retrieved the walkie-talkie from his jacket pocket. 'Hal to camp four. Come in, Todd.'

There was a pause, then Todd came on the line. 'Go ahead, Hal.'

'We can see a third light coming up behind the Sherpas. That's not you, is it?'

'You got to be joking, mate. I'm all nice and snug in me sleeping bag.'

'You bastard. So who is it?'

'I don't know. I thought we were the only team left this late in the season. He passed the camp some distance off. I called out but I don't think he heard me. He was moving bloody fast.'

'He'll have to. He's left very late, whoever he is.'

'Sorry I can't help you.'

'No problem. Over.' Hal pocketed the radio and they waited for the two Sherpas to reach them.

Eventually they arrived, Nima almost in tears of frustration at their snail's pace, Lhakpa breathing hard and looking increasingly ill.

'I'm sorry, Hal,' Nima said. 'Nothing I can do to make him faster. I try everything, persuade him, but he no go fast. He too old.'

'Not too old!' Lhakpa pulled his oxygen mask to one side and spat into the snow. 'Too sick today.'

Nima spoke sadly to Hal: 'I think he not get higher than south summit. We drop oxygen bottles there for you, then I take Lhakpa back.'

'Oh, but Nima, that means you won't get to the summit today.' Josie was distraught, knowing how upset he would be.

'Plenty other time for summit,' he said, 'but I don't leave sick friend alone on mountain. If Lhakpa go down, I go down too, make sure he safe.'

Hal nodded. 'All right. Thank you, Nima. And don't worry about your chance for the top. It will come soon.'

'When the gods wish. But we will leave two bottles at south summit, OK? You rely on that. Now go, we rest.'

He looked at Josie. 'You ready for more?'

Josie nodded.

Hal kicked his front points into the ice and continued up into the night. 'He's like his father, generous to a fault. The finest people on earth, the Sherpas, and Nima's one of the best.'

Josie didn't reply. She didn't want Hal to know she was shedding a tear for Nima. She knew how much he had wanted that summit.

60

Just after 10 a.m. Josie and Hal completed the long climb through the ice gullies and emerged on to the sharply defined terrain of the ridge. One hour earlier they had switched to their second oxygen bottles.

The physical rigours of the climb were taking their toll on Josie's body. The last session had been particularly difficult as a series of muscle cramps had attacked her. 'I've got to sit down, Hal. Let me rest.'

'I can't let you do that. Last time you sat down we were stopped for fifteen minutes. We're getting slow.'

Josie hated him for it but she knew he was right. The consistent pace of the first five or six hours had slowed to a crawl, punctuated by frequent stops as she sought to control her breathing. She slumped over her ice axe, trying to restore some strength to her legs by leaning her weight on it for a few moments.

'Let's go. The south summit is just past this section of ridge.'

Josie straightened up and willed herself to carry on, fired by the thought that Sebastian was not far away.

Sebastian. She had become so wrapped up in the process of the climb that she had almost forgotten him. The higher they had climbed the more oxygen deprivation was beginning to work its peculiar chemistry on her mind. Focus, she told herself, remember what this is all about. But that was hard.

Without realising it, Josie began to lose her grip on time, unable to differentiate between a minute or an hour. She let her mind wander – anything to diminish the deep ache in her legs – casting herself back on to a Durham river the colour of jade, to mornings in which the mist would hang precisely at the level of the rowers' arms, the eight cutting silently through it as they pulled to her call. Breathe. Breathe.

'Josie! Are you listening to me?' Hal's shout jolted her out of the dream state and back to the climb. Josie looked back down the rope in confusion, trying to remember where she had been when her body went on to autopilot. Somewhere in her deeply infected sinuses a microscopic air bubble was trying to fight its way out. She opened her mouth wide in a silent scream to relieve the pressure, feeling the sharp influx of frozen atmosphere as the movement pushed the oxygen mask away from her cheeks.

One more step. Breathe. One more step.

When they finally reached the flat terrain of the south summit Josie stood, blinking and confused, staring around her as if she expected Sebastian to be there, a ghost of ice.

There was no sign of any bodies.

They both rested for a while before Hal said, 'I'll take a look around.' He moved off, his crampons cutting crisply into the ice.

Alone, the sheer exposure of this place suddenly struck Josie. She was lying on an even patch of snow – no more than ten metres square, just a few hundred metres from the true summit of Everest. Looking up, she could see the notorious summit ridge, with its numerous steep sections. The summit pole itself was out of her eyeline.

Hal's footsteps returned, interrupting her reverie. 'I found Sebastian and Rick,' he said. 'They're together just the other side of that snowbank.' He pulled Josie to her feet and led her away towards the ridge. At the far end of the flat ground the wind had cut a shallow indentation into the ice. Two bodies were lying there, about two metres apart, both half buried by snow.

Josie could see immediately that one was Sebastian.

Not far off, his arm slightly raised as if to try to protect himself from the wind, was Rick.

'I'll leave you alone for a while,' Hal said, retreating a short distance to give Josie some space.

Sebastian was curled in a foetal position, his face half nestled into the faded nylon of a wind suit, the lower part of his body completely covered. Josie pulled the fabric back from his face so she could see him more clearly.

She had thought about this moment so many times that there was no sense of horror at the partly mummified corpse that lay before her, no feeling of revulsion at the sun-blackened skin, the skeletal claws that were once the hands of the man she loved. There was only the slightest odour – a hint of sweetness so slight that Josie thought she might be imagining it. The features were still recognisably Sebastian despite the tightening of the skin against the skull. The eyes were frozen shut and what remained of his hair had been bleached pure white by the intensity of high-altitude radiation. The muscles around the mouth had atrophied, pulling the lips back from the teeth in an ugly snarl.

Josie took off her outer gloves and stroked his face, the tanned skin as hard as parchment to her touch. 'I had to come, Sebastian. I know you'd have wanted me to.' She was quiet for a while before whispering again: 'I can't tell you how much I miss you. It's been so difficult to get over all this when I didn't know where you were . . . didn't know anything about the place that killed you. But now I do and I think I understand what made you come here.'

For a while Josie stayed very still. 'Do you remember the poem? The one you sent me once?' She pulled the sheet of paper from her top pocket and read the words written there:

> 'They who are near me do not know that you are nearer to me than they are.
> They who speak to me do not know that my heart is full with your unspoken words.
> They who crowd in my path do not know that I am walking alone with you.
> They who love me do not know that their love brings you to my heart.'

Josie paused for a long moment as the emotion of the moment swept her. 'That's how I'll always feel. That my heart will always be full of unspoken words for you. And that's all I want to say.' After some minutes Josie stood, her legs shaking.

Hal came over to join her. 'You OK?'

'Yes, I'll be fine.'

Hal kneeled by Rick's body and searched the pockets until he found the guide's camera. 'There might be some useful shots on this . . . give us an idea who was where in the group as they got higher,' he told Josie. He put the camera in his rucksack, then searched the body once more until he found the hand bearing the ring Deborah had asked him to retrieve. The finger it sat on had atrophied and he slipped it off easily. Hal put the ring carefully in his pocket and turned his attention to Sebastian, tearing back the frozen rucksack flap to examine the contents.

'Look at this.' Hal pulled open the neck to reveal the top of an empty oxygen bottle. He tugged it out a little, rolling it to reveal Rick's name written on it in black marker. 'Rick gave Sebastian his last oxygen bottle.'

'He did that?'

'It doesn't surprise me. Rick would give his final drop of blood to save his clients.'

'But where are the others?'

'I don't know. They could have stumbled off the ridge in the white-out. Or they might have been carried off this edge by an avalanche. You see how steep it is here?'

Josie nodded.

Hal reached further into the rucksack. 'There's something else in here, feels like Gore Tex or Dacron.' He pulled out a corner of brightly coloured fabric. 'Oh, maybe it's the paraglider . . . he was going to try to fly, you remember?'

'You're right. I forgot he was planning that.' Josie looked around her. 'Do you think he could have done it from this place?'

Hal scanned the flat area and nodded. 'Good a place as any. That run-off ice slope there would be the one to slide down. It would be hairy as hell but a good pilot could pull it off.' Hal tried to yank the fabric out further from the pack but the way the rucksack was frozen against Sebastian's back meant it would have disturbed the corpse. He left it and stood to take out his camera. 'Do you mind if I take a photograph of the bodies? That bottle is exactly the type of thing that might help Deborah when she gets to court. That and the fact that Rick stayed with his client to the end.'

'Of course.'

Hal took a few pictures.

Then Josie asked him: 'Maybe I should check his pockets?'

Hal nodded.

Josie reached forward to try to free the zip on the breast pocket of Sebastian's wind suit. It was frozen solid. 'Can you help me?'

Hal crouched beside her and helped her undo the zip. The pocket was empty. Josie tried the one on the other side of the suit, which opened easily. Inside was a long piece of white silk. Josie ran the fabric through her fingers. 'You think he meant to put this on the summit?'

'Probably.'

'To think he got so high but didn't reach the top. In a way that's one of the saddest things of all. I'd like to take this there for him.'

A flurry of spindrift blew across the body. Josie brushed the powder grains of snow from Sebastian's face. 'You'll always be in my heart, Sebastian.'

She stood. 'I'm ready,' she told Hal.

He looked up the ridge, considering something for a while. Eventually he asked: 'How about the summit?'

Josie did not hesitate. 'Yes.'

'Sure you're up for it?'

'How long do you think it will take?'

'If you keep the same pace, another hour – maybe two.'

'It's what Sebastian would have wanted.' She tucked the silk scarf into her pocket. 'Let's do it for him.'

'And for Rick.'

Josie stepped in behind him, sensing the ground rise as her legs began to kick into the slope.

The summit. The words set her heart racing even more powerfully here than they had at base camp. If she had to crawl there on her hands and knees, Josie wanted it now more than ever. She let her head drop down, watching the bright-yellow painted claws of Hal's crampons as he began again to move relentlessly in slow motion up the slope in front.

Josie braced herself for the pain.

61

'Can someone get these fucking lights turned down? It's like a sauna in here.' Mike padded a handkerchief against his brow.

The *Daybreak* studio was way too hot – the air-conditioning problem that had bugged them since the technicians were sacked had never been properly solved and today it was worse than ever. Mike could feel his shirt beginning to cling to his back, the tungsten heat off the racks of two kilowatt lights was more than the air-conditioning could handle. Twice already he had asked for the system to be cranked up but the heat was still rising. The only person in the room who didn't seem to be feeling it was the stand-in presenter Tim, sitting on the sofa waiting for the news to end, looking as cool as a cucumber.

The control centre went quiet as Tim got his cue, 'Thank you for joining us once more at the *Daybreak* Everest Expedition control centre. We're still waiting for news on the satellite connection to Josie and Hal. Meanwhile we do have a live link-up to camp four where the rest of the team are waiting. What's the latest, Todd?'

Todd's voice came in loud and clear: 'The news is that Josie and her guide are making good progress up the final summit ridge, but slightly slower than anyone anticipated. If all goes well it seems likely that they will be reaching the top within the next hour.'

'Thank you Todd.' Tim held up a series of newspapers to the camera. 'For now we can take a look at some of this morning's papers. The *Daily Mail* has Josie on the front page here with the title HEADING FOR THE TOP OF THE WORLD; in the *Sun* there's also a front-page photograph of Josie with the headline GO JOSIE GO. In the *Mirror* she's on page three and four with a long feature about the *Daybreak* expedition and there is also coverage in *The Times*, the *Telegraph* and the *Guardian* . . . So the world is watching, but still no news from Everest. Just to remind you, we have had confirmation from the expedition that Josie and Hal are making their summit attempt right now and we should be hearing any time whether or not they have achieved that incredible objective.

'Meanwhile, while we're waiting, we go to Barry, our resident vet, for more tips on how to keep the pet in your life happy . . .'

62

The oxygen cylinder was black against the snow. Josie's crampon points nudged into it with a small metallic chink. She stared at it dumbly for a few seconds, then fell on to both knees to rest. The sudden movement brought stars before her eyes.

A wave of nausea threatened her, the taste of bile filling her mouth. She stared at the cylinder, wondering whom it had belonged to. It had been there for years, she decided, seeing that one side was devoid of black paint where the prevailing wind had scoured it down to the aluminium. A series of symbols was stamped into the metal and it took her a while to recognise them as Russian.

'Time to move,' Hal told her.

She raised her hand to plead for a few more moments, lifting up her torso as the nausea passed in a single mouthful of foul-tasting fluid. She let it dribble down into the bottom of the oxygen mask and breathed the oxygen, relishing the purity of the taste as it cleaned away the acid rancour of the bile. Then she looked ahead, her heart sinking as she registered the immensity of the challenge still to come. The ground here was steeper even than it had looked from the south summit, more committing psychologically, with big exposed drops on each side. The fixed ropes snaked along its length, placed earlier in the season by other teams.

Hal pulled out a power bar from his fleece. He snapped it in two and passed Josie half.

She waved a hand to decline.

'Take it. Come on. You have to force this stuff down, right? You're going to need this energy later on.'

Josie took the high-energy bar and eased the oxygen mask away from her face just enough to slip the tablet of food into her mouth. It was frozen hard and, wary of cracking another tooth, she let the warmth of her mouth thaw it out before chewing and swallowing.

Hal reached once more into his pack and retrieved his water bottle in its padded thermal case. He unclipped the top attachment of his oxygen mask and let the plastic snout hang away from his mouth while he drank a few sips of the juice. 'Take some.'

Josie fumbled with the clip of her mask for some moments, then let Hal do it for her. He pulled it gently away, aware that the hard plastic shell had scraped away the skin on the bridge of her nose. She gulped down the juice.

'Let's go.'

Josie hauled herself up on the rope and shakily continued, forcing herself to concentrate on the thin red filament of nylon, trying not to let her eyes be pulled to the sides. She was beginning to realise that she had underestimated this last push along the ridge.

'You can do better. More steps.'

Josie raised her head and gave a slow nod. She curled her fingers around the serrated teeth of the axe head and lifted it, sensing rather than feeling the metal through the four layers of gloves.

Step and breathe. Breathe. Breathe.

Step and breathe. Breathe. Breathe. Breathe.

Step. Josie sucked the oxygen deep.

Hal stopped. They were standing at the foot of the steepest section yet. Hazily, Josie realised this would be the Hillary step, ten metres of demanding climbing, protected by a fixed rope.

Hal checked that her jumar clamp was in place and began to ascend.

Josie waited for his call, then forced her body upwards, swinging her ice axe into the face and levering herself on it with shaking arms. An outward explosion of gas. Panting uncontrollably she felt her head sagging down once more, only to be jerked up by an angry tug from above.

'No rest here, Josie.'

Josie pushed her crampon spikes into the crumbling snow and stretched her leg up on to a protruding rock. Her whole body was shaking with the strain as she pushed up.

Another blow of the ice axe, two more moves and she made it, collapsing on to the flatter ground at the top, grateful for the chance to breathe.

Hal let her lie there, until the walkie-talkie suddenly crackled to life in his pocket.

'This is Hal.'

'Todd here. How you going up there, Hal?'

'Slow but good. Just made it up the Hillary step.'

'How's Josie?'

'Thought she was losing it a while back but she's still moving in the right direction.'

'You know what the time is, don't you?'

'Can't say I've checked my watch for a while.'

'It's almost one o'clock.'

'It is? Shit, I lost track of that one.'

'One o'clock is turnaround time remember?'

'You're right.'

'What are you going to do?'

Hal looked up along the ridge. The summit pole was still not visible. 'Give me some time. Let me talk to Josie.'

'What's he talking about?' Distracted by the pain in her sinuses, Josie had not concentrated fully on the conversation.

'We've got a problem, Josie. We hit the turnaround.'

Josie stared at him dumbly as she tried to register the meaning of his words.

'We're too slow. And late. You remember I told you if we hadn't topped out by one we were out of here? I don't want to risk bringing you down in a night descent.'

Only then did Josie realise what the implications of his words were. A sense of disbelief engulfed her. 'You're not serious? Tell me you're not serious about that?'

Hal said nothing.

Inside Josie the disbelief escalated rapidly into anger. 'No! You can't do that to me. Not now. Look how high we are. I can't believe you can even think about it.'

'It's brutal I know . . . but the hard fact is that you are moving too slow.'

'I'll get faster. I can do it. I promise you I can make it.'

'And the weather . . .'

'The weather's clear. There's nothing to stop us. How far are we from the summit anyway?'

'If you pick up the pace we can make it in thirty minutes. If.'

'I will never forgive you if you turn me back now.'

'Don't say that.'

'Please, Hal. Please.'

Hal looked up at the ridge once more, then out to the horizon.

Josie waited, watching him intently. 'For me, Hal. For me.'

He did not respond, but continued staring out over her shoulder with an intensity that caused her fear, even though she could not sense why. Intimidated by his silence she let her eyes rest on tiny details, the beard of frozen spittle cascading from the outlet valves of the oxygen mask, the rippling movement of the fur lining to his hood as gusts of wind caught it. Only one patch of his skin was visible, a triangular area of cheek left exposed where the oxygen mask fitted imperfectly against the goggles. The skin was scorched and black, the colour of overcooked meat. It reminded her of Sebastian's dead body.

Hal clicked on the walkie-talkie once more. 'Hal to Todd. We're going up.'

'That's pretty bold, mate.'

'I know that. We'll call from the summit. What's the status of the Sherpas?'

'Yeah. They'll be back down here pretty soon. I can see them through the binoculars. They made it to the south summit so the oxygen is there waiting for your return. Oh, and that other climber is still coming up about an hour and a half behind you.'

'Any more ideas on him?'

'No. But he's a fucking robot. I haven't seen him rest once. He's getting late too.'

'Well, that's not our problem. We'll call from the summit.'

'Good luck. Over and out.'

Josie reached out and touched Hal's arm. 'Thank you.'

'Thank me when we're back down in camp four.' He turned and continued to climb.

Josie took a deep breath and followed on.

63

'All your points in! Keep moving.'

Dimly Josie could sense that the angle of the ice now sloped awkwardly away from the face. The rope pull intensified. She placed her feet carefully sideways, bending her knees in a crabbing motion to plant home every one of the ten crampon spikes. Four more steps. A wave of anger engulfed her as she felt the insistent pull on her waist. When was Hal ever going to let her rest?

Kick in. Breathe. Breathe.

Kick in. She could feel her kidneys throbbing inside her. Breathe.

Josie plunged in her ice axe and fell to one knee, her head resting on her gloved hands as she struggled to draw in the life-giving air. She felt his arms under her shoulders and found herself uncertainly on her feet. They stood there for some minutes until her dizziness subsided. Then Hal changed his position and moved at her side with his hand clutching her harness at the back. *Like a dog*, she thought, wondering at his strength as he half pulled and half pushed her along the now flatter terrain of the ridge.

Then he paused. 'Look up ahead.'

Josie squinted through the frozen lenses of her goggles and saw the flags of the summit pole for the first time, a fluttering splash of colour sitting above a final rise in the ridge. Her throat tightened, her heart stumbling for a beat as a rushing wave of adrenaline engulfed it. They were close now. Really close.

Frustrated by the distorted vision she had lived with for so many hours, Josie pushed her goggles clumsily up on to her forehead in a hurried movement, feeling her retinas burn with the new intensity of brilliantly defining light. 'Hal!'

He remained motionless.

She shouted again: 'My feet are freezing.'

Raising his arm, Hal peeled back the fabric layers and checked his watch. Then he turned and looked up the ridge. He took hold of the front of her harness and they began again, the ridge steepening once more.

'Every metre up . . .' Josie felt the pulsing of blood in her temples as the over-thick liquid fought to circulate through her.

Move. Breathe, lungs stretching to the point where she felt sure they would explode through her ribs.

Move. Breathe.

'Is a metre less to go.' Rest.

She could hear Hal, strangely distant above the rising bluster of the wind, even though he was right next to her: 'OK, Josie. OK! Look how close. One more time.'

She buried her head into his shoulder, letting him take her weight.

'No way! Keep it going. Look at it, Josie.'

Josie pulled her head back and squinted up the ridge. He was right. The summit pole, with its garland of prayer flags and devotions, was now just a few metres further up. In the bullying wind the saffron and scarlet silks seemed alive, as if they were trying to tear themselves from their tether. To Josie's eyes, bruised and reddening, they looked like birds of paradise, fluttering to escape.

Adrenaline coursed once more through her body as she watched the fragile pennants. Hal let her rest for a few more moments. Josie still wouldn't allow herself the luxury of believing. Not yet.

'Stop dreaming, Josie. Let's finish it.'

Josie dragged her mind back and clenched her fingers inside her four layers of gloves. They were solid with cold and she winced with the pain as tepid blood coaxed the tissue back to something like body temperature. She looked steadily in front of her, lifting her head as high as she could and straightening her back. As she took the first step Hal fell in behind her.

Breathe. Another step, swing the feet out in an arc to avoid snagging the other boot. Breathe. Breathe.

'Don't . . .' Josie punched through the pain barrier with an explosive grunt. Breathe. Breathe. Breathe. Breathe. '. . . stop.' She looked down, willing her legs to move.

Two more steps. The ridge was levelling off now as the summit pyramid gave way.

Breathe. Breathe. Breathe. Breathe. Josie was laughing silently, internally, to herself. The laughter welled inside her as two more steps came just ten seconds apart.

Josie took one more step and placed her hand on the summit pole. It was rigidly fixed and she used it as an anchor to pull herself up. Hal moved steadily up beside her.

'Everest is yours, Josie!'

They stood side by side, recovering, leaning on their axes for support. Josie could see the faint imprint of Tibetan prayers inscribed into the fading flags beneath her. A bright-orange oxygen bottle and some abandoned television camera batteries lay nearby. The view was the most perfect piece of natural theatre in the world. Josie was speechless with awe as she looked to the south. Seen from her vantage point, the mountains around her seemed to plummet sheer to the centre of the planet, the ridges to be sharpened steel, razor edges ripping the sky.

To the north was not so clear, Josie realised, clouds filling a significant part of the sky. But nothing could dull the intense joy of the moment.

She pulled the silk scarf from the pocket and tied it gently to the summit pole. 'For you, Sebastian,' she whispered, 'with my love.'

64

Hal helped her manoeuvre into a position where she could sit, legs on either side of the sharp bank of compacted snow. She kept her hand on the pole, looking out to the south.

'I'm going to bump up your oxygen level for a short time.' Hal opened her rucksack. 'Four litres. You're going to need it for the interview.' He clicked the regulator round from its flow rate of two litres a minute to four.

Josie felt the increased flow of oxygen immediately, the extra gas suffusing warmth into her body, chasing dark shadows out of her mind, bringing a wave of euphoria with it. She sucked it down deep, relishing its richness, then reached up and pulled Hal gently towards her. They embraced clumsily, oxygen masks clashing. 'We made it, Hal. We really made it.' Josie felt the tears freezing even as they crept into her eyes. She rubbed at her frozen lashes, forcing them apart.

Hal looked out to the north. 'We got work to do. Then we move fast. I'm not so happy about the look of those clouds.'

Moving carefully around the clutter of debris on the summit, Hal sat facing Josie on the other side of the pole. He slipped off the shoulder straps of his rucksack and pulled out the walkie-talkie. Removing an outer wind-proof glove to free his fingers sufficiently to operate the switch, Hal clicked on to transmit and held the mouthpiece close to his mask. 'Hal to camp four. Hal to camp four. Todd, do you read me? Over.'

There was a hiss of static for a few seconds. 'Loud and clear, baby. This is Todd. You'd better have some good news for me. I lost you on the binoculars.'

'We're on the summit.'

A cheer erupted from the handset, Todd's whoops of celebration resonating thinly through the tiny speaker. 'That is the best news ever, Hal! Josie OK?'

'Pretty good.'

'OK. Listen. Just a minute ago I had Rachel call up from Vancouver to find out how you were getting on. I think she's still on the satellite line. You want me to patch her through?'

'You bet,' Hal told him.

'Hal?' Rachel's voice sounded hesitant and nervous.

'On the top of the world.'

'Hey, fantastic! Oh, I'm so pleased for you, Hal, and for Josie too.'

'Thanks. How's things at Deborah's?'

'Perfect, but we've been a little stressed waiting for news. Deborah and her kids all send you both their love. Oh, wait, Deborah's just asking me something . . . oh, did you find Rick?'

'Rick's and Sebastian's bodies were together . . . it seems that Rick gave Sebastian his last bottle of O's. We got Rick's camera and Josie had a chance to say goodbye to Sebastian as she'd hoped. We haven't found any of the others but I think they were probably blown off the ridge.'

'All right. I'll tell her that. We'd better get off the line now. I know how . . .'

'Hey. One last thing.'

'What?'

'Well, this might surprise you, but I have a question for you.'

'You do?' Rachel's voice was puzzled.

'Will you marry me?'

There was a yelp of joy down the walkie-talkie. 'What? I don't believe you, Hal, you're so outrageous. You ask me that from the summit of Everest? How wonderful. The answer is yes.'

Hal laughed. 'That was one of the things that kept me going.'

'I'm in tears here, Hal.'

'I love you.'

'Me too.'

'Over and out.'

Josie patted Hal on the back. 'Congratulations,' she said. 'I never knew you were such a romantic.'

The walkie-talkie crackled again, this time with Todd's voice. 'I'm going to patch up the satellite link to *Daybreak* right now. Those guys have been chewing their fingers to the bone waiting for you to get there.'

'Roger that. Standing by . . .'

65

'We've got the call!' The words came from the director in the gallery, fed into Tim's earpiece. 'Connecting you live to Everest in five seconds.' He turned to the camera as the vet finished his outlink. 'Thank you, Roger. Well, from high jinks in the poodle parlour we turn to high links on the summit of the world. We've just had the news that Josie Turner and Hal Maher are standing on the top of Everest right now! Thanks to the wonders of modern technology we should be able to speak to them direct. Do you hear me, Josie?'

'Tim?' Josie's voice came across the studio speakers loud and clear.

'Josie. You're a hero! Everyone here at *Daybreak* sends you heartiest congratulations. What's it like up there? What can you see?'

Josie projected her voice as loudly as she could, ignoring the protesting thump of pain in her throat as each word was formed. 'Right now I'm looking out across the greatest peaks of the Himalayas and I'm the happiest woman in the world . . .' She broke off for a moment as she fought off a coughing fit. 'I want to thank everyone at *Daybreak* for their support. I could never have reached the summit without you.'

'Thank you, Josie. I'm sure every one of the millions of *Daybreak* viewers will be moved by what you say. You may like to know, by the way, that our viewing figures have soared since we started covering your climb. You've been creating quite a bit of press over here. How was the final section?'

'More exhausting than I can tell you. And terrifying. It's steep as hell and . . .' There was a loud crackle of interference on the connection.

'Sorry, Josie, we didn't quite catch that last section. Can you repeat, please?'

This time there was no answering voice.

'Hello? Josie? Do you hear me . . . ?'

The seconds ticked past.

'This is the *Daybreak* studio calling Everest.' Tim forced a nervous smile. With a quiet click the satellite line went dead, leaving him with nothing but white noise being pumped into his earpiece.

66

An avalanche sent a pressure wave of shock through the air, a sharp explosion as hundreds of thousands of tons of ice raced down the Kanshung face beneath them. Josie peered into the cloud but could see nothing.

'It's just a serac collapsing.' Hal cocked his head to one side as the rumble died away.

'Try the connection again.' Josie could feel her buttocks and thighs beginning to deaden as the ice chill seeped up through her down suit.

Hal called camp four. 'What's happening, Todd?'

'Satellite link went down.'

'Goddam.'

'We're working on it. Hal, just to let you know we have a barograph read out down here and it's falling like a stone. There's a front coming through fast from somewhere. Could be one of those unexpected lows the Met guys can't spot.'

Hal looked out to the north. 'Yeah. Roger that. There's definitely cloud building and the wind is picking up. We'll be down as fast as we can. Over.'

'OK. You're the Bergführer. Don't forget the cache of oxygen at the south summit.'

'Two bottles, right?'

'Yeah. Nima and Lhakpa just got back here. The bottles are in position.'

'All right. How you doing on that call? It's getting cold up here.'

'Soon as we have it, I'll be back on.'

Hal shifted impatiently. 'Let's do the filming.'

'OK.'

Hal brought out the lightweight digital video camera. He tied his rucksack to the summit pole with a short sling and took several careful steps back down the slope to frame up some shots.

'Hey. I nearly forgot the flag.' Josie rummaged through the internal pockets of her down suit, retrieving a crumpled square of cloth. She unfurled it, turning it so the words '*Daybreak* Everest Expedition' faced the camera. She posed as he took the footage, bracketing the exposure to allow for the extreme levels of light.

Hal shouted up: 'Can you take the oxygen mask off so I can see your face?'

'Oh, God.'

'Come on, Josie. We can't see if it's you or King Kong behind that thing.'

'OK.'

He crabbed slowly up the ice and unclipped her mask.

Josie let it fall to one side of her face and tried to turn the convulsive gasping into a smile as he panned from the mountains to the summit pole. She held up the *Daybreak* flag in a triumphant sweep of her arms. 'Made it!' she shouted. 'Feeling on top of the world!'

'OK. That'll do it.'

Josie replaced the mask, experiencing a surge of relief as the flow of oxygen resumed.

'Camp four to summit. Do you read? Camp four to summit.'

Hal grabbed the handset. 'This is Hal.'

'Todd here. We've got an update for you. We still can't get a response on the satellite link.'

'This is a major pain in the ass, Todd. We're freezing our tits off here. I want to get Josie moving. Like in the next few minutes.'

'How's the weather looking? We've got less than fifty metres visibility here at base.'

Hal ran his gloved hand through the prayer flags, which were now hanging loosely from the pole, untroubled by the wind. 'Wind's died down for the moment. But Josie's not getting any warmer. Tell them if they can't make the connection in the next five minutes we're starting down. Over.'

'No!' Josie snatched the radio from him. 'Todd! You have to get that link. We can hang on if that's what it takes.'

'Roger that. Wait my call. Out.'

Todd's transmission cut abruptly. Josie handed back the radio.

Hal looked out into the void for a few moments. 'I say when we leave, Josie. That's my decision, not yours.'

'You run the mountain. I run the PR remember?'

'You can talk to the world from base camp.'

'The summit broadcast is part of the package. I owe it to *Daybreak*.'

'And I have to get you off this mountain alive.'

A sudden rush of wind whistled across the summit, causing them both to hunch down their bodies for protection. The prayer flags flew momentarily into life, then died again as calm returned.

Hal stood and moved away. She could hear the faint click and motorwind of his stills camera as he photographed the scene behind her.

Trying to extinguish the tight knot of anger inside her, Josie stared out to the north where, she now realised for the first time, Everest's plume was starting to run. She gazed into the spectral cloud of ice, blinking hard to clear the microscopic granules that pricked and spiked against her eyes. For minutes she sat motionless, mesmerised by the ebb and flow of the curling system as it stretched away to infinity. What had Hal called it? A rotor. She had to dig deep inside her half-frozen brain to find the word. That was why the ice crystals moved in that beautiful loop, the summit ridge had put a spin on the wind. Wasn't that what he had said?

Josie closed her eyes as a crackling flash of pain seared at the back of her retinas. It flared for a second more, then was gone. She shook her head to clear it, then gasped as it burned again. The ski goggles. A shockwave galvanised her into motion. She clutched wildly at her forehead, fearing for a terrifying second that they were gone. Her frozen fingers snatched clumsily against the plastic frame, trying to drag the tinted glass down. The elastic was snagged, hooked or twisted on to some part of the oxygen headband by her neck.

Breathe. Breathe. Breathe. Josie forgot her control and began panting as she pulled the goggles up and clear from her head to reposition them. The lenses were still frozen. She held them in front of her to brush away the ice with her GoreTex outer gloves. One fumbling moment, one split second as her deadened hands lagged a nerve pulse slower than the signals from her brain.

The goggles fell, skittering in a series of short bounces down the steep ice before dropping over the edge of the ridge out of sight. Ten thousand feet. Josie felt the dense surge of panic well up within her as she imagined them falling, tumbling, impacting hard against ice and rock. She placed both hands around the summit pole and gripped it with all her strength.

She heard the crisp ice steps as Hal worked his way back up to her. Please God he didn't see it, Josie prayed. He moved his body into the sitting position on the crest. 'Can you still feel your feet?'

'Yes,' Josie lied.

'How about your hands?'

'Bit cold. But I'm keeping the circulation going.' Josie held up her hands and showed him she could still flex them.

'Another two minutes and I'm taking you down.'

Josie fought off a coughing attack. 'Really. I'm fine.'

'You're fine because I pumped up your regulator to four litres. When we leave here I'll have to knock you back to two. Then you're going to feel it.' He pulled out the walkie-talkie. 'What the fuck are they doing over there? Come on, goddam it!' Hal beat his arms across his chest to try to raise a glow of warmth. 'We are sitting in a minus-sixty-degree freezer here. Someone speak to us!'

Josie felt the needlepoints of pain once more, dancing across nerve endings in the back of her eyes. She screwed them shut, biting her lip behind the oxygen mask until the sensation passed.

The walkie-talkie suddenly clicked on.

'Here we go.' Hal shuffled closer to Josie.

A hiss of radio interference came on the line, followed by Tim's voice, startlingly clear: 'This is *Daybreak* expedition control in London. Do you hear us, over?'

'This is Hal Maher on the summit of Everest reading you loud and clear.'

'Yes!' Once more the sound of cheers rang from the walkie-talkie. 'This is London. We've had a problem with the satellite link but we're back with you now. Can I speak with Josie?'

'I hear you.'

'Josie, how are you feeling? Does Everest live up to your expectation?'

Josie laughed. 'You might say that. Climbing this mountain has been the most incredible challenge of my life. I had no idea it would be so tough. But standing here now, it all seems worthwhile.'

Tim's tone shifted down. 'As I understand it, you visited the resting place of your late husband today. If you can bear to talk about such a deeply personal moment, can you possibly describe how you felt?'

Josie paused, searching for the words. 'I know a lot of people have criticised my motives for this expedition, accused me of being ghoulish for wanting to visit Sebastian's body. All I can say is that I spent time with him today and those were the happiest moments I have had since he died.'

'Amen to that, Josie. I think we all understand how you feel. Let's move on to Hal. You've guided to the summit of Everest five times now, that's a record for an American guide. How did Josie do?'

'She was great. I've never seen such will-power. It's been a pleasure to climb with her.'

'How long will it take you to get down now?'

'Hard to say but we should be moving right away. All I'm thinking about is getting her back safely.'

'We'll leave you to it. Godspeed from *Daybreak* and over and out.'

The line went dead, leaving just the bluster of the wind as it played around the ridge.

Hal checked his watch. 'Time to move.'

67

The wind was rising, Josie knew that much. And, as it did so, the cold was cutting deeper.

Breathe. Breathe. Breathe.

Then the pain hit. Josie screamed into her oxygen mask as the burning stab rippled like St Elmo's fire across the back of her retinas, a blowtorch flame of agony igniting nerve endings she never knew existed. She stumbled a few steps behind Hal, feeling with her feet for the route she could not see.

As she descended, she turned her face full into the increasing force of the wind, believing in a moment of insanity that it could reach into her and turn the fire into ice. Her reflexes fought back, slamming the eyes shut against the pulverising ice grains and jerking her head down, involuntarily seeking shelter in the soft down of her protective suit.

The weather was deteriorating fast and they had descended just thirty metres down the ridge. Josie felt so tired she could barely move, her progress slowing dramatically as the temperature dropped. Now she had to sit. What was happening? It should be so easy to go down. She couldn't fathom why it was all so hard.

Hal crouched over her on the windward side, his body rocking slightly as he shifted his weight to counter the thrust of the wind.

'Hal! My eyes!'

He screwed his head down so she could hear his shout. 'Where are your goggles?'

'I don't know.'

He pulled back her hood. 'They're gone.'

He patted his hands against the pockets on her suit, searching for the tell-tale bulk of the plastic frame. 'You lost your goggles? Jesus *Christ*! I told you *never* to take your goggles off. Now you're becoming snow-blind.'

'Give me yours,' she begged him. 'Let me borrow them.'

'The damage is already done,' he told her. 'If I give you mine we both get snow-blind and then we really have got a problem.'

Breathe. Breathe. A second wave of acid sparks exploded in Josie's eyes. Pressure began to build in the soft tissue of her cheeks as tears tried to force their way through frozen ducts. Another blast hit her. She could feel the tension of the straps biting into her flesh as the oxygen mask was almost ripped off her face. Only the steady grip of Hal's hand on her waist harness prevented her from being blown backwards off the ridge.

He stood above her with his shoulders hunched, bent over his ice axe like an old man over a walking stick. 'Move! This weather is coming in fast.'

Josie rolled on to her side, then pulled her legs up beneath her, willing the frozen muscles to move. She hooked an arm around Hal's leg to stabilise herself as she moved on to all fours. Etched into the ice in front of her were the deep indentations of his crampon spikes. Josie watched them fade and disappear in seconds, scrubbed out by the eroding blast of driving ice. The pain in her eyes subsided to a dull ache.

Hal would not let her crawl, the ridge was too steep. Josie raised herself on to one knee and felt him lift her bodily to her feet, his raw strength surprising her now more than ever. Leaning into him for protection, she took one faltering step. Then another. She gave up trying to look into the white-out, there was nothing to see. Hal shuffled forward, dragging her, bent double, at his side with her head buried deep in the down hood of her wind suit.

Now the blowing ice was as hard as gravel. Josie could feel it being forced down her neck, penetrating the thermal layers and pricking against her skin in the small of her back.

Shuffle forward. Breathe. Breathe. Breathe.

She sensed the uncertainty in Hal's step as they hit a steeper incline. Josie had to bend her knees to maintain her balance. Then he stopped. She could tell by the movement of his arms that he was cleaning the encrusted ice from his goggles. She risked a look out from inside the hood and by chance caught a moment when the intensity of the blizzard faltered, revealing a blacker mass far below.

The sickening realisation churned in her guts as the desire to step forward swamped her. There was a drop in front of them.

Breathe. Breathe. Breathe.

The drop. Take the step. The voice inside her screamed at her to do it.

'Hal! We're on the edge.'

'I know that.' Hal pulled her backwards a few steps and let her rest as he stared intently into the perfect blank, searching for the smallest visual clue to orientate him. 'What on earth?' His cry caused Josie to look up.

Just a few metres away, a climber emerged from the growing blizzard and headed slowly towards them.

'There's someone climbing up,' Hal told Josie, 'but who the hell . . . ?'

68

The climber stopped without acknowledging them, hunched over his ice axe, body angled into the wind to counteract the blast. For two minutes or more he stayed motionless. Then he carried on towards them, each footstep bringing him just a few inches closer. He was less than an arm's length away before he showed any signs of recognising their presence. He stood shivering uncontrollably, his wind suit and oxygen mask covered in a thick coating of ice.

It took Hal some moments to fathom who the flint-grey eyes belonged to. 'Andrei?'

The Ukrainian climber leaned forward, suddenly galvanised into action. 'How far to the summit?' His shout was whipped away by the storm.

'What?'

'How far?' He pointed upwards wildly.

'You'll get blown off the ridge! Go back down.'

'No!' Josie could hear the panic in Vasylenko's shout. He pulled a yellow plastic camera from his pocket and waved it in front of Hal, ranting almost incoherently. 'I need a photo. On the summit. Come back up with me. Ten metres, maybe less.'

'No way. It'll take you at least an hour to get up there.'

Andrei grabbed Hal by the shoulders and made as if to push him back along the ridge in his fury. 'I have to have the photograph. One photograph. They won't believe me. Like K2 all over again.'

'Do you think I'm crazy? We're going down.'

'For me! For me! One photo. Do it, my friend.'

Ignoring the battering wind, Hal squared up to him, so close to the Ukrainian's face that their ski goggles almost touched. He yelled the words slowly. 'Andrei. Listen carefully to me. I know you're strong but if you keep going up into these conditions you are going to die. Do you hear me? You're not thinking rationally. Get off the mountain while you still can.'

'The summit is here! A few metres, nothing more. You think I can turn around now?'

Hal manoeuvred Josie around Vasylenko and pulled her several steps down the ridge in the direction the climber had come from. His torrent of abuse was quickly swallowed up by the roar of the storm.

When they looked back he was little more than a grey shadow through the driving snow. Josie saw him take one step in the direction of the summit, then a fresh flurry of spindrift engulfed the ridge and he was gone.

Josie sucked as hard as she could on the mask. There seemed to be so little air. A ring of stars danced around her head as she fell on to the ice.

'Stand up!' Hal shook her so hard she could feel the impact of her skull against the ice. 'We're not far from the fixed ropes. You're doing well, Josie. Keep it going.' His voice was almost exhausted from the continual shouting.

Josie tried to move but her legs would not obey the command. Hal pulled her up on to her knees, then hoisted her upright in a bear-hug. She stood unsupported for a few seconds, then lunged forward again on to her knees.

Hal bent down next to her, breathing hard from the exertion. 'I can't carry you, Josie. You have to get off this mountain on your own two feet. Now get up and walk.'

Josie shook her head slowly from side to side.

Hal looked at her in confusion for some moments, then reached for her oxygen line. Halfway along the rubber tube the valve indicator could be seen. He rubbed the glass to remove a layer of ice and saw immediately that the red pea-sized ball inside was lying idle. 'Shit! You're out of oxygen. I never put you back down to two litres when we left the summit. How could I have been so damned stupid?' He began to unclip Josie's oxygen mask, releasing it at the three attachment points and tucking the frozen piece of equipment deep into the recesses of her down suit. Then, removing his own mask, he placed it against Josie's mouth. 'Hold it to your face with your hands.'

Josie did as he instructed, drawing deeply on the oxygen, feeling the miraculous gas permeating every cell in her body with new life.

Hal brought out the walkie-talkie, turning with his back to the storm to protect it as best he could from the spindrift. He swallowed to bring some moisture to his dehydrated mouth, then spoke as loudly as he could to be heard above the wind rush. 'This is Hal to Todd at camp four. Do you read?'

There was no response.

'Hal Maher to *Daybreak* camp four. Do you copy?'

A barely audible voice replied. Hal had to pull his hood to the side to get the handset against his ear to hear it. 'Hal! This is Todd. Jesus it's a relief to hear your voice. We've been trying to get you for the last hour. We thought you might have been blown off the ridge. Is Josie all right, over?'

Hal paused to draw breath, beginning to feel dizzy as the loss of his oxygen supply struck. When he spoke, his words were slurred. 'She's . . . OK. We're about halfway along the ridge. Near the fixed ropes. We're on the last quarter bottle of gas. Listen, Todd, I need to know exactly where those two cylinders are at the south summit. Talk to Nima. Find out precisely where he left them. We have less than three metres vis up here. I may have to dig them out.'

'Roger that.'

'I'll call you when we get down there. I'm switching off to save battery power, OK?'

'Standing by.'

Hal put the handset away and helped Josie to her feet. The oxygen had restored some strength to her legs and she no longer burdened him with her weight. 'We're going to share this, OK?'

Josie nodded but he could see the fear in her eyes. He gently pulled the oxygen mouthset from her and placed it over his own face for a minute or so. Then he returned it and indicated they should move.

Holding the mask to her face with her left hand, Josie felt him take her right arm and lead her onwards into the wind, the two of them bent double against the unrelenting power of what was rapidly becoming a full-out storm.

69

The light was fading fast. Hal was struggling to make out anything through the darkened glass of his goggles. He had to hold his wrist right up close to see the watch face through the blackening storm. 'We got twenty minutes of daylight left. Keep moving, Josie. We can't stop here.'

Josie nodded sluggishly but made no effort to take a step. A small voice reached him: 'Help me stop it, Hal . . .' Crying out in a sudden howl of pain, Josie began to scrape at her eyes with the hard frozen fabric of her outer gloves.

Hal had to take his hands away from the rope to force her to stop. He put his arms round her, holding her tightly against him as she tried to force her hands back up to her face. Then she stopped struggling and pushed her head into the protection of his shoulder, her body stiffening as each wave of agony hit.

Lifting the goggles from his eyes, Hal scanned the section of ridge beneath them, cupping a hand against the side of his face for protection as he tried to focus. All he could see was the fixed rope descending into a shifting world of blacks and greys. He clapped Josie on her shoulders to get her attention. 'Time to go.'

She looked up at him, the whites of her eyes shockingly red from retinal haemorrhage. 'Rest?'

'No.' Hal checked her sling was attached to the fixed rope and moved a few steep steps down the ridge. He hit her hard on the back of the leg with his ice axe. 'Move this leg. Now!'

Shocked into motion, Josie moved the frozen limb forward a few inches. Hal grabbed the front of her waist harness and pulled her down towards him in a series of hesitant steps. Then, moving again to her side, he forced her as fast as he dared down the steep section of ridge, using the fixed rope for support.

Out of the gloom, the level terrain of a snow platform appeared, the terrace marking the dip between the sharp section of ridge and the rise of the south summit. Hal could see the huddled shapes of Sebastian and Rick nearby. He unclipped Josie from the rope and caught her fall as she collapsed on to her side. He arranged the hood of her suit to give her face maximum protection as she curled up, instinctively, into a ball to retain as much body heat as she could. 'I'm going to look for the oxygen.'

Hal heard a muffled 'OK' as he crouched down close to her to shout into the walkie-talkie: 'Hal to Todd.'

'Go ahead, Hal. Where are you?'

'Near the south summit. How do I find the gas?'

A blast of wind whipped away the answer.

'What? I don't hear you.' Hal pushed the handset right against his ear to hear the shouted response.

'On the west side. About five metres down.'

Hal turned off the unit and pulled a Granola bar from his pocket. Ripping off the foil wrapper with his teeth, he snapped it in two and pushed half into Josie's mouth. 'Stay right here. I'll be back as fast as I can.'

Standing too fast, Hal had to pause as stars flickered across his vision. Then he stepped over Josie on to the slope beyond, chewing the energy bar as he went to force down precious calories. Hardly visible in the rapidly failing light, the fixed ropes stretched away to the right. He knew they would take him too low to find the oxygen stash, which was less than thirty metres from where he now stood. The bottles were higher than his current position and the thought of coercing his deeply fatigued body to ascend once more sent a wave of despair through him.

Hal knew what was happening, he had been here before. Oxygen starvation was shutting him down. Anger began to well up inside him as he summoned the will-power to climb. How was he supposed to find the oxygen when he couldn't see his hand in front of his face? How the *hell* was he supposed to climb when his feet were so completely frozen? How had he let himself get caught by this *fucking* storm? By now they should be reaching the safety of the top camp. Hal imagined how it would feel to crawl out of the wind into the sanctuary of a tent, of a sleeping bag folded around him, of his fingers defrosting as he curled them around a steaming mug of tea. The fixed ropes were beating from side to side, whipping against the face. Hal watched them in a near trance, feeling their pull.

Deep inside him he felt a creature stir itself, a creature he had met before on other mountains. Uncoiling, it roused itself from a very long sleep and began its work. Hal had a name for it. He called it the altitude weevil, a blind white worm of a creature with – he imagined – the forked tongue of a snake. The altitude weevil began to whisper, a soft, hissing sound like the escaping gasses of a steam engine at rest: 'Look at the ropes. Where do you think they're going? They're going *down*, Hal. Down to safety. Down. To life.'

A massive clap of thunder ripped through the air.

'You want to live?'

Hal couldn't take his eyes off the rope.

'Clip yourself on. You've got the strength. If you do it on your own, four hours. That's all it'll take. You know the route.'

Hal felt the muscles in his neck tense as he tried to resist another urge.

'Turn your head, Hal.'

He looked back at Josie, a faint dark huddle, motionless and still, already partially covered with drifted snow.

The weevil was whimpering, excited, pleading, breathless: 'She's not going to make it, Hal.'

Hal closed his eyes, breathing deeply and fast.

'Come on, Hal.' Then, in the tiniest imaginable voice, a slow exhalation, no more than a child's breath: 'You've done it before.'

Hal felt a shout from somewhere inside him. 'No!' He stepped back on to the platform, beating Josie's back with his fists. 'Josie! Josie!'

Her head shifted to acknowledge him.

'We're going to make it, OK? We're going to make it! You have to believe that, OK? I'm going to get you off this mountain alive. Don't let go of that.'

Hal returned again to the slope, desperately trying to remember the topography of the bulging false summit. He chose a trajectory and moved away from the snow ledge. He climbed with his eyes screwed shut to protect them, smashing the ice axe deep into the slope and using what remained of his upper body strength to gain some height. Reaching an exposed section of rock, he paused for breath. He calculated he had gained five metres of height and guessed there were at least twenty metres of traversing to do before reaching the distinctive hump where the oxygen had been left.

He left the rock, striking out on to new ground, but came to a halt after just a few steps. Something felt wrong on his left boot. He shone the head torch down and found that his left crampon had wrenched free from its straps and was now dangling uselessly on to the surface of the snow. 'Son of a bitch.' Hal cursed this piece of bad luck. It was not unusual for crampons to become loose but the timing was as bad as it was possible to get. He knew that resecuring the iced-up metal spikes on to his boot would be an infernally difficult task – if he could achieve it at all with frozen fingers. He also knew that if he tried to continue with just one crampon attached, a fall would be virtually unavoidable once he was back on hard ice.

Hal swore again. He realised, as he looked with a surge of increasing anger at the dislodged crampon, that this could be the small piece of misfortune that sealed both their fates. Refitting that crampon could mean the difference between life and death . . . for them both.

70

Hal backtracked, descending through the deep snow to the exposed area of rock he had rested at before. Losing height was a depressing necessity – he knew from experience that he would need hard terrain to push against to refit the crampon.

At the rock, several hard blows from the ice axe removed the balled-up snow, which had accumulated on the base of the boot. Similar blows cleared the metal frame of the crampon. He placed it on the flattest section of the stony surface and positioned his boot on it with some difficulty. At the back of the crampon a tensioning device was designed to lock into a groove in the boot moulding. Unable to feel any sensation in his fingers, and hampered by the now feeble glow of his head torch, Hal fumbled to get it in place. Believing he had it, he pulled the plastic lever up hard. It was out of line, the crampon skidded sideways off the boot, causing him to lurch forward into a near fall.

Hal could feel the blood pumping in his head as he stooped to retrieve it – stars making frantic orbits across his field of vision. He repositioned the crampon – resisting with difficulty the urge to succumb to his anger and throw the thing off the mountain and be done with it. This time he got the alignment right, the boot stepping firmly into the frame, the back clamp clicking into place correctly. Hal peeled off his outer gloves to the thinnest inner layer and threaded the upper securing strap into the two alloy rings on the third attempt.

It was done.

Hal stood upright into the full brunt of the wind, confused and dazed after the period of intense concentration the operation had demanded. He stared up the incline towards the south summit, dreading the moment when he would have to commit once more. But commit to what? Why was he climbing up when he should be going down?

For a moment Hal experienced total disorientation, every function of logic and memory scrambled into a fuzz of forgotten objectives.

The oxygen. The cached bottles.

Hal remembered. But he wished he hadn't. The very thought of reascending the face, of wading to his groin in the clinging powder, of digging into the snow to extricate the bottles . . . ?

Time passed.

Then he wrapped the ice axe sling round his wrist and took the first of the steps back up the slope, his body aching, protesting as it had never done before.

71

Josie let her mind drift – away from the excruciating pain of her eyes; away from the biting cold that was seeking to destroy every cell of her body; away from the endless wait for Hal to return.

Time and place had ceased to have any meaning at all. She had given up trying to imagine how many minutes, hours or days Hal had been away, given up trying to remember where she was – or why. All Josie knew was that she had to find an escape route somehow and it was her mind that was about to find a way out.

She found she could change her surroundings at will. It was easy enough and much less painful than trying to put one foot in front of the other. That was for fools.

A few words from Hal floated into her mind and made her smile. Don't treat the mountain as an enemy, he had told her, treat the mountain as a friend. Josie liked that, it made a lot of sense, but which mountain? Josie tried to remember the name of the mountain she was on but soon gave up.

The penetrating wind was the first and greatest of the enemies. Changing it into a friend was deliciously easy, Josie found. How stupid she had been, wasting all that time worrying about how cold the wind was when in reality it was blowing warm air at one hundred miles an hour: a giant industrial heater. Josie had seen one once in a warehouse – a gas-fired device which pumped out a jet of unimaginable warmth. She remembered how good it had felt to stand before that blast and that was what it felt like now. The shivering had stopped. That has to be a good sign, she decided.

Through the distortion of ice that had grown around her eyes, she could see a dark shape lying on the terrace. It was just visible through the driving snow.

Sebastian.

Was that really Sebastian or was she imagining it? She rolled on to her front and began to crawl towards the body. But this was perfect

– Josie was laughing inside – that Sebastian should be here too, to comfort and care for her in this place.

Baby you're so cold.

He was so cold. Why was Sebastian so cold? Josie placed her cheek against his. She would warm him with her body, she decided, as she entwined herself as closely as she could.

She dreamed their embrace into a sleeping bag, into a cocoon of warmth so intense it was almost too much: of a fire in a Sherpa house, the excited eyes of the children gathered round it glinting in the orange light; of a village filled with the sound of laughter.

Of Sebastian laughing, kissing her tenderly.

But what about the noise? That was another enemy, wasn't it? The roar was debilitating. It nagged. It was corrosive. Josie had her hands cupped over her ears but it still punched through.

She forced her mind back to the village, back to the security of that place where warmth was dripping from the walls, where she lay in a glorious bed with Sebastian.

Somewhere in the night skies above the village the sound of a jet aircraft was approaching. Josie couldn't understand what the pilot was doing. He couldn't land in the dark on that strip. The rush of the engine noise increased in volume as the roar intensified. Now Josie was sure the pilot had made a terrible mistake. His engines were powering him right into the lodge. The sound was unbearable, intrusive, obscene. She pushed her hands against her ears but the roaring was inside her.

Then she felt the wind rushing around her face, the patter of the snow granules against her skin. She tried to open her eyes but could see nothing. She could sense that she was alone with Sebastian. Utterly alone, only the roar of the storm for company.

She curled herself back into the foetal position by his side, content. She took one of his hands in hers, curling the warmth of her living flesh around fingers that were frozen as hard as iron.

I love you.

What did the shrinks call it? Josie had a moment of lucidity before slipping away once more. Closure. That was most definitely the word.

72

Hal hauled himself on to the ridge a few metres from the south summit and retched a mouthful of semi-digested Granola bar on to the snow. He placed his hands against his temples, trying to squeeze away the pulse of the altitude headache. He felt detached from the panting noise he could hear, unable to believe that the rapid-fire breathing was his own.

The climb had driven new blood into the frozen cells of his hands and feet, stirring them painfully back to life. Hal clenched and unclenched his fingers inside the gloves, biting his lip as the frost-damaged tissue protested. He had to keep the fingers working – he would need them to screw the fresh oxygen supplies into the regulators. If he could find the bottles.

The wind was stronger on the exposed skyline, the cold blowing another tiny percentage of life out of him for every moment of inactivity. He shone the head torch on to his watch. It had taken almost one hour to retrace his route up the slope, a climb that he could have completed in less than ten minutes at sea level.

Josie. Hal suddenly thought of her. The brutal struggle to reach the south summit had taken him through so many pain barriers that he had blanked her from his mind. With a shock he realised he had left her for too long – far too long.

Would she still be conscious when he got back to her? Would she still be there? Hal knew how easily victims of altitude sickness became disorientated. If she believed she had been abandoned, Josie might try to move off the ledge where he had left her.

The paranoid thought pressed him to move away, down on to the softer snow of the slope that ran beneath him. Hal fought to remember Todd's words; what had he said about the position of the bottles? He stepped further down the slope, realising that he would have to take extreme care; the pack here was loose – classic avalanche conditions.

He began to traverse, striding first for ten steps one way then dropping down one pace and returning for the same distance in the other direction. He counted the steps under his breath and, knowing the oxygen cylinders would be at least partially buried, dragged his feet, hoping to knock against metal. Then it happened. His crampon spikes struck an unseen obstacle buried beneath the surface. His hopes rising, Hal scraped away the snow and shone the torch on to the exposed metal cylinder. It was olive green and obviously old – one of the thousands of discarded empty bottles littering the peak.

He resumed the search, traversing down a further step, moving with great care not to trigger an avalanche as he waded through another area of thigh-deep powder.

Ten minutes passed, fifteen. Hal could feel his entire body running down into a sluggish form of slow motion as he mechanically continued. Increasingly frustrated, he began to probe in the snow with his ice axe as he moved, trying to increase the odds of finding the cylinders. 'Help me find them!' he screamed at the wind.

Soon he was on the verge of blacking out from the extreme demands he was making of his body. It was now nineteen hours since he had set out with Josie from camp four and his body was desperate for rest. His gut instinct told him he was out of time. He couldn't risk leaving Josie any longer. A deep vein of fear ran through him as he considered what state she would be in by the time he returned to her.

He set off towards the snow platform, following the ridge line by keeping the sharp crest on his right-hand side and dropping down the slope, navigating by instinct alone.

Fifteen minutes later he stepped on to the platform, his head torch illuminating the still figure of Josie where she lay in Sebastian's arms. 'Oh, God.'

She was still lying in the foetal position, her face nestled out of sight beneath Sebastian's down suit. She was as immobile as he was, the bright colours of her outer clothing barely visible beneath the crystallised shroud of ice that now covered her.

If Hal hadn't known better he would have thought they were both dead. 'Josie!'

She did not respond.

'Wake up!'

Hal pulled the stiffened fabric of the wind suit back, shining the torch directly on to her. The face that he was looking at was barely recognisable.

Josie's eyes were two inflamed slits, the skin around them grotesquely puffed. The pupils barely dilated as the light hit them.

'Who is it?' Her voice was a rasping croak. 'I've been having such beautiful dreams.'

'I'm sorry I was away for so long.'

For the first time in hours the wind dropped for a few moments, falling away and leaving them in unaccustomed quiet. Hal could speak without having to raise his voice. 'We're going to get you back safely, Josie. You and me are going down together.'

'Why? What's the problem?'

Hal braced himself and tried to pull Josie away from Sebastian. She clung on hard, but he was stronger. He hauled her a few metres and cradled her head in his arms.

She turned towards him in confusion. 'Where's Sebastian? What have you done with him?'

The wind began its furious assault once more as Josie started to scream out loud: 'I'm blind, aren't I? Something has made me blind. I want to get my eyes back. And I want the pain to go away! Sebastian!'

Hal hustled her to her feet, striking her hard on the cheek with his hands to get her attention. 'Don't lose it now, Josie.'

She stumbled one awkward step forward, reaching the slope where the fixed ropes would begin. Then she lost the support of her legs, crashing down on her backside and forcing Hal to step backwards to keep his balance.

They were still on the platform, but only just.

She lay prone, making no attempt to protect her face from the full brunt of the wind. Hal yelled at her, hitting his hands repeatedly against her cheeks, harder than before. Desperation and anger gave him the strength to raise his voice so he was sure she could hear. 'Listen. If you stay here you are going to die. Do you hear me, Josie? Get up and move!'

Illuminated by the dying glow of the head torch, Josie's face remained impassive, as serenely indifferent as a death mask.

That was the moment when Hal knew. He had seen it before, the terrifying finality with which the human body could switch off at altitude.

Hal had gone beyond the point where his will-power alone could keep him standing. He lowered himself stiffly down and rested with his back to Josie, letting his mind blank out. There was no pain from his fingers and toes, they were too frozen for that. He let his eyes close, burying his head between his knees, forcing them against his ears to create a silent world of his own, away from the wind rush of the storm.

73

When the walkie-talkie clicked on, the voice was almost inaudible. Jammed into the camp four dome tent, Todd, Nima and Lhakpa struggled to decide if what they were listening to was someone trying to talk, or a trick of the wind outside as it blustered against the fabric of the flysheet.

Todd scribbled the time on a page of his notepad – 21.54. 'This is camp four to Hal. Is that you?'

The hiss of transmission noise came back. Todd adjusted the squelch control, tweaking it in the hope of better reception. 'Hal Maher. Do you read?'

Hal's voice came through: 'That you, Todd?'

'Yes.' A wave of jubilation ran through the tent. It had been more than four hours since the last transmission from the summit team. Todd pressed the transmit button. 'This is Todd. Where are you, Hal?'

'Up high.' He sounded drugged, lethargic, slurring from a combination of altitude and fatigue.

'Can you be more specific?'

There was a long pause before Hal came back again. 'I couldn't find the gas.'

'Shit! It was right there at the south summit.'

'That's where we are.'

'You're still at the *south summit* now?' Todd could not keep the crack of emotion from his voice.

Hal's reply was inaudible.

Todd spoke again: 'Hal. We need to know about Josie. How is Josie?'

There was no reply. The seconds ticked by with Todd swearing beneath his breath. 'I repeat. We need to know about Josie's condition. Do you read me, Hal?'

'Josie's right here.'

'Is she conscious?'

'She's alive.'

'Can I speak to her?'

'She's sleeping.'

'That's not good, Hal. Can you wake her up and get her moving?'

There was no reply. Then Todd remembered the syringe of dexamethasone he had given Hal just as he had left camp four. The powerful steroid was capable of rousing victims of altitude sickness – the benefits were temporary, lasting only an hour or less, but in this case it might get Josie on her feet. 'Hal. Have you still got the dexamethasone shot? Can you give it to Josie to bring her round?'

Hal's breathing came through for several seconds, laboured and fast, before he replied: 'She's hit the wall, Todd, but I'm not going to give her the dex while it's dark. There's no point when we can't move. I'll save it for daylight when we can see where the hell we're going.'

'Can you get her to the fixed ropes?'

'Not tonight. We'll make it through the night and come down at first light.'

'The storm is going to kill you if you're not moving. You'll be dead by morning, Hal. You know you can't do that.'

Another pause before Hal came on again. 'What time is it?'

'It's ten o'clock. You have eight hours before daybreak. Eight hours.'

'Can you send anyone up with some more bottles?'

'With the conditions the way they are? If Nima and Lhakpa go out into this white-out they'd never find the other side of the col.'

'We'll get through the night. And wait for the Sherpas to arrive.'

'You've got no shelter up there. As far as we can determine this storm is going to run all night. If the Sherpas leave at dawn they won't be at the south summit until one, two o'clock in the afternoon – they're both exhausted, Hal. They can't move fast.'

Hal made no reply.

Todd looked at the other two. They could not meet his stare. 'God help me', he whispered, 'for what I'm about to do.' He clicked on transmit. 'Hal. You have to think rationally. If Josie's unconscious then perhaps she can't be saved.'

'I can't leave her, you know that, Todd.'

Todd raised his voice. 'I'm just reminding you that you can't carry her down. No one's going to blame you if you have to leave her. You did everything you could and now's the time for hard facts.'

'No way, Todd. You remember how we did it on K2?'

Todd cast his mind back to the climb they had shared on the world's second-highest peak. He knew instantly what Hal was referring to – the ice shelter they had dug out of a slope to survive a storm. 'I remember that, Hal, but it was different – completely different. We were one thousand metres lower, we had plenty of oxygen and we were both in good shape at the start of a climb . . . not screwed up like you are at the tail end of a monster summit day a hop skip and a jump from the summit of Everest. Think about it! You might as well be on the moon there, Hal.'

'I've got a stove with me and some food. Josie's head torch has got some juice left in it. I'm going to eat a power bar and get my strength back up.'

'You stubborn idiot. Spot the difference. There's one of you, with a near-comatose, inexperienced client . . .'

Hal's transmission cut across him. 'I'm going to dig out a bivouac.'

'Don't waste your strength. If you've got anything left inside, use it to move down.'

'I'm turning the walkie-talkie off, Todd.'

'No, you're not. Don't you do that. Listen to me, Hal.'

A faint click came through the speaker.

Todd screamed: 'Hal!'

The line was dead.

Todd turned to Nima.

The Sherpa held his head in his hands. When he looked up there were tears in his eyes. 'I go to find Hal,' he said, anger sweeping across his face. He made to leave the tent.

'Not now,' Todd told him. 'Too much storm. You see nothing. If the storm stops then you go.'

'No. Hal needs me now.' Nima ripped back the tent flap, exposing the savage storm outside.

'Are you crazy? If you go out into that we'll never see you again. Then more people dead. Be sensible, wait for light, then go with Lhakpa.'

Nima slumped back, knowing in his heart that Todd was right. 'Then I pray to the gods.' He began to mutter beneath his breath.

Seconds later the satellite phone began to ring. Todd braced himself and picked up the receiver.

74

'Todd? Do you hear me? This is Rachel in Vancouver.'

Oh, God, Todd thought, *this is going to be bad.* 'Rachel. Yes I read you. Speak as loud as you can, there's a lot of wind roaring around the tent.'

'Are they down yet? I just wanted to check. Deborah and I have been sitting here drinking champagne and I suddenly felt bad – like what are we celebrating when we didn't even bother to check they got down? Can I speak to Hal? Or is he sleeping?'

'Rachel, Hal and Josie are not back in the camp yet.'

Rachel stuttered, 'Not back? Then . . . where are they?'

'They're going to be spending the night up high.'

'Up high? How high?'

'Rachel, we have white-out conditions here. They can't see to find the route right now. But I'm sure they'll make their way down just as soon as it clears up . . .'

'They can't see? Is it a storm?'

'Just after they left the summit it blew in.'

Rachel sounded detached, ripped cruelly out of her euphoric state. 'Like Sebastian and Rick,' she said. 'It's all going to happen over again, isn't it?'

A new voice suddenly broke in: 'Todd?' It was Deborah.

'Reading you.'

'What the hell's happening?'

'They're benighted on the summit ridge.'

'In what conditions?'

'It's not the worst I've seen on Everest, but it's bad.'

'Have they got shelter?'

'Hal was talking about digging a bivouac.'

'Oh, my God. Can you patch us through to Hal?'

'I don't want to do that. His batteries are getting low.'

'OK. I understand. All right.' Deborah was going to be the strong one, Todd recognised by the way she sounded.

Rachel came back on the line, tearful, her voice strained and loaded with dread: 'Don't let them die, Todd. Do anything to save them.' Then a thought hit her. 'Is Nima there?'

'He is.'

'Let me speak to him.'

Todd handed the young Sherpa the handset.

'Yes, this is Nima.'

'This is Rachel. I'm Hal's girlfriend. We've never met but Hal often speaks of you. Nima, if you have it inside you . . . can you go up to rescue them?'

'I will try,' he promised. 'I will do everything for Hal.'

'Thank you, Nima. I'm depending on you, do you understand? You could make the difference.'

'I understand.'

Todd took the handset again, 'I want to save this power cell. We'll call you when we have any more news.'

'All right. We'll wait here.'

The line went dead.

Todd felt dreadful. He could picture the scene in Deborah's house following the call, the two women consoling each other, Rachel facing the possibility that she was about to lose the man she loved, Deborah with the weight of two lives on her shoulders. He looked at Nima. 'I'm never coming back to this mountain, Nima.'

'And me too. If Hal die I never come back. My father killed. Now . . . ?' He unzipped the tent flap a little and looked out into the storm.

'How's it looking?' Todd asked him.

The Sherpa shook his head.

75

Hal pushed the sharpened tip of the ice axe into the steeply angled wall. He was standing less than ten metres from Josie's position on the western side of the crest. The ice was iron hard, too dense to be easily cut away. An experimental blow with the cutting edge of the ice axe blade merely scratched the surface. He swore, taking two more steps on to the incline and shining the head torch on to another section. He tried it with the axe.

The same story. Hal had begun to doubt that he would find a suitable place to dig, he had been criss-crossing the face for almost half an hour probing and testing with the axe.

He pushed the tip in again. This time the ice felt different, softer and more granular. He twisted the axe and raised it to strike a downward blow. The broad edge bit deeply into the face, producing a quantity of loose crystals. Hal tested a metre to the right. The conditions were the same. The slope was perfectly angled to be cut into.

Encouraged, he began to scrape slowly at the face, drawing the axe down in long sweeping movements, eating away at the compacted snow. He found a rhythm and kept to it despite the intense muscle ache of his arms and shoulders, and the dull pain in his lungs as he demanded more oxygen than the altitude could deliver. He worked by feel, finding that the easist section to scrape away was producing a roughly circular area approximately a metre across. After ten or fifteen minutes he rested, trying to suppress the urge to vomit from the exertion. He had scraped a hollow about ten inches deep into the face.

'Too slow.' Hal knew he had to push himself harder. He picked up the ice axe and began again, increasing the frequency of the blows as the snow texture hardened. Breathe. Breathe. Breathe. He had to use the haft of the axe to smash into the surface, loosening it into chunks, which he then raked out.

The hole deepened further, the granules of eroded ice flying as Hal powered into the face. Gradually the composition of the snow changed again – Hal began pulling out book-sized blocks.

Unexpectedly, the ice axe plunged into a part of the face with no resistance. Confused, Hal shone the head torch into the scraped-out area, squinting to try to see any detail through the blowing snow flying around him. 'Holy shit.'

Hal could scarcely believe what the head torch revealed. A hole the size of a cigarette packet had opened into the face. There was a hollow area behind. Increasingly excited, he pushed in the axe and began to pull at the edges. It was easy work to enlarge it and after three or four minutes he had excavated it wide enough to push his head inside.

By the light of the torch Hal saw the best sight of his life. The interior was hollowed out into a coffin-shaped space about a metre high which, with some work, would allow two people to lie side by side. Drifted snow filled one end but Hal knew he could soon clear it. For the first time in hours he savoured a few moments of protection from the wind blasting against his face. 'There is a God, man. There is a God.'

Now, the peculiar ease with which he had excavated into the mountain made perfect sense. Hal realised he had been cutting into the entrance hole of an old bivouac site. He looked at the walls of the interior, noting the axe marks where whoever had built it had scraped a bigger space.

'Great job.' Hal was stunned by his good fortune. He had often been lucky in his climbing career but this was uncanny. What were the chances of stumbling on an old bivouac site like this?

And who had it belonged to?

Hal knew of at least six or seven instances in the history of Everest when climbers on their summit day had been forced by bad weather to bivouac near or on the south summit. Several had dug big snow holes such as this one. The discovery gave Hal a new shot of optimism. Now he had a fighting chance of getting Josie through the night.

He put the axe to one side and began to open up the entrance with his hands. The loosely packed snow crumbled away with little resistance and he quickly scooped it out so that he could push his upper body into the cavity. He began to clear out the drifted snow from the far end of the shelter, pushing it out down the face behind him like a burrowing animal.

When he was satisfied he had created enough space, Hal wriggled backwards to exit the bivouac and carefully crossed the slope back to the platform where Josie lay. He knew there was no prospect of getting her on to her feet. 'Josie. I found a shelter. I'm going to pull you across the slope for a while.'

She made no movement.

'Do you hear me?'

Her hand lifted a little, then flopped back down on to the ice.

Hal bent down and placed his hands under her arms. Shuffling awkwardly backwards, he dragged Josie against the full force of the wind for several steps until he reached the edge of the platform. 'OK. Now we're going on to the slope.' Hal knew that this was going to be precarious. He would literally be holding Josie's life in his hands. If a violent blast came through and he lost his grip she would slide off the mountain to oblivion.

He stepped backwards, praying that he would be able to keep his balance.

Rest. Breathe. Breathe. Breathe. Power backwards a few more inches. Rest. Breathe. And so on. And on. Hal had no idea how long it took him to haul Josie across the ten-metre distance but it felt like hours. By the time he got her to the bivouac entrance his world was spinning and Josie was dangling almost vertically beneath him. He drew a few enormous breaths and with a last supreme effort hauled her up in a single movement, turning her so that the top part of her body was leaning into the bivouac entrance.

Hal collapsed against her, resting his face on the soft fabric of her down suit. He felt as though he had just sprinted three marathons back to back.

'Hal?'

'I'm here, Josie. Stay calm. You have to help me now. I'm going to take off your pack.' He released the straps of her rucksack and looped the pack around the ice axe to secure it. 'Now, push yourself up into the shelter.'

'I don't understand.'

'Just lift your leg up and move inside the hole.'

He pushed her from behind as she lifted her knee stiffly on to the lip of the entrance. Josie slid into the snow hole head first and lay full length on her side. Hal pushed her pack in and followed it with his own, which he dumped on top of her. Then, pushing her cramponed feet away to the side of the shelter, he climbed in beside her.

How to seal the entrance? Hal took Josie's rucksack and jammed it across the hole, half covering it. It was an imperfect seal through which bursts of spindrift still blew, but the worst of the wind was excluded.

Hal collapsed on to his back, a wave of relief overwhelming him as he lay by Josie's side – finally out of the punishing wind. He cradled Josie's head in his arms, close to tears. 'I'm going to make you warm now, Josie. Going to get you through the night.'

'Are we in the camp?'

'Yeah. We're in a camp. A five-star camp.'

Hal shone the head torch around the interior. Whoever had built the snow hole had done a professional job. He found it was high enough for him to sit upright next to Josie.

Now they had a fighting chance.

76

A niche had been carved out of the ice wall big enough to take a gas cooker. There were signs that someone had used the space for that purpose, an iced-up tea bag was solidified into the floor and there was a brown stain, as if a pan of drink had been spilled there.

Hal pulled off his gloves and scrutinised his fingers. They were frozen but had sustained no more than frostnip – the waxy texture of the skin indicated surface damage but the deep tissue was still safe.

He undid the front of his wind suit and unzipped the down suit within. He placed his hands under the thermal layers into the warmth of his armpits and counted the minutes as the fingers thawed out. The relief that he had not so far suffered frostbite went some way to compensating for the pain the process involved.

Leaving Josie to sleep for the moment, Hal pulled his rucksack up on to his legs. He opened the main section of the pack and brought out the few precious items which, he knew, would now play a critical role in their chances of survival.

For every single day, of the thousands of days he had spent in the mountains as a professional guide, Hal had carried a basic emergency kit with him. How many times he had cursed the extra weight on the hundreds of climbs that had gone to plan. How many times he had packed his rucksack and been tempted to leave them behind. But he never did. That was one of the reasons why he was still alive.

Placed in a pile, it looked anything but life-saving: a superlight Gore Tex survival bag, a cut-down foam sleeping mat, a burner unit for cooking with, a full canister of butane gas, a small aluminium pot and two red survival packs, each containing one thousand five hundred calories of mixed high-energy rations. Hal knew the combined weight precisely. It was two point nine kilos.

He unrolled the Gore-Tex survival bag and began the awkward task of placing it along the length of the shelter floor. He had to roll Josie against the ice wall to push the fabric beneath her. Then he did the same with the cut-down piece of foam, placing it widthways so they would both benefit from its insulation.

Next, fluids. Hal knew they were both critically dehydrated. He had to get at least a litre into each of them if they were to stand a chance.

Food would come later.

He picked up the burner unit and checked the black rubber O ring seal was in place in the valve. Then he screwed the unit into the thread in the top of the new Epigas container, hearing the tiny hiss of escaping gas as the seal shut tight. Snapping an ice screw off his belt, Hal scraped hard shavings of ice off the wall of the shelter into the aluminium pan. When it was half full he placed the lid on top and put the pot on the cooker in the niche. Hal found his lighter in an inside pocket and held it against the burner unit. He opened the valve, flicking his thumb against the flint in quest of a spark. The flint was sharp and after twenty or thirty strikes there was blood running from his broken skin. Deprived of oxygen, the gas was reluctant to fire even when he did manage to make a spark.

The shelter filled with the nauseating stench of uncombusted butane as he repeated the process over and over. Hal began to fear that when he did get a spark the loose gas might be dense enough to create a fireball.

Finally, he got the burner to catch.

Hal watched the ring of blue flame roar into life, then – despite himself – fell asleep, waking with a start ten minutes later. For a panic-stricken moment he had no idea where he was – the head torch had fallen from his hand, leaving him with little light to see by.

The storm was still blowing spindrift through the gaps at the far end of the shelter. Their legs were covered with a thin dusting of snow.

Next to him the cooker was burning, the last of the ice just melting in the pan. Hal didn't need to protect his fingers from the heat as he lifted the aluminium pot off the gas – the metal was nowhere near hot enough to damage his skin.

He poured a little of the warm liquid into the plastic mug and ripped open one of the sachets of chocolate powder from the emergency ration pack. He tipped it into the mug, stirring it into a paste with his knife, then added the rest of the fluid. It smelled enticingly sweet. His body craved the sugar and the warmth it would bring. But Josie had to come first. 'Josie.'

She stirred next to him.

'You have to drink.'

He raised her head with his right hand and tried to hold the mug to her lips.

Josie turned her head away.

'Wake up.' He pulled her upright again and held the mug beneath her nose. 'Smell that. It's hot chocolate. I want you to drink it now.'

Josie parted her lips, letting the fluid enter her mouth, swallowing it in small gulps. He got one third of the contents inside her and waited patiently as a coughing fit racked her body. Then he resumed the task, making sure not a drop was spilled.

When the mug was empty Hal turned his attention back to the cooker. He packed the pan with more snow and put it on the burner to begin the process of melting once more.

Getting calories into Josie was his next priority. He opened the emergency ration packs and considered the contents. Sugar would provide the fastest hit; each pack contained a 200-gram bar of mint cake – peppermint-flavoured compacted sugar. He unwrapped both bars and fed one to Josie in small pieces before eating his own. The benefits were fast, within minutes Hal could feel the sugar being absorbed into his bloodstream.

Later he would boil up the foil sachets containing ready-cooked food – one was filled with beef goulash and another with a fruit compote.

Josie's hands were the next priority. Hal pulled off the four gloves on her right hand, struggling with the last silk layer, which was frozen stiffly in place. Her flesh was icy to the touch. Josie was passive, still only half aware of what he was doing.

He let out a low whistle as her fingers were revealed. He had been expecting damage but not this much. Only her little finger and thumb were untouched. The other three fingers were grossly distorted with the fluid-filled blisters that indicated first-degree frostbite. At the edges of the blisters Hal could see the tell-tale encroachment of black tissue. The necrotising effects of gangrene would set in if he didn't act fast.

Hurriedly he ripped off the gloves from Josie's left hand. It was even worse; all four fingers were blistered. Moving carefully in the confined space, Hal shifted his position until he lay full length next to Josie. He took her hands and placed them under his armpits, shivering as the frozen tissue drew heat away from his skin.

Josie began to murmur, calling his name in a low voice several times. Hal knew what was happening: the pain of thawing out her hands was pulling her out of whatever dream state she was in. Ten minutes later Josie was conscious enough to talk. 'What's happening? My hands are burning. First my eyes, now my hands.' Instinctively she tried to pull them out – away from the pain.

Hal locked them in position. 'Stick with it, Josie. Just a little longer. Can you move the fingers?'

'No.'

Josie pushed her face into Hal's shoulder and bit into the fabric of his suit as the warm blood seeped back agonisingly slowly into the tissue of her hands, capillary by capillary, cell by frozen cell.

Hal used the time as best he could, scraping more ice from the walls of the snow hole with his knife and adding it to the melting pot.

As soon as Josie could command her fingers to move, Hal let her withdraw her hands. He showed her how to continue the warming process herself.

Now the second pan of water was ready. Hal chose the remaining chocolate powder and prepared the drink, this time adding a sachet of muesli to the liquid. He retrieved a small plastic spoon from the side pocket of his rucksack and stirred the concoction. He allowed himself precisely half the fluid and, as closely as he could estimate, ate half the warm muesli. The rest he spooned into Josie's mouth. 'Josie?'

'Uh-huh.'

'You know what we did with your hands?'

'I know how it felt.'

'We're going to have to do the same thing with your feet.'

She said nothing.

Hal crawled forward to a position where he could reach Josie's feet. He unlaced the double ring fastener on the crampons and pushed down the quick release at the heel to free them. Then, cursing as the frozen fabric of the laces bit into his fingers, he proceeded to undo the boots.

The plastic outer shells came off first, followed by the softer inner boots. Inside that, Josie's feet were locked into three layers of socks with a Gore Tex vapour barrier between the silk layer and the first layer of Capilene. Hal put the socks into an inner pocket of his down suit to keep them warm as he removed them. When he got to the final silk layer he paused. He was deeply fearful of what state Josie's feet would be in.

Hal knew that finding the bivouac had dramatically increased their odds of survival. But if she couldn't walk, Josie was as good as dead.

She had to have the use of her feet. Hal pulled the frozen silk fabric away from the flesh, praying under his breath . . .

77

Josie felt the sweetness of the warm liquid against her lips as Hal offered the mug once more. She propped herself on her elbow to drink, finding to her surprise that she had the strength to hold the mug herself. Her fingers felt alien, bloated and distorted, the skin stretched tight by the build-up of fluid inside. She drank the liquid quickly and felt Hal take back the mug. She heard the scraping noise as he shaved more ice off the wall into the pan to begin the melting process all over again.

'I'm going to heat up the meals,' he told her.

Josie nodded. Speaking was a big effort for her.

Her feet were still aching from the brutal process of defrosting. After the hours – or was it days? – it had taken him to massage them back to life, Hal had replaced the socks and the inner boots, and told her she would be able to walk in the morning. He could have been lying, Josie knew, but as she was unable to see the condition of the frostbite herself she had no choice but to take his word. What she did know was that both her hands and her feet felt as she had never known them to feel before – as if they had been sewn back on after a botched amputation.

Her eyes had stabilised, more or less. The searing acid attacks of earlier had now been replaced by a dull, thumping pulse of pain, which stubbornly refused to go away. There was a gritty texture to the tissue, as if someone had thrown a teaspoon of sand into each eyeball.

Josie shivered. The snow shelter was just warm enough to keep her body core at a level to sustain life but she was definitely not what she would call warm. She shifted on to her side, then on to her back, but no one position was any warmer than another. The cold was all pervading and it wasn't going to let her go.

The hiss of the gas cooker resonated through the shelter: white noise. Josie felt her mind slipping back into another escape route;

what did they call those things in space? A weird name for them. Wormholes. That was what she needed. A wormhole to suck her out of this reality and spit her into another.

'You're doing fine, Josie,' Hal told her. 'You're going to come through this, OK?'

Josie held out her hand and felt him take it in his. He raised it upwards and she felt the warmth of his breath as he blew gently on to the fingers.

Hal let Josie rest. He had forced as much food and liquid as he could into her body and the sleep would help restore her strength for the descent. If she had any strength left to give. He checked his watch. It was 3.30 a.m. He realised he had left it far too long since the last radio call down to camp four. They would be going out of their minds with worry. He found the walkie-talkie in the side pocket of the pack and switched it on. 'Come in, Todd.' Hal had to turn the volume right up to hear the reply, the batteries were on the way out.

'This is me. What's happening, Hal?'

In all the years they had spent together on expeditions, Hal had never heard Todd so distraught. 'I have to keep this quick, man. There's not much juice in the radio. I found a bivouac site near the south summit. We're going to leave here at first light. You have to get the Sherpas to come up and meet us as high as they can with some oxygen and fluids. Do you copy?'

'I read that, Hal. What kind of state is Josie in? Are you sure she'll be strong enough to get down?'

'I'm loading her up with calories so she has to be in with a fighting chance. I'll give her the dexamethasone shot just before we leave.'

'Is she conscious?'

'She's sleeping.'

'What about frostbite?'

Hal looked at the waxy texture of his fingers. The greenish-coloured skin was beginning to puff up and blister. 'Tell the doc he's going to have two patients.'

'Roger that.'

'Have you spoken to Rachel?'

'She called. I spoke to her and Deborah. You can imagine how they are. Rachel wanted me to patch her through to you but I didn't think we could spare the battery power.'

'You did the right thing. If she calls again, tell her I'm in control of the situation and give her my total love, OK?'

'Hey, one more thing, Hal.'

'Go ahead.'

'I'm so sorry for what I said earlier. Maybe it was too soon to tell you to bail out. But if it gets to the stage where Josie can't move . . .' Todd struggled to find the words.

'I know what you're saying.'

'I'm signing off now. Nima and Lhakpa will be coming up just as soon as they can get themselves together.'

'Over.'

All was quiet but for Josie's irregular breathing.

Hal sat for a few minutes trying to work out what had changed. Then he realised – the rumble of the wind had eased away. The holes in the makeshift doorway were no longer blowing with the steady blast of spindrift. The storm had blown itself out.

Hal leaned back against the ice wall of the shelter and tried to think rationally. If the weather was clear when they exited the shelter then surely he stood a chance of getting Josie down? But did she have another day of effort inside her? Hal was not at all sure.

Next to him, Josie murmured, unable to sleep as she found herself increasingly suffering from the cold. Chill fingers of frost had begun to work their way beyond the easy targets of fingers and toes, deeper into her legs and arms. Hal tried to warm her with his body as her shivering began to get violent. She could sense what he was doing but felt no benefit. To her, the cold was an assailant – an enemy intent on destroying her. Josie began to fear that the cold was now so deep inside her that she would never chase it out again.

78

Nima tightened the shoulder straps on his rucksack and stared up into the night sky as he waited for Lhakpa to finish his own preparations. Todd was standing beside him outside the tent, shifting restlessly from one foot to the other as he attempted to keep warm. 'What's the time?' Nima asked him.

Todd checked his watch. 'Four thirty.'

'Getting late.' Nima shook the top of the tent with his gloved hand. 'Hurry!' he called to Lhakpa.

The silhouette of the ridge was just visible in the thin cast of starlight, the snow glowing with a weak luminosity against the ebony black of the night. 'Storm finished,' Nima said. 'But now plenty soft snow. Not good for fast climb.'

'I know. And bad for avalanches.'

'You have walkie-talkie for me?'

'I don't. This is the last one with any power left.'

'Dangerous. We have problem we can't tell you.'

'I know. But there's nothing else we can do.'

'Not good.'

Nima bent down and pulled back the flaps of the tent to see if Lhakpa was ready. His fellow Sherpa had taken over two hours to prepare himself, moving with irritating slowness as he donned his down suit and struggled to fix his boots. Nima spoke rapidly in his own language: 'Get moving. The day is nearly here.'

'I'm moving as fast as I can,' Lhakpa snapped. 'You want to go ahead that's fine by me.'

Nima tried to quell his anger. He knew that Lhakpa had suffered badly from altitude sickness over the last two days and that he had already been exhausted from carrying up their load to the south summit. He was an older man, with less energy to spare. Nevertheless, his recalcitrance was beginning to wear Nima down. 'Let me help with those,' he offered, crouching into the entrance of the tent to assist Lhapka with the cumbersome task of stretching his neoprene gaiters over his plastic boots.

Finally Lhakpa was ready. He emerged from the tent and pulled the hood of his high-altitude suit tight around his head for protection. 'How high we go?' he asked Todd aggressively.

'I don't know. If Hal manages to get Josie moving then they'll come down towards you. That's the best case. The worst . . . if he doesn't get her out of the bivouac, you have to get to the south summit.'

'Climbed to south summit yesterday,' Lhakpa reminded him. 'Left oxygen already. What happened to oxygen?'

'I don't know. No one knows. But their lives are depending on you.'

Lhakpa returned to his native tongue. 'If he can't find the oxygen, it's not our fault,' he muttered angrily to no one in particular. 'We did our job. No one asks Sherpas to go to the south summit twice. I've been to Everest many times and never . . .'

'Be quiet,' Nima told him, angry himself now. 'It's not our job to wonder what happened. It happened like that. Now both depending on us. We stay here, they die. You want to go back to the Khumbu and everyone in your village knows you left them to die? Where's your strength?'

Lhakpa pulled his hood to one side and spat noisily on to the ice. 'Why you no go?' He stabbed Todd in the chest with his hand. 'You never go high.'

'My job is here,' Todd said. 'If I leave here, then no one to run communications. Then no one knows who is dead or alive. I have to be on the end of this radio to talk to Hal if he needs us.'

Lhakpa turned away with a sigh.

'Are we on or not?' Todd turned to Nima, unsure whether Lhakpa was even now about to pull out.

'We go.' Nima pushed Lhakpa gently away from the tent.

Uttering a silent prayer to the gods, Nima led the way across the col, heading towards the snow ramps for the second time in two days, the dead weight of the three oxygen bottles pulling down on his spine and bringing an ache to his legs even on this flat ground. 'Today is a day to be strong,' he told himself. 'That is what my father would have wanted.' Behind him he could hear Lhakpa breathing hard, his breath coming in short bursts, peppered with the occasional swear word as he tried to keep pace with the younger man.

79

'Wake up, Josie.' She felt her body jerk as something tugged at her shoulder. 'It's time to go.'

She realised a cooker was hissing nearby. Why had Hal lit the gas again?

'Josie. It's light. Time to move.'

Then her mind ripped her back to the last place in the world she wanted to be. Josie held up her hand and felt the hard contact of the ice ceiling.

Her eyes had improved a little, now she could see dim images of her surroundings, the light filtering from the entrance of the snow shelter, Hal crouched over the stove next to her.

'We made it through the night, Josie. Now we're going to get one last brew inside us, we're going to get our boots and crampons on and we're going down.' Hal added a handful more ice to the slowly heating pan of water and shuffled forward to the entrance. He kicked out the top layer of snow from the hole, pulled Josie's pack inside and poked his head out. 'Want to know what I'm looking at?'

'OK.' Josie forced herself up into a sitting position, the muscles in her back horrifically stiff from lying all night on the hard ice floor.

'I'm looking at a clear day. Not much blue sky out there but it's clear enough to navigate our way down the fixed ropes. The Sherpas will be on their way up now. We'll meet them in a couple of hours and then we'll cruise down to camp four.'

'I still can't see much.'

'That won't stop us. I'll sort out the harness and get you clipped on to the ropes. I'll guide you down every step of the way.' Hal took out the syringe Todd had given him and removed it from its plastic case. 'Now don't move while I give you the steroid.'

He squirted a fine jet of the clear liquid into the air to clear the needle and then injected it right through Josie's many layers of clothing, directly into her thigh.

Josie didn't flinch as the needle went in, but the effects of the steroid were fast and dramatic, rather like a fainting victim given smelling salts. 'God, I can feel that working,' she told Hal, 'like waking up from a deep sleep.'

She felt a tingling sensation as the steroid ran through her, energising exhausted tissue in every part of her body.

'It doesn't last long,' Hal warned her. 'An hour at most, so we have to move fast.'

'My fingers feel like they're going to burst.'

'Let me see them.'

Josie held up her hands and let Hal pull off her gloves. The blisters had increased in size, the skin at the edges blacker than before. Hal knew that it was critical to get Josie to some basic medical attention within the next twelve hours. He also knew that giving her that news would not be good for her morale.

'How are they?'

'They've stabilised. Looking good. They'll be swollen like that for a while but they should work out fine.'

Josie was feeling ever more alert – enough to see through Hal's words. 'I'm going to lose them, aren't I?'

'Not if you're prepared to fight.' Hal replaced the gloves carefully.

'Hold me, Hal. I'm scared. I want to be sure you're really here.'

Hal embraced her as best he could in the confined space of the shelter. 'I want you to be positive about what we're about to do, OK?'

'I don't know if my legs are going to work.'

'Don't think like that. Compared with how it could be we're in very good shape. We've had a full night of shelter, fluid and food.'

Hal checked his watch. It was seventeen minutes past 6 a.m. The two Sherpas would now be on their way up the steep ice face from camp four with the relief supplies of oxygen and fluid. He packed his rucksack and turned to the tricky task of getting Josie dressed. Her plastic outer boots were next to his own by the entrance. Hal positioned himself with her feet in his lap and slid the hard shell over the softer inner boots. Her feet had swollen in the night so that he had to use force to get them fully on. The laces were a problem: the cords had frozen together in a ball. Hal picked at the iron-hard strands with the numb ends of his fingers, cursing continuously beneath his breath as the work reopened old splits in the skin.

Then it took a good five minutes blowing on his fingers to defreeze them enough to tackle his own boots.

The crampons came last, they also gave Hal a problem. Both the sets of metal spikes had acquired a coating of ice, which was now set like concrete. Hal laboriously chipped the excess ice away with his knife. When he had finished, he snapped the crampons on to both sets of boots and checked that Josie's harness was still correctly fastened in place round her waist. 'I'll make a fast call down to camp to let them know we're moving out.' Hal switched on the walkie-talkie. 'Hal to Todd.'

'This is Todd.'

'We're kitted up and moving out of the bivouac.'

'That's a big relief, Hal. We're in cloud down here; what have you got up there?'

'It's clear. Are the Sherpas on their way up to meet us?'

'Affirmative. They left at four forty-five this morning.'

'Nothing more to say. I'll give you a progress report later on. Out for the moment.'

'Over and out.'

Hal cut the transmission and pulled his pack to the entrance. 'Are you ready to go?'

Josie stirred herself to a sitting position.

'OK. I'm going to exit first. You shuffle forward and crawl out after me. Remember it's steep terrain out there so get yourself planted on your feet on the ledge and don't move anywhere until I tell you to. I'll put you on a short rope. You get that?'

'I guess.'

'We traverse across the slope to the fixed ropes and then we'll be singing and dancing all the way down to the col.'

'OK.'

'So let's move.' Hal turned his head to the entrance.

And froze.

A face was staring into the shelter.

'Oh, my God.' Hal recoiled, breathing heavily from the shock.

'What is it? What's happening?' Josie was confused by Hal's sudden cry.

'It's OK. Just stay calm. I'll sort this out.'

The face staring at Hal was so ravaged by frostbite it looked as though it had been burned in a fire. The eyes were nothing more than slits in the midst of huge swellings, the whites bloodshot and the pupils dull. The frostbite damage was by far the worst that Hal had ever seen – and he had seen much. The nose and cheeks were blistered jet-black – the skin the colour of charcoal. Blood seeped from the pores where the cells had frozen, expanded and burst their contents to the surface. The lips were blue, indicating severe hypoxia, and beneath them the beard had accumulated a mass of ice. The central section of the beard was stained red from the blood that seeped from the mouth in a continual frothy spume.

With some effort the climber parted his lips, ice cracking around them as he did so. 'Help me.'

Then Hal realised. 'Andrei? Jesus Christ, Andrei, is that you?'

80

The climber made no response, merely swaying from side to side, small red-flecked bubbles emitting from his mouth each time he breathed out. Hal watched him closely, unable to tear his eyes away from the horror of the frostbitten face.

'Speak to me, Hal. Are the Sherpas here?' Josie was disturbed by the long silence.

'It's not the Sherpas. It's Andrei. He's in a hell of a state.'

'Andrei? Who is Andrei?'

'The Ukrainian we met on the ridge. He's been out all night in the storm.'

'Are we going to move?'

Hal made a fast decision. 'Andrei. Can you hear me?'

The Ukrainian shook his head.

'We're going down to camp four. I'm going to help you as far as I can but I have Josie with me. You remember her? I'll be looking after her on the fixed ropes but if you can descend with us I'll make sure you stick on the right route. Do you understand?'

Andrei began to raise his arm and Hal could see his hands for the first time. He realised that what he had thought was a black glove was actually Andrei's fingers. His hands were completely consumed with frostbite. In the right hand, clenched by fingers that were locked into position, was a yellow plastic object. At first Hal thought it might be a radio of some kind but as Vasylenko raised the hand to his face he saw it was the same cheap plastic camera he had held as he passed them on the summit ridge. 'No photo.' The Ukrainian stared at the camera just inches from his face.

'Andrei. Never mind about your photograph. That doesn't matter now. The storm is finished. We can all go down. Move aside and I'll help you get to the fixed ropes.'

'No!'

In a clumsy movement Andrei raised his left arm and pushed his ice axe into the shelter, narrowly missing Hal's face. Then he began to scramble into the entrance.

Hal placed his hands on Vasylenko's shoulders, blocking him. 'Andrei, you don't have time to come in here. You are running out of time.'

'Don't tell me this. You have bivouac. You want to keep bivouac.' Andrei began to push hard against Hal's arms, forcing his head and shoulders into the shelter and pinning Hal against the back wall. Hal pushed back as strongly as he could but the power of the Ukrainian was too much. Andrei brought up his hands and began to beat them wildly at Hal, striking his head and shoulders with the frozen limbs, the camera still gripped in the right hand. 'Let me! Let me!'

Andrei twisted his upper torso, releasing his shoulders from Hal's grip. He lunged forward until half of his body was inside, then, using his knees to lever himself against the entrance wall, he forced the rest of his body into the space. His crampons dug into Hal's leg as he kicked his way in, ripping the down suit and cutting through the thermal layers to puncture four holes in the calf.

Andrei came to a halt, half smothering Josie and with his feet resting on Hal's lap. He was panting furiously with the effort, spraying specks of blood against the ice wall.

'OK. Now rest. Now rest.'

'I can't breathe, Hal.' Josie was struggling to free herself from the weight that constricted her.

Hal pushed Andrei to the side and lifted the feet away from his lap so that the Ukrainian was lying prone alongside Josie in the position he himself had occupied through the night. Hal was now jammed, sitting upright with his knees against his chest, right by the entrance. 'Fuck this.' Hal pulled up his protective suit to expose the wounds on his calf. The puncture holes went deep into the flesh but his blood was so thick from dehydration that they leaked only the merest trickle of fluid.

Intimidated by Hal's silence, Josie spoke. Her voice was thin and filled with fear. 'Are we going now?'

Andrei reacted violently as he heard her words. 'No leave! Help me! Look my hands!' He pushed his hands towards Josie's face.

'She's snow-blind, Andrei. She can't see anything. Show them to me.'

Vasylenko put his hands inside his down suit and turned away from

Hal. 'I don't want.' He let out a groan of pain and began muttering in his native tongue.

'Hal. Let's go now.' Josie's voice held a new urgency. 'The shot's not going to last for ever. I feel strong enough to get out.'

Hal looked down at the Ukrainian. He was lying on his side, shivering violently, with his eyes screwed shut. A stream of Russian was tumbling from his lips. Hal felt nausea welling up in his throat. The brief struggle with the other man had left him dizzy and exhausted. He collapsed against the ice wall and tried to remember a time when he had ever felt so tired.

'What are we waiting for?' Josie had to raise her voice to make herself heard above Andrei's muttering.

'Let me think.'

'About what?'

Hal exploded in a burst of anger. 'Give me a fucking chance, Josie! Things are changing around here. I have to think my way through it, all right?'

'No, it's not all right.' Josie began to shuffle her way forward on her backside in an attempt to reach the entrance. 'We're leaving. I am *not* going to die here.'

'And Andrei?'

Josie swung her boots awkwardly over the prone figure of the Ukrainian but could not manoeuvre over him further in the confined space of the bivouac. 'Hey! Wake up. Out of my way. Move!' She beat at his legs in frustration. Andrei remained motionless. 'Help me, Hal.'

Hal did not acknowledge her.

'Are you listening to me?' Josie pushed angrily at Vasylenko's legs once more, weakened fast, then slumped back, gasping for breath. 'This is your fault,' she told Hal. 'We did everything right. We were *ready*, for Christ's sake. Why the hell did you let him in?'

'I couldn't stop him.'

'And now? What do you suggest? We stay here and freeze to death?' Josie tugged insistently on his wind suit to get his attention.

Hal thought for some time, then roused himself to speak, his voice slurred and thick with fatigue. 'Option one. The two of us leave now.' Hal gestured at the inert climber. 'And if we do that. He dies.' He reached out to hold Josie's hand. 'Option two. We do everything we can to keep Andrei alive. The Sherpas arrive with fresh oxygen in about four hours and we all go down. Nobody dies.'

'He's nothing to do with the equation. He got himself into this shit. He's not our responsibility.'

'What if it were you lying there now? Would you really want the only two people in the world who could save you to walk out and leave you to die?'

Josie made to move for the entrance once more, jamming her back against the ice wall to give her leverage to pass over the Ukrainian. 'I'm not here for a moral argument, Hal. I came here to climb a mountain and now I'm going down.'

'And what if it were Sebastian?'

Josie froze, her body caught mid-movement, her back arched and rigid. A hiss of breath exhaled icily into the air. 'How can you possibly say that now?'

'Because it's the only way I can think of to make you see. Someone is out there, waiting on the end of a telephone line to hear if this man is dead or alive, just as you did. Now tell me if you think we can walk away.'

Josie fell back into her position next to the wall, deflated, spent. Even now she could feel the effects of the steroid wearing off.

'I'm sorry. That was a cruel thing to say.'

Josie rubbed her eyes. The snow-blindness was almost gone, and though her eyes were bruised and sore she could see the contours of Hal's face for the first time. She watched as he turned his gaze back to the entrance. 'So?' Josie asked him.

Hal remained silent, staring out of the snow hole entrance. Ten thousand feet below he could see a glacier weaving a trail along the valley floor, pointing the way to the green foothills. The scene was illuminated by a thin scatter of sunlight, filtered through a high cloud. 'I can't leave him,' he said finally.

'Oh.'

'If the Sherpas are going strong they should make it here in the next few hours with the O's. I'm going to radio Todd and tell him there's a change of plan. We'll wait here, revive Andrei with the gas and we all go down.'

Josie had no energy left to fight. With infinite weariness she lifted her legs off the Ukrainian climber and wriggled backwards into her lying position against the wall. 'Hal?'

'What?'

'I will never forgive you if you let me die.'

Hal patted Josie's leg, aware that she had drifted immediately into sleep. 'Priority number one,' he murmured, fighting a wall of fatigue. 'Everyone goes home.'

Hal tried to fix his mind on the task. Use the walkie-talkie. The radio was in a breast pocket, accessible by the mere action of lifting an arm and freeing the Velcro fastening. Hal tried to raise his hand but it felt as heavy as lead, as fixed to where it rested as if it had been nailed. He tried to curl the fingers of the hand but the message could not beat a path through the frozen tissue. Hal found his mind wandering as he stared distractedly through the snow hole entrance. Then an overwhelming desire to sleep overcame him. 'Everyone goes home.' He muttered the words again before passing into a state somewhere between deep sleep and unconsciousness.

81

Nima cursed his lack of a watch as he looked at Lhakpa fighting to make progress up the fixed rope towards him. Judging by the way sunlight was flooding into the gully it was already mid-morning. Since leaving the top camp the pattern had been the same: Nima painfully breaking the trail through soft snow, making good progress and then having to wait interminably while Lhakpa made heavy weather of following up. Now, impatience bit into Nima almost as strongly as the cold. 'Climb! You can rest here,' he shouted. 'I have tea for you when you get to me.'

Lhakpa showed no sign that he had heard the younger man but slumped theatrically over his ice axe. Nima could hear the high-pitched whistle of the older man's breath as it exited the perforated exhaust valve of his mask.

Nima turned to look up behind him, squinting into the brilliant light. 'Where are you, Hal?' He sighed. He had expected to see the two climbers coming down towards them by now. There was nothing, not even a scattering of tiny falling ice particles, which would tell him someone was moving above but out of sight. Nima wondered for a moment if they had somehow missed Josie and Hal in the dark. But looking down at the col he could see no tell-tale sign of movement.

Some minutes later, coughing and retching dramatically, Lhakpa finally reached the small snow platform Nima had chosen to stop on. He fell on his side in the snow, managing to gasp out the words: 'Where are they?'

'I don't know.' Nima scanned the slope above once more.

'We should have met them.'

'Maybe the woman can't move.'

Lhakpa swore loudly and hacked up a blood-filled mouth of phlegm, which he spat out on to the snow. 'You see that?' he said, pointing weakly to the bloody ball. 'I'm killing myself for these people. And for what? They'll be dead by the time we arrive.'

'No they won't.'

'They treat us like animals.' Lhakpa spat again.

Nima pulled the thermos flask from the side pocket of his rucksack and poured a small measure of the sweet tea into the lid.

Lhakpa took it with shaking fingers and downed it in one. 'I won't go on,' he said. 'I'll leave my oxygen here. This is the limit.' He turned his head, swearing beneath his breath, ashamed to meet Nima's eye.

Nima glared at him angrily. For a moment he felt like picking Lhakpa up and shaking him, so intense was the fury. But then he crouched down, brushing the snow away from his friend's face where it had collected on the cheek. 'I understand,' he told him. 'Don't be ashamed. You got the oxygen as high as you could.'

Now Lhakpa turned to face him, grateful for the sympathy. 'I would climb if I could, Nima. But I am no longer young like you.'

Nima pulled off Lhakpa's rucksack and took out the two full oxygen bottles, leaving the partly consumed one in place. 'You have enough gas?'

Lhakpa nodded.

'So go,' Nima told him. 'I will continue.'

Lhakpa struggled to his feet. 'It will be for nothing,' he said.

Nima poured some of the tea for himself. 'You will not say that when I return with them alive,' he insisted.

With a grunt, Lhakpa put on his pack. Then, without a farewell, he pushed past Nima and began to descend the fixed ropes, his slightly stooped figure caught in the full glare of the sun.

Nima watched him go with a heavy heart, knowing that worse was to come. He knew their progress had been too slow. There were still at least two hundred metres of vertical ascent to go in the gully before the gentler ground leading up to the south summit and the snow was deep. Nima opened the main compartment of his rucksack and placed one of the extra oxygen bottles beside the three it already carried. The other he tied carefully to the fixed rope and stood upright so it could be spotted easily on the descent. He picked up the pack, straining with the weight. Then, muttering a half-forgotten prayer beneath his breath, he set out up the deeply packed slope, hoping at every moment to see the silhouettes of Josie and Hal appear above him.

82

'Hal. Come in. Hal. Come in. This is Todd.'

Hal came slowly out of the sleep, disorientated until he realised where he was. He pulled the unit towards his mouth and somehow got his thumb against the transmit button. 'Hi,' he croaked.

Silence.

'Hal, I couldn't hear your voice, but I think we heard a click. Can you confirm that?'

Hal clicked the transmit button again.

'OK. That was a response. I think what's happened is your walkie-talkie battery is too weak to transmit voice. If you can hear me, click once.'

Hal clicked the button again.

'That's great. Hal, I can see no sign of you two coming down. Can you confirm that you have left the bivouac?'

Hal made no response.

'I don't hear a click,' Todd said. 'Does that mean you are still in the bivouac?'

Click.

'Shit. Is Josie still with you?'

Click.

'Is she still alive?'

Hal tried to lift his head to check her but was saved the effort when she suddenly coughed.

Click.

'Thank God. Listen, Hal, Lhakpa has turned back but Nima is still coming. Do you copy that?'

Click.

'If he can carry enough gas to you, can you still get Josie down alive?'

No response. Hal tried to draw himself out of the mental paralysis the altitude had brought on.

'I repeat. Hal. Is Josie going to be able to walk?'

Click.

'That's good. That's really good. Now when Nima gets close, Hal, I'm going to ask you to get out of the shelter so that he can locate you. We can't afford to lose time while he stumbles around trying to find your bivouac.'

Hal focused his eyes on the case.

Click.

'You're going to go out on to the south summit so he can find you. Do you think you can do that?'

Hal tried to imagine how it would feel to try to get out of the shelter.

Todd's voice came back, angry: 'Can you do that, Hal?'

Click.

'You have to fight, Hal. You have to fight.'

Click.

'Over for now.'

The line died. Hal lay for a long time looking at the walkie-talkie, his breath freezing on to its leather case.

Fight. Or die.

He knew he was losing it. And he knew also that he should do something about it. But what *could* he do?

In front of him Andrei's face was directly on Hal's eyeline, hideously contorted, his eyes intermittently wide, then screwed shut as he descended further into madness. Hal pushed the Ukrainian away from him with his feet. Apart from a louder grunt than usual, Andrei did not resist, partly rolling so his face was no longer visible.

Then Hal saw it. The action of rolling Andrei over had dislodged the rucksack, which had been jammed behind him: Andrei's rucksack. With a sudden shock Hal realised he had not checked it. How could he have neglected this? Hal had no idea what was going on with his mind but he knew he would now have to find the strength to look inside the pack.

Cursing himself, he leaned forward and pulled the rucksack out from its position. It was a Berghaus 'Hot ice' model, like his own, forty-litre capacity with a drawstring top. It was heavier than he had expected. Taking off the glove on his left hand, he used what sense of touch remained in his fingers to undo the plastic clips on the restraining straps. He clasped the drawstring toggle in his teeth and loosened it.

Inside was an orange oxygen cylinder.

He looked at it in total confusion. Josie's name was written in black marker on the side. He checked the gauge. It was full.

Hal pulled out his regulator from the pile of gear next to him and, painfully slowly, managed to get it screwed on to the thread. He cranked the gauge up to two litres a minute and, holding the mask against his face, breathed in deeper than he had ever done before. The oxygen ran through his body, re-energising him almost immediately.

He kicked the Ukrainian's body. 'You fucking thief, Andrei. If you weren't half dead already I'd kill you.'

Then he shook Josie's shoulder hard enough to rouse her a little. 'Josie. Wake up. Wake up and have some air. We have some fighting still to do.' Hal's lips cracked into a smile as he looked at the oxygen cylinder on his lap.

Hal let Josie breathe for ten minutes, then switched the mask to Andrei. At first he struggled against the plastic held up to his face but Hal had it firmly in place, forcing him to take the oxygen. Ten minutes later he took his own turn once more. He checked his watch. Eleven o'clock. The oxygen would keep them alive for a few more hours but not much longer.

Where the hell were the Sherpas?

83

Nima found himself wading in softer snow, heavy powder that had collected in the lee of the slope. Each step broke through the thin crust of ice on top, plunging him in to his waist. He floundered upwards for a few more strides, panting with the exertion, forcing his knees up to his chest and kicking down as deep as he could into the pack to find hard terrain beneath. He tired rapidly; lifting each leg – and its heavy boot – out of its trough required more strength than his exhausted thigh muscles could supply.

After some metres a big gust of wind knocked him off balance. He fell awkwardly to one side, his outstretched arm sinking deep into the snow, both legs twisting painfully in their slots as his waist pivoted into the fall. Even in his debilitated state, Nima was alert enough to know he was risking a bad injury on this terrain – the seemingly soft snow was clamping each leg upright with surprising force. He could feel from the pressure on his shins that he had come close to fracturing a bone.

In considerable pain, he rolled sideways and on to his back, raising his head and shoulders to compensate for the downward orientation of his body. Using his hands, he pulled the right leg out of its trap but to raise the left required more strength – the front of his boot had created its own hollow from which it now stubbornly refused to be drawn. Shifting position slightly, he forced the leg backwards, pointing his frozen foot as best he could to ease it out. It came free suddenly in a cascade of broken ice chunks, leaving him sprawled in an ungainly heap on the snow slope, half buried in the powder.

He lay for some time, cursing Lhakpa for turning back. This climb was bad enough for two. But alone? He could feel his will-power draining as he thought of Lhakpa reaching the camp on the col, heating himself food, holding his hands close to the flame of a cooker to warm himself. Why hadn't he taken the opportunity and turned back too?

Now Nima cursed himself. It might all be pointless, anyway. What if Lhakpa had been right about that? If Josie and Hal were already dead? Nima flexed his back to ease some of the nagging pain of the rucksack, then looked up the slope, trying to judge how far. It looked like hours more work. Uttering a big sigh, Nima realised he had to make a decision before he froze.

With an enormous effort he pulled himself upright, his body stooped under the weight. Just contemplating the climb made his legs tremble. He was on the edge of giving up.

But he didn't. One painful step after another, Nima began to climb, resting to breathe after every two or three steps.

84

The oxygen was long gone. The morning had stretched into afternoon. Hal watched the faltering rays of light through the entrance hole. Clouds were thickening around the flanks of the peak and night was just a few hours away.

And then?

Hal could not project his mind forward to think of the following dawn if they had to stay in the shelter. They were already on the most fragile margin between life and death. With no warming rays of sunlight on the slopes it was getting colder again, the cold creeping into their bodies, freezing the fluid in vulnerable cells, locking their muscles in position, pushing the process of altitude sickness one step nearer.

The walkie-talkie buzzed into life, the signal incredibly faint as the batteries gave their last pulse of power. 'Hal? This is Todd. Do you read me?'

Hal picked up the instrument, curling his swollen fingers around the unit with difficulty.

'If you can hear this, click the button.'

Click.

'OK. We're looking good, Hal. We can see Nima through the binoculars and he's just a few minutes from your position. Be ready for him.'

Click.

Todd was in tears. 'We're praying for you both. Over for now.'

Hal placed the walkie-talkie in his top pocket and, feeling dazed and weak, tried to move his legs. The creeping effects of frostbite had – he was now sure – begun to strike his feet. Bright lights flashed in his head as he moved forward to shake Josie's shoulder. 'Josie,' he croaked. 'Nima is coming. You have to move again.'

Josie grunted and turned further into the ice wall.

'Don't go back to sleep. We're leaving for good.'

Hal sat back, feeling nauseous. What next? He tried to get a little order into his mind. How long had Todd said he had? And which direction would Nima come from?

Andrei suddenly screamed loudly.

Hal decided to try to get the Ukrainian out.

'What are you doing?' Josie half raised her head in confusion as Hal began to shift.

'Nima is almost here. I'm getting Andrei out first.' He realised immediately that this was not going to be easy. The Ukrainian was lying flat along the ice wall, blocking him from moving. 'Andrei!'

Vasylenko flinched as he recognised his name.

'Andrei, we're going to go down. Oxygen is on the way.'

Andrei moaned loudly, still sucking on his frostbitten fingers and rocking back and forth in his agony.

'Stop making that sound.'

Suddenly there was a noise from the slope outside. It was faint, but Hal thought it was a shout.

'Nima!' The first attempt was little more than a whisper. 'Nima! In here!' Hal's voice found some residual power, rising almost to a shout.

Suddenly, footsteps were cutting through the ice on the slope. 'Hal?'

Nima's face appeared at the entrance, his eyes clouding with confusion for a second as he saw the three tightly packed figures in the bivouac, then burning instantly with relief when he spotted Hal. 'You alive? I not too late?'

Hal leaned forward and held Nima's oustretched hand in his own, almost lost for words as a wave of intense relief swept him. 'You made it . . . you made it . . . I can't believe you kept going . . .'

'Who's this?' the Sherpa asked, gesturing to Andrei.

'He came in for shelter. We have to get him down too.'

'Frostbite very bad.' Nima recoiled as he saw Andrei's face.

'Josie too.'

'Josie,' Nima called to her. 'Wake up now. I have tea. I have oxygen. We go down.'

Josie roused herself so she could see him. 'Nima? Is that really you? You came for us?'

'Don't talk. No time. Nearly dark. I get this one out, OK?' Nima began to smash at the side wall of the shelter with his ice axe, enlarging the entrance hole rapidly then reaching in to grab the Ukrainian's shoulders. With difficulty, cursing the lack of space, he manoeuvred Andrei into an angle in which one big pull would slide the semi-conscious climber out of the entrance. He did not protest.

Nima took Vasylenko's waist harness in his hands. Then, tensing his shoulders, he hauled on him with all his strength. Andrei shifted a few inches, the smooth fabric of the wind suit helping to ease the friction. Now his shoulders were wedged in the entrance hole. Nima had to beat at the ice with his boots until it was wide enough to allow him to pass. With one final haul he slid the Ukrainian out of the bivouac, holding him firmly as he collapsed on to the small snow platform outside the shelter.

'What happens?' Andrei cried out, staring around in shock and confusion at the sudden flood of light.

'Be still,' Nima told him, moving downslope to block him from rolling off the small ledge. Unclipping a titanium ice screw from his harness, he screwed it into the slope and fastened a short sling on to Andrei's harness to secure him.

Then he turned back to the shelter, where Hal was struggling to straighten his legs. 'Let me help you,' Nima said. Taking Hal's legs, he swung them round to the entrance so they dangled out on to the slope. He could hear the cracking of his joints as the frozen ligaments in his knees and ankles began to work.

As slowly and awkwardly as an insect emerging from its cocoon, Hal let Nima drag his protesting body to the entrance and pull him out until he was sitting on the platform next to Andrei. Hal sat for some minutes, massaging life back into his cramped limbs, then, feeling like a child taking his first step, he rose. Nima embraced him tightly and for a long moment they stood holding each other. 'Thank you, Nima. Thank you from the bottom of my heart.'

'No problem.' Nima smiled at him. 'You my father. If I no come maybe you get mad with me!'

Then they turned to the task of pulling Josie from the shelter.

85

With just thirty minutes of daylight remaining, Hal and Nima were putting the final touches to the equipment that would keep them alive during the descent.

Hal had been unable to achieve much. Nima had done the lion's share of the work, fixing the oxygen masks to the new cylinders and installing them in the individual rucksacks. Hal had forced Josie to drink a full cup of heavily sweetened tea and she now lay resting, fully prone on the snow, breathing from one of the full oxygen cylinders at four litres a minute. Saturated with oxygen at this maximum rate, she had soon come out of her comatose state and was looking more alert as each minute passed.

Hal was also benefiting from the hot tea and oxygen, but Andrei had violently rejected it, knocking the cup out of Nima's hand when it was offered and motioning to throw the oxygen cylinder away. 'No give me!' he yelled at Nima. 'I no need.'

'Take it,' Nima told him calmly, 'or you not get down.'

Andrei thrust his grotesquely swollen fingers in Nima's face. 'You see?' he screamed. 'He do that!' He pointed to Hal. Then he went back to sobbing in his native tongue, clenching and unclenching his destroyed hands by his sides and looking blankly towards the setting sun.

'He crazy,' Nima said.

'I know. But we take him,' Hal replied.

'You sure? Josie cannot use her hands. Maybe she needs us both to help on fixed ropes.'

'I'll take Andrei, you take Josie.'

Nima glared at the Ukrainian with distaste. 'OK,' he agreed reluctantly.

They made a final check on their harnesses and assisted Josie to stand. She gasped out loud with the pain as blood began to circulate in her feet.

Getting Andrei upright was a more difficult task; he struggled as they tried to grasp his arms.

'Andrei. You have to do as we tell you now. Or we will leave you.' Hal tried reasoning with him.

Vasylenko shrugged them off and got awkwardly to his feet. 'Don't care,' he told them. 'Don't care anything now.'

'I'll put him on a short rope,' Hal said.

Andrei did not resist as Hal took a short length of rope and attached it with a carabiner to his harness.

Nima did the same with Josie and they were ready for the descent. 'You can walk?' he asked her.

'I don't know.'

'You no walk, you no live.'

Josie took an experimental step, almost tripping as her legs buckled.

'I hold you.' Nima held tight on to her waist harness and Josie began to shuffle forward, gaining confidence as she felt her body starting to work.

Between the bivouac and the top of the fixed ropes was a narrow ledge etched into the face. It was a natural fault line, some thirty metres long, and the logical way to traverse the steep ground back to the more gentle gradient of the south summit. They set out along it, Nima and Josie first, Hal and Andrei some five metres behind.

Suddenly, Andrei stopped dead. 'Summit!' He gestured to the rising ground ahead.

'That's not the summit, Andrei. We're going down.'

'You lie. You want stop me go summit. Now I go summit.' He pulled hard on the rope as he tried to climb directly up the slope, jerking Hal at the waist.

'*No*! We go down.' Hal reached towards him to restrain him from moving.

Andrei took two clumsy steps up the incline.

Hal grabbed his shoulder to block him.

'I go summit. For photo. For photo!' Andrei began to nod rapidly, like a pecking bird, his blackened and bleeding nose casting tiny globules of dark blood into the air. 'Yes, that good idea now.'

'Not a good idea.' Hal tried to twist Andrei back.

Andrei started to choke, his chest convulsing in one great spasm after another. His face went bright blue. Hal instantly thought he might have swallowed his tongue. Vasylenko began to scream, turning and kicking Hal with his spikes.

'Nima! Help me!' Hal cried.

Before the Sherpa could come to Hal's aid Andrei jumped forward unexpectedly, his forehead smashing into Hal's shoulder and his arms windmilling in an attempt to barge him out of the way. A flailing hand caught Hal in the stomach, winding him and throwing him momentarily off balance.

Andrei leaped up on to the steeper ground once more, his steel crampon spikes scraping against the ice as he scrabbled for a purchase on the iron-hard slope. He was pushing strenuously against Hal now, trying to dodge past him. One foot slipped but he threw his weight forward to compensate, stumbling back for a metre or so and clasping Hal's leg with both hands.

From the corner of his eye, Hal could see Nima starting back along the ledge to help him.

For a heart-stopping moment his leg held Andrei's entire weight as he scraped the sides of his spikes against the ice, dangling almost free above the slope. In that instant he thought he could still hold his fall.

As if from another world, Hal could hear Josie screaming.

But Andrei twisted his body away, like an animal trying to wring itself free from a trap, sending his centre of gravity out even further, ripping Hal's hand from his shoulder while the other snatched at his waist harness.

Hal and Andrei fell, locked together, in a tumbling confusion of metal and fabric and flesh, away down the ice run towards the drop.

86

Hal felt himself fly through the air, falling momentarily through free space, then striking the ice a shattering blow with his right side. Then they were glissading down the face, their bodies turning and spinning.

Hal felt his snow goggles and his oxygen mask tear from his face as Andrei impacted briefly into him, then they tumbled apart once more, Hal briefly aware that the grunting high-pitched noise he could hear was the sound of exhaling air as Andrei was beaten against the ice.

Melted through the ice were several outcrops of rock. One flashed past – and another, the razor-sharp stone just inches away from Hal's path. Then he hit one, the stone slicing through his clothing and ripping into his leg. He felt the bone break.

A second later they were approaching the drop. Hal braced himself for the sickening plunge into the depths.

It didn't happen.

Instead, with a shock that threatened to cut him in two, he felt himself lurch to a stop, his pelvis twisting abruptly as the waist harness bit hard into his midriff. In the violence of the impact every scrap of breath was forced from his lungs. Winded, he gulped for air as he tried to comprehend what had happened.

A gasping noise told Hal that Andrei was still attached to him and that he too had been brought to a halt. He looked down to find that the Ukrainian was hanging beneath him, dangling over the ten-thousand foot drop on the short length of rope tying them together. His weight was straining Hal's spine to the point where he felt it was about to break.

Hal reached down and forced his frostbitten fingers to unscrew the carabiner holding them together. It snapped open with a small metallic chink.

With a last guttural gasp of terror Andrei vanished into the gloom with no more sound than a slight hissing of Gore Tex fabric against the ice, gravity ripping him away from the ridge and out into the tumbling black void of the south-west face where he fell, unheard, to the uncaring embrace of the glacier at the base.

Hal lost consciousness as he watched Andrei fall.

87

Nima and Josie stood fixed to the spot, absolutely motionless as Hal and Andrei slid away from them. The two men were out of sight in seconds, leaving just a line of deeply etched abrasions in the ice where their crampons had scratched into the surface. Then there was nothing. No scream of terror, no impact of flesh on rock, just the ever present bluster of the wind.

After a while, Nima leaned forward as far as he dared to try to see down the fall line. He could detect no sign of the two men, nor did he expect to. From his vantage point he could see nothing that would stop them from pitching into the abyss. In their fall, they had passed over an overhanging lip of ice, a feature that now blocked Nima's perspective and meant he had no sight of Hal, suspended a further distance below. Nima unclipped his oxygen mask so he could call: 'Hal!'

His cry echoed around the vast amphitheatre of the western cwm. 'Hal!'

They waited, praying silently for a response, a muffled cry, anything.

When nothing came they were not surprised; the two men had fallen to their deaths, of that they were certain. They stood, heads bowed, unsure.

Minutes passed. The sun was setting. In a short time it would be dark, compounding the problems of the descent.

Josie felt a need to act – to pray – to call out something to someone. But no words came. She merely stared, as Nima did, out into the darkening drop into which the two men had been pulled.

Nima was the first to speak. He talked to her shyly – it was the first time he had been alone with her. 'Camp four,' he said, gesturing to the narrow trail to safety. 'Walk please.'

Josie stepped forward, her mind still reeling. Had she really seen it happen? Josie had had the illusion that she had been watching the horror unfold on a screen, that this disaster was happening in another dimension, at another time, to someone other than Hal.

Now it replayed through the oxygen-deprived, already damaged cells of her mind, like a repeating terror of the night: the sound of the sharpened spikes scrabbling against the ice, Andrei screaming for the summit.

Hal was gone in that violent moment of insanity.

Josie took one more step towards the fixed ropes, Nima falling in behind her, his hand reassuringly firm on her harness. There was no sense of sorrow, of remorse, just the brutal knowledge that the mountain had taken him as it had taken so many others. It didn't matter who you were, Josie now realised, your identity was as meaningless in this place as a single gust of wind.

For the next ordeal it would change nothing. Nima would manage her, cajole her, feed the tea and oxygen into her like a mother caring for a child. The hours would pass in a haze of pain, as her legs carried her down through the gullies and across the unending flatland of the col.

She would fight while she still could – fight her way down and out of this place . . . with Nima's help. But even if she lived, she knew that she would always belong to the mountain now. Like Hal, she had gone too far into this forsaken place. Something inside her was as cold as the rocks and ice from which the mountain was made.

88

The pain of his broken thigh brought Hal back to consciousness just as the sun was setting. There was still enough light to register his surroundings. He turned, looking frantically up the slope. 'Nima!'

He half expected to see the agile figure of the Sherpa abseiling down towards him. But there was no movement above, just the jutting, angular presence of whatever had caught his fall. A tree? A branch? But how could it be? Then Hal focused his eyes closer and realised.

It was not a rock that his harness had snagged on, it was the frozen torso of a climber, half buried in the snow, one arm sticking at a crazy angle from the ice, the face twisted into a mummified contortion of horror, the skin black from the relentless solar radiation. He must have died on the ridge, Hal realised, and been swept off by an avalanche or the wind to become embedded in the slope.

Hal reached up and grasped the dead man's hand. He thrust the ice axe in next to him and hauled himself up so that he could rest his head against the corpse, feeling closer to that dead man in that instant than he had ever felt to any living being. Trying not to faint from the pain in his leg, Hal levered himself higher and twisted the harness free from where it had snagged.

He waited while his breathing recovered a little, summoning the will-power to commence the climb. Then he swung the ice axe into the face, kicked in his left crampon as hard as he could and inched his way upwards, the broken leg trailing behind. He used an ice screw as a makeshift second axe, digging it as hard as he could into the face with his left arm, ignoring the shooting spasms from the base of his fingers.

Time ceased to matter. It was the nearest he had ever achieved to total focus, complete commitment. He knew that if he made the slightest error he would die there and then. His good leg shook uncontrollably every time he pressed his weight on to it, the muscles so close to their limits that they had virtually nothing left to give. He was beyond fatigue, beyond exhaustion but he kept the ice axe swinging, one blow after the other, gaining a few inches of precious ground, then heaving up and trusting the crampon to support the progress.

Darkness came and all Hal had to measure his progress by was the increasing pain from his leg and the gradual weakening of his arms. Periodically he called for Nima, knowing that it was a shout in vain. There was no reason for them to linger in that place and Hal guessed the Sherpa and Josie would be well into their descent, a third of the way down the gullies or even more. He passed the snow lip, dragging large quantities of powder on to himself as he cut through the slight overhang forcing his way on to the hard ice of the ramp.

Here he paused for a considerable time, resting on the easier gradient, blacking out once more for he knew not how long.

By the time he reawakened, a sliver of moon was moving across the night sky. When clouds weren't obscuring it, he could just make out the dark shadow of the bivouac entrance against the snow. He began to traverse to the right, heading for the mouth-like shape. Inch by inch he climbed, oblivious to anything but the all-consuming desire for shelter as the moon transited half of the sky.

The bivouac. Hal dragged his shattered leg up the final steep mound and collapsed into the flat sanctuary, retching mouthfuls of bile on to the compacted floor. He just had enough energy left to scan the interior. Nima had left very little. Half a foam mat, two empty oxygen cylinders, the empty gas cooker and the dead walkie-talkie. Hal dragged out the foam mat and laid his head on it. Then he took the walkie-talkie and fumbled with the casing with his swollen fingers. After a painful battle, he eased the leather flap open and retrieved the battery. He unzipped his wind suit with difficulty, placed the battery against his chest and zipped it up again.

And that was the margin.

Would a few hours of warmth regenerate the battery to make just one call? And would anyone be listening?

Hal slipped rapidly into unconsciousness.

89

Josie woke into a cocoon of green light, filtering through the side wall of a tent, a sleeping bag of snug down wrapped in a tight embrace around her. Somewhere nearby was the sound of voices – the Sherpas and Todd, talking softly but urgently. She felt devoid of being, separate from herself, deprived of all familiar points of reference now the world had ceased to be ice and rock. Only the oxygen mask was the same, the hiss of gas feeding her body as it had done through the night.

Half-constructed images flickered in her mind: torchlights bobbing across the col; Nima calling to Lhakpa; the texture of fabric as she was helped into a tent; the white bandages being wound around her fingers; the sharp intrusion of the hypodermic syringe as it entered her arm. An empty phial was discarded on the tent floor next to her. Josie focused on it. Morphine. That was why she could feel no pain in her hands or feet.

She heard the sound of footsteps crunching across the ice and a moment later Nima's head came in through the tent flaps. He looked older, she thought, with deeply etched rings of fatigue in his face.

'You sleep?'

Josie nodded, not trusting herself to reply.

Nima unzipped her sleeping bag and propped her upright while he helped her to drink some tea.

Her lips were so swollen with blisters she could barely sip the fluid. 'Nima. Thank you,' she whispered.

More images came back: the endless fixed ropes stretching down into the dark; Nima's shouts as he bullied her to continue.

'Hush. Save for later,' the Sherpa replied gently. 'We not safe yet.'

Nima left as Todd came in. He, too, looked as if he hadn't slept for a week. 'Josie, are you strong enough to talk?'

Josie nodded as he unclipped her mask. 'Go ahead,' she croaked.

'What the hell happened with Hal?' Todd asked her. 'I got what I could from Nima but he's too upset to say much.'

'There was another climber . . .' Josie tried to recall Andrei's name but failed. 'Hal was trying to save him but he went crazy . . . They fell.'

'Where did they fall?'

'Right down outside the bivouac.'

'Off the south summit?'

'Yes.'

'It was Andrei, wasn't it? The Ukrainian guy? That worthless fuck killed Hal.'

Josie sighed, 'Yes . . .'

'Jesus.' Todd looked away, tears springing to his eyes. 'He'd done it, Josie. He'd pulled you both through. Nima would have got the pair of you down if it hadn't been for that . . .'

'I know.'

'And that's what makes me so mad.' Todd let the tears flow freely. 'What am I going to tell Rachel?'

Josie tried to imagine how much time had passed since her arrival at the camp. 'She doesn't know?'

'Not yet. We've released the news that you've been brought down to camp four. All we've said so far is that Hal is still missing.'

'Oh.'

Todd looked at her hard. 'Josie. I know this is a tough moment. But I have to ask you. Is there any way Hal could have survived that fall? Could he still be up there, injured, in a crevasse, for example?'

'Oh, God, how do you expect me to . . .'

'To know? Because you saw it with your own eyes. I have to make decisions here. I have responsibilities to the Sherpas, to myself – we've all been too high too long – and not least to get you to medical care. But once we pull out of this camp that is it for Hal. He's dead. You understand that?'

'Yes.' Josie hated him for pressuring her when she had never felt weaker. 'Wait. I'm going to be sick . . .'

Todd dragged her to the tent entrance where she retched painfully. As the spasm subsided she found she was looking up at the mountain. Storm clouds were gathering once more on the high slopes.

'Could he still be alive?' Todd asked her again.

Josie watched as the summit was covered by a block of cloud. 'I don't think so,' she whispered.

'OK, I'm going to get Rachel on the satellite phone and tell her. She may want to speak to you.'

Josie did not reply, but allowed herself to be pulled to her feet and half carried to the communications tent.

As they passed Nima and Lhakpa, Todd gave them a nod. They immediately began to pack up the tent Josie had just vacated.

Todd dialled the numbers and waited for the connection to be made. He put it on the loudspeaker option so Josie could hear. 'Rachel?'

Rachel's voice filled the tent, sounding strained but composed. 'Go ahead, Todd. You have news from Hal?'

'The worst possible news. I have to tell you that Hal is dead. He was killed in an accident on the south summit yesterday evening.'

All the confidence drained from Rachel, her voice catching as she spoke. 'In an accident? He fell?'

'That's right.'

There was a tense silence.

'Rachel?'

'Hal wouldn't fall. He knew the mountain too well.'

'He was trying to help another climber.'

'There was someone else up there?'

'There was. He sheltered with Josie and Hal in the bivouac.'

'And that climber fell with Hal?'

'Correct.'

'And Josie?'

'Nima managed to get her down to camp four. We've had her sedated overnight and she's coming down with us now. She has first-degree frostbite to her hands and feet.'

'Can I speak to her?'

Todd covered the handset while he asked Josie: 'Do you think you're up to it?'

Josie sighed and let Todd hold the handset to her face. 'Rachel, this is Josie. I . . .' She tailed off, knowing that any words were pathetically inadequate.

'Don't worry, I don't want the words, I want the facts. How did Hal fall?

'The climber Hal tried to save. He was delirious. I'm so sorry, Rachel . . . there was nothing could be done.'

'Did you see Hal's body?'

'Well . . . no . . . you see he fell far away down the slope.'

'So he *could* still be alive? No one saw his body, right?'

Josie paused to consider her response. 'We called him. There was no reply.'

'Have you tried the walkie-talkie again?'

Todd took the handset. 'The walkie-talkie's dead. It has been for more than twelve hours.'

'Is there anyone who can go up one more time?'

'No way. We've pushed it to the limit, Rachel. No one has the strength now.'

'Oh.'

'We've got to get Josie down.'

'So even if Hal is alive you're abandoning him?'

'That's not fair. We're ninety-nine point nine per cent certain that Hal died in that fall.'

'And that point one of a per cent?' Suddenly, Rachel was crying. 'Oh, shit. It's just if there's a chance . . .'

'I understand, but we're out of choices now.'

'If you were going to try one more walkie-talkie contact when would it be?'

Todd checked his watch.

'On the hour. In thirty-five minutes . . . but there's no . . .'

'Let me try it. Patch me through so I can try one last time.'

'There's no point.'

'Let me try. Just one more contact. If there's any way Hal can pull through this he will . . . we owe it to him.'

'It's going to delay our departure. I'll have to leave the satphone up. Let me talk to Josie.' He turned to her. 'It's your call. An extra thirty minutes might mean another toe or finger lost by the time we get you out of here. That's the bottom line.'

Josie looked at her bandaged hands. Blood was already beginning to soak through the gauze where the tissue was suppurating. 'Let her do it,' she told him.

'Rachel, we'll try it. Call me back on this number in thirty minutes and we'll patch you through. But I'm telling you, you won't get any response, the walkie-talkie's dead and I'm afraid so is Hal.'

'I'll feel better if I try. Thank you.'

'You understand we can't wait beyond that?'

'I do.'

Todd replaced the receiver, terminating the call. Then he pulled back the tent entrance to look up at the peak. 'We're really pushing it now,' he said to Josie. 'If this weather deteriorates much further we're into an epic to get you down.'

90

Hal was so cold when he came round that he could not tell where his flesh ended and the ice began. He registered daylight, blinking as his eyes pulled the world into a blurred sense of shape.

He pulled his hands out from their refuge inside his down suit and considered them. Frostbite had eaten another few millimetres into the flesh of his fingers, blackening them almost to the middle joint. They looked like the hands of a ghoul, but after a little clenching he found he could still move them.

He checked his watch. It was five minutes to ten.

The battery. Hal suddenly recalled his last actions on reaching the bivouac. He had to get it into the walkie-talkie or he would miss the 10 a.m call. Hal retrieved the battery and held it against his cheek momentarily. He could feel from the temperature of the plastic casing that his body heat had warmed it a little but would it be enough to kick-start the exhausted cells into a last burst of power? He slotted it into the walkie-talkie and watched the seconds ticking past on his watch: nine fifty-nine and forty-five seconds.

Hal turned the 'on' switch. The unit beeped faintly as the sound of weak static hissed from the speaker. Hal placed it against his ear, waiting for a voice to come out of the ether. He did not waste power trying to transmit, knowing that the spent battery would not provide the strength to do so. The best he could hope for was to click the button by way of response. And even that was likely to shut the battery down.

He waited, still watching the face of his watch. Ten o'clock came and went. Thirty seconds . . . forty. Hal had no idea if his watch was accurate or not.

Then, Rachel's voice was with him. 'This is Rachel calling Hal Maher. Rachel calling Hal Maher. Can you hear me, Hal?'

His heart racing, Hal clicked on the transmit button, hearing the static begin to fade as the battery dribbled out its last milliamps of power.

'I'm not sure if that was a response or not . . . it was a click but it was so faint.' Rachel's tone had changed, Hal could hear her trying to maintain her composure. 'Hal. If you are still alive, click now . . .'

Hal pressed the button, praying it would deliver.

A further pause.

'Now I don't hear anything. Maybe I was mistaken before.' A thought occurred to her. 'Maybe your battery is dying. Hal, if you can hear me, click!'

Hal clicked so hard he burst the frostbite blister on his thumb.

The volume fell away until it was barely audible, but he could still hear the desperation in Rachel's next words.

'Hal . . . I believe you might be alive . . .' A crackle of static swept the transmission '. . . Fight for me . . . don't give up . . .'

With a small pop of interference the walkie-talkie died. Hal stared blankly at the lifeline. He knew there was no prospect of re-energising the batteries again. He had failed. The signal had not been strong enough for Rachel to be sure she had heard it.

Hal looked out of the bivouac, experiencing now for the first time the real fear that he was going to die in this place. What were those last words? 'Don't give up . . .' Hal let his eyes draw across the slope until he saw the shape buried in the ice, the small darkened bump that he knew was Sebastian's body.

To die here like that?

91

While the two Sherpas began to dismantle the tents Josie scanned the slopes, tracking and retracking the route of the fixed ropes, hoping against hope that something would move . . . some speck would firm out of the void and turn itself into the figure of a man . . . coming down.

'It was nothing.' Todd touched her gently on the shoulder.

Josie turned angrily to confront him. 'It was a click. Rachel heard it. We all did. He's alive.'

'You said it yourself. He can't have survived the fall.'

'So why did the walkie-talkie click like that?'

'I don't know but I don't think it was Hal. It was just a bit of interference, a random bit of static . . .'

'He's up there. And he's waiting to be rescued. We have to do something.'

'Like I just explained to Rachel' – Todd tried to keep the impatience from his voice – 'no one here is in a position to go up again. Getting you down is going to take everything we've got. Even with three of us I'm not sure we can do it.'

'Rachel's right. You're abandoning him.'

Todd snapped: 'Josie. We're all fucking dying here, OK? I have personally been sat above eight thousand metres for four days and nights. We're out of food and cooking gas. We have no more oxygen. The way my body feels right now I doubt I can survive another night. And look at the Sherpas . . . what do you think they can do now?'

Josie looked over to Nima and Lhakpa where they were packing the gear. Even in her own debilitated state she could see they were both moving like automatons, their every movement sluggish and apathetic. Periodically Nima would pause, staring strangely out into space and murmuring mournfully.

'Hal's dead, Josie. You have to come to terms with that and think of yourself now. You need hospital treatment. Fast. I've ordered up a helicopter. It's going to pick you up at camp one and take you straight to Kathmandu.'

Josie felt a wave of intense fatigue as the effects of the drugs began to wear off. Her legs buckled and she sat, heavily, on the ground next to Todd. 'I'm sorry. I'm too tired to think. I just couldn't face Rachel unless we had done every last thing.'

Todd prepared a syringe of dexamethasone.

'I know how she feels, you see,' Josie murmured, trying to will herself into another place as the needle went into her thigh.

Then came the descent, time distorted by the drugs, pain suspended in a haze of exhaustion until Josie did not know when she was standing, stumbling, or being pulled.

Between them, Todd, Nima and Lhakpa half carried, half man-handled Josie's unresponding body along the thousand metres of fixed ropes leading down the Lhotse face. It was a retreat of fifteen hours, an exercise of brute strength as the three men took turns to take her weight.

Josie's awareness diminished as the afternoon became a bitterly frigid night, the guttural exchanges between the three men gradually reducing to the point where all she could hear was their laboured breathing and the odd explosive curse from Lhakpa. Sliding for the most part on her back, her spine and coccyx became beaten and bruised, even through the padding of her down suit.

At some point she was aware of arriving at a tent, of hot tasteless fluid being poured down her throat, of a choking mouthful of cloying chocolate. New voices joined them, other Sherpas from the team who had come up to camp three to assist with the evacuation.

An argument erupted between the men but she could not fathom its cause. Then they were out into the night, mobile again, Josie lowered metre by metre down the face, the back of her head jolting against the irregularities of the slope, her woollen balaclava ripped off and lost unseen in the night.

With daylight came the bergschrund, the crevasse that marked the end of the Lhotse face and the beginning of the glacier. Josie descended the short ladder herself, trusting Todd beneath her to guide her frozen feet on to the rungs. Then they were on easier ground, with six hours of hard walking between them and camp two.

Nima and three other Sherpas took it in turns to carry Josie on their backs. She could not feel her hands to hold on properly and a second Sherpa had to follow behind to ensure she did not topple backwards. She rode in darkness, a scarf tied round her face to protect her eyes.

The miles were measured in a succession of bone-shaking passages, the Sherpas gradually tiring beneath her until they could manage less than five minutes in each session. The temperature rose and Josie was almost warm. Nima was endlessly caring, remonstrating loudly with his fellow porters when they accidentally jolted her – or, worse, stumbled so she was dumped in a pile on the ice.

They reached camp one at the top of the ice fall: a desperate collection of wind-blasted tents, half collapsed under the weight of snow, their interiors squalid after their two months of habitation.

Josie lay, unflinching, as a doctor from one of the other teams unravelled the bandages on her fingers. She tried not to notice his sharp intake of breath as the damage was revealed. 'Nothing we can do here,' he told Todd.

There were urgent conversations into a radio. Todd's voice raised into a tense tirade with someone in Kathmandu. 'We pay cash,' Todd kept repeating. 'We pay dollars to pilot. Dollars.'

Then, unbelievably, the muffled clatter of a helicopter coming up the valley, the distinctive rotor chop echoing around the cwm, alien and invasive in a place which normally knew only the sound of the wind.

'Get her into the helicopter.'

Numerous hands, stronger than the ones before, lifted Josie and brought her out of the tent. They began to carry her across the ice towards the waiting aircraft.

'Wait,' Josie commanded.

No one heard. The downwash of the helicopter rotors was creating a small blizzard of noise, which drowned her voice.

'Stop!' Josie forced the shout.

The porters came to an uncertain halt.

'What's up?' Todd pulled the scarf from her face, stooping to hear her better.

Josie screwed up her eyes against the light, squinting as they sought to adjust from the dark world she had been inhabiting. 'Let me see the mountain.'

'The helicopter can't wait.'

'I want to say goodbye.' Josie hissed the words so that Todd would understand.

He nodded sharply and instructed the Sherpas to help Josie to stand. She swayed uncertainly on her frozen feet, but one by one they let go.

The mountain was clear of cloud, bathed in the bronze light of late afternoon. Josie let her eyes follow the familiar fluted lines up that serpentine, glittering ridge. There was the summit, appearing so firmly planted in the heavens that just to imagine she had been there seemed an affront to some undeniable law.

Hal was there somewhere, that she knew. Turning her eyes towards him this last time was the closest Josie was going to get. She didn't feel separate from him, she had travelled too close to the edge of her own destruction to allow herself that. Instead, she felt absolutely in tune with where he was, so much so that her original idea – to whisper a few words of goodbye to him – was clearly not necessary. He would see her from wherever he was. You can see a thousand miles from the summit of Everest. Wasn't that one of the things he had told her?

Josie bowed her head, fighting against the light, shifting her eyeline down to where a haze of heat shimmer was hanging lazily above the ice of the glacier. It was pulsating, distorting the air into impossible pools of water, a mirage higher than any other.

Then she saw it.

From one of those pools a shape was trying to define itself. It was dark, sticklike, rising from the mirage to offer an excalibur to the gods. Josie blinked. For a second she thought she must have been mistaken. Then it moved again. An arm raised, almost hidden among a confusion of moraine and boulders, bearing not a sword but an ice axe. 'Todd. There's someone out there.'

'Don't be ridiculous.' He scanned the glacier but could see nothing. 'Come on. There's a limit to how long this helicopter can wait at this altitude.'

Josie saw the arm again. 'There is! There's someone there.' Insanely, she set off across the glacier towards it, her frozen feet refusing to respond, tripping her into a fall. Todd and the Sherpas picked her up.

'Josie. Stop it. You're going to damage yourself more.'

'Follow me.' Josie struggled to leave them once more but they restrained her, trying to turn her back to the helicopter.

'It's Hal!' Josie twisted and pointed towards the tiny object.

Todd scanned the glacier, seeing nothing. Then one of the Sherpas gave a cry and began hurrying away.

Now Todd could see it. 'My God. There *is* someone there.'

Josie sat on the ice and watched as Todd made as fast progress as he could, picking his way through the maze of crevasses and threading around the boulders in pursuit of the faster Sherpas. She saw them stop, huddle close around something for what seemed an age. Then they were coming back, bearing a figure swaddled in a bright fabric, which was hung between them like a hammock. They held it reverently, shuffling awkwardly with the weight it contained.

Josie pulled herself upright, coaxing her limbs to move and throwing her arms out wide to balance. Then she was among them, the procession coming to an uncertain stop as she half fell into their midst. Todd was saying something but the pounding of her heart drowned his words. Instead she locked on to Nima's face, noticing that it was shining with a type of shocked radiance.

'Hal alive! Hal alive!' he cried.

They placed the bundle on the ice where Josie could kneel. Inside was Hal, wrapped in what she took initially to be the fabric of a tent. His eyes, at first clouded with pain, shone with recognition when he saw her.

'How could I ever doubt?' she told him. Josie rested her face against his, her bandaged hands clutching him clumsily in an embrace as she held herself tight to him.

'I wouldn't want you to be the only one to walk away from this,' he whispered.

Then he was crying, pulling Josie closer again. 'Call Rachel,' he managed to croak. 'Tell her I'm alive.'

'Give him fluid,' Todd instructed.

Josie stood back as Nima took an insulated bottle of meltwater and pressed it to Hal's lips. He gagged as he forced it down.

He whispered some unheard words to Nima as he lay.

'But how . . . ?' Josie looked up at Todd in confusion.

'It's a paraglider,' Todd said, 'but God alone knows where it came from.'

Then Josie understood, fingering the material wonderingly in bewildered recognition. 'I've seen this before. It's Sebastian's. It was in his rucksack.'

Todd stared at Hal in amazement. 'He flew down. With Sebastian's paraglider?'

A Sherpa ran across from the helicopter, shouting as he came: 'Pilot say two minutes. No more.'

Todd was galvanised into activity, organising the Sherpas to pick Hal up once more. Josie was bundled between Todd and Nima, resting her arms across their shoulders as they lifted her with locked hands.

Beneath the helicopter rotors there was no more chance for conversation, even a shouted one. One of the Sherpas produced a knife and Hal was cut from the harness he was tangled in. It was clear from the way his legs lolled strangely to one side that both were now broken.

Josie was bundled into the rear of the cockpit, lying on the aluminium floor. Hal was heaved in beside her like a sack of potatoes. There were no seats and only a simple restraining strap to hold on to.

Nima was the last to stand back. He held Hal's hand until the final moment, then turned away with tears in his eyes.

Todd waved everyone clear. He could not close the door. There was no door. Every ounce of surplus weight had been stripped from the craft. The rotors changed pitch, biting aggressively as they obeyed the pilot's command, the brittle roar of the jet engine becoming a scream as the Alouette rose smoothly two metres into the air. Then it was gone, swooping low over the ice fall and heading down the Khumbu glacier, leaving just a lonely echo behind.

Josie drew Hal closer to her, pulling his head to her to protect him from the windrush coming through the space where the door should have been. Wordlessly, they watched as the grey ice gave way to green fields, the terraces caught in relief by the last dying rays of the sun. A village flashed past beneath them, the children running excitedly and waving at the low-flying machine. Josie imagined she could hear their shouts.

Then Hal was pointing, his hand withered and black as a crow's wing.

Through the window of the helicopter Josie could see what he was gesturing towards. It was Everest, visible for a fleeting moment amid darkening clouds. Then, as her tears began, she watched the clouds race across the face until the mountain was gone.